This is a work of fiction. All of the characters, organizations, and events portrayed in the novel are either products of the author's imagination or are used fictitiously.

Spell Borne Book 1 in the Lointaine Fairy Tale series.

Copyright © 2022 by Auden Llyr

Cover art by David Gardias
Formatted by Sophie Hanks

First published under the title Sub Rosa in June 2022 by little independent artists, LLC

Second Edition 2023

All rights reserved. No portion of this book may be used or reproduced without written permission from the publisher or author, except as permitted by U.S. copyright law. For information regarding permission, write to auden@audenllyr.com.

Dedication

This book is dedicated to all the women
who refuse to stay on the path…

Content Note

This book is based on fairy tales, from the gentler Disney versions to the significantly darker older versions. Please be aware that this book contains the following:

- profanity
- blood
- abuse
- violence
- homophobia
- internalized homophobia
- life changing injury
- drug use
- sex
- sexual assault
- trauma
- discussion of pregnancy
- animal death (hunting)
- death
- dead body

PROLOGUE

A human might have thought the smell was barbecue. The aroma was certainly enough to make me salivate. I gave a quick swipe with my tongue to make sure I wasn't drooling. It wouldn't be dignified.

Tendrils of the scent twined through the depths of the forest. The thought of barbecue distracted me from following an elusive odor. I had been trying to parse its essence for the last half hour: part scaly reptilian, part halitosis, and a hint of musky skunk. But all that was forgotten as the charred pork smell curled into my nostrils. The previous scent was well ground into my fur. I'd puzzle over it later. It wouldn't hurt to check out this other smell . . .

My nostrils quivered as I tested the gusting wind. The perfumes of the forest washed over me in waves: the earthen leaf litter, the bright astringent musk of a bobcat marker . . . There! Sweet raw meat, coppery tang of blood, voided bowels, and fresh decay. Fresh decay, was that an oxymoron? What a random thought — I flopped my head from side to side to dismiss it. I would be off chasing a squirrel next if I wasn't careful.

I bounded through the trees, following the scent map across a deer path, over a slight rise, and then hunkered down for a belly crawl through a bank of bracken ferns. God — why couldn't I manage to be quiet like the Pack? I sounded like I was marching over potato chips in combat boots.

The smell swamped my senses. I must be close, it should be . . . There. Hmm. I had suspected I would find one body, but I hadn't expected the second.

The rumble of a growl started in my chest. Stop that! You are trying to be stealthy!

I crept from under the ferns — eyes on the humans, ears cocked toward the forest, while conducting an olfactory reconnaissance. It took only a second to determine the man was dead. I sunk my teeth into his camos and pulled, yanking on various pieces of clothing, while fiercely quashing my curiosity about the fascinating smells wafting from the fabric folds. After much tugging and pulling, the man was no longer crushing the smaller form beneath him.

I felt the Magic arrive. It made every hair on my body stand at attention — not a comfortable sensation with the amount currently covering my body. The clouds, which had been scudding across the sky, cleared. Golden sunbeams fell into the glade, giving the whole scene a luminous quality you might find in a Romantic-era portrait of a napping nymph. The body was even posed in the sleep of the innocent, with a hand tucked beneath her cheek.

It was a good effort by the Magic, but the same light, that made her unhealthily pale skin into pearl dust, also highlighted the dripping blood, blue bruises, and dirt smudges. I can't even see a full range of colors as a canine, so the Magic was wasting a lot of effort. I snorted again as the swell of magic subsided.

Distraction over, the identity of the comatose human hit me so hard that I actually hopped backward.

Fuck!

I dislike using that word, as it generally shows a lack of creative variance in a person's vocabulary, but sometimes it is the only word that will do. Right now, it was a litany in my head. The detached part of my brain was already sorting through the implications and planning ways to offset the upcoming problems. I wondered idly if I would have the balls to point out to Roselle Dalton that I was right. Probably not.

She was still breathing, but unconscious. I stuck my cold, wet nose under her chin into the petal soft skin of her neck, and nudged ever so gently. No response. Triage: being unconscious for more than a few moments indicated brain trauma, so potential concussion, broken arm — obvious when the bone is sticking out of the skin — bruised or broken ribs from being crushed, maybe spinal damage? Unlike the guy, she didn't have any burns.

She needed help now, and I was in the wrong form to provide it. I couldn't change back quickly enough, either — I wouldn't make it out of the woods myself, let alone have the energy to carry another person that far. And clothes — clothes would be a problem. Naked guy carrying an unconscious girl, what could possibly go wrong?

Ugh, *fuck, fuck, FUCK!* I was going to have to pull a Lassie. What had I done to deserve this? I licked her pale freckled cheek, more for my own reassurance than hers, and then I was off.

CHAPTER 1

"Good afternoon, Chief Duncan." I decided to break the ice with a breezy greeting as I entered the room. Start things off on the right foot as it were. I wasn't going to allow the chief's stare to unnerve me like last time. I was stronger than that.

He did stare. I detected a hint of him being thrown off by my entrance. Hah!

He finally nodded a greeting, cleared his throat, and gestured to a wingback chair. "Please have a seat, Ms. Hughes."

I bristled, even as I tried to talk myself out of being irritated. Perhaps he was unaware of the proper etiquette for the situation. Four weeks ago, I wouldn't have had a clue myself. It was the host's job to ask people to take a seat. The library was my favorite spot, and the one place I was usually left alone. For him to claim it as his own, however unwittingly, grated. I found myself unreasonably defensive at the invasion of my home territory.

I was tempted to sit in a different chair, even though I liked the one he indicated. When I was a little girl, I thought it was a throne. It wasn't particularly fancy, but it was covered in burgundy velvet and had the same general shape as an illustration in one of my fairy tale picture books. On second thought — or was it a third thought at this point? — given the recent revelations of my grandmother, maybe I shouldn't sit on anything resembling a throne. Wait! Was I seriously thinking this hard about whether I should sit in a damn chair?

I sat, just to end the mental babbling. *Uh oh*. I had debated with myself for too long. Chief Duncan was looking at me strangely. Yup, this conversational gap was getting to be awkward. This tangential dithering of my brain had to be one of the worst consequences of my accident.

I smiled sunnily at the chief. Why no, officer, I wasn't eyeing the chair as if it might bite me.

He shifted uncomfortably in his chair, as if unsure whether I was a threat. I wasn't used to that as a female. Huh, being considered mentally unbalanced had its upsides too . . . My smile became a fraction more genuine.

The chief's disgust with being unnerved was obvious. He glowered from his leather armchair. I happened to know his chair was nowhere near as comfortable as it appeared. It had been my grandfather's favorite seat, and its padding was molded to his shape. Grandmother claimed she couldn't find a chair she liked enough to replace it. I didn't think she ever would, and it perversely gave me hope for our relationship.

The chief finally stopped staring and shifted his large frame the inch or two the chair allowed. I was willing to bet he had been a linebacker in high school. For that matter, it looked like he could still play a mean game, despite his gray hair. I wondered if the officers under his command were supposed to meet his standards of physical fitness, or if he only had unreasonably high expectations of himself.

The petite policewoman, seated on the couch to his right, couldn't have been more his opposite. She radiated wholesomeness. She could convincingly go undercover as an apple-cheeked dairymaid if you just threw a kerchief over her dark hair. She smiled sweetly at me. I was so grateful for the small gesture that it surprised me. I told myself not to get too excited. She was probably setting up to play the good cop. It was pathetic I was so easily manipulated.

Chief Duncan finally broke the awkward silence. "Ms. Hughes, this is Officer Ramos." He rolled the R in her name beautifully; I was surprised he had it in him to be so culturally sensitive. "Officer Ramos, Loren Hughes." We shook hands and exchanged pleased-to-meet-yous.

"I wanted you two to meet because Officer Ramos has been assigned to this case. She will be your contact person in the future." She slid a card toward me with her cell phone number meticulously circled, so the ink didn't cover any other text.

"In case you think of anything else you want to share with us, you have my contact information now." She smiled at me again.

The chief waited expectantly, so I nodded again. I was beginning to feel like a bobblehead. I let the silence stretch. Was the awkward pause meant to intimidate me into telling him everything he wanted to know? I wished it was that simple.

Chief Duncan lost patience with the waiting game first. "We have some new evidence in the case. But first, we need to ask if you have remembered anything else about that day, Ms. Hughes?"

"No, sir."

He stared at me, "So you have nothing to add to your statement?"

Did he pretend his gaze was boring into my brain, to uncover all the secrets I was theoretically keeping?

"No, sir." Sugar wouldn't melt in my mouth.

Awkward, but the chief was going to have to do better. So far, this was easy compared to dealing with my grandmother.

"When we last spoke, you stated you never met the deceased before the day in question."

I didn't bother reaffirming the obvious. How many different ways did I need to say it? I had no idea who the dead guy was, or why he was there in the woods that day. I reconsidered his question. Was he trying to trick me?

"That is correct, although I don't know if I am comfortable with the term 'met.' I suppose our bodies met, but we didn't introduce ourselves or anything." I was careful to keep my voice level since the words themselves could be taken sarcastically. I was never sarcastic . . .

Chief Duncan raised an eyebrow anyway.

"Would you mind going through everything from the beginning for me, since I am new to the case?" asked Officer Ramos. Her tone was sweeter than I liked my coffee, which was saying something. "Perhaps that will help fill in some of the gaps we seem to have. It may also help you remember details you may have forgotten."

I wanted to groan, "The whole thing, again?" I glanced at Chief Duncan, hoping he would veto the idea — hoping he would say we didn't have the time for it. I was not in luck. Chief Duncan was nodding.

"That might be useful. You were still on pain medication when we last spoke, and your responses to our questions were . . . disjointed."

Well, that was a nice way of saying I sounded like I should be committed to psychiatric care. Given the painkillers I had been on, I wasn't sure the concussion was to blame.

I took a deep breath, "Right. It was August thirteenth." It was easy to remember the date because the accident happened on my birthday, and Grandmother hadn't let me forget it ruined her plans for my birthday dinner. "I was out in the woods, sketching."

"Sketching?" The two officers were amusing in stereo. I stifled a smile. Chief Duncan was skeptical. Had we not covered this before? I racked my brain, trying to remember those initial fuzzy hospital days. I must not have explained before, given that reaction . . . It was scary when you couldn't trust your brain.

"Yes, sketching." I modulated my tone, so I didn't give too much of my mental state away. "I'm an artist – a technical illustrator. I have a client publishing a botany text. He commissioned some fern pieces."

"We didn't find any drawings at the scene. There weren't any in your pack, either." I wasn't sure if the accusatory tone was meant to imply it was my fault the evidence was tampered with, or if he thought I was lying. Either way, it didn't matter if the chief had impugned my honesty. Really, I wasn't going to let it bother me. I just like to grind layers of enamel off my teeth for no reason . . .

Lying to yourself is hard.

"My sketchpad was with my things at the hospital. I assumed you didn't need it since you didn't take it." I shrugged.

Chief Duncan looked more disgruntled, which I wouldn't have guessed was possible. "That book should have been handed over to us along with your pack. We need to take it into evidence."

Another personal item confiscated by the police, how many years would it be before I got it back? I wished I had the nerve to ask permission to scan it first. I could see if perhaps they would let me do it at the station. I didn't want to lose the twenty or thirty hours of work my sketchbook represented, especially with the setback of my broken arm.

"If you'll excuse me, I will go get it for you." The smile on my face couldn't have been pretty; my jaw was clenched so tightly, it was triggering a headache. I almost collided with Ms. Millie as I entered the hallway.

"Done already?" She sounded surprised.

"No," I responded. "They want my sketchbook. I'm not sure they believe I was drawing out in the woods. Plus, it's apparently evidence." The long day caught up with me, my shoulders slumping out of their Grandmother-approved-posture.

"I know where your sketchbooks are. I will bring them along with a plate of cookies. I know how to soften Chief Duncan up. Why don't you head back in and finish so you can manage a nap before dinner?" Her eyes shone warmly with amusement at her deft manipulation of the chief, and I suspected, of myself as well.

"Thank you, Ms. Millie." I gave her a quick hug. "I hope my grandmother realizes how lucky she is to have you around!"

"Oh, you!" She was still chuckling at my flattery as she left. "Shoo." She gestured toward the library.

"Yes, ma'am."

I was able to reenter the library with a serene smile on my face. Raised eyebrows greeted my empty hands.

"Ms. Millie offered to get the sketchbooks so we could finish talking," I explained as I resumed my seat on the throne, ankles neatly crossed and tucked under the seat.

"That's helpful. So, you were out hunting plants to draw . . .?" Officer Ramos prompted.

"Yes. I only have a few clients right now. I was planning to accept more commissions once I finished my master's degree." I motioned with my left hand to my right arm in its brace. "That plan is currently on hold." For reasons other than just the broken arm, but they didn't need to hear about all the ways my life was going to pieces.

"Besides the commission, I also wanted to have some pieces to add to my portfolio. The weather was so lovely, I was working whenever I could. That morning, I was looking for ferns and mosses to sketch."

Chief Duncan frowned. Did he realize it made him look constipated? "So, you hiked off-trail, in unfamiliar woods, for ferns? Doesn't your grandmother have some of those here, in her acres of gardens?"

"She might. I didn't think to ask. I wasn't staying here then." Be patient, you are tired and overreacting. I repeated it like a mantra. It was his job to be suspicious, and there was a lot more going on than I knew about. I was grumpy about it myself. I tried not to let my frustration creep into my voice.

"I enjoy being in the woods, and I prefer to draw plants in their native habitats when possible. I know some orienteering, and I can assure you, I took all the proper precautions. I had basic emergency supplies with me. I told my roommates the general area I would be working in, and when I should be back."

"You don't look like the outdoor type."

Well of course not – certainly not in the frilly white nightgown Grandmother had brought to the hospital, and not in this dress, either. It seems the chief didn't know it was possible to change clothes.

"Whatever makes you say that?" I asked innocently, making certain to widen my eyes slightly.

The chief must be one of those men with whom you were either a sweetly clueless wearer of pink frills or a tomboy who might possibly know something about the manly pursuits of cars, sports, and hunting. Obviously, crossing the boundaries between the two possibilities was suspicious activity, but if I let his notions of proper female behavior derail the conversation, we would never finish. That thought didn't stop me from wanting to make him squirm as he failed to fit me into one of his neat little mental boxes.

"Anyway..." I continued faux blithely, "I wanted to find a granite outcrop, as I needed a *Diamorpha smallii* specimen, and they are known to grow in a shallow substrate. Of course, I wouldn't have passed up a cryptogam either, though I planned to finish illustrating the vascular species first. But I got distracted when I found a pinnate pleurocarp specimen at the bottom. You know, it is just fascinating how those outcrops end up supporting zonal vegetation so different from the surrounding areas. Oh, but I am getting distracted! Don't let me lecture you!"

Not a bit passive-aggressive, nope. I shook my head at my antics. I took great glee in upending the chief's mental image of me – I imagined him trying to add a lab coat to a frilly ball gown. Was it too obvious what I was doing? The corner of Officer Ramos's mouth was twitching like she wanted to smile.

"The early light was perfect, so I took some photos, then set up my watercolors. I believe I had out viridian, sepia, and ochre."

Chief Duncan had been leaning back broodingly in his chair, with his fingers steepled in front of him. He startled me when he bolted upright. "You had a camera?"

"Yes, sir." Shouldn't he have known? "It was in my backpack, along with everything else. Do you know how long you'll need to keep my sketchbook and my camera?" I couldn't remember what pictures were on my camera – other shots of plant specimens were guaranteed, but hopefully nothing too weird or embarrassing.

Chief Duncan's tone was flat, without even the briefest emotion flitting through. "I can't answer that, Ms. Hughes. I don't recall seeing a camera in evidence. I would like for you to write up a list of everything you had with you that day. It will help us determine what might have been overlooked. We secured the scene quickly because of an impending thunderstorm."

"Does this mean my camera has been lost?" My voice sounded tight and unnatural. Way to play it cool, Loren.

Another uncomfortable shift in his chair, then evasively, "I am going to need to go back and review the evidence before I can let you know."

I turned his words over in my head and prodded the idea. He knew instantly there were no sketches in the evidence, so I didn't believe he had forgotten my camera. How was he so calm when it appeared somebody lost evidence? Did he assume I was wrong about it being in my bag? Trying to sort out all the options was impossible. I didn't have enough information – or energy.

Officer Ramos cleared her throat. "Why don't you continue."

"Um, okay. I got caught up in my work. I don't know how much later it was – maybe an hour – but I heard a loud rustle, like tree branches shaking overhead. At first, I thought it was a couple of squirrels chasing each other or something, but it got louder. I know some animals in the area can be dangerous, and I didn't want to be lying on the ground if a bear or mountain lion was nearby. So, I stood up to see if I could figure out what was going on." I didn't mention stumbling as I stood because my foot had fallen asleep while I was absorbed in my work. "I managed to look up just in time to see something large falling toward me. After that . . . well, I don't remember anything else clearly until the hospital."

Officer Ramos pounced, "You said the next thing you remember clearly. Do you remember anything *un*clearly?"

Damn. Why couldn't I get the knack of thinking things through *before* they popped out of my mouth? I didn't particularly want to share that bit of information. The heat of a blush rose in my cheeks, which probably seemed suspicious. "I know it sounds ridiculous, but I remember regaining consciousness for a few seconds, and there was a wolf. It sniffed me and licked my face."

Officer Ramos ever so slightly raised an eyebrow. "Are you sure it wasn't a dog?"

I considered it for a second. Then reluctantly shook my head. "I don't know. It was pretty big."

"How much brain trauma did the doctor say you had, again?" Chief Duncan asked. He was just full of tact.

I shrugged. Honestly, I didn't think it sounded like something a healthy brain came up with, either. "The doctors said it was a challenge to know exactly how much damage there was. I was unconscious for about an hour and a half, but it was two days before I could remember anything about the accident. My memory seems back to normal now, but it's hard to say. Didn't you talk to Dr. Aatos about all of this?" The doc had been surprised at how quickly I was recovering. I was just grateful something was going well for once.

It was Chief Duncan's turn to shrug. "Patient confidentiality. They wouldn't tell us anything."

"Oh." I couldn't think of any reason not to share my medical records with the police. I was all for cooperating so they could find out what happened to that poor man, but I didn't trust things not to get twisted in some way that got me into further trouble. With how things had been going recently, I'd check with Grandmother's lawyer first.

"Do you still have gaps in your memory?"

"Just the parts when I was unconscious. I remember everything else."

"So you don't remember meeting the deceased ever before?"

"No, sir." I should record myself saying it, then the chief could play it back the next twenty times he wanted to ask me that question.

The chief pulled a photo out of his folder. "What about this man — do you recognize him?"

I dutifully looked at the picture. It was not a close-up of the charred dead body like the last picture the chief showed me, but it was still disgusting. It was a trophy shot of a man standing with one leg propped triumphantly against the side of a dead elephant. I was having difficulty getting past the elephant's drooping eyelids with their absurdly long lashes, to even notice the man. When I was able to finally focus on the human, I couldn't stop myself from rolling my eyes.

The hunter resembled a caricature of someone on safari. He was dressed from head to toe in shades of khaki, including a bushman's hat, a safari jacket, and a linen vest with too many pockets. Knee-high boots and a ridiculously oversized rifle completed the outfit. It was beyond overkill. Unless maybe the photo was older, from a time when it was culturally acceptable to kill endangered animals for sport?

From the color processing, it wasn't that old, though it might have been touched up and reprinted. How long ago was big game hunting in Africa the thing to do? This guy would have to have been mummified for that to be the case . . .

"When was this picture taken? Should I be imagining him as older? This guy looks like an extra from *Out of Africa*." Was I mistaken, or was that a muffled laugh from Officer Ramos?

"No, the photo is current." The chief's answer was curt.

"But isn't hunting elephants illegal?"

"As a huntsman, that is what I would have expected, but apparently you can get a permit if you pay about sixty grand." He sounded disgusted. I wasn't sure if it was with me sidetracking the discussion, or with people paying ridiculous amounts of money to kill peaceful herbivores solely for sport. "Ms. Hughes. The gentleman in the picture. Do you recognize him?"

I dutifully peered closely at the man's face again. I waited for even a glimmer of recognition. I shook my head. I passed the photo back to the chief; I didn't want to look at it any longer.

"I'm sorry. I don't recognize him." More staring silence. "So . . . is he the dead guy who crushed me?"

Officer Ramos nodded. "His name was Charles Gifford." They were watching for a reaction, but the name meant nothing to me. I shrugged and shook my head. Mr. Gifford sure had managed to cause a lot of trouble.

The chief nodded at Officer Ramos. She had set up a laptop while I was examining the photo. She turned it around so I could see the screen.

"This is footage from a security camera, taken three weeks before the incident," the chief informed me.

I watched as an Audi – no wait – *my* Audi pulled up to a gas pump. The car was a gift from my father for my sixteenth birthday; it was in excellent shape for its age. I wish I hadn't thought of my father, as it led to thinking about how we weren't speaking. Even distracted, I didn't have too much trouble placing the location of the video. It was the last gas station on the main highway before the turnoff that led to Lointaine.

I had almost forgotten about managing to get tangled in the gas hose. Look at that grace. How delightful for the chief to find evidence of my inadequacies. The man on the other side of the pump stopped filling his vehicle to assist me. It was a scene straight out of *The Three Stooges*, except I guess we were missing Curly. A minute later, I was free, and the gentleman helped brush me off. We talked for a few seconds before he went back to gassing up his oversized SUV. I topped off my tank and pulled away before he finished. I vaguely remembered he made some joke about needing to fill up before leaving civilization. It had seemed weird given that his vehicle would be at home in a jungle. You did have to drive through the mountains to get to Lointaine, but we were talking about paved roads through the Blue Ridge Mountains, not an icy pathway through the Himalayas.

Why were we watching this? The video footage wasn't high quality, and it certainly didn't contain a close-up of the man's face. It might have been the same man shown in the photo . . .

"Do you still claim to not know him?" the chief demanded.

"Was that the same man?" No response from the chief, but Officer Ramos nodded. "Until you showed me the video, I didn't remember any of this. I wasn't there for five minutes! He helped me when I got all twisted in the gas hose." The chief's eyebrows were climbing his forehead in disbelief. They resembled fuzzy caterpillars having seizures. The inappropriate mental image made me want to burst out laughing, which was at odds with how frustrated I was. "I barely spoke to him other than to say thank you!"

I pulled the shreds of my composure together, determined not to lose any of the ground regained in the last few weeks. Even if I had to fight for every last iota of control, I was determined that the side effects of my concussion were not going to be permanent.

"So, you expect me to believe you both just happened to meet at the gas station – where he put his hands all over you, 'helping,'" he made air quotes, "before you both came into town the same day. Then later, you happened to be in the same part of several thousand acres of woods, where you magically ended up together on the ground, sharing a blanket?"

I was astonished as the implication hit me. He thought the creepy hunter guy and I were a couple! I guess he had been pushing the angle before, but I hadn't noticed because of the painkillers. Or – and this was more likely because the idea was so ridiculous – it would never occur to me. I closed my mouth when I realized it was hanging open.

The chief leaned back in his seat and clasped his hands, pleased with himself. "That is an awful lot of coincidences, Ms. Hughes. Now, if it happened that he was in town to meet a woman he was having an affair with . . ." He spread his hands apart as the sentence trailed off. It was an arrogant, scripted gesture that left me with no patience. "If you explain things to us now, it will be much better than if we find proof later you are lying. I understand accidents happen, although this one sure seems like it was a doozy . . . I must admit I am extremely curious to hear what happened. I will do my best to make sure your, ahem, *relationship* doesn't get mentioned to your grandmother."

"Relationship?" A red haze was creeping into the edge of my vision. I had been ready to laugh when he first mentioned his ridiculous notion, but my emotions rapidly changed as the obnoxious charade continued. If I hadn't been so angry, the intensity of my reaction would have scared me.

"We didn't have a *relationship*. From what little I know of the hunter guy, I wouldn't want to be his friend – let alone be intimate with him." Just the idea caused ripples of disgust to creep over my flesh. "Ugh!"

"Gifford's secretary said he was particularly excited about this trip, and jokingly mentioned he was hunting something special this time. Since it seems he has killed everything from grizzlies to giraffes, there doesn't appear to be anything in North Carolina that would fit the bill. The only thing in season here is deer, and only for bow hunters. Gifford didn't bow hunt. Best I can figure, it was a crude joke and he meant he was hunting some tail of the human variety. Namely, you."

I struggled to keep my composure.

Millie knocked on the door before entering with a plate full of cookies balanced on top of a stack of sketchbooks. "Here we go. I wasn't sure which one you wanted, so I brought them all." She winked at me before turning to beam at the chief. "Oatmeal-fig-flaxseed cookies — I know they are your favorite!"

I was ready to name Ms. Millie my personal Saint of Timely Interruptions. That was way above and beyond any "other duties as required" that might be a part of her housekeeper position. The anger drained from my body like a balloon deflating. She put the stack on the coffee table in front of me. As she left, she gave me a significant glance I couldn't interpret. Chief Duncan gave a tired sigh and, in an unconscious gesture, scrubbed at his eyes briefly. I bet he would have hated that I noticed the sign of weakness.

I reminded myself I would be grumpy too if it was my job to sort out this mess. Trying to see things from his side wasn't helping me deal with his behavior. I sighed. It would require a monumental effort, but I was going to be gracious. It was more important that I like my own behavior than to show my displeasure for his. Here goes . . .

I practically had to mentally staple the smile on my face, but I offered the chief the elegantly arranged plate, "Cookie?" He grimaced before taking one, and I decided I won that round.

Now for the sketchbook . . . Even though several of the sketchbooks had equally battered black covers, I knew exactly which one the chief wanted. Millie bringing the whole pile of books hadn't been subtle, but it couldn't hurt to reinforce the idea that I was an artist.

I pulled one of the books out and flipped through it, so the sketches were easily visible. Ooh, still life – see, a real artist here. I grabbed another book at random. I opened it and flipped a couple of pages before I realized what I was flashing around the room. I could feel my skin blushing a flaming red, all the way to the tips of my ears. This sketchbook was not full of ferns and flowers;

it was from my nude figure drawing class. When I froze in shock, I managed to leave the book open to a full frontal of a nude male model. Hello! Penis!

I slammed the book shut. Well, that'll show them what a fine artist I am. I hastily found the correct sketchbook and passed it to Officer Ramos, who failed to hide her grin this time. She passed the book to Chief Duncan to put in a large plastic evidence bag. It seemed a little late for that now.

He started to speak when the ringing of his cell phone interrupted him. He barked as he answered, "Yes?"

Was the chief losing his hearing? I was easily able to hear both sides of his conversation. Apparently, the report on Gifford from the medical examiner's office was finally available.

"About time," grunted the chief. "Why were they dragging their feet?"

"Well . . ." The reluctance of the poor man on the other end of the line was tangible. The chief's face tightened further. Millie should have brought him prune cookies. "There were some oddities the medical examiner was hoping to resolve, but she wasn't able to."

"Like what?" As the chief snapped the response, I wondered if the people at the station had argued over who would have to play the part of the messenger. Whoever drew the short straw might not have been lucky, but they were smart. I was going to have to remember the tactic of calling with unfortunate news when dealing with Grandmother.

"The burns were superficial. They probably weren't enough to kill him like we initially believed."

"Then what did?" The chief's words remained clipped.

The person on the other end hurried to offer further information, words racing over each other, "M.E. says blood loss, but the only wound was a bite on his leg, made by serrated pleurodont teeth."

I could tell he was reading the last few words. They didn't flow smoothly off his tongue, and he was over-enunciating them.

"Best the M.E. could figure, it was made by an enormous iguana, or perhaps a shark – which doesn't make any sense. But it shouldn't have done enough damage to kill him before he could get help, except the toxicology folks found snake venom in his system. That may have made him bleed out from the leg bite, but there are no signs of a snakebite on the body – although it could have been in the hunk the shark took out. But it doesn't make sense that he was bitten by a snake and a shark in the same place . . ." He trailed off weakly. "Anyway, the M.E. won't sign off on the death certificate – marked it as pending."

The chief started to cuss and looked up to see both of us staring at him. Officer Ramos found some important notes to make in her files. I glanced away too, pretending to study a mischievous gargoyle perched on a bookshelf.

"Mark, I will call you back. I'm in the middle of an interview here." He ended the call and glared at Officer Ramos. "This is exactly the sort of bullshit I was talking about!" I kept my eyes lowered, but noticed Officer Ramos's notes included 'sharks: research aquariums and private owners.' Really?

"And you!" The chief's glare turned toward me and then swung away as the library door burst open. Grandmother sailed into the room like a warship, Millie trailing in her wake. Ah, Millie's earlier look had meant she was going for reinforcements.

"Chief Duncan, perhaps I should have used smaller words. Loren has a concussion. You weren't to upset her. You will cease speaking with my granddaughter immediately. I will not have you venting your frustrations on her."

I turned back to Chief Duncan with macabre fascination. I expected his head to explode with this opposition. At the very least, turn red, veins bulging all over his forehead – probably end up with someone needing to call an ambulance for a coronary or some such thing. What happened was scarier. Chief Duncan's face shut down and didn't show any emotions. His voice, however, was like a shard of ice.

"Mrs. Dalton, I would like to take this opportunity to correct a notion that you seem to have. To begin with, you are not the queen of Lointaine. You do not rule its residents, and you certainly do not rule me. I do not care that you descended from a royal bastard." Oh, he enjoyed that double entendre.

My mouth was hanging open, but I couldn't seem to find the muscles that worked my jaw — if Grandmother was correct, I'd be catching flies any second now. Had Chief Duncan just challenged her? Even forces of nature like the weather seemed to fall in line with my grandmother's wishes; she regularly planned outdoor gatherings without a concern or a backup plan. And yet the chief was throwing down a gauntlet . . .

"Furthermore, this 'curse,'" another set of air quote gestures, "of yours does not only affect your family. It affects us lowly peons, too. When things go wrong, we seem to be the ones who get trampled. Or have you already forgotten the events of this past year? If you all would stop being so high and mighty, wrapping things in a web of secrets, I might be able to do my job and protect people. You are not above us, and you are not above the law. If either of you has withheld any information pertaining to this case, I will have you arrested for obstruction. Enough."

Ooh . . . It sounded like they'd butted heads in the past. His words suggested the chief knew about Louis and the Magic. He might even believe it was real. That was interesting. Was the same true of everyone in Lointaine?

Grandmother's face remained impassive throughout this speech, aside from a slight tightening around her mouth. "Thank you for sharing your opinion. However, we are done here for the day. Loren is still in a delicate state. I will not allow you to tire her out by harassing her further with your spurious notions. If you need anything else from her, you may speak to our attorney."

She followed her pronouncement with a small, sour smile of social triumph that contained no joy or warmth. She had won this skirmish, but she wasn't happy about it. That was smart, because I think she – or perhaps I should say we – made an enemy in the process. Chief Duncan slammed his folder shut.

The coup de grace came with a fluid motion toward the library door, "Mildred will show you out."

CHAPTER 2

They were gone, all of them. I had been heading downstairs to confront Grandmother when I decided I should check one last time. After all, it was possible my abused brain just blanked out the previous three times I looked.

I reviewed each shelf in the closet. I wanted something comfy to change into so I could curl up and recuperate from the interrogation. But nope — not a hint of frayed denim or stretchy cotton could be seen.

Damn. Unfortunately, it seemed like my brain was working just fine. I froze. Wait, I didn't just think that, did I?

After spending three weeks clawing my way back from my concussion — not to mention having outrageous family secrets dumped on me — how was it possible to be upset my brain was functioning properly? Grandmother was not good for my mental health.

"Grandmother Rose!" I hollered, not caring a bit that she would consider yelling across the house the very height of rudeness. I did keep my muttering about high-handed, interfering, presumptive relatives to myself. The impending discussion would be antagonistic enough without adding name-calling to the mix. A sharp stabbing pain lanced from my temple to a spot just behind my ear, a sign I needed to calm down. Right. Deep breaths.

I heard the door open and turned to see Ms. Millie come in. "What is all the fuss about, Loren?" She didn't seem terribly concerned. The question was asked over her shoulder as she straightened one of the umpteen pillows on the bed.

"Where is my grandmother, Ms. Millie?" I spoke more sharply than I intended. I wasn't angry with Millie, but I needed her to focus on me instead of housekeeping. This was of greater importance than making sure the embroidered roses on the pillows lined up.

"She is downstairs in the library with Connor. He stopped by about something or other." Satisfied with the military precision of the gauzy bedding, she finally turned toward me. "Why do you ask?"

"All my clothes are gone."

Millie came over. She looked at the dresses, skirts, and blouses hanging in the closet. Confusion and concern warred for control of her face. "Sweetie, your clothes are right here." I could practically see her trying to recall my neurologist's phone number.

"No," I said emphatically, just managing not to stomp my foot like a three-year-old. Another deep breath. "Ms. Millie, these are the clothes Grandmother picked out. *My* clothes are gone."

"Oh."

I had an awful thought and crossed to the dresser. I took a deep breath and opened my underwear drawer. A peek was all it took. I slammed the drawer closed.

"Where are my clothes?" Surely Millie knew what happened; I couldn't imagine Grandmother handling cardboard to pack my things away in boxes.

Millie swallowed nervously. "The people from the thrift shop were here earlier. I didn't realize . . . I mean, I am not sure, but I think . . ."

I tried hard to wait for her to finish, per Grandmother's rules of polite conversation, but when she faltered, I just turned and walked off. I pounded down the steps. I didn't care if there were snide comments later about sounding like a herd of elephants.

Grandmother Rose had pushed one too many buttons today, so I didn't bother knocking before bursting into the library.

Grandmother did not appear pleased at the intrusion; however, she quickly replaced the irritated glare with one of her trademarked gracious smiles. "Loren, I was just about to send for you. Connor has been studying the town's history with the tales. I expect he will be able to answer some of your questions."

Huh. Interesting, I hadn't known that about him. Not that I knew Connor well . . . I'd only run into him at the few social events I'd felt obligated to attend recently. No, wait, Loren. Stay focused. Remember you are angry!

I nodded a greeting to Connor. "Good afternoon."

Turning, I addressed my errant relative. "Grandmother, I need to speak to you," I gestured toward the hallway. "If you could excuse us, Connor?"

I expected Grandmother to argue about leaving a guest unattended. After all, it was highly improper. Perhaps she was trying to avoid a scene. I probably wasn't hiding my anger well. I wasn't the least bit sorry.

I barely waited for her to get close enough to pretend we were having a private discussion. "What did you do with my clothes?" I hissed. I should have waited; Grandmother paused in the doorway when I started talking. So much for keeping this private.

"Your clothes?" She had leaned in to hear my whisper, then straightened so quickly that she looked like she was riding one of those bouncy spring animals at a playground. I wished she would take one more step so I could close the door.

"Yes, my clothes. My jeans, my t-shirts . . . All the clothes you disliked, and thought weren't fit for my 'new position.' They seem to have magically vanished."

"Loren, I gave those beat-up old things to a local charity. You won't need them anymore. It made space for your new clothes. In addition, it will help those less fortunate. Although I do wonder if they will want your holey jeans . . ." Her tone and manner suggested I was being utterly unreasonable. She wasn't even trying to keep the discussion private at this point.

I glanced over and saw that Connor was trying to look like he wasn't witnessing our disagreement. It wasn't working. He had definitely noticed and seemed like he would be happier if he could take cover behind the couch. I felt awful for making him uncomfortable.

Guilt swirled into my anger. It was making it hard to articulate. I couldn't get through a list of all the ways her actions were wrong. Blood rushed to my head, spinning the room around me. I was going to have to sit down when what I wanted to do was yell.

Of all the things I could have said, what I finally managed to splutter was, "I can't believe you rummaged through my underwear drawer!"

"Well, it needed to be done. Some of your underthings were in deplorable shape. What if you were in an accident?"

That was her concern? Too late — been there, done that. It's not like I had been wearing my nicest lingerie while tramping through the woods. And yet, somehow I had managed to avoid traumatizing the EMTs.

I finally pulled it together enough to explain. "Those clothes were mine. They were not yours to dispose of. You had no right!" I tried not to let my dizziness show as I sat down on a chair that was usually solely ornamental. I glared. "What if I decide to leave?" She flinched. "Or if I wanted to get some painting done? I can't hike in a skirt! I still need those clothes. Get them back."

Grandmother placed her hand over her heart with a graceful bend of her wrist. "You want me to ask a charity to return a donation? That simply isn't possible."

There wasn't much I was completely sure of right now, but I was sure that letting her get away with this would set a dangerous precedent. I would have no control over my own life.

"Get my clothes back or this experiment is done. I will leave." I met her eyes, letting my threat hang. If she truly believed all the tales she had been telling, she wouldn't want me to go. Grandmother dropped her gaze first, shoulders drooping the smallest fraction.

"I can see you are going to be unreasonable about this." She sighed as if I was a six-year-old, declaring I was going to hold my breath until I got a pony. She would probably prefer buying me a horse to having frayed denim in her home. "If I had known they mattered that much to you, I wouldn't have given them away."

Something containing the word "sorry" would be the next logical step in this discussion . . . I waited, certain it wouldn't happen but hoping I was wrong, for the sake of our relationship.

"I apologize." Wow, that was stiff. Easy on the starch there.

Of course you are sorry, you finally pushed me into taking a stand. Weren't planning on that, were you? I put the thought into my eyes as I continued to stare at her. I wasn't going to relent just because she finally apologized for one of the many ways she was manipulating me. "Thank you for apologizing."

"Perhaps I can buy them back. Excuse me, I will need to make sure the boxes containing your clothes are set aside. Please see to our guest, while I take care of placing the call." She didn't wait for me to agree before she strode off.

Connor was staring assiduously at the pyramid of coffee table books. Right. I had to say something now, something to smooth over the awkwardness. I was much better at being awkward than fixing it.

"I am sorry I did that while you were here. I just couldn't . . ." Just couldn't figure out how to end the sentence apparently. Deal with this anymore? Deal with her? I didn't manage to fill in the blank.

Connor grinned at me. "It's ok. I missed the fireworks on the Fourth this year."

He was kind to try to put me at ease. Connor didn't seem like the type of person who generally noticed if you were slouching, so I could just be myself with him. I sat down and snuggled into the couch cushions. If I could just get my tight shoulder muscles to stop pulling on my bruised ribs . . . They had felt good recently, but all this stress was acting like a ratchet, tightening muscles across my back. Ahh . . . I was going to enjoy slumping for these precious few minutes.

Um, small talk. Right. I looked around desperately for something to spark an idea. Not much help, just lots of books. I could ask if he had read anything good recently? I needed to say something soon . . . Wait . . . I scanned the titles again. How had I missed it before? That entire shelf was filled with fairy tales.

Although I had spent a lot of time in the cozy room during my recovery, I hadn't explored it properly. When I first arrived at Grandmother's, I wasn't allowed to read because of the concussion. Since that restriction had been lifted, I had used all the reading time my headaches allowed to catch up on schoolwork. However, I was regretting not taking a closer look at the library's offerings. Was it rude to get up in the middle of a conversation? Connor probably wouldn't care, and I could tie it into my small talk. That seemed like a win! I got up and wandered over to the bookshelf. "Grandmother said you are studying the tales. Have you read these?"

Connor got up and came over to join me. "I believe I've read many of them."

The books were old; the ones in English all appeared to be early or original editions. Other books were in French, Italian, and German. Was that Cyrillic? I found books I remembered reading as a child: *Grimm's Fairy Tales*, the colored fairy books by Lang with gilded illustrations on their covers, Hans Christian Andersen . . . Some I knew of, but had never actually seen copies of before — Basile, Straparola, and Calvino. As I explored, I realized the entire wall contained only fairy tales. Even the oil portrait I had assumed was a distant ancestor was labeled as being Marie-Catherine Le Jumel de Barneville, Baroness d'Aulnoy. One of the volumes of her *Les Contes des Fées* was propped open on the shelf underneath. I flipped a few pages, letting my fingers enjoy the slightly fuzzy nap of the old paper.

Finette Cendron, "*Il y avait une fois* . . ." The French version of "Once upon a time . . ." The first line of a fairy tale was terrifying now that my life had been borne away by a curse, but it was also triggering hazy childhood memories. Did Grandmother tell me stories in French? Was I making things up now, or did that actually happen?

"So, how are you holding up?" Connor asked. I glanced over at him. Oops, I had left him to carry the conversation. I appreciated the effort on his part, but the question was a bit artless. Connor felt it, giving in to a nervous tick, pushing his glasses up the bridge of his nose. Logic seemed more in line with his strengths than emotion.

I shrugged, "I'm not sure." I was too drained to try to come up with a precise or socially polite answer. I struggled to find something else to say on the topic. Ideally, something that didn't result in me crying messily on his shoulder or a priceless first edition.

"Hmm." Connor paused, was he going to push the issue? "Your grandmother asked me to stop by so I could answer any questions you might have. Maybe knowing more would help?"

Would it? In the days after the accident, I struggled with vertigo. The world moved in unpredictable ways — tilting in ways it shouldn't, continuing to move when it should be still. I'd be fine one minute and then stumbling sideways the next as the Earth's center of gravity randomly changed directions.

This revelation of my grandmother's had similarly set my mental balance off-kilter. The unquestioned rules that anchored my worldviews had been cut. Plucking one tangled bit to unravel was beyond me.

Connor seemed happily absorbed, looking the books over, while he waited for a response. He ran his fingers over the spines of the books — was he sniffing one? I hid a grin. I liked the vanilla and tannin smell of old books, too.

That small connection freed the words stuck in my throat. I grinned to take a bit of the sting out of them. "You do know Dr. Aatos says I am supposed to get lots of 'physical, cognitive, and emotional rest'? I'm lost. I have so many questions, I don't know where to start."

"Um, yeah." Connor shuffled his feet and scratched the back of his neck like a child confronted with an empty cookie jar. "You know, we did check with him first. I know the timing is awful, but we decided it was better to tell you, even if it did slow your healing. We hoped it would keep you from making any rash decisions with lasting repercussions."

How in the world did they think I was going to get myself into trouble? "What, like kissing frogs?" Then, what Connor just said sank in. "Wait, you mean Dr. Aatos knows?"

Connor nodded. "He was your mother's doctor, too — during her tale."

I waved my hand vaguely at the wall of books — or more accurately, the wall of fairy tales. "So he believes all this?" Another nod from Connor. "What about you? Do you believe, too?"

"I have seen too much *not* to believe." It was official — either the whole town was delusional, or I was. I still wasn't sure which way the evidence was pointing.

"So, some leftover spell from three hundred years ago is cursing my family?" I laughed, not caring that it sounded closer to a stereotypical witch's cackle than a polite chuckle.

He shrugged. "It's one way to explain what is happening here. There are certainly verifiable elements in the story. Marie-Catherine D'Aulnoy existed and was well known for her fairy tales. We have letters she sent to Louis, your great-great-grandfather and Lointaine's founder, where she calls him her godson. Her works influenced folk tales throughout most of Europe, so why not the personal tales of people here as well? She was even called the *'reine de fees'* or 'fairy queen.' If anyone could cast a spell, the original 'fairy godmother' would be a logical choice." He shrugged. "It's possible, but I think there is something more fundamental at work. Marie-Catherine's tales are only a variable in the equation, not an operator driving it."

"Did you just use a math analogy on me?" It came out closer to an accusation than I meant it to. "Um, maybe you could tell me the answer to the equation, and not worry about the operators?"

It was Connor's turn to give a rueful laugh. He managed to be amused and self-deprecating, without a trace of bitterness. "Sorry, no. I don't have any answers, which is maddening, since I have spent years studying the subject."

Connor paused and glanced at the sofa. "It is going to take a few minutes for me to explain . . . perhaps we should sit before I get started?"

I was so tired I wasn't sure I wanted to deal with an extended — and from what little I knew of Connor — technical discussion. On the other hand, all the unanswered questions swirling around my brain would make it impossible to relax. If Connor's explanation could settle some of the thoughts that had been keeping me from sleeping, I probably needed to tough this out.

"What do you think about finding some of Ms. Millie's croissants and coffee before you explain things?"

"I think nobody turns down Ms. Millie's baking."

I didn't disagree. "If she ever opened a bakery, she would make a fortune. I can bring a tray back here, but we could also eat in the kitchen? It's a little less formal there . . ."

"Please. I always feel like I am going to break something in rooms like this."

Well, that made two of us. I hoped there were some chocolate croissants left. The million calories in one of those might sustain my brain long enough to keep up with Connor's "simple" explanation.

CHAPTER 3

"Let me get the oven preheated, and then I will show you where all the coffee things are." I held down the button to set the oven to 365 degrees, the temperature at which Ms. Millie had decreed her croissants be reheated.

"Sure thing."

There was a coffee station tucked away in one corner of the kitchen. I walked over and opened the cupboard over it. "Mugs are up here." I gestured so he could pick out the mug he wanted. "The coffee should still be hot. Sugar and spoons are next to the pot. I'll grab the cream when I get my coffee out of the fridge."

"The fridge?" Connor looked at the pot of fresh coffee confused.

"I'm stuck drinking decaf." Don't pout, Loren. It's not like it doesn't taste good. "Ms. Millie makes me a pot, and we keep the extra in the fridge. I'll just heat it up quickly." I heard the tinkling of Connor stirring his coffee as I dug around in the fridge.

"Oh right, your concussion. I should have remembered caffeine would be bad for that." How did he know everything? I had been shocked to hear that caffeine was something I would have to avoid.

I settled a small pot on the stove and dumped my coffee in. One of these days I would talk Grandmother into getting a microwave, or perhaps one of her caterers would. The burner clicked as I turned on the gas.

"Where are we sitting?" Connor asked.

"How about at the island?" The tall stools seemed better for a technical discussion than the breakfast nook. "I can grab a notepad if you will need to draw pictures for me?" I smiled as I said it.

Connor chuckled. "I think I can explain without pictures or equations. I'll fine-tune my delivery method while you finish up."

I grabbed the croissants from the breadbox and popped them into the oven. Then I set the timer for three minutes and got two plates out.

Less than five minutes later, I was out of ways to procrastinate with little domestic tasks. I turned to the island with a sigh. Connor grinned. "I should pretend to take that personally, but I won't."

"I'm so sorry! Grandmother would be horrified by my manners."

"No worries, my standards are rather lower than hers," Connor reassured me. I laughed. That was probably true of most people.

"Thank you. I'm ready to get started, really."

"Right, so like I said earlier, I don't know the exact reason Lointaine works the way it does. What I *can* tell you is every field I pursued seems to indicate something like this was inevitable. They all skirt around the edges of the idea that fairy tales are being manifested. When you put everything together, it is glaringly obvious this *should* happen: the collective unconscious, Jungian archetypes, the Aarne-Thompson system of classifying tales, Propp's morphology . . ." he paused for a breath. "Karma, quantum consciousness, cognitive metaphysics, entanglement theory . . . They all indicate a universal connectedness between tales and the people who tell them."

Suddenly, the extra studies required by my scholarship didn't seem like such a hodgepodge of subjects. My scholarship was obviously tied into all of this somehow. How had I missed the connection? Could I still blame my obtuseness on the head injury? I was getting tired of needing an excuse, even if it was legitimate. Connor was oblivious to my revelation and had continued, quite involved with his explanation. He had leaned forward intently in his chair and propped his elbows on the counter, straightening occasionally to gesture with his hands.

I wondered what I had missed.

". . . about ten years ago some researchers at Princeton started the Global Consciousness Project. They now have machines all over the world generating random numbers — zeroes and ones, a digital flip of the coin. They found that around major world events, like 9/11, the number distributions change. Machines all over the world had anomalous, non-random spikes. The researchers leading the project are hypothesizing that human reactions — the collective consciousness — are affecting the results.

"Other scientists are skeptical because there are blips in the data that don't correlate to major world events. The thing is, they don't have all the data. The other irregularities coincided with major happenings in the tales occurring here."

"That doesn't seem possible."

"Have you heard the saying: 'Watch your thoughts, for they become words. Watch your words, for they become actions. Watch your actions, for they become habits. Watch your habits, for they become your character. And watch your character, for it becomes your destiny?'"

"Yes — wasn't that Gandhi — or was it Buddha?"

Connor smiled. Gold star for Loren! Yay.

"Actually, it is difficult to say where the quote came from — it's been attributed to everybody from the Chinese philosopher Lao Tzu to Ralph Waldo Emerson, and yes, Gandhi. The basic idea is the thoughts or stories we tell ourselves end up shaping our lives — even in ways that shouldn't be possible. Mind over matter if you will . . .

"We tend to notice the extreme examples — like a depleted body somehow crossing a finish line before collapsing — but we ignore the subtle ways the same thing is true in our day-to-day lives. How many times have you seen someone ruin a good thing by telling themselves all the reasons it can't be? 'I can't take it anymore.' 'She'd never be interested in me.' 'I'm not qualified, no way they would hire me.' 'He always gets the credit.' We create the lens we see our lives through, which then affects how our lives play out."

I had surely seen people sabotage themselves, and I had also been astonished at what a sense of entitlement could get people. I nodded for him to continue.

"It makes sense that if the tales people tell themselves affect their lives, the same would happen on a larger scale. So, society should also watch its collective thoughts, because they will manifest as our collective destiny. We all understand this on some level, or we wouldn't get so upset when people have morals and values that differ from our own."

He paused to see if I was keeping up. I understood his logic, but I wasn't convinced. I nodded slowly, grasping for any missed connection. Connor sensed the hesitation and elaborated.

"I believe there is so much similarity amongst tales across the world because they evolved from the bits of our lives that play out repeatedly. For example, a woman used to be delayed in reaching full societal status until a man arrived on the scene and she was married. This stasis between maturity and being socially accepted as an adult is explored in the magical sleep of '*La Belle au Bois Dormant*.' But as the tale spread and became ingrained in additional minds, it became part of our collective unconscious, if you will — well, the universe was practically forced to manifest a Sleeping Beauty. Then someone, like your grandmother, ends up losing a century to sleep. It's the collective mind affecting matter. This town," he tapped the island with his index finger, "seems to be the place where that happens — where the Magic coalesces."

My mind was still turning over what he had said about Sleeping Beauty, but the last sentence caught my attention. "What? Why here?"

"Well I have my theories about that, too — ethnographic population distribution, ley lines, etcetera, etcetera, but you probably don't want to hear about them now. So, let's stick with the theory about Louis and Marie-Catherine. Where do fairy tales always take place?"

I considered the question. It was always in a neighboring kingdom, or an enchanted forest, or a far distant land . . . Oh right. "Umm. Far, far away? They are always far, far away."

"Do you know what Lointaine means in English . . .?"

I dredged up my high school French. "Loin . . . Wait — far away, distant?" I groaned. "Ugh — so it was Louis who cursed us when he named the valley? Not Marie-Catherine's spell?"

Connor shrugged. "Why not? He's as good a scapegoat as any. Or maybe it is both their faults."

"Why don't people just leave?"

"Well, they tried. But it didn't work. I don't think it is just the town — it's some combination of locality and ancestry. I mean, everyone would still be from 'far, far away.'"

Connor paused and shifted from side to side in his seat. He appeared to be considering exactly how to phrase things. He pushed his glasses up his nose. He didn't seem aware he had done it — it was becoming clear that it happened when he was thinking.

"It all began with your mother. She was concerned Sleeping Beauty seemed to run in the family; it did happen three generations in a row . . . She was worried it would happen to you, too. She felt becoming Sleeping Beauty derailed her life. She was engaged when she fell into her enchanted sleep. Her fiancé wasn't the man who woke her after one hundred months."

Whoa! Mom had been engaged to someone other than Dad?

Connor cleared his throat. "And, well . . . happily ever after doesn't mean everything is rainbows and sunshine. If you think about the oral traditions that fairy tales grew out of thousands of years ago, well, the people telling them were often worried about starving or freezing to death. Take those worries away, throw in some nicer clothes, existing at the top of the social hierarchy — life looks pretty good. It didn't matter if you were married to someone you could only tolerate. In an age of arranged marriages, tolerating your spouse might have been pretty good. Happily ever after doesn't necessarily mean much by modern standards." That was grim. "Although, the Magic does seem to do a slightly better job at matchmaking than people do themselves, at least when you examine empirical information like divorce rates.

"From what I can gather, your parents weren't one of the Magic's matchmaking success stories, though. Your mother wanted to take you away from the valley. She believed the Magic was contained here, and leaving would keep you from becoming a jinxt, or a princess."

"Wait, my mother is the one who wanted to leave?" I asked. "But I was told Dad and Grandmother couldn't get along."

Connor shook his head. I stared numbly out the window. Exactly how many lies had my parents told me? It was kind of like learning Santa wasn't real all over again, but about something much more important than who put the presents under the tree.

"There were a lot of disagreements when your mother announced she planned to leave. Your grandmother threatened disinheritance. Others thought her plan might work." He grew thoughtful. "Some physicists in Berkeley have been exploring some of the wilder implications of quantum theory — entanglement and wave function collapse applied to consciousness and destiny. It came to the attention of the family, and they began to theorize the Magic might be self-fulfilling. As in, if you believe you are part of a fairy tale, then your life starts to look like one."

He cleared his throat before continuing. "So, an entire princess generation was taken away from Lointaine. They were to have no contact with the family members that stayed. They were not to be told about the Magic. They were especially not to be told about their potential future as fairy tale princesses. The hope was this would disrupt the Magic enough to stop the spell. Of course, those girls would lack the skills needed to survive their quests if the theory was wrong. That is when the scholarships were created."

I was having trouble processing all the implications. My brain kept shutting down when it ran into an idea it didn't like, such as the amount of manipulation I had been oblivious to. Or how far off track my happy little world was from reality. My stomach was tying itself into knots, matching the tangles in my thoughts. "So, all that stuff about creating students versed in both the arts and the sciences . . .? Does the Soleil Renaissance Project even exist?"

Connor shrugged uncomfortably. "It does, but the princesses were the reason it was created. The town couldn't draw attention to you by only including the princesses. There is a demand for people who cross disciplines; lots of businesses were willing to help with funding."

I had been proud of the award. I guess that was just another piece of my world crumbling away. "Would I have qualified for the scholarship if its board didn't think I was a princess?" I wanted to curl into a ball, but that wasn't practical on a stool – or while wearing a skirt.

Connor shrunk a little and avoided answering my question. "You need to realize how much effort has been put into trying to protect all of the princesses. An entire 501(c)(3) was set up. There was fundraising, school administrations were cajoled into allowing special programs. The committee found professors to teach the classes and got the schools to allow guest professors. Then there were the conferences, a lot of which were sponsored by the project, and wouldn't have existed without it."

So instead of pride in an accomplishment, I was supposed to be grateful for being rescued? I wasn't the type that sat around waiting for Prince Charming to come rescue me. If I was any kind of princess, it was the self-rescuing kind. I liked my life — well, I mean I had. I wanted to howl about how none of this was fair, but I was too much of a grownup.

The truth was damning. I hadn't asked for any of that to be done on my behalf, but I had certainly been willing to accept the benefits of the scholarship. My father had insisted I major in something "useful" like business, or he wouldn't pay for my tuition. It had been one of our first major disagreements, although unfortunately not the last. The scholarship freed me to find my own path. I would never have been able to afford the schools I'd attended without help. I hadn't been too concerned with the reason it was offered — just considered it a reward for working my butt off all through high school.

Guilt and anger were distracting me from the questions swirling in my head. I set the frustration aside to process later and plucked a random question from the mess in my brain.

"You said the princesses were moved. Why not the princes?" I didn't pause, questions just spilled out. "Were there no boys this generation? And why bring just me back, unless . . . wait — are there other princesses here, too?"

Connor grinned, seeming relieved to switch the subject. "Whoa! Which question do you want me to answer first?"

Connor had a surprisingly infectious smile. I appreciated his ability to see the absurd in the situation, and I couldn't help but grin back, even though I was not amused. "Pick one."

"All right. There were boys in this generation, but the Magic is a lot easier for them to deal with. When they hit eighteen or so, they just need to pick an open-ended quest they can draw to a close when they are ready to get married. If they wait too long, the Magic starts getting a bit pushy. So far, it hasn't been too much of a problem though. The Magic has always been harder for women.

"Think about it — how many traditional fairy tales have females setting out on an epic adventure just because they felt like seeking their fortune?"

I pondered that for a moment, rifling through my mental files of fairy tales. "I can't think of one."

"Right. In fairy tales, men get to be proactive. Princesses are largely reactive. The princesses are almost always coerced in some way. Many are fleeing the threat of death or rape, or if they are really lucky — both. A minority starts their quest to save a loved one or escape slavery instead. You were sent away to avoid such a situation.

"You are back now because it didn't work. I believed I would be able to predict the *contes des fées* — that is what your grandmother calls these episodes. I was tracking all the princesses, using Schrödinger's equation and quantum decoherence theory, to predict if and when any of the story arc wave functions would collapse." My eyes were glazing over, but Connor didn't notice. "You were at the highest risk since you were the oldest and about ready to graduate — the modern equivalent of being a full grownup. Then there was your family situation . . . But things were muddied by the fact that we were trying to avoid the fairy tales. So, now we're dealing with a fate or prophesy tale subtype, instead of the subtypes more typical for the princess tales. The story is more about the impossibility of escaping your destiny, like in *Oedipus* or 'The Robber Bridegroom.' No one realized this could be a problem. I can't believe I missed it!"

I felt sorry for Connor, the guilt and frustration in his voice were so clear. At the same time, I hoped he didn't expect me to understand all the stuff about quantum theory and formulas. I struggled through my math and physics classes and didn't hold out much hope for figuring it out now.

"Because of the complications, we missed that one of the princesses we sent away was getting pulled into a tale." Connor paused, choosing his words carefully. "It did not go well. At least in Lointaine, there is a support structure in place. People believe you when you say something weird is happening — they are slightly more aware of how the Magic amplifies your personality, including character flaws."

Connor took a deep breath. "We brought you back here because of that. Honestly, I don't believe you can escape your fate as a princess at this point. If you accept that, we can remove the trying to escape fate variable from the equation, and my models will be much more accurate. That will not only mitigate any damage your story might cause, but also give you a bit of control over how things play out as well."

I was trying to integrate all the new information. It was a losing battle against the numbness settling over me.

"Loren, I know this is a lot to accept. But we just don't have time for you to be in denial right now. The accident was just the last in a string of bizarre events, wasn't it?"

I thought about how my life had been dumped upside down recently. I cringed as flashes of the last two months flickered across my mind. Each event was unbelievable in and of itself. Thinking about them all together was the best evidence of unnatural happenings yet.

I giggled and then cringed at the slight edge of hysteria I heard. "Do you understand how ironic this is? How many millions of girls would love to be told they were a princess? But the Magic is stuck with me. And I'm stuck with it." I resisted sticking my tongue out.

Connor said quietly, "Loren, it is only going to get worse if you don't accept it. Work *with* the Magic, and I believe we can expect some decent results." Slow, hot tears were prickling the back of my eyes. I didn't want to cry in front of Connor, so I just nodded.

Connor realized it was time to stop. Either he was more sensitive than I gave him credit for, or I wasn't holding it together as well as I hoped. "Why don't we call it a day? You can think all of this through. Roselle is old-fashioned. She works intuitively, and she doesn't understand the modern need for data when making a decision. I have done a lot of research on our family, and I would be glad to share it with you."

"Wait, *our* family?"

Connor grinned. "I guess that didn't get mentioned before now, did it? We are distant relatives — separated by something like eight generations and three or four branches . . . We can figure out the exact relationship tomorrow if you want. Although this many generations from Louis, it's all notional anyway — statistically none of the descendants' DNA overlap by even a whole percentage. I've got everything spread out in my home office. We can talk about it whenever you're free to swing by."

Another twist to send me reeling. Connor was caught up in this too, even if he was getting off easy because he was male. "Wait, so does that make you a prince? What is your quest?"

This time his smile was wide and smug. "Me? I am on a quest to save the distressed damsels of Lointaine from an evil enchantment. Let's see how the Magic deals with that."

He turned and strode from the room. Despite its lack of existence, I could almost see a cape swirling around him as he left.

CHAPTER 4

I felt like a cow chewing information cud en route to Connor's. Stanley, my grandmother's gardener, was playing the part of chauffeur since I wasn't allowed to drive for at least another two weeks. That meant I had too much time during the drive to mull over the facts I'd dug up that morning and reconsider them, again and again. I'd managed to chew everything over so thoroughly, it had lost its meaning.

In retrospect, I don't know what I hoped for when I searched through Lointaine's Register of Deeds, and the newspaper records at the local library. I guess I hoped to disprove Grandmother's story. Instead, the information available all seemed to make the story more plausible. On my list of supporting evidence, there was the wedding license that recorded her birthplace as Lointaine but conveniently didn't have her birth date filled in. I couldn't find a birth certificate. There was no appearance in school yearbooks or the local news before her marriage. While reading the description of her exquisite wedding dress, I had been distracted by the lost look in her eyes in the accompanying photo. It was not at all bride-like. There was even a woman with her name in the census in 1840 and 1850, but she wasn't listed again in the 1860 records. None of it was truly proof, though — it could all be coincidental, although that would be *some* coincidence.

Maybe Grandmother was living a delusional fantasy, created after finding the same census records? Her birth certificate might have been under another name. That was a stretch though, given how many people believed it had all happened, claiming to have seen her in a coma for years, even. Fairy tales being real seemed like the more plausible scenario.

I'd found nothing that proved fairy tales were playing out here, but nothing to disprove them either. I mean, how would you hide a hundred-years sleep — or even a hundred-month nap, these days? And where did that leave me?

Apparently with a headache. I decided to abandon the problem for a while. I rolled the window down, and let the autumnal air pour into the car.

I was glad I wasn't driving because I might have veered right off the road when Connor's house appeared. Good grief, talk about fairy tale dwellings. I had found the storybook village charming this morning, but this took the cake.

The house appeared to have grown organically out of the mountainside, much like a shelf mushroom on a tree. It was surrounded by a cottage garden that blended seamlessly into the surrounding forest. The multiple levels were constructed of stone, timber, and blue-gray stucco. Every detail I noticed increased the house's charm: arched doorways, gabled wood-shingled roofs, a copper weathervane, a teeny glass conservatory, flagstone walkways, and low, mossy stone walls. Fanciful turrets, leaded casement windows, chimneys, and wee balconies added a touch of whimsy.

Stanley pulled around to the side of the house and parked. He took out a dog-eared Baker Creek seed catalog, perusing its pages with the avidity most men reserve for pornography. The rasp of his fingers, dragged over the cactus-like stubble of his chin as he considered the merits of one plant variety versus another, followed me as I got out of the car. He smiled and nodded in lieu of saying goodbye.

"Hello!"

I turned and was surprised to find Connor kneeling in a clump of coneflowers. His shirt sleeves were rolled up and the hair on his arms was glinting in the sunlight. I stared. I so badly wanted to draw him. Connor waved a mangled dandelion at me. Had he been weeding? He seemed like a stereotypical geek; geeks don't plant flowers, do they? I guess I didn't have Connor pegged yet.

"You garden?" I tried to sound bemused, not accusatory.

Connor sat back on his heels and grinned, leaving a streak of dirt on his forehead as he swiped a sandy-blond lock out of his eyes. "My aunt guilts me into it." He continued as he threw the weed into a burlap bag, and collected a slew of garden tools. "She designed the gardens, and she comes by occasionally to putter around in them. I hear about it if she finds too many weeds. I think she worries I spend too much time in front of a computer screen. This is her way of making sure I get outside." His light tone let me know he was amused by her manipulation.

"I thought about hiring someone to take care of it, but it seems disrespectful of her efforts. Besides, I am a bit scared to see what she would come up with instead to get me away from my computer. Why don't you come on in? You can review my research while I grab a quick shower, so I don't run you off with my smell."

Smell? I caught a whiff as he held the door open for me. He didn't smell bad at all; he smelled of moss and coffee, maybe a hint of cinnamon — all scents I enjoyed. But I could understand if he felt grubby and wanted a shower.

I followed him inside. I looked around while Connor paused in the kitchen to pull off his boots and wash his hands in the copper farmhouse sink. I was a bit surprised by the home's interior. The kitchen was more modern than I expected from the exterior, but still fit the home's character. The ceiling beams were exposed, and the room was full of warm-toned wood and stone. Complementing these rustic notes, hammered copper pendant lights hung over the granite-topped island. The cabinets were painted sage green. Acres of countertops and a huge gas range were almost enough to make me want to learn to cook something.

"My office is through here," Connor gestured. We passed through a breakfast nook and then down a hallway. I was disappointed about not getting to explore the rest of the house, but I forgot about it the moment I caught sight of the wall in his office. It held a corkboard that was about six feet tall and eighteen feet long, positively *covered* in colored paper and a web of strings.

"This is my attempt to recreate Louis and Rosalind's family tree." He walked over to a desk and computer I hadn't noticed in my preoccupation with the corkboard. At the keyboard, he typed in a short string of characters, then spun the monitor around. "I've got everyone's tale listed to the best of my ability to determine it. That includes people that haven't had their tales yet. I'm not sure I should be documenting projections — it might alter how tales play out, but I don't know how else to test my model. Things get messy toward the bottom," he gestured to the corkboard now, "when distant relatives got married. I had to stop adding them to the board. Feel free to look through it all. I will be back in, say, ten minutes?"

I was already glued to the information on the wall and only nodded distractedly. "Uh, sure."

I heard him chuckle as he left, "Well, I will leave you to it."

Louis and Rosalind's seven children were listed in birth order across the top of the board. I began in the upper left, where I found Isabelle Catherine de Bourbon (1714), their eldest child, and all twelve branching generations of her descendants. Connor made some effort to color code the branches of the family. Each of the children was assigned a different color, but he had been forced to be creative toward the bottom. In one location, an ancestor of Eric's orange and Philippe's yellow created a new marigold line. Other color combinations (Isabelle's red and Lilianne's green for instance) were not so attractive.

People who married into the family were on white notes with a border colored appropriately for the branch they married into. Each person had two layers of notes written in a precise, angular hand. The top note contained a name, date of birth and death, and a brief note about what fairy tale the person's story followed. There was also a string of letters and numbers I couldn't figure out how to decode. The second layer of the notes contained miscellaneous details Connor seemed to think might be relevant. I wandered, randomly examining cards to get a feel for Connor's system.

It was interesting to see none of the lines died out. We were a fertile lot. Jacque's line even tended to run to sets of seven boys. I wasn't entirely certain I wanted to get married, and children were definitely not in my short-term plans. I looked for instances of childlessness. I found roughly a dozen in all — I apparently either needed a war or an influenza epidemic to remain childless. I made a strong mental note to use duplicate forms of birth control in the future.

Oh wow. I wouldn't be thinking that if I didn't believe in the Magic. I sat stunned for a minute as the knowledge spread, unfurling through my thoughts and reorganizing them. I should be panicking. Instead, I felt warmth wash over my body as I was overcome by euphoria. It was just *right*, and it was a relief to let things fall into their natural order.

I was lighter, free. I never realized how much energy it took to hold the tenuous scaffold of my previous worldview in place. How long had I been fighting that battle? It should have only been within the last few days, but I knew it had been much longer — years, even. Some part of me must have recognized the lies I was told long ago.

I stared at Connor's board. I may have accepted that the Magic was part of my destiny, but I wasn't ready to accept a starring role in *Sleeping Beauty*. I needed to figure out how to change that. I examined the board with a new determination to find anything that would help keep the Magic from sweeping through my life like a tornado through a trailer park. I was suddenly impatient for Connor to finish his shower. He needed to get back in here so we could come up with a plan.

I found Rosa Marie's descendants in pink. Whereas other lines had between eight and fourteen generations, there were only three previous generations in my tiny branch: Rosa Marie (1716-1871), Roselle (1836-), Aurore (1956-1995), and Loren (1983-). Connor appeared to try to leave white space under my name for future generations by making the lines connecting our generations very long, but Isabelle's and Eric's descendants were creeping into the space below my name. It felt a bit lonely.

I looked through the pink notes for my lineage. Each of the women was listed as a Sleeping Beauty — even me. A question mark graced my notation. I have never been so grateful for a bit of punctuation in my life. I pulled my notecard off the wall.

How many times did it take to learn the lesson of inviting everyone to a baptism anyway? I mean, did that whole bit happen at my baptism? Why not skip the whole thing? Or would that then be the thing causing offense *leading* to the curse?

Why couldn't I be stuck in a branch dedicated to a more benign tale like the 'Dancing Princesses' or even 'The Princess and the Pea?' The question triggered a spark of unease. Something about that idea was wrong — and not only because it was whiny. I turned back to the other branches, grasping for the revelation lurking just beyond reach in my subconscious. It finally struck me, along with relief so intense I plopped onto the floor to preempt collapsing. Not one of the other branches was constrained to just one fairy tale. In several instances, a tale had reappeared in several generations like in my family, but only once or twice did it repeat through three or four generations. Maybe I would be spared any pricked fingers. Another mental note: no spinning wheels! Where does one find those anymore? I guess I should avoid museums, the textile department at school . . . and no more antiquing.

Brain racing, I hopped up and tore through the recent story notes. Disney seemed to prevail, which made sense if this was some sort of collective unconsciousness asserting itself. I compared my situation to the Disney princesses. Only one fit — unless . . . I raced back to the notes. Where did he keep the blank paper? I needed a pink slip. It was time to change things.

Connor came back as I was pinning a new set of notes to the board — cards without Sleeping Beauty listed on them at all. Might as well make the best of it . . . I straightened and asked, "How do you think I would look as a brunette?"

Connor appeared stunned for a fraction of a second and then grinned. "I guess that means you are on board. What exactly did you have in mind?"

I had expected him to be confused a bit longer. I was disappointed I hadn't stumped him for even a full second, but I liked that he was willing to jump right in and play along.

I backtracked so my proposition would make sense. "I noticed that in most of the family branches, the tales that play out tend to vary from generation to generation. Seems like it's time for a change in my branch, too. I was working on figuring out an alternative fairy tale."

"Hmm. Brunette, visual reference . . . so a movie. That means Disney . . ." It was fascinating to see how he made connections. "I am going to assume you were thinking *Beauty and the Beast*. Snow White has black hair, and none of the other dark-haired Disney princesses are pale like you. Although I don't have any data on how much that or race plays into matters . . ."

I could tell I was losing Connor. I wondered how long it would take him to formulate a new set of equations.

He ran his hands through his still-damp hair. While it was wet, his hair was darker; it looked more auburn with golden highlights instead of sandy-blond.

I needed to bring Connor back to the problem at hand. "I started thinking about the Disney princesses — the movies certainly seem to have influenced the number of Snow Whites and Cinderellas that occur. There haven't been any Belles since *Beauty and the Beast* came out, probably because there haven't been any princesses since then. My life lines up with the Disney version fairly well." I ticked things off. "I like to read, I am in a small provincial town, and I only have a father in my immediate family. Perhaps the Magic has been setting me up for this all along. I can take care of the hair color . . . But where are we going to find a Beast?"

I hoped we could work around that. Honestly, if I had to be a princess, idling the time away curled up and reading seemed much better than slaving away cooking and cleaning for a step-family or dwarves.

"Hmm, that is a bit of a hairy problem." I turned from the board to Connor. His face was straight, but the sparkle in his eyes and the little crinkles around their corners gave him away.

I groaned. What a time for him to be joking! "That was a spectacularly heinous pun."

"Sorry! I couldn't help myself," he chuckled. "In all seriousness though, finding a Beast won't be a problem. In fact, I know several people who might be candidates for the job."

He did?

"Why don't we meet again in the next couple of days to talk logistics? I actually have other things I am more concerned about."

Wait, something he was more concerned about than our ability to locate a giant man/buffalo hybrid? Really? I mean, what even qualified a person as a Beast in his mind? Their behavior? People who believe they can change their partners made me uncomfortable. It doesn't work that way in real life — not that this was real life. Except it was. I got snarled in my thoughts again and sighed.

CHAPTER 5

My preconceived mental image of the local theater had not done it justice. I ought to have known that anything named after Marie-Catherine Le Jumel de Barneville, Countess d'Aulnoy, would not be rustic.

On the way to the theater, Stanley and I debated whether the lack of kudzu in Lointaine was proof of the Magic. Stanley felt strongly that it was. Somewhere during the discussion, he mentioned the theater had nice landscaping; quite the compliment coming from him. I was so distracted by checking out the plants, I didn't notice the building as we pulled up. I conceded the debate and said goodbye before hopping out of the car.

Yikes! It wasn't nearly as warm as it looked from the cozy car. Cold gusts of wind ripped my hair out of its clips. The dark strands buffeting my face startled me. I still wasn't used to being a brunette.

It wasn't until I cleared the hair from my face that I got a good look at the building. It deserved a pause for admiration, but I was forced to hurry inside since I was barely on time. I was left with impressions of grandeur and color: the verdigris of the oxidized copper gable roof, the black iron of the leading in the narrow Arts and Crafts-style windows, and the local granite's smoke, ochre, and mauve. I also had a strong desire to see it all lit up for a show. It would be something to look forward to on Saturday, a reward for all the socializing.

My footsteps were swallowed by the plush carpet in the lobby. The silence was loud. I half expected someone to be there, perhaps in the box office, or stocking the concession stand. But no one was around, and all the windows were shuttered. It gave the impression of being abandoned. This space was meant to be filled with a lively crowd. Ridiculously, I felt a bit lost, even though I knew where to go. I had been given careful instructions: second door on the right, then straight on through the auditorium. Kella would meet me there.

As I entered the auditorium, the doorway clanged shut loudly behind me. Normally I would have cringed at the noise, but I was hard-pressed to care. I was taking in the splendor — cream and gilt, lush red velvet, a scrolled proscenium arch . . . there were even private viewing boxes lining the walls. It took me a moment to realize there was music playing. Something lively and Celtic.

The lobby had been lonely, but this space thrummed with possibility. The theater was waiting for its next adventure. On the stage, a stand with a single incandescent bulb threw shadows across set pieces, reminding me that this adventure included a sinking ship and a storm. Guess I'd have to wait until the show like everyone else to see more.

I wandered down the aisle, trailing my fingers along the chairs. So many details to take in — even the vaulted ceiling was painted as a stylized night sky. I turned in a circle to fully absorb the space. Wow.

"So, what do you think?" I let out an involuntary squeak and jumped. I turned to see a woman on the stage, walking toward me. Was this Kella? If so, I wondered that my grandmother trusted her to pick out my clothing. There were dozens of tiny braids mixed into the woman's dark curls. Some were peacock blue, green, or purple. It was fantastic, but it didn't strike me as a style Grandmother would appreciate. I had heard all about how people should keep their natural hair color from her. The woman continued, "Sorry! I didn't mean to startle you!"

"No, it's all right. I was absorbed in looking at everything. It's stunning — like something out of a movie . . ."

"Almost an archetypal theater, you might say?" She laughed. "Funny how that kind of thing works around here. You must be Loren." She smiled and held out her hand to shake, "I'm Kella. Why don't you come on back? I have so many clothes for you I decided to borrow some racks from costume storage."

Kella was wearing a pale mauve handkerchief shirt covered in a feather motif. Despite her lush curves, she looked amazing in skinny jeans. This alone put me in awe of her — I never managed to wear them without feeling like a sausage. I grinned at her bare feet and teal toenails. Perhaps this makeover wouldn't be as disagreeable as I feared. It was killing me that I had just gotten my clothes back and I was letting them go again.

I followed Kella up steps set into platforms of various heights and sizes in front of the stage.

I was forgetting something necessary to be polite. Right, conversation. It was my turn to say something. What did Grandmother say again? Oh – if all else fails, ask the person about themselves or their work . . . "So, is this all for an upcoming play?"

"Yes, we're opening *The Tempest* soon. I'm hoping — Oh, watch out for those foils!" She gestured toward some swords that had been left on the stage. One of these days I would have to learn to pay attention to where I was walking. I did not need to take a header down the stairs. I glanced up once I skirted the pointy objects, and caught sight of Kella's face. Oh, man. She was pissed. I wouldn't want to be the person who had left those out. Kella visibly collected herself, and let out a sigh, "Sorry about that, I should have moved the ghost light so you could see better."

"Ghost light?"

"Yup, tradition has it that every theater building has its ghost. You know what that means in Lointaine." I gulped and looked around nervously, but Kella continued before I saw anything supernatural. "Come on back this way; we are actually heading up to costume storage."

"Up?" I looked at all the metal trusses, the dozens of ropes and cables, and the lights now visible overhead.

"The costume shop is upstairs, in the back. It keeps the clothes from getting musty like they would in the basement."

"Oh." It was a struggle to pay attention as we navigated the steep metal stairs. I'd never been backstage at a theater this large before. Sure, I had participated in the obligatory ballet recitals, before Dad talked Mom into letting me quit and take art classes. However, all I remembered of being backstage was lots of black curtains. Here, I was getting a peek at the alchemy for a show: sets being built, row after row of ropes attached to pulleys, symbols taped to the floor that might as well be occult, for all I could fathom their meaning . . . I felt a bit odd, like I was trespassing.

I trailed after Kella along a walkway and into a room used to make costumes. There were shelves of fabric, sewing machines, jars of buttons, mannequins in doublets . . . and several racks of clothes Kella was now organizing.

The purple dress in her hands caught my attention. It was a deep eggplant color, with a pleated sweetheart bodice and cap sleeves. There was even a black crinoline under the full skirt.

"Oh, that is beautiful!" I should have been facing her as we talked, per Grandmother's rules, but I was having trouble taking my eyes off the dress. "Is it part of my new wardrobe?" Please say yes please say yes . . . Is it possible to lust after a dress?

Kella shook her head. "I did pick it out for you. Unfortunately, it won't work now."

Nooo!

"Why not?" I asked as I watched her put the dress on a rack with several other items. If that was a sample, I was excited to see what I would be wearing.

"It isn't blue. I only found out yesterday that we are trying to sway the Magic toward *Beauty and the Beast*." She leaned over and fingered a lock of my hair, "I have to say, I have never seen a dye job turn out so well. You look like you were born a brunette."

"I can't get used to it." I peered into a mirror. "At the salon, I was checking out someone's hairstyle and wondering if my hair could be done the same way. I realized I was seeing myself in a mirror across the room. It's so different! I am used to being the girl next door, but now . . ." I struggled to find words to describe my new appearance.

"Now, you look almost mysterious, perhaps like the girl from far, far away?" Kella grinned as I groaned. She stopped shuffling dresses and peered at me in a way that would have been offensive if she had been a male in a bar. "Hmm. Well, this is going to be fun despite the princess limits — especially since we don't have any budget constraints to worry about."

We didn't? Who was paying for this?

She sighed, "Shopping may be forever ruined, without someone else's platinum card funding the trip."

I eyed the full racks. "Ah, exactly whose card are we talking about?"

Kella stared at me dolefully for a second before breaking out in a rich, fruity laugh. The sound was so deeply exuberant, I couldn't help but smile.

When she could breathe again, she explained while fanning her flushed cheeks with her hand. "I can't believe they didn't tell you. Your grandmother is paying for this." That seemed like it might come with some dangerous strings attached. Reading my expression, she continued, "And don't you dare feel a bit guilty about it — she can easily afford it. Think of it as making up for all the birthdays and Christmases she missed while you were away. Besides, you know she will make you miserable if you try to keep wearing your current clothes."

I caught myself chewing on my lip, a bad habit that needed to stop, according to the aforesaid Grandmother. "Um. I am not sure that her idea of what is appropriate will match mine."

"Not a problem." Kella was shaking her head. "I told Mrs. Dalton I wouldn't be your personal shopper if this was style by committee. She agreed that you and I would have the final say over what you wear."

Her firm voice became cajoling, "We are just trying clothes on — it isn't a commitment. Although, we should go ahead and get started. I have a rehearsal in about four hours and that will barely be enough time for us to get started." I was dismayed by the gentle reminder Kella was volunteering her time while in the midst of final rehearsals for a show, and that we were going to be trying on clothes for four hours.

"Oh gosh, I am so sorry. I didn't mean to waste your time."

Kella's eyebrows scrunched as she looked at me, and her mouth fell open. "I didn't mean that at all! Good grief, they didn't tell you anything, did they?"

I shook my head.

"First off, I enjoy shopping and helping people find clothes that work – helping them develop a style. I recently took five of the girls from my young actors' program shopping for their homecoming dresses. Most fun I have had in a long time! So, I would have done this solely for the fun of it.

"But your grandmother, well, I suspect she didn't want to be indebted. And she wanted a chunk of my time when I was at my busiest – right before a show. So, she made an *extremely* generous donation to the theatre company, to compensate for taking up the artistic director's ever-so-valuable time." The warm sparkle in her eyes let me know she wasn't taking herself as seriously as Grandmother did.

I still had doubts. "But . . ."

"No, really. *EXTREMELY* generous. I will never, ever, be paid this well again. Even if the money technically went to the theatre instead of me."

"But then —"

"Oh for heaven's sake – this company is my baby. It gets all my money anyway. Your grandmother was doing her best to compensate like with like. She put her granddaughter in my hands, and she wanted to take care of my child in return. For the first time in years, I won't have to stress about the cash outlay between when a show preps and when it opens. I almost feel dishonest, taking the money for something I am happy to do anyway. So PLEASE, stop apologizing, and let me help you. I sincerely enjoy it."

How could I not agree? "All right . . ."

"Here," she handed me a full slip of the palest blue. The material hung in folds from my hand. Did she want me to put this on now? Hold it for her? Hang it up? What exactly was I supposed to do with it?

When I didn't move, Kella gestured, "Changing screen is over there. Come on out when you've got it on. Unless you will be uncomfortable with me seeing you in it?"

"No, not at all." And I meant it. The slip would cover more than many dresses did. Behind the screen, I shed my jeans and t-shirt. The slip fell in cool whispers over my body.

When I came back out, Kella was digging through a pile of CDs. "Where in the world —" She triumphantly held one up. "There you are. We need the right soundtrack." She slipped the CD into the player while simultaneously directing me to stand in front of a three-way mirror. "I love jazz on a rainy afternoon! It seems like that is where the weather is headed. You okay with Ella Fitzgerald?"

Kella had shifted the racks of clothing. The closest was loaded full of dresses. The styles, lengths, and fabrics varied, but the color did not. They were all blue. I hadn't understood the implications of Kella's comment earlier. Since Belle wore a blue dress, it looked like I would, too.

"We will have a few warm days left in the year, so I have a few lightweight dresses for that. Why don't we start with those?"

I tried on several fluttery dresses, all in soft floral prints, that Kella informed me were of crepe, chiffon, and light cotton. The slip was brilliant as it allowed Kella to help me gently maneuver dresses around my bum arm, without feeling as self-conscious as I might have in my underwear.

I was originally frustrated that the broken bones required surgery, but it had turned out well. The metal plates and screws meant I didn't need a bulky cast, just a brace and sling. It also meant I'd already started physical therapy, and there was less chance of lost mobility. I had every hope of getting back to painting before the semester was finished. Besides, a plaster cast was decidedly *un*princessy.

Three dresses were discarded for not being right before one met Kella's approval. The first dress on the "yes" rack was the same blue as Belle's dress, with a slightly darker leaf shaped print. The flowing material fell from a halter-top to mid-calf, and it was gathered under the bust and around the waist with cords in a style that was vaguely Grecian. Another was rejected. Then an ankle-length sheer teal dress, splashed with oversized four-petaled ochre flowers, joined the first on the rack.

A gray-blue pleated vest dress with a white belt joined the first two. Next was an ice-blue sheath with a white art deco flower lace overlay, and two casual knit dresses to wear around the house. The dresses became a blur. Eventually, we had twelve summer-weight blue dresses, and Kella felt we could move on to items appropriate for fall and winter.

Fairy tales aside, in the last few days, I had faced a few too many uncomfortable truths. My grandmother was introducing me to levels of mastery I hadn't known existed for basic life skills, such as walking and using a fork. Silly me, I thought it was enough not to trip over your own feet, or to keep from spilling food on yourself. Not that I always managed those, even. It was becoming obvious to me that I needed some remedial education in fashion. Fabric type, weight, drape, formality . . . The only thing making this bearable was Kella's charming love of clothing. Her exuberance, as she helped me learn what was attractive on my body, saved the afternoon.

Kella went into raptures about the different shades of blue woven into a tweed dress coat and invited me to enjoy the luxurious knap of a velvet dress. She happily explained what welted and jacquard meant when I didn't know which dress she was asking me to grab. 'Jersey' and 'boat neckline' joined my vocabulary with the fourth winter dress that joined the "yes" rack. Sweater and coat dresses were easy to figure out after that. My legs were going to freeze.

The rack of clothes Kella approved of was getting full. Surely that meant we were almost done . . .

But no. We were moving on to skirts — slim pencil skirts, full skirts with crinolines, and skirts in-between made of twill, tweed, wool, velvet — and even one with yards of tulle. Several white blouses were to be worn with skirts or layered under dresses.

I surveyed my new clothes. "Um, we don't have any pants."

"I wasn't sure if you would want to risk pants. Some blue chinos would be fairly safe . . . I can order some?"

"Aren't chinos like khakis?"

"Chinos are a bit dressier. Their stitching isn't exposed, and the fabric is often a lighter weight and tightly woven. Also, the cut on chinos is slimmer. They are more princessy. And they come in blue." Her eyes twinkled as she delivered the last line.

"Of course they do." I groaned. "At least we are finished! I'm not sure I can look at another piece of blue clothing today."

Kella laughed at me. "We aren't close to done. Are you ready for accessories?"

"There's more?"

"Yup."

There were white cardigans, a wrap, and even a shawl. I had five pairs of ballet flats in either black or blue. I was also allowed a pair of blue rain boots. Simple pearl earrings in blue, pale gray, and white were to be my only jewelry. As Kella pointed out, Belle technically doesn't wear any jewelry with her blue gown. She decreed pearls were enough in line with the character to work. We had a brief disagreement about the necklace I always wore, which had been my mother's. I finally won, but only because Kella decided the rose motif made it safe.

Then there were four blue coats in various styles and a cloak in dark periwinkle.

After Kella produced the last one, I couldn't help but jokingly comment, "Oh look! It's also blue!"

Kella gave another of her wonderful laughs. "You know, we renovated the theater a while back. My heart was set on a deep teal for the seats and curtains. But all my color samples kept changing to burgundy. Those iconic red velvet curtains . . ." She gave a rueful shrug. "In the end, it was easier not to fight it. I'm saving my energy for other things that matter. It's a bit ironic you are getting to have blue now, due to the Magic. That said, here . . . I was saving these." She produced two additional dresses. "You shouldn't wear these in public, but I figured you might need a bit of variety in your color choices. They should be safe enough." One was a sliver gray with only the barest echoes of blue, the other was a blue-tinged lilac. I was glad when both fit and were added to the rack.

"Thank you! I love all the clothes we have picked out, but I haven't been so limited in what I can wear since I was in school uniforms!"

"This stage shouldn't last for long. Once you meet your Beast, we can add dresses in green and red. Later on, when you are in the final stages, we can add yellow. I already have some clothes set aside."

It was reassuring to see the racks of clothes, even if they were a bit Christmas themed. The white fur lining on a red cape looked so soft, I had to touch it. Hmm, would I get to throw snowballs at my Beast while wearing it the way Belle did? "Well, that will be one thing to look forward to at least!"

"So, we have your everyday wear taken care of. Any special events coming up?"

It was my turn to grin. "Well . . . there was some theatre thing Connor mentioned. Opening weekend for a play or something? Does that count as a special event?" I teased.

Kella clapped her hands together gleefully as she pirouetted toward the racks. "I have just the thing. The town likes to make a big deal of opening night, and everyone comes in formal wear." She stopped to give me a mock serious look, and placed her hand on her heart, "God, I love a man in a tux." Then she said something muffled by the rack of clothes she was leaning through, trying to get to another behind it.

She reappeared with a gorgeous swath of inky blue silk and soft drapes of black tulle. The dress had off-the-shoulder gathered sleeves that flowed into a wrapped front. Kella fingered a narrow velvet sash, "I should take the black sash off and replace it with white, but I can't do it. It would ruin the look. Do you want to try it on?" I laughed at her, teasing. I was already holding my arms up in a demand for her to slip it on.

I didn't care that I was grinning like an idiot. "Yes please!"

Once the dress was on, I stared at the elegant woman in the mirror. I was having problems associating myself with the reflection. I glanced over my shoulder at the low-draped back of the dress. There was definitely magic at work. I felt willowy instead of gawky for the first time in my life. As the black tulle shifted, the light gleamed off the shimmering blue silk underneath, shifting it from cerulean to seafoam to navy. It was captivating. I was captivating. I have never managed that before in my life.

I didn't notice Kella leave to rummage through her stacks again until she returned with a pair of black velvet pumps. They were the perfect finishing touch. The dress wouldn't need to be hemmed with the extra inches they provided.

I gave Kella a spontaneous hug. "Thank you! I have never felt so beautiful before!"

"You're welcome! I had a lot of fun myself! Let's get you out of this before we put any serious wrinkles in it." I reluctantly let her help me out of the dress. "Now, what are you going to wear home?"

"How about this one," I asked as I pulled out a dress with an A-line silhouette constructed from fabric with a subtle linen texture. It had a wide flat collar that matched the shape of its scoop neck. Was it still called a Peter Pan collar if it was that low? I gathered my confidence. I had to master dressing as Belle — the stakes were too high to mess this up. "With this blouse?" I daringly suggested a combination Kella hadn't already put together as an outfit. I needed to see if I properly understood the rules.

"Why don't you try it on so we can see what it looks like?" Kella suggested.

I pulled on the blouse, hoping its scooped neck was cut low enough so that only its three-quarter length puffy sleeves would show. I breathed a sigh of relief when the bodice of the dress covered the blouse.

"Nice choice. It is perfect for Belle." The words were praise, but Kella had a furrow forming between her eyes. Finally, she laughed ruefully. "It wasn't feeling correct, but I figured out why. We need to do this again when you are finished. It will be fun to pick out a wardrobe that is actually for you."

It was such a relief to hear someone suggest that this was a role I was playing. Perhaps being costumed in a theater was appropriate, because this was a temporary role, and at some point, I would get to leave it behind. Not that Grandmother agreed. She acted like she was correcting character deficits on my part each time we met for a "lesson." My eyes were getting hot and prickly. I didn't want to let all the critiques make me cry; it would be like admitting they were correct.

I could see how everything I was being taught might be useful. At the same time, I wasn't sure I wanted to live in a world where it got applied on a regular basis. It seemed so artificial. Don't get me wrong, I value that society has rules that make it safe for me to walk the streets. At some point though, you needed to stop with the layers of polite veneer, or there would be more of it than your *actual* personality. Later, when all this was through, I could figure out which parts of the role I wanted to permanently incorporate into my character and ditch the rest.

I gave Kella a wobbly smile. "I am going to take you up on that. Although I really do like some of the clothes we picked out." I wouldn't be lying on the ground painting in any of it, but I might keep some pieces for occasions like meeting with clients.

"I'm glad to hear it. We should have enough here to get you started. But if it ever seems like you don't have anything appropriate to wear, let me know — the sooner the better. Also, don't hesitate to ask if you need a second opinion about an outfit."

I glanced at the three racks of clothes I was going to have to squeeze into my closet. Barring formal events, I had trouble believing there was anything I wouldn't be prepared for.

"I will do some shopping for winter. We can plan on having you back in about a month for another round." More clothes? Seriously? But Kella continued before I could protest, "And I believe it is about time to meet your grandmother. She doesn't seem the type to appreciate being made to wait."

She headed toward the door as I fingered the gown for Saturday.

"Don't worry, I will have someone drop everything by your grandmother's. It wouldn't be princessy of you to schlep piles of clothes around, now would it?"

"I feel like I should at least be carrying a wrapped parcel and a hat box or something, out with me," I commented with the tiniest bit of a grumble, reluctant to have so little to show for the afternoon's work.

"Ooh, how deliciously Parisian of you. I think even your grandmother would approve of that." Kella grinned over her shoulder at me. She paused to plug a cord into the wall. The bare bulb I noticed earlier on the stage lit up. "We might have a hat box in the prop department if you want me to try and rustle it up for you."

I laughed, "Thanks, but I don't want to keep Grandmother waiting. I am nervous enough about what she will say as it is." I was rolling my eyes to myself over this when Kella stopped dead and turned toward me. I managed to slide to a stop in my new flats right before I would have plowed into her.

"You do realize, that despite the fact your outfit is just about perfect, your grandmother will find something wrong with it." Given how close we were, I couldn't fail to meet Kella's eyes.

I sighed and nodded. "You're right." I left unsaid the fact that knowing something, and not letting it bother me, were two different things.

"Mm-hmm, so I see," Kella said, before continuing up the aisle toward the lobby door. "Tell you what, no matter what your grandmother says, give your new look until Saturday evening. I guarantee that everyone else's reaction at the theater will be more indicative of how successful your makeover has been."

I didn't have any choice but to play out the whole princess thing, even if Grandmother hated my clothes. "I promise I won't let my grandmother run me off course in the next three days. Close enough?" I asked with a smile.

"It will do for now."

Grandmother came through the front door as we entered the lobby. Kella and I shared a smile, amused at our perfect timing. I saw Stanley outside, shaking out an umbrella.

"Mrs. Dalton, what a delight it is to see you again!" Kella said.

Grandmother barely glanced at me before thanking Kella for her time and effort. I especially appreciated her comment about how she knew it couldn't have been easy. If I hadn't seen the light dancing in Kella's eyes, I would have melted into the lush lobby carpet in mortification. I was relieved to find I believed her when she said, "It was my pleasure!"

I did a slow, and for me, extremely graceful spin. "Well, what do you think?"

A sigh was not the reaction I was hoping for.

"It is better than blue jeans, but I will be glad when we move away from the whole *Belle et la Bête* idea."

I shared a look with Kella, acknowledging that Grandmother's words fulfilled her prediction. I almost broke out laughing, which turned into a stifled, unladylike snort.

"What is wrong with Belle? She likes books. She is amazing." Kella asked, just a touch too innocently.

"That isn't the point. Come along. It is time for us to head home."

Well, what *was* the point? Grandmother hadn't ever hesitated to point out where I was going wrong in the past. It was curious that she was being squirrelly about telling me now. I was going to have to pin her down later to figure out exactly what was going on.

I waved cheerfully to Kella as we left. There would be plenty of time for probing questions on the way home.

CHAPTER 6

"I'm sorry. I tried to be patient, but I keep hitting walls working on the model for your tale." The words popped out of Connor before I had even completely entered the vestibule. "Do you have some time to talk, so I can get some information from you? I can't predict the function collapse without more data."

"Oh. Umm . . . Well, Grandmother is out at her gardening club meeting, so Ms. Millie and I planned to have sandwiches in the kitchen. We could talk and eat, if you'd like to join us for lunch?"

"Is it lunch already?" Connor looked down at his watch. "It is. Good. Work won't even notice I'm gone, in that case. Yes, please. I'm always happy to eat Ms. Millie's food!"

I led Connor back into the kitchen. "You mentioned work . . . I know you are a physicist, but nothing else about your job."

"I work for IBM on quantum computing. Remotely, most of the time."

"That sounds interesting." That was a polite lie. Truthfully, I would be in over my head in under a minute with any further explanation of what he did.

"Unfortunately, I can't talk about what I do much, because of confidentiality agreements."

"I had no idea quantum physics had anything to do with computers!"

Ms. Millie had laid out bread on the counter before she pulled a multitude of sandwich toppings from the fridge.

"Can we help, Ms. Millie?" Grandmother would be horrified by Connor's offer, but I found it sweet.

"After you wash your hands. Both of you." That wasn't a pointed look or anything.

"Yes, ma'am." Connor was already on his way over to the sink.

"Loren, would you get the blue plates down when you're done?"

"Sure, how many?"

"Four, please."

"Oh, is Stanley joining us?"

"He is."

"Now, what can I do to help?" Connor asked as he dried his hands.

"Chop these, please." Ms. Millie plopped veggies on a cutting board. They looked to be fresh from the house garden. I noticed that Ms. Millie got the homemade pickles out, too. Those were usually saved for fancier events, like when Grandmother had company for tea. Interesting... Was Ms. Millie treating Connor as a formal guest, or a favored one?

As we worked to make sandwiches, I couldn't help but laugh at the absurdity of the toppings Connor heaped on his sandwich. "Who puts hard-boiled egg slices on their sandwich?"

"I do. You should try it! Your sandwich is sad because it's so boring right now." He frowned at me on behalf of my sandwich, including some big puppy dog eyes.

I considered my sandwich with its mayo, baby greens, Havarti, and turkey. "Thanks, but I'm good."

Stanley came in the backdoor, toeing his boots off on the mat kept there for him.

"It doesn't have to be boiled eggs — how about some avocado?" I shook my head at him — not with the mustard. "Or some cucumber, bell pepper?"

"No, thanks." Connor sighed at my refusal and added them to his sandwich.

By the time he finished, his sandwich was three times as high as mine. Stanley eyed the sandwiches with interest as he washed his hands.

Connor wasn't done yet. "What about you Ms. Millie? Any cucumbers or bell peppers needed over there?"

"I am having a salad, so I will take some. But after fifty years, I have learned exactly how Stanley likes his sandwich. It is just fine as it is."

Stanley walked over and put his hand on Millie's shoulder. "I like to think I can learn new ways to surprise my sweet Petal." Eyes twinkling, he snagged some of Connor's boiled egg slices and slipped them into the sandwich Millie had made for him.

Ms. Millie chuckled and her cheeks turned pink. She bustled away into the pantry and returned with chips. So that's where she hid them!

She put some on Stanley's plate before offering them to Connor. He passed them to me. I put them on my sandwich, looking at Connor with narrowed eyes. "This is not because you are pressuring me. I've been doing this since I tried being a vegetarian in middle school." Plus, it left room on my plate for a side salad so I could pretend to be healthy.

We settled in at the island with lemon fizzy waters. Everyone was hungry, so there was a lull in the conversation as we applied ourselves to the food. Connor eventually broke the silence, diving into the questions that drove him to visit. "I have had some time to consider the logistical pitfalls I expect there to be with any story quest. What I don't know are the specifics of your situation."

"Specifics? Situation?"

"Yes, so I can determine which story arcs we need to be on the lookout for. I understand we are trying for 'Beauty and the Beast,' but there are other tales we can't rule out yet." He hopped up and grabbed a notebook he had left on the counter earlier. It was the same kind that I used for my sketchbooks, down to the spiral binding and black cover. Huh.

He opened it to a page with a list of fairy tale titles and showed it to me. "For instance, you are too old to be Snow White. She was between seven and ten depending on the version."

"That makes the prince in that story revolting!" I couldn't help but be disgusted by the pedophilia.

Ms. Millie sniffed in agreement. "The Disney version was careful to leave that part out, although she still looks very young."

"The Disney versions are almost always nicer, otherwise we'd probably still have Sleeping Beauties that were unconscious while getting raped by married kings."

Right, the Basile version that had Sleeping Beauty woken by her baby suckling the splinter out of her finger. Yikes! Thank goodness for the updates by Perrault and Disney! If ignorance was bliss, then it was definitely a bummer I learned so much about fairy tales while working on my thesis.

Connor pulled a set of folded pages out of the notebook and opened them up. "Although, I don't think we can completely dismiss the older versions as options for Loren's tale."

"Maybe you two could figure out who the prince might be by checking therapists' offices. Don't forget the prince also fell in love with her when she was dead. That doesn't sound like a healthy start to any relationship." Connor and I stared at Ms. Millie.

"Don't forget about where he makes the evil queen dance in red hot shoes at the end," Stanely added. "Not the sort of husband we want for Loren."

Ms. Millie caught our looks and chuckled. "Why wouldn't we keep track of the fairy tales? Even the unjinxty need to be on the lookout in this town."

Unjinxty? I was trying to sort out what that meant when Stanley interrupted my thoughts.

"I'm glad Loren isn't likely to be Snow White." Stanley offered. "'Beauty and the Beast' is much better than that, even before Disney."

Connor recovered first. "I agree." He unclipped his pen. "Right. Shall we see what we can do to help steer the Magic that way?"

I nodded and gulped my mouthful of sandwich.

"Have any animals spoken to you in the last few months?"

"No, never." Talking animals were not an auspicious starting point.

Connor made a big slashing motion on the first page and flipped to the second. Was that a flow chart?

"Have you come across any objects that seem magical in any way?"

I assumed he didn't mean the ordinary magic of opening a book for the first time or the smell of freshly sharpened colored pencils. "Not that I know of."

While Connor pursued his chart, I pulled his notebook over and looked at the equations scrawled across the pages. Lots of Greek letters — even the one that looked like a little trident — and lots of wavy lines graphed. I had no hope of understanding this . . . I flipped a few pages.

What was this? The scrawled note in the margin read:

Science Slam, 4820 Blackbirds
Saturday 8:45
fix tardigrade line - drive home word cute used to undercut survivorship more forcefully

The rest of the page was filled with columns of rhyming words. Did Connor write spoken word poetry? Even with a science-themed poetry slam, I was struggling to picture it. I guess there was more to Connor than I knew.

"What about fairy godmother types?"

"Umm, Kella and her clothes?" I wasn't in the right mind frame to answer his question. I closed his notebook, filing away a mental note to quiz him about poetry later. Any other fairy godmother types in my life? Umm. "Ms. Millie saved me from Officer Duncan." Ms. Millie turned pink as I suggested this; Stanley beamed as he finished his sandwich.

"Hmm, I'm not sure I should count those. But I won't dismiss them just yet, either." Ms. Millie made a small noise and got up from the island. She started puttering about, tidying the sandwich fixings away. Connor didn't seem to notice.

"I also have a human godmother." How odd that I needed to make that distinction. "In case it matters. I rarely hear from her, though. She and my mother had some sort of falling out."

"Well, you can't blame her," Ms. Millie said. "That ridiculous woman as good as cursed you herself. I know people were getting antsy during your baptism, but there was no need for her to tell everyone to calm down, since there was no way to stop you from ending up in an enchanted sleep, no matter how much they worried."

Connor stilled. "I didn't know about that."

"Me either."

"Does it matter if you are planning to steer things toward a different tale anyway?" Ms. Millie asked.

"I'm not sure. I'm going to have to consider if it is enough to tilt things toward 'Sleeping Beauty.' If you think of anything else that might tie Loren to a fairy tale, could you let me know? Er, let us know?"

"Certainly."

Connor looked down at his checklist, "Have you seen any magical creatures?"

"What, like fairies?"

"Well, yes. But anything remotely magical . . . Like seeing a lizard in a campfire, or a horse that might have looked like it had wings for a second? Or even Bigfoot?"

"Nothing like that. Wait – does Lointaine have those?"

"I don't know specifics, but I can introduce you to someone studying Lointaine's magical creatures at some point if you want to learn more."

"If you keep an eye out, Stanley seems to think there might be a nisse that helps around the grounds. He occasionally leaves a bowl of oatmeal in the potting shed."

How fascinating. I'd have to see if I could catch a peek.

"Well, let me know if you see anything magical. Especially any ogres or man-eating giants."

"Seriously?"

"I don't want to make any assumptions. And there are lots of ogres in fairy tales. Even in the original 'Sleeping Beauty,' the prince has a mother that is an ogre who tries to eat her babies."

"Umm, yeah. No ogres. I haven't come across anyone more than about six-foot-five since I got to Lointaine."

"Great. Next, any boyfriends? Girlfriends?" He looked at me out of the corner of his eyes. "Any significant others of any kind?"

Stanley chuckled and got up. "That's my cue to head back outside."

"Don't forget these," Ms. Millie handed him his thermos, and a cookie wrapped in a napkin.

"See you later, Mr. Stanley." He waved goodbye as he closed the door, mouth full of cookie already. I turned back to Connor. "No significant others. The last one dumped me while I was buried in my thesis."

Connor made a disbelieving – or perhaps a questioning – noise, through a mouthful of sandwich. I elaborated for clarification. "He said he hadn't realized he was 'so high maintenance,'" I made air quotes, "but that he was just going to have to accept that about himself. He said I obviously didn't have enough time and energy to devote to him." I rolled my eyes. "He didn't seem to care when I explained the situation was temporary. I can't believe he had the nerve to make my crisis about him. So I didn't chase after him. And oh – wow!" I noticed Connor pop the last bite of his sandwich into his mouth, "You ate that entire sandwich? And the chips!"

"Don't forget the pear."

"What pear?"

"This one." He pulled a pear out of the fruit bowl centered on the island. "Want one?" he asked around a bite.

I laughed while shaking my head. "Where are you putting it all?"

He shrugged. "I have a ridiculously high metabolism. I can't seem to keep any weight on." Oh, you poor baby. I will be sure to cry for you later. Snarky thoughts must have shown in my eyes; he changed the subject. "Back to the topic at hand, your ex sounds like a real di– um, jerk." He glanced over at Ms. Millie, who didn't seem to notice the near slip.

I grinned. "Yup. But let's not waste any time talking about him. What else do you need to know?"

Connor paused and searched my face. He was making me nervous. "I don't do interpersonal stuff well . . . Are you really okay, or is this one of those times I need to let you tell me about it and offer a tissue?"

I couldn't help but laugh at his earnest question. "No, I promise I am fine. Thank you for the offer, though. We can go back to getting you your data."

Connor examined me, I suppose for evidence of glistening eyes or a runny nose. Deciding he could believe me, he moved on. "In that case, I need you to tell me everything the Magic did to get you here. And please don't worry about what I might think. Remember, I expect the Magic to do horrible things to force you into seeking your fate."

I snorted — delicately, but a snort nonetheless. Grandmother would have been horrified. "I don't think there is anything in my past that warrants that kind of disclaimer. I mean, it hasn't been a bed of roses, but it isn't anything I can't work around with time and elbow grease. As for getting me here, that was all the scholarship. I finished everything else required for graduation. I only need to finish my thesis and this semester of scholarship classes. Those classes were supposedly here so we could study Appalachian folk tales." Had they been lying about that, or was it a ruse to get the princesses to Lointaine?

Connor tensed. "Hmm . . . That doesn't sound promising."

Huh? It was bad I had a solid reason for coming to Lointaine? I didn't have time to process that before he motioned for me to continue. "Sorry, I didn't mean to interrupt. We can discuss it after you tell me about your recent life."

I considered the request. "I can't list every bad thing that has happened in my life. Where should I start?"

"At some point, there was one event that was the beginning of everything else going downhill – a point when you weren't able to recover from one setback before the next one came. Start there."

That clarified things a bit. "That would be the fire at the framing store. I lost seven pieces for my thesis project." I ticked them off on my fingers, "The pumpkin, one of the apples, two of the rose pieces, the rampion, the pea, and the wheat."

Connor choked on his bite of pear. When he recovered, he asked, "Rampion? I am almost scared to ask. What was your thesis project?"

"I thought you were on the scholarship review committee? Don't you know?"

"No. Those duties rotate." He shrugged. "I wouldn't ask if I knew."

I could feel myself blush. "Oh! I was putting together an exhibit of botanical illustrations of plants with major roles in fairy tales. There were also coordinating interpretive panels. Besides discussing the obvious literature ties, the panels summarized things like how the plant was used historically, and any symbolism that was associated with them. I have spent the last year studying fairy tales. Ironic, isn't it?"

Connor groaned. "How the hell did that get by your committee? They were supposed to steer you away from any topics involving fairy tales. No wonder your story quest began." His expression was comically fierce. I was glad I wouldn't be answering for the oversight.

"To be fair, I didn't call them fairy tales in my proposal. I used terms like fable, folk legend, oral tradition, and mythology because they sounded more scholarly. A lot of people think fairy tales are just for kids." I rolled my eyes. If they read any of the originals, they would change their minds.

Ms. Millie slipped a plate of cookies on the island before heading out of the kitchen.

Still shaking his head, Connor asked, "What happened next?"

"I kept losing the spaces I arranged to host the show. The first gallery got an offer from a famous artist; that took precedence over my work. The art museum wanted to host it, but they didn't have an opening in their schedule. I found out the history museum had space to fill, so I beefed up the historical references in my panels, and they agreed to host the event.

"But then the executive director was suddenly put on bed rest during her pregnancy. Emilia Larkin, the woman who took over as acting director, didn't like the project. She didn't bother reviewing my pieces before she told me the whole thing was childish and a waste of her time. She was only letting the project continue because the board of directors had already approved it."

Connor made a motion for me to continue with his free hand.

"It seemed like she did everything she could to sabotage the project. I was out of town at a friend's wedding when I got a call from her in a snit. She claimed I hadn't emailed her the paint color for the gallery wall. The painters were there, and no paint. Never mind that she should have ordered the paint the morning before and discovered the missing information then. I re-sent the email immediately. When I got back, I found that instead of a lovely soft yellow named Old Parchment, the walls were screaming pink — imagine bubblegum, or Pepto-Bismol and Barbie Dream houses. She got two numbers in the paint code reversed when she called the paint shop, and she didn't realize anything was wrong when she saw the color on the wall.

"I thought I handled things fairly well." He didn't need to know I'd hidden in the bathroom while I pulled myself together — not emerging until all signs of my frustrated tears and near panic attack had vanished. "I volunteered to oversee the repainting myself. Emilia said there was no money for repainting the walls. I offered to pay for it, and she declined. She said she didn't have time to deal with supervising the repainting. At that point, I decided to do it myself. I bought the paint and rounded up some friends to help. We were halfway through the second coat of paint when she found out.

"She stormed into the gallery yelling about insurance and how I was flouting her authority. Somehow, my going against her private ruling on the matter was making her look bad in front of her staff. She didn't understand why I wasn't respecting her judgment. She called me several rather nasty names. I held my temper and told her she was behaving unprofessionally. She turned as pink as the walls had been, and shook the ladder I was standing on. One of the buckets of paint fell on her head. She blamed it on me — accused me of pushing it over on purpose — but I was clinging to the ladder to keep from falling off!

"After that, she complained to the board. She told them either my show went, or she did. Unfortunately, they didn't have much choice at the time. As sorry as they were, it would have been extremely disruptive for them to try to find another interim director.

"I called my father, hoping for some advice and help to brainstorm about where else I might have the show. But it turned out he had already heard the entire story because he and Emilia were dating — which is absurd! She is only four years older than me! Also, she is so different from his other girlfriends. It sounds silly, but I sometimes wondered if he dated women who could help me when he couldn't. Like when he dated a personal shopper right before prom, or the time he dated an artist . . . But with Emilia, it is the exact opposite!

"Dad didn't realize I was the person Emilia had been complaining about for weeks. I had talked to him about my project several times. I still can't believe he didn't put it together when she was telling him about everything. To make matters worse, he took her side! He said it was selfish of me to ask the history museum to continue with the project, with an interim director in charge. I tried to explain it wasn't just about me. The show had been advertised to both the history and art museum members for months. It was a fundraiser for the botanical gardens, too. They had already arranged to have live specimens of many of the plants made into centerpieces for the opening night. But Dad didn't care.

"Then he told me I was lucky she wasn't pressing criminal charges for throwing paint on her. How could he believe I would do that? I didn't even go through a rebellious teenage phase! How could he believe I would act that way? But he said I needed to grow up — that once I got out in the real world, I would see not everyone thought my 'little paintings' were important. He ended the call by saying I had better learn to get along with Emilia because she was important to him. What did he mean by that? More important than me? How could she be so important when I didn't even know they were together? He hung up without saying goodbye. We haven't talked since. He didn't even call after the accident to check on me, and I almost died!"

Now I needed a tissue and a shoulder to cry on, but Connor was too absorbed to notice. He had flipped his paper over and was scrawling a frenzy of equations. I couldn't find any tissues, so I blew my nose on the corner of a paper towel while peeking at his notes. I knew enough to guess it was some sort of calculus, but that was it. Any time math has more Greek symbols than actual numbers, my brain shuts down. Occasionally, he would cross whole lines out and backtrack. When he finally surfaced a few minutes later, it was only to ask, "Does Ms. Larkin have any children?"

Huh? Is that what all his equations were about — Emilia? Why was everyone so concerned about that obnoxious woman? "I don't think so."

Further scribbling. Finally, his head popped up.

"We need to be very careful if you are hoping to push things toward 'Beauty and the Beast.' With your mother dead, you aren't set up to be Sleeping Beauty. But, there is the family precedent to consider, and you were unconscious recently. Although, it wasn't in a significant increment of time like one hundred days, which seems like the pattern the Magic would follow — a hundred years for your grandmother, and a hundred months for your mother. Oh, but it may have been one hundred minutes . . ."

"But nobody kissed me to bring me out of it — no EMT on bended knee at the hospital playing the role of the prince. Wouldn't I be in a relationship now if I was Sleeping Beauty? My tale would be over."

"Hmm, good point. But I'm not comfortable saying it's not still a possibility."

"I am," I muttered under my breath.

"Of course, if you end up with a stepmother, that changes everything."

"What? Not her!" I hadn't considered Dad marrying Emilia. "Ugh!" I didn't bother suppressing an unladylike groan.

"And with how distant your father is becoming, we could even call you an orphan, or consider tales where the daughter is kicked out of her home as a potential plot point."

"Wait, so my father taking Emilia's side isn't his fault – it's the Magic's fault?" The heaviness that had been weighing me down since the fight began to lift. But with Connor's reaction, my mood plummeted. He was shaking his head.

"After reviewing case studies, I would almost say the Magic concentrates, or distills, personality. Have you ever studied wave interference?"

"Umm, I vaguely recall something about it."

"It's like that. A person's character is one wave, and the Magic is another that matches it. The two stack on top of each other, amplifying personality traits — making the person *more* of what they already are. I'm almost positive the Magic doesn't make people do anything. It may tempt them by putting them in situations to test their character. It may do everything possible to free the darkest, nastiest, most selfish, parts of a soul — but there is always a choice in which path to choose. Since these are fairy tales, those that resist and stay pure of heart are eventually rewarded. The Magic punishes those that let their baser selves take over. You need to remember that as we move forward. Give drinks to thirsty beggars and such."

"How can you say the Magic doesn't force you to do things? I don't want to be a princess. I don't want to get married and have children."

"Well that's different, you were born a princess. Nobody gets to control how they come into the world. As to marriage and children, if there is no part of you that wants those, then that won't happen. Happily ever after doesn't necessarily mean married — even the Disney versions gloss over the weddings. As far as the Magic is concerned, this is more about finding love than getting married. Pretty much everyone wants to be loved."

I couldn't argue with him, especially since I had just celebrated being able to blame a lack of loving support from my father on the Magic. Rage, and the burning unfairness of the situation, were causing my head to throb. I wanted to yell at Connor for being right, perhaps tell the Magic where it could stuff its pink princess dress code. None of that would help, though. I would still be in the same situation.

"Maybe Stanley has some weeds I can rip out of the ground or something," I muttered to myself.

I finally surprised Connor. "What?"

I shrugged, "Sorry, I am a bit frustrated at the moment. That would at least be a constructive way to deal with it." Although destroying something one-handed might further frustrate me, rather than helping clear my foul mood.

"Hmm, while I applaud the thought," he stuck his nose in the air and assumed a prissy tone, "princesses do not weed." He continued more earnestly, "Cinderella weeds. I seem to remember Belle has a bit of a temper. You could be less constructive?" He waggled his eyebrows at me, "Yell! All joking aside, if we are trying to sway the Magic toward Belle, you need to be in character at all times." He looked at me pointedly.

"What, now?"

"Yes. The sooner we can collapse the possibilities into the desired path the better. You need to start living the part at all times, to help steer the Magic where we want it to go." Connor shifted in his seat and glanced away, "Speaking of which, your grandmother has indicated you might need some assistance with some of the finer points of acting the part of a princess."

I groaned. "Seriously?"

"So, we made some arrangements to help you with that."

"Whoa! What does that mean?"

"Your grandmother has agreed to take care of deportment and etiquette classes; she said something about a cotillion teacher? So for the time being, it would be easier if you stayed with her. There will be other classes to help with skills such as hosting parties and managing a large household."

"But there's no time for extra classes! How am I going to find time to complete my thesis? I still have paintings to finish!"

"You can't finish your paintings now anyway, can you?" Connor glanced at my arm in its sling. "Don't worry, it's all worked out."

"It is?" I was incredulous. How had they worked everything out, if they hadn't known what I wanted?

"Yes, the scholarship board is willing to work with you. They won't be able to just excuse you from your classes, as it would set a precedent that might cause problems for the foundation in the future."

"I realize that," I muttered.

"If you agree to the etiquette classes to replace the official scholarship classes you missed, then they will grant you an extension for your thesis. You would have until the end of the spring semester."

I had already approached the scholarship committee about the possibility of an extension. If they denied my request, I could rework the interpretive panels so they didn't mention the missing pieces. Then I would have done the show in a basement if necessary. I didn't want to showcase less than my finest work, but it would be enough to fulfill their requirements. So while I appreciated the offer, I resented the attached conditions. I was tempted to tell them I didn't need the extension. Except I'd have to make up the classes anyway. Ugh!

Connor continued. "The committee will also tweak some of the topics for the symposium sessions. A lot of business skills conveniently overlap with those you need. Your next symposium session will be switched to event planning, which will cover party hosting skills. Hiring practices and management basics will stand in for how to run a household. Then, since the symposium sessions end on a lighter note, we will finish with ballroom dancing lessons. That is easy enough to justify because you never know when that skill will be needed at a fundraiser. We also lined up a therapist that knows about the Magic because—"

"You have everything planned out. What if I stayed in denial about the Magic?" My temperature was rising with my temper.

"We believed something would convince you. Besides, you would have had to take the courses even if you didn't believe."

Whoa, he wasn't sugarcoating it at all. I didn't know which was worse — knowing there was blatant manipulation I couldn't avoid or the feeling that everything up until now had been behind-the-scenes machinations.

"Doesn't it seem manipulative that you convinced me to work with you by offering to help control the direction the Magic is taking, yet you are dictating my every move?" My tone was sliding toward icy.

Connor shrugged. "It's not any sort of systematic collusion. We had time to prepare. It seemed silly not to. You are the one who came up with 'Beauty and the Beast.' We just planned to help you through whatever tale occurred with the fewest problems. Did you have a different plan you wanted to implement?"

I let my exasperation show. "No. I haven't processed everything yet. How could I have a plan?"

"Loren, we meant this to be reassuring. The Magic is a lot to absorb, and we didn't want you to be overwhelmed and alone while coming to terms with the situation. Why don't you consider our plan a default option? If you think of something else you prefer, we can change directions then."

"It is hard to argue when you are being so reasonable," I grumbled, trying to keep the bitterness out of my voice. It wasn't Connor's fault I was in this position. He had spent a lot of time and effort trying to help. I tried to be gracious, but my clenched jaw probably ruined the effect. "Thank you for all your help."

Connor burst out laughing. "Why do I get the feeling you would rather tell me to go to hell?" I started to splutter, but Connor didn't give me a chance to speak. "No, no — don't worry about it. I appreciate the effort on your part. You are very welcome. Now, one more thing. We need to get you out and about, meeting the people in town, so we can fill all the roles in the story. Some of your lessons will help a bit, but I would be honored if you would join my cousins and me at the theater. I have tickets for the opening night of *The Tempest* this weekend. Between the three of us, we can introduce you to a fair cross-section of the town's younger adult population; your grandmother isn't likely to have the same connections in the twenty- and thirty-something crowd."

Oh, tempting. It took me a few moments to realize I was weighing pleasure against the non-existent duty of my course load and painting schedule. Old habits die hard, I guess. "That sounds lovely. When does it start? Where should I meet you guys?"

Connor gave me a baleful look that stretched, as I tried to figure out what he was getting at. Oh, right! I was supposed to be a pretty, pretty princess. My shoulders drooped from their Grandmother-approved posture. "What time shall I expect you to pick me up?"

CHAPTER 7

By the time Saturday evening rolled around, I was ready to kiss Connor for giving me something enjoyable to concentrate on for a few hours. Physical therapy, being made over as Belle, and etiquette classes with my grandmother were making me question my life choices.

The etiquette classes were especially horrific. Today I had spent three hours learning how to properly glide across the floor because apparently I usually "clomped across it like a pachyderm." As a bonus, we covered how to properly sit and stand up, because Grandmother couldn't believe Mrs. Minchkin hadn't covered those topics with me yet. I was desperate for anything that resembled fun.

Ms. Millie helped me into what had to be the most gorgeous gown in the entire world. I didn't even care that it was blue. When I saw myself in the mirror I gave Millie a spontaneous, one-armed hug to celebrate. I looked amazing.

I mean, sure it took a whole team of people a week of intense effort to make me this attractive, but I was sure as hell going to enjoy it. When Grandmother came into my room after a peremptory knock, I was still grinning at myself in the mirror like an idiot. She was dressed to attend the theater, too. Even next to her glitzy outfit and glittering jewels, I felt like I held my own.

Kella was a miracle worker. I made a mental note to send her a thank you note along with some other appropriate token of my appreciation. Perhaps my first-born child? Flowers couldn't express enough gratitude.

Grandmother frowned as she reviewed my outfit. I hid a smile. I was as perfect as I got — she was proving Kella correct. "Loren, that jewelry simply will not do."

Before I could protest, she turned and stalked from the room. I met Millie's eyes in the mirror, mystified. I started to take the pearls off. "Should I try the navy instead of the gray?"

I looked over the corkboard filled with pictures of outfits sanctioned by Kella. I was sure she had said the pearls were neutral and acceptable with pretty much everything.

"Just wait a minute dear, I imagine your grandmother had something specific in mind."

I drew a calming breath and caught sight of the pink notecard I had stolen from Connor, pinned up amidst the blue and white outfits. I'd added a big red 'X' through the Sleeping Beauty notation. A gentle reminder that it was worth the etiquette lessons, and the poking and prodding, to avoid a hundred-month coma — or even a hundred-day coma. The one I had already experienced was bad enough. Maybe I should add some other positive things to the board? Pictures of books and libraries, perhaps a magical rose? My thoughts were interrupted by Grandmother striding back into the room.

Millie was correct. Grandmother had a black velvet box. She set it on the dressing table, opening it with a dignified flourish to reveal sparkling diamonds. She clasped the cuff around my wrist and then put earrings in my palm.

"These will correct the problem. Although," she tilted her head slightly to the side while reviewing my image in the mirror critically, "I believe we will leave the necklace off. It would be too much."

Impulsively, I turned and hugged her. "Now I really *am* perfect!" With the diamonds sparkling against the inky blue silk, and the delicate wisps of black tulle, I was a goddess of the night sky.

"Careful dear, you don't want to muss anything." The words were a bit cool, but to my surprise, I saw a slight smile as she carefully set me far enough away that the skirts of our dresses didn't touch.

Ms. Millie was looking a bit misty-eyed as she enjoyed the scene. She was searching in her pockets, probably for a tissue, when the phone rang. The interruption was well-timed, as it stopped anyone from putting on an emotional display that would embarrass my grandmother — including her. Millie excused herself and answered the phone. I barely heard her, "Good evening, this is the Dalton residence . . ."

I checked my clutch to make sure I hadn't forgotten anything. I added my lipstick, and after some consideration, the powder — better safe than sorry. I was rising to my feet when Ms. Millie came back in.

"That was Connor at the gate."

"In that case, I guess I should head downstairs." I was turning to leave when my grandmother sighed.

"You will do no such thing. Connor might not be an actual suitor, but you will treat him with the same courtesy as one. Besides, it is good practice in showing someone how you are to be treated."

I was forced to pause, what did that mean? Confusion must have shown plainly on my face.

"Loren," Millie said gently, "Even I know you need to make an entrance. Why do you think your grandmother gave you extra deportment lessons this morning?"

Grandmother nodded and serenely glided along the hall exactly as she had tried to get me to do all morning. I lurked at the top of the stairs.

I didn't have to wait more than a few minutes for Connor to arrive, but if he had taken much longer, I might have ended up twisting permanent wrinkles into the delicate tulle overlay of my gown. While I waited for Ms. Millie to get Grandmother, and then sat through the polite chitchat, I mentally reviewed my earlier lessons. Chin lifted — no looking at the stairs. Foot placed flat on the stairs at a fifteen-degree angle toward the banister. Then I should shift my weight from the back foot to the front foot, hand lightly trailing the banister — not holding it in a death grip, even if I was sure I was going to fall in these heels.

I didn't want to keep Connor waiting too long, especially with Grandmother. When there was a slight pause in the discussion, I took a deep breath before tackling the stairs. I don't know if it was the Magic, or the dress, or the hours of practice, but I floated effortlessly — light as thistledown. A glow of happiness and accomplishment lit my face. The thought that Grandmother would not approve of my broad smile made me want to laugh. I checked to see if she was frowning at me, but neither she nor Connor had noticed me. Well, that figured. I paused to give them a chance to notice my presence.

"I am aware that this is the best course of action; it is the only reason I agreed to let you escort Loren. However, that doesn't mean I am not cross that you are the one introducing her to Lointaine society." Connor opened his mouth to protest, and she waved her hand for him to stay silent. "I am telling you this not to suggest a change in our plans, but to explain how perturbed I will be if you do not bring her by my box during the intermission. There will be plenty of time for her to meet your young people, even if you manage to spare five minutes for an old lady like me." Oh, that sounded just the tiniest bit bitter.

"I would be honored to escort Ms. Hughes to your box, Mrs. Dalton." Wow, putting on our frosty formal fronts, were we?

"Thank you, Mr. Tierney." With that, Grandmother turned and finally saw me standing on the stairs. "Loren," she managed to conceal most of her surprise, "Well, don't dawdle on the stairs." I smiled benignly at her. She might be fussing, but her secret was out. If she wanted to introduce me to society, that meant she was proud of me. I managed to float down the rest of the stairs just like a fairy tale princess — well, except for the tiniest bobble at the end, where the last stair was a smidge higher than the rest.

"Please try to remember all your lessons tonight, dear."

"I will, Grandmother." I leaned in to kiss the soft crepe of her cheek. The scent of her perfume curled around me. As I drew back, an invisible trail of rose, ylang-ylang, and pear connected us.

The perfume was another hint at Grandmother's softer side. She had been wearing Patou's 'Joy' since my grandfather gave her the first bottle as a young bride. I suddenly wanted to make my grandmother proud. Not because of some childish need for her to approve of me, but because I was beginning to love her. In theory, you have to love your family, but I found that wasn't true, especially when one hasn't seen a person in over twenty years. Maybe there was hope yet for a non-adversarial relationship.

I was a bit dewy eyed from this revelation, and flushed from the pleasure of not tripping and falling down the steps, when I turned to Connor. "Well, shall we head out?"

Connor gulped audibly and bowed before offering his arm — properly, I noted, in front of his chest and not out to the side. I guess he was as nervous about all of this as I was. Did he get lessons for this too, or had he been "raised properly" from childhood? I placed my fingers on his arm, lightly to avoid putting creases in his snazzy tuxedo jacket, and turned to wave at Grandmother. She was grinning, a bit wickedly actually. "I do believe Mr. Tierney, that you may be in trouble."

Connor glared and sighed before leading me toward the door. At the last minute, he turned and said, "It was never her eligibility that was in question."

The tight smile on her face faded into a softer one and she gave him a nod. "I see."

Well, I didn't. "What was that all about?" I asked Connor, as he held the car door open for me. I was glad the question distracted him, as I was not at all graceful as I sank into the car seat. If my dress were shorter, I would have been flashing my underwear like a pop star.

"Well," he paused as he walked around the car to get in on his side, "let's just say your grandmother and I have a difference of opinion as to who might be eligible for the part of the prince in your tale. Don't worry though, I plan to make sure you meet as many eligible men as possible, and then trust that you and the Magic will make the right choice."

"Oh." His faith in me was a bit scary. I hadn't made the best choices of boyfriends in the past. Perhaps it was time to change the topic. "So, when are we meeting your cousins?"

"At dinner, which is where we are headed now."

"Where are we eating?" The question was generic, but I couldn't come up with any better conversational gambits. I had expected his sporty car to make ridiculously loud *vroom vroom* noises, but instead, it was so quiet that the silence hung heavy in the air. "I'm sorry, that wasn't the right thing to say, was it? You would think after three hours covering the art of conversation and learning about," I paused to make air quotes, "'the eloquent silence,' that I would manage better."

Connor laughed. "It seems like a reasonable topic of conversation to me. We have reservations for the terrace restaurant at the Mountain Grove Resort. We were lucky to get reservations. Liam — that's one of my cousins — coordinates with them a lot through his business, and he pulled some strings to get us a table."

"That was nice of him."

"Both he and Henri are looking forward to meeting you." He cleared his throat. "Actually, I should warn you that most people in the town are curious. Everyone wants to know why you came back, and whether or not your tale has started yet."

Everyone knew about the tales? I let out something that was a cross between a groan and a laugh. "No pressure though, right?"

Connor spared me a glance. "Well, I could see how it would feel that way. But for the most part, you will only be getting introduced to people and exchanging basic pleasantries. Cook up an answer for 'How are you liking Lointaine so far?' and you will be set."

"Well, that is a loaded question if I have ever heard one." I smiled to take the sting out of the comment.

"Try some variant of, 'It's such a lovely town, I can't wait to' and fill in the blank with whatever seems appropriate. It answers the question politely without saying anything. To be polite, you may have to respond to questions, but that doesn't mean you owe anyone personal information you don't want to share. In fact, such shallow answers tend to be best in general." A tinge of cynicism colored Connor's voice.

"I will keep it in mind." I didn't want to elaborate for fear of poking any sore spots.

The quiet stretched.

"Sorry. I just don't like people as a whole. My whole life, I have been prodded by well-meaning relatives into interacting with society in ways I didn't want."

"I take it you are an introvert. I thought I was comfortable in a social setting, but all these new rules of Grandmother's make me feel like I have been running around with my skirt tucked into my underwear all along." Connor laughed at the image. "She seems to believe everyone in Lointaine has the same expectations as she does, which means I am toast. We don't have to go to the play you know. We can go hide somewhere instead. Like a bookstore! I bet Lointaine has an amazing bookstore." I gave Connor a big grin while raising my eyebrows and nodding maniacally at him in a dare to take me up on the offer.

Connor chuckled. "Your grandmother will kill me if I don't bring you to her at intermission. No one has standards quite as Mrs. Dalton does." He paused for a moment. "I think she is so strict because it is one of the few ways she believes she can prepare you. She doesn't like feeling helpless."

"I will have to remember that the next time she is exasperated with me."

"Did you know she used to make excuses to come by my office and sneak peeks at your file?"

"She did?" I couldn't imagine my proper grandmother engaging in such skullduggery.

"She would wait until we were in my office, and then ask for a drink. Once I figured out what was going on, I made sure to take extra time getting it."

Oh man, that was so sweet — of both of them.

"I don't know whether learning more about your grandmother would make her easier to deal with or not."

As much as I wanted to know everything, it was an invasion of my grandmother's privacy. If she wanted me to know, she would tell me.

"Why don't we settle on me trying to be more patient with her?"

"All right."

That damned quiet car again. "So, how about that sports team, music group, most recent book you read . . . Help me out here."

"Changing the topic, are we?"

"Yes, any topic is fair game as long as it isn't serious."

"No pressure though, right?" He was grinning.

"None intended." I teased back. "We could play favorites instead."

"Favorites?"

"Oh come on, it's not that hard to figure out. I say something like 'book,' and you tell me your favorite, and I reciprocate. You go next with picking out the topic. Classic getting-to-know-you banter."

"Oh, *Cannery Row* then."

"What?"

"*Cannery Row*. It's my favorite book."

"Oh." Duh. Exceptionally bright tonight, aren't we? I thought about the book. "Why that one?"

He shrugged. "Doc and the 'Black Marigolds' poem. When I read that, I knew Steinbeck must have felt like Doc at some point, and it meant at least one other person knew how I felt. Plus, if there was hope for Doc, then there was hope for me. Stuff like that makes a big impression when you are fifteen." He gave a self-deprecating shrug.

I remembered the ending now. "That was such a poignant ending, that poem . . ."

"'Black Marigolds' — I can quote it for you if you like." What an impish grin. I should have realized he would have it memorized. "You know, not many people I know have read that book. It doesn't seem to make the school reading lists around here. Isn't it your turn to share now?"

I groaned. "I don't know if I can pick a favorite book. I just threw that out there as an example. Besides, how can I pick one after your answer?"

"Well, at the very least you have to share something profound and book-related."

Hmm. "*The Princess Bride* may be the only book/movie combination where I thought the movie was better than the book. Although, I may need to reconsider that, given what I have recently learned. I am feeling a bit snarky about perfect fairy tales myself right now."

He laughed. "That's close enough to count, I guess. So, now I am supposed to pick something to ask what your favorite is?"

"Yes."

"Well, I believe I will have to hold my question in reserve for use at a later time. We have arrived." He pointed off to his left as we turned off the main road. The hotel was a cross between a mountain lodge and a castle. Its warm lights twinkled at us, peeking through leaves and branches. The irreverent line, "Have fun storming the castle!" popped into my head. Well, here goes nothing . . .

CHAPTER 8

When we pulled up to the valet stand, I managed to be much more graceful getting out than I was getting in. It helped that I remembered to keep my knees together, so I didn't flash anyone or snag a foot in my skirt. The valet's respectful, appreciatively wide-eyed look was a lovely bonus.

Connor led the way through the hotel lobby to the restaurant. When Connor told the hostess we were with the Randolph party, her cool efficient façade became warm and almost bubbly. His cousin must tip well for such a reaction. As we approached the table, I quickly realized that tips had nothing to do with the hostess's reaction. Connor's cousins were arresting. Talk about tall, dark, and handsome — and did I mention the broad shoulders? I was focusing so hard on not starting, my brain dearly wanted to analyze their features for a drawing, that I almost tripped over my own feet.

Both men stood as we approached so Connor could introduce us. "Ms. Hughes, please permit me to introduce my cousins: Mr. William Randolph and Mr. Heinrich Randolph." The introduction was so formal I fought the urge to curtsey, and inclined my head to each gentleman instead.

I held my intact left hand out to William because he was closest, although his magnetic appeal might have had me offering my hand to him first anyway. Instead of shaking my hand, which would have admittedly been a bit awkward, he leaned forward with a flourish to kiss it. A tousled lock of hair, shining with hues of polished wood — chestnut, maple, and oak — fell forward as he did so.

His lips were supposed to hover above my hand on a first introduction, but he wasn't playing by the rules. He turned my hand over and kissed my palm. As his light stubble brushed my wrist, shivers spread in a warm wave across my body. My brain refused to develop an appropriate introductory comment. Instead, it rolled over, baring its belly and begging to be scratched.

What was wrong with me? Sure, he was easily the most handsome man I'd ever met — including the ridiculous studio session I did illustrating a romance novel cover — but his greeting was overdone almost to the point of being obnoxious. Why were my knees turning into jelly? Being asexual, I never, *ever*, react to someone like this just because they were handsome. If this was the Magic pushing me at someone, it was obnoxious.

"I'm enchanted." His deep voice coiled through the air and raised goosebumps along my skin. Every raised hair on my body was straining toward him.

He raised a devastating eyebrow (how the hell does an eyebrow manage to be devastating?) above topaz colored eyes. They glinted — inviting me to share in his amusement. "Now Connor, what kind of an introduction is that?"

A proper one, at least according to Grandmother, retorted the small, tart part of my brain that wasn't turned into mush. I was glad the thought didn't pop out of my mouth, as I hadn't been sure my filter didn't reside in the part of my brain that was apparently out of commission.

He continued to hold my hand, which wasn't proper. Of course, it wasn't proper for me to pull my hand away either. "Please call me Liam. William is so . . . formal." He winked as he said it. I wanted to groan at the performance, but I was also trying not to start drooling.

Oh Loren, get it together!

Heinrich came to the rescue, holding out his hand so that Liam was forced to drop mine. The corner of his lip lifted in a sardonic smile at his cousin's maneuvers. "My friends call me Henri. I hope you will, too." After Liam's maneuvers, I felt the need to offer him my hand with the knuckles up to be kissed. He held my hand lightly in his and — with a minute bow, properly brushed the air above my knuckles with his lips. His understated performance seemed suave after Liam's more over-the-top display. Not that he wasn't amused by the formality too — it showed in sparks flashing through his green eyes, reminding me of light hitting a gemstone. Perhaps a peridot?

Henri was handsome too, although in a harder, chiseled way. With his sharply angled jaw, slashes of cheekbones, and dark hair, he was a black-and-white charcoal sketch to Liam's soft-focus pastel.

"Fine," Connor's voice held a light note of exasperation as he completed the introduction, "Liam, Henri — this is Loren," he let a pregnant pause hang in the air, "Roselle Dalton's granddaughter." Liam and Henri chuckled while looking slightly sheepish.

I briefly pondered the differences in my reaction to the two men. Why wasn't I attracted to Henri, despite his being equally handsome? It wasn't that he wasn't being friendly . . . It was difficult to pinpoint exactly, but it was almost as if he was radiating cool detachment to Liam's suggestive warmth. I gave a mental shake and kicked myself into social gear. "It is a pleasure to meet you both."

Connor gestured toward my chair and held it out while I seated myself. I managed to raise my skirt just enough that it wasn't tight or caught under a chair leg as my seat was scooched in, a small miracle considering I had to do it one-handed. I might be getting the hang of this! Oh no, did thinking that jinx it? Ugh, focus, Loren! What's next? Small talk . . . What were safe topics again?

"Liam, I understand you arranged for our reservation tonight. That was very kind of you."

"It was my pleasure. After all, it gave me a chance to meet Lointaine's newest resident."

I was saved from more over-the-top comments by the arrival of our waiter. Water was poured and our napkins were placed on our laps. He delivered his spiel about the day's specials and left us to consider our options.

Connor interrupted my internal debate about whether an appetizer would allow room for dessert when he cleared his throat and asked, "Loren, would you like me to order for you?" Huh? I found myself blinking excessively while I tried to process his request. Even Grandmother didn't insist on that anymore.

"I don't think that . . ." I was trying to figure out how to politely decline when curiosity struck. "What would you order for me?"

"Umm, the poached pear salad with grilled chicken?" He was practically squirming in discomfort.

I gave in and laughed. "Thank you for your ever-so-kind offer but I believe I will order for myself."

He was baffled. "But the etiquette book your grandmother sent . . . Would you have preferred the cranberry goat cheese salad?" Hmm, Grandmother at work? I might have to forgive him for his assumptions after all.

"I don't like eating salads for dinner. My family tends to eat them at lunch."

Henri and Liam were still laughing at the look on Connor's face as the waiter came back to take our orders.

When the waiter asked for my order, I told him, "I'd like the bacon-wrapped, blue cheese stuffed figs for my appetizer. Then the steak au poivre and the cauliflower au gratin." Connor seemed more and more confused as I ordered. I gave him an innocent look and batted my eyes for good measure. "I think I will skip the salad course to save room for dessert."

Liam was having trouble breathing from laughing so hard that he waved the waiter toward Henri. Henri looked at the waiter with a straight face, "That sounds excellent. I believe I'll have what she's having, hmm, along with the blue crab salad." That salad tempted me too — pomegranate and citrus dressing, yum! What sort of lecture would I be setting myself up for with Grandmother if I asked to try a bite when it came?

Liam pulled himself together enough to order with a gesture toward Henri, "The same thing as him please." Then he also ordered a bottle of red wine for the table.

Once the waiter left, Connor almost accused me, "No wonder I couldn't order for you. I've never been out with a woman who didn't order a salad."

Was there a proper reply to that? I didn't feel like coming up with one, so I lifted one shoulder in a sort of elegant shrug. "I just ordered what I felt like eating."

Liam was staring at Connor in disbelief. "Always salads? Isn't that a bit clichéd? You might want to check your math." He rolled his eyes. "Loren, you have to watch out for these theoretical physicists and their quantum numbers."

"Is this a first date phenomenon, or truly an every single time kind of thing?" Henri asked with mock seriousness.

"How many dates are we talking about anyway? Two?" That seemed like a bit of a low blow from Liam, but neither of the men commented on it. Must be a family thing to pick on each other.

Connor flushed, finally seeming to catch on that what he said was a bit uncouth. "Well, I meant at least a salad along with their main course. After all, it is a fairly healthy habit."

Sheesh, admit you were a bit of a jerk and get it over with. I practically cooed, "Oh, maybe I should add a salad to my order." I cocked my head and pretended to consider for a few seconds. "On second thought, perhaps the two vegetables coming with my entrée are enough." I vapidly blinked my eyes for effect. Liam snorted his water and started choking.

"That seems sensible." Henri commented, "And the steak is a good choice because you need a high protein intake to help your arm heal."

Liam recovered to scoff, "When did you change specialties to become a dietician?"

Henri responded to the snide teasing calmly. "Eating a diet high in protein is standard advice after surgery, just like keeping incisions out of the sun. Any surgeon would know that."

"Even the plastic ones, huh?"

"It's reconstructive, not —"

"Now children . . ." Connor intervened, shaking his head. "You two make me grateful that Bree is so much younger than I am. Talk about sibling rivalry!"

"Wait, I thought you were cousins." Why did I think that again? I knew they were Connor's cousins, but that didn't mean they weren't brothers themselves. Was it from the family tree?

"Technically we are both."

Connor clarified. "Liam's parents died when he was young. Aunt Margarete and Uncle Nick adopted him, and raised him along with Henri."

"Oh. I'm sorry. That must have been awful." It was almost impossible for me when Mom died when I was eight – did that count as young? I couldn't imagine having lost Dad, too.

"Thanks," Liam responded. He cleared his throat, "So, tell me about yourself, Loren . . . I get the feeling that Connor and Henri know more about you than I do."

Change of topic, I could respect that. Although I didn't know why he believed Henri knew anything about me. "Well, I am working to finish my master's degree in technical illustration."

"Your grandmother said you were an artist," Henri mused, "but she didn't mention the technical part. I would love to ask for your advice about an article I am writing at some later point. But I don't want to bore anyone by talking shop . . ."

When had he talked to Grandmother? I guess he did know a bit more than Liam. "I would be glad to try to help, but I haven't done much in the way of medical illustrations before."

"What do you illustrate?" Liam was fighting to stay in the conversation.

"Recently I have been focusing on plants."

"Botanical drawings, huh? There is a boggy area on one of the club properties with some pretty amazing pitcher plants. If you would be interested in seeing them, I would be pleased to take you." Wow, that was a kind offer for someone that was practically a stranger . . . I blinked vapidly for a moment before pulling together an answer. Nice poise, Loren.

"That would be wonderful. I don't have any pitcher plants in my portfolio. I could probably manage to take some pictures if nothing else." I stopped to groan. "Of course, I will have to go buy another camera first. My last one seems to have been lost by the police somewhere."

"Hmm." Liam didn't seem willing to let the outing go so easily. "We could find one for you to borrow. I know the club has a high-end one around somewhere for trophy shots."

"What club is this?" He said the word 'club' with a sense of pride that let me know it was important to him. It seemed like a good conversation starter. Grandmother said the secret to excelling at conversation was to let the other person talk about themselves.

"Just–" Liam started to answer, but Henri cut him off.

"Liam is too modest to tell you, but he is the owner and manager of an exclusive international hunt club. He does such an exemplary job; he has a waiting list a mile long and can't seem to stay ahead of the demand — no matter how many zeroes he adds to the membership fees."

I could see aw-shucks-it's-nothing written all over Liam's face. I wouldn't have expected him to be modest.

Henri apparently couldn't take the modesty. He made a mock serious face and said in a snooty tone, "Bringing back the grace and elegance associated with the colonial era of big game hunting . . ."

Liam chuckled. "Have to do something to justify 'all those zeroes.'"

"That on top of a physicist and a doctor! What an amazingly talented family you all are."

"Just don't ask us to sing," Henri grinned. "We sound more like dogs howling at the moon than anything human." I liked that he could laugh at himself. Connor and Liam stared for a moment and then burst into laughter as well.

"Must be an inside joke there." I smiled to let them know I didn't mind being left out.

"You could say that–" Connor was interrupted by the arrival of bread and the guys' salads. Conversation waned to generalities as we applied ourselves to our meal, and in my case, remembering which knife to use when. I was grateful for the distraction as I was beginning to find my reaction to Liam uncomfortable. I couldn't seem to stop staring at him. It was awkward.

After a few moments, I needed a new distraction. "It sounds like you travel for work, Liam. Have you traveled anywhere interesting recently?"

"Well, I took some clients to South Africa to hunt buffalo a few months ago; it's been mostly stateside otherwise recently." Liam happily talked about his work. Score for Grandmother and her lessons. Of course, maybe that was bad if I was going to have to listen to hunting stories. Eww. And while we were eating . . .

"Didn't you head to South Africa recently too, Henri?" Connor asked. Thanks for the save, Connor!

Henri replied with a self-deprecating smile, "I'm sure Liam's trip was more interesting." I wasn't sure I agreed.

"Do you like to travel too, Henri?" See, I could do polite discussion.

"I mostly travel when I volunteer for Doctors Without Borders."

"What was it this last time? Cleft palate repairs?" Liam asked.

"No . . . Um, something that doesn't make for good discussion while eating." Henri frowned at Liam.

"Oh," Liam replied. The exchange effectively killed conversation until dessert was offered and reluctantly declined. Apparently, there wasn't time. Connor promised the pre-theatre party would have something chocolate.

I teased Connor as we stood to leave. "The molten chocolate torte sounded amazing. I am holding you to your promise. After all, I skipped my salad to save room for something chocolate!"

Henri threw his head back and laughed, and Connor shook his head at us, preoccupied with looking over Liam's shoulder while Liam signed our bill. Connor pulled out his wallet and passed some money to Liam. "We should leave a larger tip, the service was excellent."

Liam frowned, ready to argue. Henri jumped in, "Why don't Connor and I go get the cars brought around? We can meet you outside in a moment."

Liam absentmindedly took the money from Connor and put it with the check, as he addressed Henri's suggestion. "Why don't I go with Connor? I had something I wanted to ask him about anyway."

"I'd be happy to escort Loren."

That was a bit of a relief because I wasn't sure I trusted myself alone with Liam. Henri was thoughtful about my arm too. He took my wrap as it was brought back to the coat check counter, draped it over my shoulders, and then pulled my hair out from underneath. It would have been awkward to manage with my bum wrist, so I appreciated his help maintaining my facade of gracefulness.

I smiled at him in gratitude, "Thank–"

Henri started in at the same time. "It's great to see Connor laugh. You are good for him. I was starting to worry about him. Thank you." He was beaming at me.

"Huh?" So much for not appearing graceless, here I was with my mouth hanging open again. My brain caught up with the suggestion. "Henri, do you think Connor and I are a couple?"

"Aren't you?"

I shook my head. After making sure no one was close enough to hear, I responded, "No, he is helping me through my *conte des fées*. I need a Beast to avoid being Sleeping Beauty, and he doesn't begin to qualify. He said he knew someone that might work."

Henri was surprised, shocked almost. "I think I understand." That sounded almost grim. I was pretty sure he and I weren't having the same understanding.

"I'm not sure I explained it well."

"Don't worry. I will discuss it with Connor. Here, why don't we head out?"

When we wandered outside, it appeared as if Liam and Connor were having another intense conversation.

"I don't care, I want this chance," Liam demanded.

Connor saw us approaching and sighed. "I will discuss it with the relevant parties."

"Thank you." Liam turned to me with another million-watt smile, "Loren, let me get your door for you."

I managed to slide into the car gracefully this time, despite the distraction of having to slide past Liam's body.

It almost killed me, but I resolved not to ask about what was obviously a private discussion. "So . . ." Connor tensed as I started to ask him my question, probably assuming I was going to quiz him about Liam. "What is your favorite poem — perhaps one you've written?" He laughed and pulled away from the valet stand.

CHAPTER 9

As soon as we got to our box in the theater, I tapped Connor's forearm with my program. "Those mini pumpkin torts were delicious, but they weren't chocolate. You still owe me dessert."

"How was I supposed to know they were going to do something different this time?" He laughed.

I harrumphed in response as he seated me. "All those people to deal with and no chocolate."

"You did beautifully," Henri said as he sat at the far end of the row. Although polite, his tone lacked the warmth it had when he thought I was dating Connor.

"Everybody loved you. I wasn't sure if we were going to be able to get away," Liam agreed, as he helped me take off my wrap.

"Thank you for making it so effortless. Apparently, all I need is three people fielding my small talk and I can make appropriate casual conversation!" Liam and Henri chuckled politely, only to be shushed by Connor as the play began.

I snuggled into my seat. I was looking forward to enjoying myself a bit. Excitement washed my previous worries away — engaging with the show was far superior to engaging with people. A flash of lights and a boom of thunder introduced the eponymous tempest.

I fell into the story. As sometimes happens with amazing art, I felt a flush of anticipation, and the hair on the back of my arms rose. It was almost as if my entire body was trying to become more sensitive to better absorb the experience. Then the ship capsized. Blinding light exploded across the theater, lighting every nook and corner of the stage, not to mention the entire audience. It was immediately followed by a deafening crash of thunder that left my ears ringing. Several audience members shrieked and there was a murmuration of comments rippling through the crowd. The last few seconds of special effects were a lot to absorb, but they were undeniably impressive from a technical perspective.

I sat stunned, already feeling wrung out. At this rate, I wasn't going to make it through the entire play. I worked on collecting myself as we sat in total darkness, wondering how long we were going to be kept in suspense. Wow, I was going to have to remember to tell Kella what a fabulous director she was.

After a minute, there was a knock on the door of our box, and an usher with a flashlight came in.

He leaned over Henri's shoulder and whispered, "Dr. Randolph, we are having a medical emergency. It may be a heart attack or a problem with the gentleman's pacemaker. Kella thought you might be able to help."

Henri immediately got to his feet. As he left, I heard him ask, "Have you called 9-1-1?"

Did they delay the play for the medical emergency? Another minute crawled by. Then two.

Finally, the wait was over. Someone was coming onstage with a lantern. The effect was dramatic with the theater as dark as it was. Wait, shouldn't there at least be aisle lights on?

"Ladies and gentlemen . . ." I recognized Kella's voice. She lifted the lantern so the fragile nimbus of light flickered across her face. "I am afraid the effects at the end of that last scene were supplied not by us, but by Mother Nature. It appears the theater was hit by lightning. Unfortunately, we have lost several pieces of equipment that are essential to the play. Tonight's performance will have to be postponed. All tickets for tonight will be honored for open seats when we resume production. We will update our website as we have more information. At this time, we must ask that you exit the building in a calm and orderly fashion, following the direction of your ushers."

Well, I hadn't expected that.

Connor's voice drifted out of the dark. "Seems like we will have the chance to get you some chocolate after all."

CHAPTER 10

The brownie sundae was everything Connor promised it would be. It was almost enough to make me forget how overdressed I was.

"So, do you wear tuxedos to soda fountains often?" I teased Connor.

He grinned at me over a brownie sundae dubbed 'The Colossus.' "Desperate times call for desperate measures. I promised you chocolate and a show and managed neither. I had to remedy the situation somehow."

I licked the hot fudge off my chilled spoon before responding. "I think I might be able to forgive you. This is amazing. However, I won't be held responsible for your demise if Grandmother finds out you brought me here. Her lessons today didn't cover how to perch on a swiveling stool or eat caramel sauce properly. I am probably supposed to stir three times counterclockwise, or something like that, to make sure nothing is dangling off my spoon before I eat." And she wouldn't approve of scraping the bottom of the bowl either — but there was no need to point out my unladylike eating habits after the salad incident.

Connor laughed as I hoped he would. He had been withdrawn since dinner. I thought he'd been dreading mingling at the theater, but he was still brooding.

"That's better. I was beginning to think you regretted having to introduce me. All those people to deal with . . ." Connor was shaking his head, so I paused to give him a chance to finish his bite. I likely would have talked with my mouth full if I had something important to say.

Finally, he sighed. "Not at all, it was a bit fun, actually." Oh well, high praise indeed. I managed to hold back a snort. "We may have a bit of a twist in our plans, and I am trying to figure out the ramifications."

"Like what? Maybe I can help? After all, this is my life we are talking about." Was it possible to damage your eyes while rolling them? If so, I might go blind before this whole thing was over.

"I am not sure I am ready to discuss it yet."

I copied a facial expression of Grandmother's and raised my eyebrow imperiously.

"I will soon. I promise. It's just that it involves some family mess on my end. I need to make sure it won't create more problems than it will solve."

I can't believe the eyebrow thing worked for me. Family messes, ugh. I understood those.

And speaking of his family . . . "Did you know Henri thought I was your *real* date tonight?" Connor's gaze popped up from his ice cream, forgetting about the spoon suspended midair, and leaving his mouth hanging open. "Don't worry, I straightened him out."

He cleared his throat and put the spoon down with a loud clink. "What exactly did you tell him?"

"That you were helping me look for a Beast." Connor groaned. He dropped his head into his hands and pushed his fingers through his hair before straightening.

"Um, did I say something wrong?"

"No, I did. I assumed certain people would read between the lines and that others wouldn't. I am going to have some groveling to do later. For that matter, I have some to do now."

"Really?" Wrinkling my nose in confusion felt weird with this much makeup on. It diverted my attention a bit.

"Yes. I am sorry for any awkwardness that arose from my not being more clear with my cousins. I told them that your tale was starting, and I needed help introducing you to people. But I didn't tell them which story you chose. That may have caused some issues."

He took another bite of his sundae. "Blargh — I forgot to ask them to leave off the butterscotch." He stared moodily at his ice cream. "You know what, forget it. It's not my job to keep him out of trouble. He's an adult, and I told him this is a mistake. It's not my job to talk him out of this." He was muttering to himself more than talking to me.

He finally included me in the discussion. "Right, so I'm going to explain everything." He opened his mouth to continue but no words came. "Except I can't. Give me a minute."

He pulled out his phone and started tapping on it. Seriously? I occupied myself playing with my spoon and pondering whether Grandmother's eyebrow trick would work again. Did it lose its effect if it was overused? Hmm.

When he finished on his phone, he explained. "I want to tell you everything . . . But I can't without sharing secrets that aren't mine to disclose. I'm working on getting permission."

A moment later his phone beeped. He read the screen and showed it to me.

The phone was open to a text conversation with Liam. HOW MUCH CAN I SHARE WITH LOREN? was on the first line. The response read ANYTHING YOU NEED TO.

Photo by Julya Mirro Photo by Julya Mirro me tonight and asked me to see if you would give him a chance to be your Prince Charming. He pretty much begged."

"Liam wants to date me? I didn't think I was . . ." Classy? Sophisticated? Glamorous? 'I didn't think I was high-maintenance arm candy for a charming globetrotter' felt rude. Yes, glamorous was the best I was likely to do. ". . . glamorous enough for him." It wasn't that Liam was a bad guy, but it seemed like he might have certain expectations of a significant other that I didn't match.

Connor was practically squirming, he looked so miserable. "It's not actually about you, it's more about the opportunity you represent." Well, that was flattering. I started to be irritated, but realized I was in a similar situation of wanting to date a guy for an attribute, and not for who he was. I suddenly felt sleazy.

The thought must have shown on my face; Connor hurried to continue. "Oh man, that didn't come out right. It's just . . . Liam is related to Henri through his mother and is not a descendant of Louis. The Magic seems to be strongly tied to Louis's genes — so he's probably not a prince. He's always been hung up about being the odd one out or feeling like he's not being included."

Connor took a deep breath. "Perhaps more importantly, Liam's parents had what could optimistically be called a rocky relationship. I know his father was verbally abusive, but I suspect he was physically, too. They likely would have gotten divorced if they hadn't died. Liam has recently been feeling pressured to marry. He is worried about marrying the wrong person and repeating his parents' mistakes. He thinks if he marries you, then the Magic will ensure true love and a happily ever after."

Wow, Liam had gotten a raw deal in life. I felt for him, but pity was a ridiculous basis for marriage. The bottom line was it didn't seem like we would be a good match. Although there was that odd attraction. . . Was the Magic pushing us together? That didn't seem right though, based on Connor's earlier lecture.

"If the Magic doesn't change people, how can it ensure a happily ever after?"

"It doesn't change *people*. The best I can figure, it tends to be an outstanding matchmaker when it isn't resorting to brute-force tactics." That sounded ominous. "Also, don't forget that the Magic tends to leave people in fortunate situations once they are married. That said, the Magic sometimes seems to be more concerned with making a tale *happen* than the people involved. I suspect Liam is wrong. But I can't convince him of that. Honestly, I think he will end up as Gaston."

"Oh . . ." I'd been so focused on the roles of Belle and the Beast, I hadn't considered all the other roles that would need to be filled. "Wait . . . but doesn't Gaston die in the end?" And what about my father getting thrown into an asylum? Did it make me an awful person if I was okay with that if the tradeoff was avoiding a new stepmother like Emilia Larkin?

Connor sighed. "Well, it doesn't explicitly show that in the Disney version. Gaston could have fallen into a conveniently out-of-sight river and lived. There's that whole trope about the villain not quite being dead and showing up later at an inconvenient time. Or it might be an allegorical or spiritual death. Something like the death of a hope or dream, a long-held belief . . . Or, he could die to the town, his business could die, he could die to his family . . . Well, you get the idea."

"What?" I squeaked. I swallowed and took a quick breath; I needed to present a rational argument to Connor. That is what he would respect. "No! I won't be responsible for anyone dying!" Yup, calm and logical response. Way to go, Loren.

"I don't think —"

"No, listen. We will have to change which story we try for. We can't kill anyone, even allegorically!" I racked my brain for alternatives that could have *No people were harmed in the telling of this tale* scroll across the screen at the end of the movie. The rapidly spinning gears in my brain slowly ground to a halt as I ran out of viable options.

Connor had been watching me, waiting with a look of pity, for me to come to the realization that he must have had ages ago.

"Shit! This is so unfair. What the hell is wrong with us that our tales are so violent?" No matter what direction I tried to take, someone was going to get hurt. If I insisted on helping to choose my fate, I would be responsible for putting people into roles that might bring them harm.

Connor shrugged. "We are trying to mitigate the damage. That is why so many plans were already in place. I know it made you feel like you were being managed, but, well . . ."

I waved at him to stop. I got it.

"I mean it though. I can't be responsible for someone dying. You have to tell Liam he might get cast as Gaston. If he knows, he can be prepared. He doesn't have to fight — shit I cannot believe I am saying this — fight the Beast to the death."

Connor was quiet for a few minutes. "I will make sure Liam is aware of the potential outcomes. If he still wants to try, will you consider it?"

I hesitated. It felt wrong. I was the one in a pickle. It seemed like I was trading my safety and well-being for someone else's.

"Loren, I am sure he will be willing to take the risk. He was pretty determined."

Well, that fit the profile of Gaston — more interested in what he wanted than what I did. He also struck me as a tiny bit self-absorbed and chauvinistic.

"All right," it came out as a sigh any sullen teenager would have been proud of. "I will give him a chance, but we have to keep trying to find a Beast. Last I checked, Liam lacked the hair for the part."

I meant it to lighten the mood, but Connor looked like he was about to start squirming in his seat again.

"Okay, spit it out," I demanded. "What aren't you telling me?"

"Liam was born with extra terminal hair — he has hypertrichosis. That is part of the family secret."

My brain blanked. "I don't understand, terminal hair? Do you mean Liam's hair is going to die? Like baldness? But congenital, it's been a while . . . like zombie hair? Or does he wear a wig?"

Connor grabbed his napkin while I was talking. He was laughing and trying not to snort ice cream up his nose.

"No! We are talking werewolves, not zombies!"

"What?!" I yelped before leaning in and hissing, "You did not just say werewolf!"

Connor raised his eyebrows sardonically.

A tiny part of my brain watched as the rest of me lost it. "Oh, come on! First fairy tales and now werewolves? What's next? Are you going to tell me there are vampires, too?"

Connor shook his head. "Not that I am aware of." He stopped talking and I could see his mental wheels whirring. "Although, I wouldn't dismiss the notion out of hand. I mean if the fairy tales are manifested . . ." He trailed off as he started considering the possibilities.

We weren't going to get distracted by the theoretical possibility of vampires. "Connor!" My tone was a bit sharper than Grandmother would approve of. Was I going to have to wave my hand in front of his face to get his attention?

"Sorry. That third train of thought distracted me for a second. I was – "

"Wait, third train of thought? You were having two before?"

"Well, two, and the conversation."

"Wow. Okay." That explained so much. It was even busier in that brain of his than I'd guessed. "I'm sorry – I interrupted. Please continue."

"Right. So, I was wondering about how the oral tradition before vampires and werewolves were split into distinct creatures affects the possibility of vampires manifesting despite their absence from fairy tales. They are making a rise in pop culture . . ." I raised an eyebrow, speaking of distracted . . .

"Oh, right. So, I meant terminal like the kind of hair on your extremities. Hypertrichosis is an abnormal growth of hair. Terminal just describes the hair type. So, in terminal hypertrichosis, the extra hair is like the hair on the top of your head. There is also hypertrichosis involving vellus and lanugo hair, which is barely visible – like peach fuzz hair." He gestured to his face. After a sigh, he pushed his fingers through his hair. It was now disarrayed — and not in a fashionable way. He leaned in closer and spoke quietly, "The condition is also known as 'the werewolf syndrome.'"

"No. It isn't possible. Liam wasn't covered in hair."

"Laser hair removal." He might as well have added a "duh" afterward for how obvious he felt the answer was. "They did a darn good job, too."

"Okay, but he doesn't turn into a wolfman during the full moon or anything, right?" I was off on my own musings now. Was the Beast post-hair still a Beast, as far as the Magic was concerned? It took a second for me to notice the grimace on Connor's face.

"Actually . . ."

CHAPTER 11

So, I ended up agreeing to date a werewolf. Pondering the implications of werewolves led to dawdling over lunch the next day. The fact that Grandmother generally didn't visit the kitchen had nothing to do with it, really. When Grandmother actually came into the room, I decided it was karma for lying to myself about why I was lingering in the kitchen. I needed a better hiding place.

Wait. Did she know about the werewolves?

"Loren, dear, please don't slouch." Without pausing for me to straighten, she plowed forward with the conversation, "I have decided to hold a fundraiser for the theater. That lightning strike caused a great deal of damage."

Just when I was ready to declare her a wicked witch, she goes and does something like that. "What a wonderful idea! I am sure they will appreciate it!"

"I am glad you agree. I talked to your instructor and got your event planning assignment changed so you can assist me. I am thinking we'll do a masquerade ball for Halloween."

. . . And then she went and ruined it. There was no point in commenting on her going over my head to my instructor and having my assignment switched. She wouldn't understand why I was frustrated, even if I took the time to explain. The impossibility of the task deserved a comment though. "But that is only two weeks away!"

"That is exactly why I need your help, young lady. It is a bit short notice, but we will manage to fill the ballroom anyway. Don't worry. I already have things well underway. The most important thing in planning a proper event is to delegate."

My mouth dropped further and further open as she ticked the list off on her fingers. "Mildred has already contacted the company we use for cleaning to secure additional help for that evening. I have already arranged for valets. First thing tomorrow morning, we will meet with the caterers. Kella has offered to help with finding appropriate costumes for the household and musicians."

Someone had been a busy bee this morning.

She continued, "All that is left for you to handle is advertising the event, decorating the house and ballroom appropriately to match the theme, and potentially handling some rentals." Oh, was that all? And wait, what theme?

"Theme?"

"Yes. I cannot believe how little the girls were wearing for Halloween last year. I decided to have a period event to keep it from being a problem. After some discussion with Kella, we settled on a Victorian steam theme."

"Do you mean steampunk?"

"Yes, didn't I just say so?"

"Grandmother, do you know what steampunk is?"

"Of course," she declared with a hand wave, "Kella explained it is like a Jules Verne novel. She said it would be a popular theme, and it means I can have something along the lines of 'appropriate Victorian attire requested' on the invitations."

I hid a grin. I imagine Kella was fairly vague while explaining steampunk culture, but there was no way I was about to rock that boat.

"Speaking of attire, I would like you to help Kella retrieve some costume materials from the attic this afternoon. We have trunks and trunks of outdated clothes stored there, and she is welcome to whatever she can find. My parents packed my trousseau away for me, but it wasn't appropriate by the time I was married. I will be glad to finally see it being put to some use."

Ouch. Grandmother was usually velvet-coated steel, but an evanescent fragility settled over her when she mentioned that particular bit about her past. "Of course, Grandmother. I will be pleased to do whatever I can."

She gave a satisfied nod and turned to leave. Right before exiting she casually added, "I know you won't be able to carry boxes down from the attic, so I asked Connor, Liam, and Henri to come help as well. Everyone will be arriving at two o'clock. We will serve our guests tea before putting them to work."

I groaned as I glanced at the clock. There was only a half hour before the torture began, and I wasn't dressed appropriately. This was surely another one of Grandmother's etiquette tests. What did one wear that was appropriate for both afternoon tea and schlepping?

I pondered. Ha! It was a trick question. Obviously, a princess wouldn't do any of the schlepping. I needed to go dress for tea.

It took longer than I hoped. The dress I chose had a sash that tied in the back. In retrospect, it was a poor choice. My right hand still wasn't working as well as normal. I came down the front stairs as Millie was welcoming Kella at the main entrance.

"Loren!" Kella gave me a hug before thrusting a gift bag toward me, "I thought this would be appropriate for this afternoon's drudgery." Her grin was mischievous, and she was practically dancing in excitement. She clapped her hands together as I opened the bag.

"Thank you!" Out came a tangle of white straps. After some shaking, I found myself holding an apron lifted straight from Belle's outfit. Even as I groaned, I joined in the belly laugh Kella was having at my expense.

"Thank you. It's perfect."

Kella curtsied. "I agree! That's why I couldn't resist."

"Why don't you take Kella through the salon, out to the porch?" Millie asked with a grin at our antics. "The boys are already there with your grandmother."

"By all means," Kella said, "We should certainly go rescue them!"

Millie swatted Kella's shoulder with a tsk. "Go on you two. I'll be along in a bit with more cookies. The boys will have polished the first plate off by now."

"Don't they know they are supposed to start with the savory offerings?" I cringed thinking about the lecture the guys might be getting on proper tea etiquette. Except Grandmother giving them a lecture would be rude, wouldn't it? Perhaps they were safe.

"You wait," Millie replied. "Those cookies are gone."

"Oh, the horror!" Kella deadpanned. She and I were still giggling when we entered the salon. Kella stopped me. "Wait, let me straighten your hair bow. Don't want to give your grandmother any ammunition." She winked at me before heading through the French doors to the patio.

The boys were indeed seated already, but they stood when we joined them. I had to spend a lot of mental energy to avoid staring at Liam. A beam of sunlight seemed to have devoted itself to him, pooling around his chair and setting off the red glints in his hair. How was it possible to look just as yummy in casual wear as in a tuxedo? I could feel my cheeks warming as he greeted me.

I remembered to place one foot slightly behind the other and sink slowly into my chair while lifting my skirt slightly. But my spacing was off, I was too far forward, and almost missed the edge of the seat. I wonder what the etiquette is for picking yourself up off the ground.

Kella gave me one final glance and a wink before gracefully sinking into her wicker chair without even a creak. Then in a calculated move, she crossed her legs at the knee and lazily swung the top leg back and forth a bit. I had to give her points for the elegantly pointed toe. Grandmother glanced over and paused for a long second before continuing her greeting, probably having a vapor fit internally.

I stared at the flowers in the center of the low table. Besides being a safe place to look to avoid drooling over Liam, the arrangement epitomized my grandmother's careful management. It was the perfect height; we wouldn't be talking over or around it. It gave a subtle nod to the fact that autumn was rapidly approaching, with pot-bellied rose hips, velvety coxcomb, heavy-headed sunflowers, and of course Grandmother's signature roses in dusky hues. However, the addition of vibrant ranunculus, kermit mums, and clusters of petite white star-shaped flowers declared it was, in fact, decidedly not too late in the year to be enjoying tea on the patio.

Any serious discussion was put on hold as tea was poured. Anxious as I was, I was awed by the innate grace of my grandmother as she handled the heavy silver teapot. I would say that she made it look like a dance, but that implies the movements were choreographed. Her grace was more organic, like the elegant glide of a swan across a still pond. Afternoon tea was a religious experience for her, a prayer to the gods of all things civilized. I could tell she was finding comfort in the familiar ritual. I wished I could say the same, but the ceremony was not part of my routine.

I was having problems remembering my grandmother's lectures. I was grateful she didn't expect me to pour. Simply trying to recall the mechanics of drinking tea was threatening to make me break out in hives. If I had to remember how to pour as well, I would be in the middle of a nervous breakdown. I knew not to let the spoon hit the side of my cup as I folded in the sugar — not stirred, mind you — but what did you do with the spoon afterward? And the cup handle was supposed to point a certain way on the saucer, wasn't it? I guess I had been too focused on getting my six o'clock to twelve o'clock folding motion perfected when that information was covered.

I knew the saucer was to be held in my left hand, but I couldn't grasp the handle properly with my right given the sling. What was the etiquette for a broken arm? My ears started ringing and my body broke out in a delicate sheen of perspiration — not sweat; ladies do not sweat according to my grandmother. Glisten or glow didn't seem strong enough, so I was left with perspire. Perhaps we princesses sparkled. I nearly snorted to myself. Ugh, the arm brace was going to be slimy by the time this was done.

The solution came to me as I clumsily accepted the heirloom Meissen teacup and saucer (whose delicate floral pattern, of course, coordinated nicely with the arrangement on the table — or was it the other way around?). I decided I would set the cup and saucer on the side table next to me. Not drinking the tea was probably a faux pas itself, but it was less likely to be noticed than if I upended my tea in my lap. My oh-so-properly placed slip of an Irish linen napkin would not protect against the contents of an entire teacup. As a bonus, if I wasn't going to drink the tea, I didn't have to fold in any sugar to make it palatable.

I peeked toward Grandmother's plate. I knew savories first, but . . . that's right, sandwich first. I caught Grandmother's delicate wince as Liam snagged a teacake from the middle tier of the curate stand. Her gaze turned to my plate to assure herself I hadn't made a similar mistake. I received an almost imperceptible nod for my choice. Even while she was glancing at me, she reached out and gently rapped Liam's knuckles. "Young man, I know you know better than that! Your aunt would be horrified."

Liam had the sense to swallow before answering. Then he took a very proper sip of tea. I couldn't help but watch in fascination as his lips curled around the edge of the cup in a kiss. I did not envy his cup, I didn't — honestly. Why was I like this?

"Actually ma'am, she would be more horrified to know she was missing out on Ms. Millie's cakes." He winked at Millie who came out to replace the cookie platter that was, as predicted, empty of anything but crumbs. "They are simply impossible to resist."

Grandmother shook her head at him, but it was with a tolerant grin. The flirt had even gotten to her!

I was appreciating the contrast between the crisp spiciness of the thin radish curl garnish and the creamy mayo in the chicken salad when Grandmother set her cup and saucer down.

"Kella, would you send the Foundation's membership roster to Loren so she can get the invitations out as soon as possible? I will add other names as I see appropriate."

"Certainly. I will email it tonight."

Ouch. She was right that we needed to get the advertising done yesterday, but we were going to have to pay for rush printing and use pre-done artwork to get things done in time. I couldn't believe I was going to be reduced to using clip art. Ugh! Ick! Maybe one of the folks I went to art school with would be able to do something with a quick turnaround? I tried not to choke as I swallowed the sandwich hunk that morphed from a tasty treat to a lump of sandpaper. I wish I had brought a pad and pencil with me. Starting a to-do list would help push back the overwhelming anxiety threatening to swamp me. My vertigo was acting up too.

"Grandmother, what sort of budget are we talking about? I am concerned about the extra costs involved in trying to get anything done that quickly."

"Well," Grandmother glanced at Kella, "I have decided to cover the event costs as my donation to the theater's Foundation. I was planning to tell you to spend what you needed, but your instructor said for this to count for your grade, we had to have a budget. So, you have fifty thousand dollars. If you come in under that amount, I will donate the remainder to the Foundation."

I choked on my sandwich but finally managed to splutter, "Really?" I just couldn't imagine having that much extra money lying around to donate on a whim. I was glad I wasn't drinking my tea. I would have spewed it across the table when she mentioned that figure.

"Yes, it seemed reasonable. We are hoping for at least two hundred people. At five hundred dollars a ticket, we should raise at least a hundred thousand. That isn't counting any extra donations, publicity, or new members the event attracts to the Foundation. Your teacher should be satisfied with the cost per dollar raised." The last bit sounded exasperated. "I can't believe he was so insistent on worrying about that." She sniffed.

I hadn't been thinking on a grand enough scale. Grandmother wasn't fond of half-measures, apparently. I was trying to figure out a response other than giggling hysterically when Henri broke the stunned silence. "I can help. I know a printer, and I bet I can get him to do things for you at cost. I'll reach out and let you know."

Liam wasn't one to be outdone. "There should also be an auction. I bet I can get the hotel to donate a weekend stay and a day at the spa. My business will donate a weekend at one of the hunt clubs." He glanced at Kella, "Perhaps season tickets to the theatre?"

She nodded and responded, distractedly and haltingly. "We could manage that. Let me think about it . . . I bet I know other people who would be willing to donate things, too."

The event was blowing up in my face and I hadn't even been involved for an hour. "I am not sure I will have time to handle an auction as well as the rest of the planning." There weren't enough lists possible to make me feel like this was all feasible, no matter what my therapist said.

"Remember Loren, delegation is the secret to coordinating any gathering." Grandmother's haughty tone became dulcet as she turned a predatory gaze toward Liam, "I imagine you would do an excellent job organizing a silent auction." Her smile reminded me of a shark.

I had to give Liam credit. He didn't even blink before responding, "Of course, Mrs. Dalton. It will be my pleasure to assist Loren. I am eager to spend time with her." He beamed as he said it. I tried to respond but didn't manage more than a quavering grin in response. Things were sure getting messy quickly.

"I'm glad to hear it. I believe I know some people who would make donations to an auction as well. I will write out a list while you all work in the attic."

"Speaking of which, I believe we should get to it. We have a lot to accomplish." Kella was smiling, but her tone was firm.

"Yes, sir!" Liam joked as he stood up and saluted. Then he held out a hand to help me stand. His touch sent goose bumps along my arm. He turned up the wattage on his smile and tucked my hand into the crook of his arm before asking grandmother, "Will you think me an unbearable heathen if I take a cookie with me, Mrs. Dalton?"

Grandmother wrapped a cookie in a napkin before handing it to Liam. He tucked the cookie in his jacket pocket before turning and saluting Kella. "Awaiting further orders, sir."

She responded with a sigh and made a shooing motion with her hands. I heard her mutter, "I didn't have enough coffee this morning to deal with this."

As soon as I thought we were out of my grandmother's hearing, I turned to Kella. "Steampunk?!?" I hissed. Grandmother had excellent hearing and I wasn't risking anything. "I don't know whether to think you are a genius or an idiot!"

"What?" Henri sounded amused. "How did I miss that?"

Connor groaned. "Steampunk? How did you get that past Mrs. Dalton?"

Liam came up behind the group, trying to fit napkin wrapped cookies in his pockets. "What did I miss?" When he noticed our looks he said, "Hey, I brought enough to share."

Kella shook her head. "I don't know what got into me! I was awake practically all night with the firefighters checking the building for potential electrical fires. Then — after hours on a Saturday night mind you — I had to try to arrange for three different people to come out to inspect the structure, the electrical system, and the plumbing. I still have to inventory how much of our electrical equipment is fried. Two hours after I finally got to sleep, your grandmother called with her plan and wanted me to put everyone in costumes, that," she paused to make air quotes, "'covered them appropriately.' I wasn't thinking straight. It was just a way to make the project fun and a bit more bearable."

"You set me up to try to make steampunk accessible to a bunch of older socialites who can afford a $500 ticket!"

Kella groaned again. "How was I supposed to know she was planning on charging that much!?"

As we entered the attic, I turned to her and raised my eyebrow. "You do realize who you are talking about?" I wouldn't have known either, but I wasn't letting her off the hook. She had known Grandmother much longer, after all.

"Two hours of sleep Loren! I wasn't thinking straight. Besides, your grandmother's winter ball is *the* event of the year. People might actually pay five hundred dollars for a chance to attend one of her parties. Any which way, I promise we will figure out a way for this to work."

I sighed. "I am going to hold you to that." I paused. I was being a grump. "Sorry. Honestly, if I didn't have so much else going on and a broken arm, this would be fun."

Henri grinned, "That's the spirit. Besides, overcoming impossible tasks should be a snap for a Disney princess."

We all groaned.

Connor's brow furrowed as the rest of us laughed. "Actually, this could be a problem. If Loren is going to lock her tale into 'Beauty and the Beast,' rather than say 'Cinderella' or 'Rumpelstiltskin,' she is going to have to focus on delegating tasks, and make sure not to do too much of the actual work herself."

Henri frowned. "I hadn't thought of that. All joking aside, also remember you are still healing."

"You all must have missed what my grandmother was saying downstairs. She is planning to pull off *the* event of 2009 in only *two* weeks. That is fourteen days! Besides, to whom exactly am I going to delegate tasks? The furniture? In case you didn't notice, they aren't talking . . ." the word "yet" almost escaped from my mouth.

Liam looked at the group as if daring them to disagree with his next statement. "Us. We are now your unofficial fundraiser committee. I bet we each have a couple of hours a week to spare. We can all give ourselves fancy titles later." No one argued and there were even nods. Wow! He had roped everyone else in. If nothing else, I was impressed by how much he was taking charge. Was he trying to endear himself to me?

"As I said, we are going to make it work," Kella said, voice muffled as she dug through the bottom of her bag. "I have interns I can assign things to."

"I'm booked solid during the day, but if you have stuff that can be done outside normal business hours, I can help then," Henri added.

"Thank you." That emotional fragility from the concussion was making itself known again. I tried to sniff delicately, as princesses weren't supposed to sniff at all.

"Loren, take a seat." Kella pointed to the floor distractedly while going all Mary Poppins, up to her elbow in her purse. Did she want me to sit on the ground?

"I've got this," Liam said. After a glance around, he pulled over a wingback armchair for me. He made a dramatic bow, "Your throne, m'lady."

I nearly jumped as he delicately touched my elbow to help me to the chair. My skin lit up and fizzles radiated outward to my shoulder and fingertips. My reaction was surely something to consider.

"I seriously cannot take you all today," Kella muttered. "Ah, here it is." I was handed a notebook and pen, cutting my thoughts short. "You get to keep an inventory as the rest of us do the heavy lifting. After we finish here, we can come up with a plan on how we are going to magically pull this whole thing off. In the meantime, point us in the direction of the clothes."

I looked around the attic, peering past the furniture relegated into its corners. "Could someone open the windows? It will make it easier to see." Liam rushed to do my bidding with Connor and Henri not too far behind. Sunbeams created cascades of light filled with dancing dust motes. The sight made my nose tickle.

I finally spotted the row of cedar chests Millie had described. "I think those trunks are the ones we want. And there is a wardrobe, too."

"All right," Kella took charge, "Let's drag them out into this clear area, and see what we have."

Liam muttered, "If anything."

Liam and Connor worked to drag one trunk out while Kella and Henri grabbed another.

"Maybe we should check to make sure these are the right ones before dragging any more out?" I felt guilty for not doing any grunt work and wanted to minimize unnecessary effort.

"I can't wait to peek into these," Kella said. "Even if everything is ruined it should still be fun."

"You just love clothes," Liam accused as he opened the other trunk.

"It's true." Kella owned the accusation. She turned toward me, "I actually wormed my way into a History of Fashion course. I talked my advisor into counting it toward a theatre degree by claiming it would help with costuming period pieces." Her grin was unrepentant as she carefully pulled the first item out.

Kella gasped. She held up a white shift. "Look at the lace on this." I had heard people less reverent in prayer.

"Huh." Liam was rooting around in another chest. "I thought they sewed everything by hand back then."

"They most likely would have." Kella absently commented.

"But this one has a tag!" He was poking around what appeared to be the waistline of a — you guessed it — blue dress. Even here I couldn't escape.

"What does it say?" Kella asked as she examined the embroidery on the shift.

"Worth and Bobergh . . . and something in French, an address?"

Kella gasped and practically teleported across the attic. "HolyMaryMotherofGod! Liam — put that down, carefully."

"I didn't know you were religious," Henri was teasing Kella, but I noticed he too was peering intently at the gown.

"You don't understand, this is a House of Worth gown." Liam raised an eyebrow, and Kella sighed. "A court dress made by Charles Worth sold at auction a couple of years ago for over a hundred thousand dollars."

Liam finally put the gown back, acting as if it might explode if it was jostled too much. Kella yelped and lunged. She carefully folded the gown back into the trunk. Her hand hovered over it as if she wanted to stroke it, like a mother avoiding touching a sleeping baby for fear of waking it.

"I don't think we should open these here. Maybe we can move to a cleaner room downstairs?" I barely caught her muttering, "And find some white gloves to wear."

We relocated to the salon. As Liam, Henri, and Connor shuttled the trunks, I took the chance to quiz Kella. "Are these dresses actually that big of a deal?"

"Well . . ." she grinned, "They probably aren't going to sell for a hundred grand, but I needed Liam to listen. However, if that dress is any indication, most will be worth at least a couple thousand dollars each. Some of them probably belong in a museum."

"I'm not comfortable wearing something like that to a party." I was guaranteed to spill an entire bottle of red wine on myself or perhaps the caterers would accidentally provide a plate of spaghetti with red sauce just so I could spill it on my historically significant, one-of-a-kind gown.

"Don't worry, I don't plan to loan out anything that belongs in a museum."

"What are we going to do for costumes then?"

Kella shrugged. "I never expected your grandmother's attic would provide all the dresses we needed. We will rent some, get some modern dresses and make them over, borrow from Civil War reenactors and modify the gowns slightly . . . We will find a way to make it work . . ."

She trailed off as she started removing an item wrapped in unbleached muslin from one of the chests. Elusive wisps of lavender and rose wafted toward me.

"I cannot believe how carefully all of this was packed," Kella commented as she pulled a sachet out. "Oh, there is a book here, too!"

I peered over Kella's shoulder at the handwritten pages. It appeared to be a journal. She opened it to a random point in the middle.

Kella started to read aloud, "'I wrote before of how skirts have become wider than you would believe possible. If you will recall, it was when I explained the new foundation garments. I am so pleased to report to you that over the last season, styles have changed and crinolines have become very sensibly diminished. A fashionable shape now has extensive padding added to the back of the skirt and almost no volume in the front. It seems that over the course of a hundred and some years, I have pinched and padded every part possible — panniers, hair pads, stays, and crinolines. One wonders what fashion will demand next. I have added one of the new crinolettes to keep your trousseau *au courant*. It has tapes and lacings so it can be adjusted to fit with each of the new dresses as well. I did so enjoy picking them out for you.'"

Kella paused and skimmed the pages. "'Blue silk faille evening gown with white silk ribbon braids' . . . 'a walking dress in cotton piqué of the palest green with cream cording' . . . 'lilac muslin day dress with lace trim' . . ."

She paused and waved her hand in front of her face a bit – staving off tears?

"Oh, that is so sad." She began to read again, "'My dear, I am fearful your slumbers will last a full hundred years. I will never have the chance to see the beautiful woman you will become, to be there to rejoice with you as you marry and bear children, or to mourn with you as you face inevitable grief. This is a sorrow I find difficult to escape. I imagine you may find it ridiculous I make such preparations, solely in case your slumbers are shorter than anticipated. If my arrangements are not needed, perhaps the dresses can be remade. Please forgive my folly as it allows me to keep your presence close to my heart. Even if you never wear these dresses, I can imagine the tilt of your head as you read this diary with your fingers touching the same pages that I do now. Perhaps later these words will allow you to keep me close to your heart as well.'"

She paused before flipped back a page. "It is dated 1867. It seems your great-grandmother continuously updated her daughter's trousseau . . . I feel like I am intruding on something private. I wonder if your grandmother has read this?" Kella carefully set the book aside.

"It doesn't seem like the kind of thing you would pack away. I will give it to her later."

Kella nodded, "We ought to get to work anyway."

Three hours later, we had unpacked just two of the trunks. Not so neatly listed by my left hand were a dozen each of embroidered chemises, nightdresses, cotton stockings, and sets of linen drawers. There were nine camisoles, three pairs of silk stockings, three bed jackets, two dressing gowns, two dozen handkerchiefs, and a pair of corsets along with assorted gloves, boots, sleeve puffs, and house shoes. Fourteen petticoats of various weights, fabrics, and levels of trim filled most of the list of underclothing.

All the clothes were exquisite. Love showed in the meticulous detail and trim work on even the most mundane objects, but the best things that came out of the trunks so far were the dresses: a wool winter outfit, two silk day dresses, one evening dress, a tea gown, and an opera dress complete with glasses.

As we pulled the last item out of the second trunk, Kella finally admitted defeat. "We are going to have to take your grandmother's advice, Loren." I laughed at how disgusted she sounded, even though I didn't know what she was referring to. "As much as I want to, I don't have time to do justice to this project. Or the skills, if I am honest . . . I am going to have to find a professional historian to deal with these trunks. Why don't we switch gears? Maybe see if we can figure out how to make steampunk palatable for your grandmother's posh party patrons."

CHAPTER 12

We started out by arguing over a logo for the event, eventually deciding on two jack-o'-lanterns carved to resemble comedy and tragedy theatrical masks with some steampunk accessories added. The group left determining what looked best to me.

Liam continued to fall lower in my esteem over the course of the afternoon. He was a bit of a malicious tease. He tricked Connor into trying on a nightgown by saying it was a dress shirt he might be able to wear for the party, and then joked about him being a cross-dresser. Connor simply glared, took the nightgown off, and rehung it.

He then pretended Henri wasn't hefting his full share of the heavy crates, joking about being the manlier of the two. Henri flushed when he saw I overheard. He hefted his side of the box higher to make it obvious that Liam was lying, but didn't say anything.

Liam poked at Kella by questioning her directions. He asked why the waists of the dresses weren't narrower. Didn't they have corsets because being thin was fashionable like it is now? He even added a significant glance at her curves. Kella ignored the overtones and explained that extreme lacing was the equivalent of modern eating disorders. She delved into details of the social construct of women as fragile creatures in need of extra support through the history of the corset. Liam regretted his question long before she was done. I found it fascinating though.

I wondered why no one got more upset. Then, I began to understand as we got into the plenary session. The same talent that allowed him to pick at their most vulnerable weak spots was now turned, and he used it to draw everyone out to their full potential. He was thinking creatively about problems before the rest of us realized the full extent of an issue.

It was during our planning meeting that Liam redeemed himself. He was on his phone all afternoon, which I assumed was a way to get out of work. Instead, he had been lining up other pledges for the silent auction. He also got the hotel to agree to lend and deliver tables, chairs, and linens for the event — cutting our costs by several hundred dollars before the meeting even started.

Liam jumped from having a jack-o'-lantern themed logo to the idea of having a steampunk themed pumpkin-decorating contest tied into the town's Fall Festival. He said it would be sensational advertising. When I protested the extra work of finding judges and handling entrants, he laughed and said festival goers themselves would vote by putting coins into the jars of their favorite entrants. Bills could be placed into rival jars to counter votes. All proceeds from the jars and a high percentage of the entry fees would be donated to the theatre. Apparently, it was an old fraternity fundraising trick. The winner would be awarded a pair of tickets to the party. Kella grudgingly admitted it was a decent idea, and offered her intern to handle keeping track of the entrants at the festival.

He also suggested having a photo booth with a professional photographer and themed props like goggles, parasols, fascinators, top hats, monocles, and overly-geared pocket watches. He suggested a brief workshop to teach people some of the simpler Victorian dances then interspersing them throughout the evening.

While Liam bubbled and enthused, Henri and Connor were making their own, quieter, contributions. Connor offered to put together a website. Henri called his printer friend and arranged a substantial discount. Henri was also able to suggest a photographer. A phone call proved he was free and would be willing to do the event if we covered the printing costs, and he could include business cards in the envelope with the photos when they were delivered at the end of the evening.

Kella added touches that made everything else work, like suggesting the photographer disguise his modern camera to look like an old-fashioned one. She also suggested having dance cards for the ladies. At one point she stepped out and made some phone calls. When she came back, we had performers — an aerialist, a fortune teller, and a fire juggler. They would perform in return for being allowed free entrance for themselves and a guest to the rest of the event. She also promised her design team to help with the decorating.

I frantically took sloppy wrong-handed notes, praying I could pull all the separate pieces together. I also reined in Liam when his flights of fancy became too wild. We would not be doing blimp rides. There would also be no haunted walk with a headless horseman throwing his head — and leaving a trail of horse excrement and pumpkin seeds strewn through my grandmother's prized gardens. There would be no murder mystery, complete with an actor portraying a steampunk Sherlock Holmes, interrupting the evening's entertainment. Just when I thought he was done, he would pop up with something new. His best idea involved having the hotel chef issue a challenge to the other area chefs to enter the pumpkin decorating contest to see who the best carver was.

By the end of the planning session, all that was left was dealing with the caterer, the florist, and all the decorations. Oh, and getting invitations out ASAP and magically pulling it all together on the day of the event. No problem though, right?

CHAPTER 13

I was delivering the invitation design to the printer the next day when Mr. Lamont, my Grandmother's lawyer, called and ordered me to find time to stop by the police station.

"I know you have been busy, but if you don't find the time to look over the evidence log soon, Chief Duncan is threatening to bring you in himself."

"But I did go once! Neither Officer Ramos nor the chief was there. I haven't had time to get back between classes, planning the fundraiser, physical therapy – and I've just been so exhausted which Dr. Aatos says is from the concussion. It stinks to not have any energy, and need a nap like a toddler . . ." I trailed off weakly.

"Mmm hmm." He was unimpressed. "Find the time, Ms. Hughes." He didn't say goodbye before hanging up.

So I relinquished the last bit of free time in my schedule that afternoon. My spotty brain and I were going to go tell the police what they had managed to overlook or lose. Should be loads of fun.

When I got to the station, I was directed to Officer Ramos's desk.

"Good afternoon, Officer Ramos."

"Hi! It's a pleasure to see you again, Ms. Hughes!" Maybe the attitude at the previous meeting hadn't been a front. Either that or I could expect 'bad cop' to come around at any moment. Speaking of which . . .

"Are we expecting Chief Duncan to join us?"

"No, it is just the two of us this afternoon. I have the conference room reserved so we can spread out if we need to."

After closing and then grabbing her laptop, she hopped up and led me to a room that was a classic example of early municipal decor. Even horrid bubblegum pink paint would improve it, and that was saying a lot, coming from me.

There was a box and clipboard laid out on the gray conference table. With a gesture toward these, Officer Ramos explained, "I can't let you touch anything, but I thought it might be helpful to have your bag here as we went through things. I can imagine what is in a bag more easily if I am looking at it, personally."

"That makes sense."

I glanced over the list. Wow! Did I really keep that much stuff in my bag? Hmm, guess so, I flipped through the pages and nothing on the list jumped out as not belonging there.

"Let's see, we have your clothes from the hospital." She pulled out a plastic evidence bag containing folded clothes. "I assume we have everything here? Pants, short-sleeve shirt, sports bra, underwear, socks . . ." She glanced at me for agreement while messing with the list on her computer. I nodded. "Anything else you were wearing that day?"

"My hiking boots, obviously." She nodded and pulled another bag out and set it to the side while I thought about what else I wore that day. "I also had a blue jacket, but I don't think I was wearing it – it was probably in my bag or on the blanket." The jacket was an ugly electric blue color with reflective piping accents. I only wore it because it was highly visible. Officer Ramos dug through the box and pulled it out and set it to the side, too.

"What about any accessories? Jewelry, watches, hats?"

"I was wearing the necklace I have on now." And if they tried taking that, there was going to be trouble. I had chosen it from my mother's jewelry box when she died and hardly removed it since. "I wasn't wearing a watch, earrings, bracelets or anything. I didn't have a hat on, but there should be one in the bag.

I did have an elastic hair tie holding my braid together." Speaking of hair, it had worked its way loose again. Just like in the Disney movie. I mentally stuck my tongue out at Belle's animators as I tucked the strands back in. Were we going with the Disney version?

Officer Ramos checked through her list and made a note. "Any chance you remember what color the hair tie was?"

I shook my head. "I have never been able to keep track of those. I keep extras in my purse and car and don't even look half the time when I grab them."

"I understand. First thing we have found missing though. Probably lost by the EMTs or hospital staff. Did you carry anything in your pockets?"

"No. I was lying flat on my stomach to take pictures and what not. Stuff in your pockets makes for uncomfortable lumps." I was speaking unusually slowly, struggling to formulate complete answers. I didn't want to forget something and have it held against me later. "I would have had my lens cap in my back pocket while it was out, but would have put it back on the camera when I was done."

"All right, tell me about your backpack. Anything attached to the outside?"

"Yup, jingle bells."

Officer Ramos's head jerked up. "Bells?"

"You know, for bears?" The blank look continued. "Bears don't like being surprised. I tend to get lost in thought when hiking and forget to make sure to be noisy. The bells make sure they hear me coming . . ."

I almost giggled out loud, bells to keep the beasts away . . .

"Oh. Hmm, okay." Officer Ramos wasn't amused. Connor would have gotten it. "What else would be on the outside of the bag?"

"Let's see, in the left-side pocket there should have been a set of colored pencils."

"And in the right side pocket?"

"A small first aid kit."

"Do you remember what was in it?"

Did they really need me to go through all of this? I couldn't possibly see how this was relevant. I suppressed a sigh. "I'm pretty sure that day was the first time I used the kit. Maybe we could find a list of what came in it? Then the only thing that should be missing is one of the antibiotic cream packets and a bandaid. I got a splinter from a blue flower, and my hand started swelling up. I think it may have been flax, but that shouldn't grow in the woods of North Carolina. I meant to look up what kind of flower it was later, but I didn't remember until now. Actually, there is a picture of it on my camera."

Officer Ramos looked bored.

"Umm, sorry. I guess you didn't need to know all of that."

She tried to look interested. "It's okay. But why don't we continue? What was inside the main section of your bag?"

So I continued in exhausting detail: bug spray, waterproof matches, pocket knife, tissues, paint rag, travel watercolor kit, brushes, a stainless steel water bottle — which had been sitting with the water in it for weeks now growing heaven knows what bacteria, a compass, tube of lip balm, camera, cell phone, pepper spray, and most importantly, my sketchbook.

We added two paintbrushes, the small cup I rinsed my brushes in, and my kneaded rubber eraser to the list of missing items.

"How carefully did you go through everything?" I asked. "My kneaded rubber eraser always gets stuck to the blanket. Did anyone shake the blanket out?"

Officer Ramos reviewed her notes again, frowning. "I don't think they did. It was starting to rain at the scene, so a lot of things were bagged and brought back for later examination." That seemed sloppy to me, but I guess there hadn't been any reason to believe the death was anything but an accident until the irregular autopsy report. Maybe it wasn't a priority?

She stalked to the door and hollered, "Hey Joe, can you come help me out for a second?" She turned around and looked at me. "It would be better all around if you didn't handle any of the evidence." Yeah, you mentioned that already. Your trust makes me feel all warm and fuzzy inside. I leaned back in my chair and crossed my arms.

In the minute or so it took Joe to join us, she packed the rest of the evidence bags back into the box. When Joe entered the room, she took the box and the blanket to a long table on the other side of the room. Wearing gloves, they removed the blanket and carefully unfolded it. The red blanket was made of heavy wool and was a fire safety blanket in its previous incarnation. It had once been a part of a friend's camping equipment. I liked it because it was easy to clean and didn't mildew. On the downside, the slightly scaly surface acted a bit like Velcro.

The officers located and bagged the rubber eraser I noticed was missing, along with the block of viridian watercolor that was always falling out of its little well in my travel kit. They also found several leaves and some bark. I might have been able to point out more bits of vegetation, but I was too busy staring at the stains on my blanket. At first, I thought it was all mud, but with a shift in the lighting, I realized the more blackish stains had a rust undertone. It was blood, and there was lots of it. There were even shoe prints — maybe from the rescue personnel? I was glad it wasn't my job to sort out the mess. I was also pretty sure I didn't want the blanket back at this point. They could keep both it and my water bottle. I made a mental note to replace them.

Joe found a seedpod of some sort. I probably could have identified it, but as I glanced over, I noticed what appeared to be part of a paw print. Except it was huge . . . Were werewolves that big?

Unfortunately, Joe noticed too. "Whoa! Does that look like a paw print?" He peered at the print, and then took the blanket and folded part of it over, matching edges to reveal a full print. "Hand me that ruler please, Alyss." Officer Ramos passed the ruler over and Joe snapped a couple of pictures of the print. I was stunned to see the print was more than six and a half inches long and about six inches across. That was one damn big dog. Perhaps I hadn't hallucinated the wolf? That was still some big wolf though . . .

My voice was a bit hoarse as I asked, "Any idea what kind of dog has paws that big around here?" Maybe they knew about a giant German shepherd and I wouldn't have to worry about covering for the werewolves.

Officer Ramos's glance at Joe deferred the question to him. He cleared his throat before answering. "Not that I am aware of, but I've got a buddy who is a biologist I can ask. I know there are some red wolves in the area that are part of a conservation effort." At his fellow officer's look of disbelief, he explained. "It's caused some tension with the local farmers and we have gotten some calls about it. But I didn't think they got this big." Did he realize he had used the past tense?

"Ms. Hughes, didn't you see a wolf?" Why couldn't she have forgotten that? Had a werewolf been involved somehow? Either in killing Mr. Gifford or perhaps in my rescue? How had we been found in the middle of the woods anyway?

"Ms. Hughes?" Oh, Officer Ramos was staring at me, waiting for me to answer.

"I wish you would call me Loren." And then because I couldn't ignore the question forever, "Maybe. I was in and out of consciousness, though. It was hard to focus properly. I said wolf, but it might have been a dog? Aren't there breeds that look similar?" I racked my brain for an innocuous explanation. "Aren't Huskies white and gray — they can get big, right?"

Joe was shaking his head. "That wouldn't have been a red wolf. They are tawny — not white and gray. Malamutes are pretty big though. Maybe it was a malamute."

Right.

Would asking questions seem suspicious? Maybe not asking would be more suspicious. Besides, Belle was curious . . . "Was Charles . . . Shoot – what was his last name again?"

"Gifford, Charles Gifford." Officer Ramos supplied.

"Was Charles Gifford bitten by a dog? Maybe he was running away from one and fell off the overhang . . . I would be tempted to run from any dog that big."

The two officers exchanged glances. "We aren't allowed to comment about active cases without getting the information cleared first," Joe finally responded.

"Right," I agreed. "It's just if there are giant dogs running around in the woods attacking people, well, it would be good to know." Were the police looking in all the wrong places?

Officer Ramos piped in, "I will check the report and ask what information we can share with you. Don't worry, if there is a risk to the public, we will be sure to let people know."

Well, I wasn't going to hold my breath if Chief Duncan was involved. "Right. Well. Thank you." Anything nice to say? Nope. Okay.

So . . . I made a play of looking at the clock on the wall. "Goodness. Did you have anything else you needed from me right now? I need to leave soon, or I will be late for my appointment over at Thistle Dew Nicely." I groaned internally as I said the name. What a pun!

"Oh, sure! We are done here," Officer Ramos responded, "Say hi to Lilly for me!"

"Absolutely." Of course someone named Lilly worked there. It seemed like Connor wasn't the only person in Lointaine that appreciated a bad pun.

CHAPTER 14

Wednesday evening, Kella arrived before the guys did for our planning session. I jumped right in before we had an audience.

"So, you seemed to know exactly which steampunk artists to call for the fundraisers."

"Yup, I know most of the actors within a hundred miles, and then some . . ." She was only giving me part of her attention as she pulled out her planning folder.

"Hmm, and you knew exactly who to go to for costumes, and all sorts of props for us to borrow. Even had some on hand . . ." Kella finally looked up from her notes. "Admit it, you are a covert steampunk enthusiast!"

Kella snorted and gave one of her delightful belly laughs. "What, as in I have a secret panel in my closet full of leather corsets covered in gears?" She wiped her twinkling eyes.

"Do you?" I was guessing 'no' from her reaction, but I was curious.

"No. Sorry to disappoint you. My ex-roommate is into steampunk. I called and grilled her." I grinned and was about to reply when we were interrupted.

"Who's disappointed?" Liam asked as he and Henri entered the room.

I wasn't about to tease Kella further in front of Liam. I winked at her before Liam came into the room far enough to see.

"I was just explaining to Kella that the florist was doing some beautiful arrangements with all sorts of unusual plants like cabbages, succulents, artichokes, and mosses in addition to the usual Victorian flowers. She is using some other things like cogs, and coiled wires, and putting all the arrangements in glass cloches and terrariums." I was over explaining — I have always been a bad liar. Shut up, Loren. "Kella was commenting that Grandmother might be disappointed there weren't more roses included."

"Hmm," Liam had that dangerous look he got before proposing another one of his ideas. "We should have flower girls selling posies like they used to on the street."

It was inappropriate, but I didn't have the energy to explain the historic socioeconomic factors to Liam, especially when he might not care even then. How could I get him to drop the idea? "I don't know . . . We already have a lot of pay-for add-ons available. I don't want people to feel like we are nickel-and-diming them after they already spent so much on their tickets. We would have to do something else for free, like the dance workshop beforehand? No, we can't change that, it's on the invite."

"It wouldn't be fair to change the terms with any of the other vendors, either," Henri stated.

"Just because the photographer is your friend doesn't mean he should get special treatment," Liam countered.

"Maybe we could add the flower arrangements from the tables to the silent auction instead, Liam?" I jumped in to keep the discussion from escalating. Besides, it seemed like a good idea once I thought of it. So far, the flowers were our biggest expense after the caterer, and I liked the idea of recouping some of the cost.

"We can number the tables so people know which they are bidding on, and have pictures available with the bidding sheet."

Liam's sour expression changed with the suggestion. "Sure, sounds like a good addition. We could have small tasteful cards on the table to let people know they are available . . ." He finally sat and made a note in his own folder.

He didn't even glance up when Connor walked in. "Glad you could join us." He was in a mood — was it because I vetoed his idea? I didn't really want to date someone I had to pussyfoot around all the time. I turned awkwardly in my chair and smiled at Connor in greeting, hoping to ameliorate Liam's jibe. Next time, I needed to sit facing the door.

Connor didn't notice me. He was frowning at his watch. "I am right on time."

Henri chuckled. When we all swung to look at him, he abruptly tried to make it sound like he was only clearing his throat. It wasn't convincing.

"We should go ahead and get started," I suggested. This was going to be fun . . . I felt more like a kindergarten teacher than a coordinator. "Why don't I go first?"

I went over the flowers again to update Connor, and showed everyone the pictures on my new cell phone of some of the bits and bobs the florist had pulled out during our meeting. I looked around and decided we needed a few extra seconds for ruffled feathers to finish settling, so I segued into a discussion of the other decorations.

"We could get more use out of the pumpkins from the carving contest by using the entries as part of the decorations. Maybe we could do some hay bales and branches with fall leaves as a base to display them. They would go around the portico where everybody will be arriving, and also in the back, around the patio. Then we could put luminaries along the drive and through the gardens, and transition from the luminaries to lit pumpkins. Any pumpkins that weren't meant to be lit could be put right around the entrances, where it is brighter."

Liam grinned, "That will make for romantic walks in the garden." Kella rolled her eyes. I almost groaned but caught myself. With all the work to get ready for the party, I had almost managed to forget I agreed to go out with Liam (and his ego, apparently). I didn't mean to be contrary, but all the hints about how interested he was were starting to be a huge turnoff. Even if he was ridiculously handsome . . .

I didn't want to date Liam. The problem was we hadn't actually scheduled our date yet. That made it hard to come up with an inoffensive reason to back out. Would Liam still do his part for the fundraiser if I did? Rather an awkward position to be in. It felt dishonest to string him along, but by the same token, I did agree to give him a chance and I hadn't done that yet. I told my conscience we could wrestle with the issue later. Right now, I needed to tune back in.

I listened as everyone gave status updates on their tasks. So far, everything was on schedule. I prayed Grandmother was correct in assuming people would pay five hundred dollars a ticket for the party. But what if they couldn't? Ticket sales were lower than I'd like, although it was possible not everyone had received their invitations yet. But what if people were booked with other parties? I was haunted by the mental image of a party with only five or ten people pinballing around a room set up for two hundred.

I interrupted Kella with my musings. "You guys, I have been wondering — what if we can't get enough people to buy tickets? We should also solicit businesses for sponsorships. They would get seats as a benefit of their donation? That way, it would be tax deductible for them. Is that correct? I don't know tax law. We might be able to raise more money even . . . A ten thousand dollar donation could get a company a ten-person table, which would also double the money raised. A five thousand dollar donation will get you four tickets. Kella, the theatre has a newsletter, right? We could promise a special full-page spread that listed event donors . . . ?"

Although Kella started out looking irritated when I cut her off, she now seemed relieved. "I love it! I didn't want to argue with your grandmother, she knows enough people that she just might be able to pull it all off — but I was concerned."

Henri grinned, "And you have already sold your first table. I know my practice will buy one."

Liam wasn't going to be topped. "The hunt club will too. I can call it a marketing expense if I fill the table with clients."

Connor grinned. "There you go Loren, ten percent of your seats filled."

"Great. Maybe we can think of a couple other businesses willing to sponsor tables. I also need everyone to take some posters and find places to put them."

I looked blankly at the table where I had left the posters that had been delivered earlier. Oh right, Millie took them to my room, trying to be helpful. "Sorry, I forgot they were moved upstairs. I will run and grab them when we are done here."

Liam jumped up. "I can get them. You shouldn't be carrying anything heavy anyway, right?"

Oh, this was awkward. The idea of Liam in my room by himself made me uncomfortable. No real reason, like a suspicion that he might start sniffing my underwear or anything, but uncomfortable nonetheless. "Thanks, that would be helpful. We can head up there in a bit, after Kella finishes her report."

A smug smile spread over Liam's face. Oh, man! Did I just suggest we head somewhere alone together — my bedroom even? And after he had volunteered to complete the task alone . . . Ugh!

"We should go ahead and get them, so we can plan who will cover which parts of town before the meeting is finished. Besides, I am sure Kella didn't have anything important to add."

While I was mentally sputtering at this rudeness, stuck in perpetual peacekeeper mode as always, Kella beat me to a response.

"I can fill Connor and Henri in about the band while you two fetch the posters if you like. In your limited role, you probably don't need to hear about it anyway." She upped the wattage on her saccharine smile and beamed at him. Oh, bravo!

"All right, we will be back in just a minute." I took Liam's arm and led him from the room before any parting salvos could be fired. I was grateful for his long sleeves, so our bare skin didn't touch. I wasn't ready to find out if the sparks from last time would be a repeat phenomenon.

"This way." Walking upstairs properly was easier than going down. I had enough concentration left over to also hope Liam wouldn't say anything too awkward. I racked my brain for a safe conversation topic.

"So, Loren, I have thought of the perfect place to take you for our first date. I trust you are free one day this weekend?"

Argh! Too late. And, seriously! Presumptive much? No graceful way to say 'no' either, likely intentional on his part. Next time, I needed to be prepared with some banal safe conversation starters like 'I would love to hear more about the hunt club!' See, that would have been perfect. Why couldn't I have come up with it sooner?

"What did you have in mind? With the fundraiser so close, I shouldn't take too much time off . . ."

"Just give me three hours. We can even make it a lunch date. I could pick you up Sunday at eleven?"

"All right." The tiny caricature of my grandmother that now hovered on my shoulder — complete with angel wings — glared and poked me. I mentally stuck my tongue out at her before giving in. "That sounds lovely." See, I could be gracious, even if I was grinding my teeth at the same time.

I didn't want to linger in my room. To avoid the problem, I stood in the doorway and gestured to the box of posters on my desk. To his credit, Liam didn't do or say anything to make the situation any more awkward. As he started back across the room with the posters, I heard a door close down the hall and turned to see Grandmother coming toward me.

"I didn't realize your meeting was concluded, Loren." Liam joined me in the doorway and her face rapidly went from friendly inquiry to hostile judgment. Powerful emotions rolled through her eyes like storm clouds, and the frown lines around her mouth hardened until they were as deep and immutable as the Grand Canyon. Uh oh. What had I done now?

Liam saw the transformation, too. "I'll, um, take these downstairs." Grandmother continued to glower. I nodded, scared to break the stony silence.

Grandmother waited until Liam turned the corner before tearing into me. "What were you doing with a man in your bedroom?"

Is that what this is about? "Grandmother, we weren't in here a full minute. Liam was just carrying the posters for me because of my arm." I flapped my arm in its splint to illustrate my point.

"It does not matter, Loren! Did you consider the implications? If the wrong person saw — or the Magic had latched on . . ." She took a deep breath, an elegant version of hyperventilating. "You need to be more careful. Any sort of intimacy you share could leave you joined to that person forever."

"But Connor said that —"

Grandmother made an agitated, slashing gesture. "Connor hasn't been through a *conte des fées* yet. All his knowledge is theoretical; he doesn't have a full grasp of the situation. I don't want you trapped in a relationship not of your choosing. Do you understand?"

Not really. How intimate was intimate? Was I in trouble from that initial hand kiss? As much as I wanted to ask, Grandmother had gone from looking thunderous to dispirited during our discussion, and I didn't feel I could press the issue. "Yes, Grandmother. Maybe we can discuss this more, later? I ought to get back to my guests."

She nodded wearily.

"I'll be careful. I promise." Before she could object, I gave her stiff body a quick hug and headed back to the others.

I barely heard her soft-spoken, "I hope careful is enough."

CHAPTER 15

Between classes and event planning, the week flew by. It came to a screeching halt whenever I tried to resign myself to my date with Liam. Of course, it didn't help that I'd been pretending it wasn't going to happen. So, now I was unprepared and left standing in my closet, wondering what to wear. Why hadn't I asked Liam where we were going? It was too late for that now. How formal would this lunch be? I mean, it was lunch — but Liam seemed the type to try to impress with a fancy restaurant, but if I was wrong and overdressed . . . Ugh!

Right, obviously I needed to wear my blue dress. The thought made me giggle. I mean if the dress wasn't right for Liam's plans, at least he wouldn't be able to resist my sense of humor . . . Of course, if he wanted to resist me, I was fine with that, too. Staying home curled up with a good book would be a lovely way to spend the afternoon.

I chose a dress I hoped wouldn't stand out too badly, whatever Liam had planned. I was going to have to remember to ask for more details about plans the next time — assuming there was a next time — so I could be better prepared. Once I was ready, I waited upstairs. See, I told the mental caricature of my grandmother, I can learn. One Loren sitting here, mostly patient even, ready to make an entrance.

I heard the melodious chime of the doorbell and waited for the greeting chitchat to die down. After a few moments, I realized that wasn't going to happen. Liam was in full charm mode and my grandmother was eating it up. I would have to hope he noticed my entrance despite Grandmother. If I struck out again, I was going to have to request another class on the topic. And wow, was I well on my way to being brainwashed. I hated Grandmother for making me care about such trivial matters. I decided to go ahead and throw Liam into my bad graces preemptively for not noticing my entrance.

Before I could go off the deep end, I took a calming breath and started down the stairs. Chin up, shoulders back, stomach sucked in, fingers trailing along the banister. It was much easier without a long skirt trying to get tangled in heels.

I kept my gaze on Liam as instructed by Grandmother. To my delight, he did notice me. Ugh, ten minutes ago I didn't even want to go out with him! What was wrong with me? He stopped talking to Grandmother mid-sentence and beamed at me the whole time. It was good to know I wasn't going to have to hate him before our date started.

At the bottom of the staircase, he presented me with a large bouquet of red roses. I noticed Grandmother was holding a smaller bouquet of white roses. Suck up. The thought held no rancor though, and I smiled as I buried my nose in my flowers. They were lovely but uninspired, typical florist roses with no scent. I murmured polite thanks and passed the flowers to Ms. Millie, who offered to put them in water along with her own. He really was turning up the charm, or perhaps he was just hoping for more of Ms. Millie's cookies.

Liam offered his arm to help me down the stairs in the portico, just as Grandmother said a gentleman would. He helped me into a low, green, sporty car. While he walked around to his side of the car, I mentally rehearsed my open-ended questions designed to carefully steer the conversation into safe waters.

We took off with a loud *vroom* noise, which I was sure Liam found satisfying. Time for ego-stroking question number one.

"What kind of a car is this? I don't know that I have seen one like it before. It certainly, uh, purrs . . ."

"It is a Phase One BJ8 Austin Healey 3000. One of only about fourteen hundred ever built. And she does purr, not like that damn electric car of Connor's." I hadn't gotten around to asking Connor about his car. Electric, huh? That explained how quiet it was. "I helped restore her. It was a project Uncle Nick and I worked on for years together." I tuned out a bit for the next ten minutes or so. The only input required of me was the occasional brief comment to keep things going.

". . . had to completely strip . . ."

"Sounds like quite a project."

". . . chrome was rusted . . ."

"Oh!"

". . . and the leather was rotted through . . ."

"What made you choose to paint it green?"

That question bought me another five minutes — I learned all about how it was the original British Racing Green and it set off the chrome work. I had plenty of energy left to admire the scenery. As we turned onto a road labeled as a scenic byway, I idly wondered where we were going.

"Well, it is fun to ride in. Where are we heading, by the way?"

"I knew you enjoyed nature and the fall colors are great. I wasn't sure if you were fully recovered yet, so something low-key like a drive seemed perfect. There are lots of waterfalls, and several scenic overlooks. If you are up for it, there are some gentle hikes. Then we can have a picnic. I also love the curves on this road." He turned and smiled his trademarked little-boy grin, and I couldn't help but smile back. There was no stabbing lust as I admired his grin, it was more as if my body melted and puddled like warm honey.

It was sweet how much thought he had put into our date. I told myself I had promised to give him a shot; it wasn't caving on my standards to do so. The logical part of my brain snorted at the rationalization.

He frowned as he turned back to the road. "You got me started talking about my car and I didn't let you get a word in edgewise." Oh, you noticed? I raised an eyebrow and made a noncommittal sound in response. "I would love to know more about you. Connor and Henri didn't seem to know much."

Well, that was a loaded statement, and he had also let slip he cared enough to do research before our date, and wasn't cocky enough to rely solely on his charm. Added to that was the fact Connor knew plenty, and apparently decided not to share. Interesting . . . I almost asked what he wanted to know, but that didn't seem safe. Time for a bit of deflection?

"I was hoping you would tell me a bit about being a werewolf, how it all works —"

"Ah, being true to character here, curious like Belle? This is the part where I am supposed to go all beastly and roar about staying out of the west wing, right?"

"But I ought to know more about the whole thing."

"Not happening. Sorry, but I'm not going to risk my chance at a happily ever after just to satisfy Belle's curiosity. Later on, maybe. But for now, stay out of the west wing." He gave a mock growl, "Grr and argh and all that. Besides, we've talked enough about me. Why don't you tell me about yourself?"

"Well, I don't know if there is much to tell. You've known my grandmother longer than I have. Other than that, there is only my Dad and me. We aren't speaking right now because I don't like his new girlfriend, who is only four years older than me." Ouch — that sounded more bitter than I meant it to. He made a sympathetic noise. Okay, safer topic. Let's see . . . "I am finishing my master's in technical illustration, specializing in botany, even though, as my father points out, the pay for medical illustrators is significantly better. And wow, I didn't realize how angry I was at my dad. Sorry, I really will change the topic. Hmm — we could talk about the fundraiser?"

He grinned. "Nope, no work today. It's okay if you want to complain about your dad. I have problems with my father figure too, so I understand. In fact, it wasn't until we started hunting together that things smoothed out between us."

"I don't think hunting would help us. I probably shouldn't be around Dad with a gun right now," I said dryly.

He burst out laughing. "I feel the same way about my clients occasionally."

"Is that why you run a hunt club now?" I hastily clarified, "Because of your uncle? Er, father?"

"I call him Uncle Nick. I guess you could say that. Uncle Nick introduced me to hunting. It was one of the first times I felt like a part of the family. Henri was always great at school and all those other things parents want you to excel at, but he doesn't like hunting. I also felt like I was in his shadow, even though he was younger than me. When Uncle Nick and I connected over hunting, I felt like I was finally better at something than he was." He grimaced, "It sounds so shallow when I say it that way. I don't mean it like that . . ."

"You felt like he finally approved of you?" I asked.

"Yes! That is it exactly. You are the first person who has understood." He gave me an intense look before turning back to the road. He reached out to gently squeeze my hand. There were those fizzles again. After a moment, he made a visible effort to lighten the mood. "Uncle Nick would approve of you." He winked.

"Ugh." I half groaned and half laughed. "Well, that would be great. I'm still waiting for my Dad to approve of something I have done." Whoa, that was meant to be light-hearted, but it came out sounding angry. STILL. UGH!

"I would tell you your Dad's opinion doesn't define your value, but I know it is easier to believe that in your head than in your heart." Liam reached over and gave my hand another squeeze. Wow. Why couldn't he be like this all the time?

I cleared my throat. "Thanks, it is kind of you to want to listen. But I would rather dwell on something more pleasant. It is too pretty of a day to ruin by talking about my family." I grasped desperately for topics. "Why don't you tell me about how Lointaine celebrates Halloween?"

Liam raised an eyebrow, but let the conversation be steered toward less-charged topics. "Well, the Fall Fest is coming up soon, over in the NoLo Art District. That is where the pumpkin carving contest results will be displayed. Let's see, there is a costume parade, pumpkin pie eating contest, local craft fair, music performances — and don't forget the locally renowned pumpkin roll, although we advertise it as world famous. Perhaps you would allow me to escort you to the fair? We can take a moonlit hayride." He waggled his eyebrows at me. I couldn't help but laugh.

"Why don't we see how today goes first?" I responded dryly. There, that was better!

"I don't have any concerns, do you?" Another of those cocky boyish grins . . . but he let the topic rest. "Would a short, half-mile or so walk be okay?"

"Is there a trail?" I asked cautiously. Needing to be thrown over a shoulder, caveman style, and toted back to the car if my vertigo got bad had zero appeal.

"It is even paved."

"In that case, I should be able to manage."

"Great." He let go of my hand and downshifted to turn off the main road into an overlook. The next hour was pleasantly occupied with a short walk and settling into a picnic. The conversation was light, centering on the food and the scenery. I made sure to tease him about the lack of a salad in the picnic fare. Eventually, the food was put away, and we lolled pleasantly on the blanket, chatting.

Between a full belly and the weight of the sunshine falling on me like a blanket, I was ready for a nap. How rude would that be? I would probably manage to bunch up my skirt in a most unladylike way if I tried to lie down, anyway. I watched as a maple leaf was caught by the wind to drift in lazy loops. For a moment, I expected it to land on me, but it settled on the edge of the blanket instead.

I picked it up and ran my fingers across its waxy surface, admiring the cacophony of reds and yellows bleeding into each other through a riot of oranges. "I wish I could paint this. Getting the colors just right would be an interesting challenge." I barely managed to not sigh.

"The foliage this year has been simply stunning. It made me think of you." Suck up, I thought again, although no negativity penetrated my mellow state. Liam was digging around in the picnic hamper again. I hope he didn't have any more food in there. I couldn't manage another bite.

"I, uh, have a little something for you." He pulled out a white paper bag stamped with an 'Artfully Yours' logo that included a painter's palette. If his slightly nervous voice hadn't gotten my attention, that sure did. I accepted it as eagerly as a three-year-old would a birthday gift. I didn't have to fish my hand around long before pulling out a large pad of paper. Its cardboard backside was facing me; when I flipped it over, I found it was Strathmore Hot Press Fine Art Paper.

He continued talking while I was examining it. "I hope I got the right things. I threw myself on the mercy of the lady at the store. She said these would be her first choice for detailed work like botanical drawings." There were other things still in the bag. Another pad of paper, this time cold press. Liam explained with a shrug, "I got both kinds, just in case she was wrong."

I chuckled. It appeared the sale's person was a saint for not having shown him all the other paper options. A box of Faber-Castell colored pencils was the next thing I pulled out. It was followed by a set of four graphite pencils of varying hardness, a kneaded eraser, and a pencil sharpener. I flattened and folded the bag as a way to discreetly check to make sure I hadn't left anything in the bag without looking like I expected additional gifts.

"These are wonderful! Thank you so much — I can't wait to use them!" I opened the tin pencil case and reverently rolled the pencils in their slots.

Liam laughed at my exuberance. "I am going to have to make a mental note to skip flowers in the future, and bring you a bouquet of paintbrushes or pencils instead." He was going to go broke if he kept buying me high-end art supplies like this – the pencils alone probably cost more than the roses.

"I shouldn't accept these. They're too much! But I am going to keep them because they are the closest I have gotten to anything creative in a long time. I can't wait to get cleared by my neurologist to do art again." I sighed. I wanted to sniff the pencils, to hold one right under my nose like a cigar aficionado would a fine Cuban. I love the smell of new pencils — watercolors too, come to think of it. But sniffing the pencils would look weird. And if Liam happened to mention it to Grandmother . . . Well, it wasn't worth it. And that was a sad state of affairs.

He cleared his throat. "I got Henri to talk to your physical therapist. They seem to think you should be fine drawing for short periods. But you need to stop if there is any pain or you start feeling any strain. The therapist suggested no longer than five or ten minutes at a time."

"Really?" I was far too excited to be pissed that apparently health privacy laws meant nothing in Lointaine. Grandmother didn't seem to have any problems accessing my health information, either.

I pulled out the carmine-colored pencil and began a gesture drawing of the leaf. I couldn't resist trying to capture the color even in such a basic exercise. The pencil slid effortlessly across the fine grain of the paper. Oh, how I had missed this! I hoped Liam didn't mind, but he was going to be ignored for the next few minutes. I glanced over to see he was propped against a tree trunk and grinning indulgently at me.

The first few lines were pure joy. By about the tenth line, I could feel concentration contorting my face. Grandmother would have said something about the frown marring my features, but I was too concerned to care at the moment. After the third time I tried to redraw the same line and it squirreled away from where I wanted it to go, I forced myself to stop and take a few deep breaths. There was no reason to panic. I decided I would finish the sketch with no expectations, and just see what happened. I hadn't drawn in a while. I couldn't expect to jump right back into things, could I?

Ten minutes later, and the image completed, I stared at the pad in shock. Liam caught my deer-in-the-headlight look and leaned over to examine my work. "Wow, that is amazing — not what I was expecting, though. This is more . . . abstract? Is that the right term? I didn't know you did abstract art."

"I don't." I didn't know what to think of the wild and unrestrained drawing on the page in front of me. It wasn't at all what I had set out to create. For that matter, it was unlike anything I ever produced before. I didn't do abstract or surreal well, at least not in the past. It was disturbing — I apparently did so with ease now.

I clamped down hard on my emotions. Being upset seemed logical, but I still wasn't sure which of my emotions were "real" and which were caused by the aftereffects of the concussion. My therapist kept reminding me that anxiety and vertigo fed off each other. Anyway, a panic attack would not accomplish anything. Surely I could keep myself together long enough to get a hold of my neurologist?

"Liam, I am sorry to cut things short, but I need to go home. I am not feeling well."

"Was it something I said?" He looked so crestfallen, I would have felt horribly guilty if there was any space left for it aside from the swelling panic.

"No, I am just exhausted all of the sudden." I lied through my teeth. I couldn't explain what had gone wrong. "Maybe we can continue our date some other time?" He relaxed with the suggestion.

"Sure. Whatever you need." He quickly reloaded the hamper. "Why don't you sit here while I take everything back to the car?"

I nodded weakly and settled back onto the blanket. I waited until he was out of sight, and then I threw the sketchbook open again. No, no panicking yet, maybe it was an aberration? My gaze skittered around the clearing for something to draw and hesitated on a sunbathing lizard. Sure, why not. I started working, outlining the rock with frantic strokes, racing to finish before Liam got back. I quickly outlined the body and then went to fill in the shape of the foliage around it. But wait, that couldn't be right. My perspective was all skewed. If the dandelion is a normal size, then the lizard had to be more than four feet long. I let my sketchbook flop to the picnic blanket in frustration. At the noise, the lizard scuttled away. Smooth move Loren, no way to figure out how far off you are now. I idly finished sketching in the dandelion as I kept an ear toward the path. Then I worked on shading in the wings. Wings?

I put the pencil down. Then I closed the sketchpad for good measure too. I closed my eyes and took a deep breath.

Lizards don't have wings. It was official, my brain was a mess, and I was in trouble. Either that or this town was getting to me. All the talk of magic . . . or, maybe this was part of the Magic? Taking my ability to support myself away so I was more like a fairy tale princess?

Would that be good or bad? Was it preferable to be manipulated, or to have lost the talent I spent a lifetime cultivating? Was this more coercion or only collateral damage? I was still mulling over the possibilities and their implications when Liam came back to escort me to the car. He didn't know I wasn't suddenly exhausted, so I tried hard not to snap at him for being overly solicitous.

My brain spun all the way home. I didn't have any attention left over to make polite small talk, and I was vaguely grateful Liam didn't expect any. He wasn't so bad when you were around him by himself and he wasn't trying to compete with anyone. I wonder if that was left over from his childhood? I guess we are all damaged in some way or another by our pasts.

Liam walked me to the door as expected. I gave him a kiss on the cheek to forestall any attempts at other intimacies, and also to hurry our goodbyes along. It wasn't a good reason to kiss someone, but it was the lesser of two evils.

Grandmother was conveniently loitering when I came in.

"Loren! Did you enjoy your time with Liam?"

"Do you have Dr. Aatos's phone number around here somewhere?"

The polite inquiry fell from her face to be replaced with concern. "Is something wrong?"

"Yes. Maybe? I don't know. I just . . . Please, can we call him?"

Grandmother crossed the room toward me.

"He serves with me on the board of the botanical garden. I have his cell phone number. We should be able to get in touch with him immediately." She patted me on my shoulder.

Once Grandmother got through to Dr. Aatos, I almost wished she hadn't. The gist of the five-minute lecture I received was that I should have known better than to try to draw. It was part of my instructions about taking it easy and not doing anything mentally stressful that wasn't required to scrape by in my schooling. I wasn't to try to draw again until HE cleared me. Just in case, he told me to call and schedule an appointment for next week — there were some additional tests we should do. When I asked if they could wait until the following week, and was forced to explain I would be pretty busy getting ready for the fundraiser, he swore and asked to speak to Grandmother.

Grandmother blanched at what Dr. Aatos said. I could only hear her side of the conversation. "Before you go any further, you need to understand Loren has to manage an event as part of her management class requirements. I was trying to help . . ." There was a long pause, then "Yes. I can certainly do that. Thank you. . . . Yes, I will see to it that she makes it in. Goodbye."

Grandmother turned to me. "Dr. Aatos isn't pleased with either of us. Why don't we go look over the list of what you have left to do for the party? You have one, right?" I nodded while she continued. "I figured, with how fond of them you are. We can pick out some things for you to delegate to me. I ought to have thought of that as a way around your teacher's requirements sooner." She was shaking her head. Surprisingly, I believed it was in disgust with herself and not with the doctor, or even me.

We went to my room where I pulled out the binder I was using to organize all the party plans. I started to put away my new art supplies when Grandmother stopped me.

"Before we get started, why don't you show me this drawing that has you all in a tizzy?"

I reluctantly pulled the new sketchpad back out of the drawer where I had intended to hide it away.

Grandmother studied the drawing for a few minutes. "Well, that is really something, isn't it? I take it this isn't what you intended to draw?"

I shook my head, afraid saying anything would let loose the sob caught in the back of my throat. It didn't matter, Grandmother caught on to the repressed emotion. I was swept into a hug that reminded me of a spider web, both incredibly strong and fragile at the same time.

"Oh my dear, please don't worry about this. I promise it will all come straight once your *conte de fées* is over."

"You think it is the Magic?" I sniffled while accepting a lacy white handkerchief from her.

She waved a hand in a Gallic gesture. "Magic, side effect of the concussion, it doesn't matter. The Magic will have to straighten it out as a part of your happily ever after." She reached up to cradle my cheeks in her hands. "You have enough to be concerned about without allowing this to affect you. You believe in the Magic now, yes?" As I nodded, she dropped her hands. "Well, have faith everything will work out for the best. You have a good heart. The Magic can't help but reward that."

I guess the question would be how the Magic rewarded that. Would it consider a rich husband and a child a more suitable reward than the return of my ability to support myself with my art? Was this just another way the Magic was trying to force a certain course of action? How was I going to get my drawings done for my thesis? My brain started skipping down the path of how to revise the text to work without the missing pieces before I could haul it back. Enough! I was sick of this lack of mental discipline. Time to get refocused.

I took a deep breath. And another.

Yes, this was a setback. But, no matter how things fell out, it wasn't like I would starve. It was time to put things into perspective. Getting married didn't mean I couldn't still pursue my art. For that matter, neither Grandmother nor my father would let me go homeless. Even if they did attach strings to their help, I was in a better position than most people would be with a concussion that erased all their training. It didn't mean my situation didn't suck, but it didn't call for panic. In fact, panicking was the last thing needed.

Grandmother apparently decided I had mused long enough. "Why don't we consider this a sign you are still healing? For now, we should focus on the more immediate tasks. If things haven't worked out in another month or so, we can worry then."

I gave my grandmother a tremulous smile. It was the only logical course of action. "That seems sensible."

"In that case, let us determine where my taking over can be useful. Then you can tell me all about your date with Liam."

"Ugh!" I buried my head in my hands, partially to avoid seeing Grandmother frown at my unladylike utterance. "I freaked out when the drawing went all wonky and cut our date short." I lifted my head, worried I wouldn't be understood while mumbling into my hands, and would then have to repeat my confession. "He was a perfect gentleman — he even bought me the art supplies."

I was ready for a tongue lashing, but was Grandmother's lip twitching? She burst into laughter. "Is that all? That is easy enough to repair. Call him later and apologize. Then ask him to escort you somewhere else."

"Wouldn't that be too forward?"

"Not at all. Well, it would be if he hadn't already escorted you on one date, and expressed an interest in doing so again. Let's see, the Fall Festival this Friday would work nicely. You can walk around downtown for a bit and have dinner. Perhaps go on a hayride afterward? Although, you shouldn't be out too late with the fundraiser the next day . . ."

"That does sound perfect. We can check on the pumpkin carving contest that way, too."

"I wouldn't usually recommend multitasking on a date, but if I recall correctly, Liam did come up with the idea." An expression crossed her face that would have been a grimace on mine; on her, it was a slight moue of distaste. One of these days I might manage to be so elegant. "I think we can make it work if you make sure to give lavish compliments about how well his plan worked. Now, let's go over your list and figure out how we will get all of this accomplished. Then I want you to take a nap."

"Yes, ma'am." I was emotionally exhausted, if not physically. I wasn't going to argue with a nap.

It was a good thing I didn't try. With the worries of the day firmly quashed, and about half of my tasks for the week taken off my plate, I felt so light, I almost floated off to sleep before Grandmother left the room.

CHAPTER 16

Wednesday evening I had my final costume fitting. I hadn't expected that Kella would be able to interest me in another blue dress, but she managed. The dress reminded me of the Mediterranean Sea; silk woven into velvet and satin that caught the light and appeared to glow from within. The overskirt was draped to show coy peaks of a frothy petticoat. It was caught up in the back in what Kella assured me was a small bustle that cascaded into a train.

I was less enthusiastic about the underclothes. Shockingly, I didn't mind the corset too much. The cage crinolinette on the other hand, complete with 40 hoops and a built-in bustle, was aptly named. It should be classified as a torture device — and that was despite the hoops being significantly more flexible than I thought they would be. Why couldn't steampunk embrace the Regency- or Edwardian-era instead? Kella made me practice walking and tackling the stairs as the skirts, hoops, and train all required management.

Then we moved on to sitting gracefully, which meant carefully spreading the skirts and maintaining a quasi-lounging position to keep the hoops from popping up in the front and crushing the bustle in the back. I was not adept. Three tries during which I showed too much leg were followed by a disastrous attempt where I slid off the edge of the chaise and hit the floor.

I started giggling at my own ridiculousness. "Ouch! That is gonna leave bruises, and in little parallel lines from the hoops, too!" I attempted to stand, but couldn't extract myself from the tangle I had made. Kella was trying to help and keep a straight face, but the last sprawl was too much for her. Seconds later, we were both helplessly shrieking with laughter in a tangled puddle of petticoats.

"Maybe you should just avoid sitting?" Kella gasped as we tried to gain control of ourselves.

I was wiping my eyes as I considered the problem. "I might be busy enough for that to work. Didn't Liam say the tablecloths were going to be floor length? Maybe it won't matter if my skirts fly up under the table."

Kella gave me a sly sideways glance, "Your grandmother would still know."

"She would, wouldn't she?" When we finally managed to stop laughing, it took a few moments of lying there, gasping for breath, before we could speak again. "Did I tell you she fired Mrs. Minchkin so she could take over my etiquette training herself? Mrs. Minchkin does the cotillion class for the Junior League! I feel less uncouth knowing that no one lives up to Grandmother's standards."

"Oh, dear." Kella chuckled. "That sounds ominous. I would offer to work with you some more tonight, but you seem like you need to be done, and I am running late for girls' night out. We should plan to practice again in the next day or two?"

I rifled through my mental calendar. "I guess I need to make time for that. Could you come over early Saturday?"

"Sure, I was planning to help with preparations anyway. Then if you like, we could help each other get ready and squeak in another lesson. Let's go ahead and get you out of those for now."

"Sounds good," I muttered through a mouthful of chemise. "I get now why there was a need for a maid to help you dress and undress, and take care of your clothes."

Kella started in on the laces on the back of the bodice. "You know, you should come with me tonight. You look like you need a break. It will be low key, just sitting around and sipping wine . . ."

Despite being tired, I was tempted. Was I tired enough that Dr. Aatos would fuss at me for pushing myself by going out? Speaking of which, "Would it be weird for anyone if I don't drink? I need to avoid alcohol with the concussion."

"I don't think anyone will mind. Nobody will have more than one or two glasses of wine anyway. Almost everyone has to be at work at some point tomorrow morning."

"In that case, I would like to come. It would be nice to make some local friends, especially since I might end up staying in town longer than anticipated." I hesitated. "Do they know about the . . ." I waved my hand futilely; realizing I didn't know what Kella called the Magic or even what her position on it was.

"The Magic. Hmm, I can see why that would matter. One or two of them do. I can point them out if you like."

"Please. I need more people I can talk to without needing to lie or avoid discussing three-quarters of my life."

"That bad, huh?"

"Yes." I swallowed and blinked back tears. "My friend Jordan called my grandmother after I tried to talk to her because she worried I needed to be dragged back to my neurologist."

Kella started to laugh but immediately clapped a hand over her mouth. "I'm sorry, that really is awful."

I sighed, "It's okay. I can see how it would be funny if it wasn't happening to me. I would be laughing if you were telling me the story."

"Well, if it matters, I don't think you are delusional. At least not any more than I am . . ." She laughed as she said it. "I'm not sure that is saying much, though."

"So, does that mean you believe in the Magic?"

"I'm not sure. I don't feel the need to be certain about what causes the phenomena around here. What I do believe is that you need to be intentional about what energy and thoughts you put out into the universe, especially in this town."

"That seems smart." It might help me focus on the positive and be less anxious. "I might steal that philosophy."

"Go for it! Oh — but be careful with the way you word things and your intensity. Otherwise, you might end up getting struck by lightning. Personal experience there obviously."

"Umm, wow."

"Yeah, I may have said 'I want this storm to feel real' too often during production meetings."

"Yikes! I'm making mental notes about what *not* to do." I thought through what I knew about Kella. Based on the comments she had made, she had been living here for a few years, but then she couldn't be a princess. So how did she know about the Magic? "So, are you one of Louis's descendants?"

"Me? I mean I have my own sort of magic," she said with a coy pose designed to get a laugh out of me. "But – no, I'm unjinxty. But my stepsisters are Louis's descendants. I was twelve when the princesses got sent away. I overheard my Dad and Connie – that's my stepmother – arguing about whether or not we should leave Lointaine. I learned about the Magic then. My having to move was just collateral damage."

How had I failed to realize the Magic would affect people outside Louis's family? "So, Liam seems to think being adopted wasn't enough to make the Magic consider him a prince. Does that mean you aren't a princess?"

Kella laughed. "No, thank god!"

"Ugh. I'm struggling to keep track of who is one of Louis's descendants, who has had a tale already, who might have one, and what role people might play or have already played. I need CliffsNotes."

Kella raised an eyebrow at me. "I think I can help there — *everyone* in town is affected by the Magic, and anyone here could get sucked into a tale as it plays out. A significantly smaller portion of the town knows about the Magic and believes in it. An even smaller portion will play a leading role as the hero or heroine in a tale."

"How can people live here and not realize there is magic at work?"

She shrugged. "Most people don't see the whole picture. They just see the side effects. Even if those are fantastical . . . well, folks explain things away."

"Hmmm."

Kella drummed her fingers on her thigh. "Okay. It's kind of like Hollywood and movies. Everyone who lives in Hollywood is affected by the movies. There may be whole extra stores for things like costumes, or your favorite coffee shop might have weird hours to accommodate shooting schedules. As you move around town, traffic might be shut down for a shoot or heavy for a grand opening. The sidewalks might be clogged with tourists or you might run across a ridiculously famous movie star. You might even end up being background for a scene. All that said, just because you live in Hollywood doesn't mean you know anything about how to make movies, or that you will be in a movie. But if you pay attention, you are likely to pick things up. And I've pieced together quite a bit since I was twelve and first learned about all this."

"Oh?"

"Let's just say some people like to brag about how they are special." She rolled her eyes. "Going to get himself into trouble someday."

"Do you mean —"

Kella blanched as I started asking and waved her hand. "I'm sorry. I shouldn't have said anything. But then, you have to know . . . Since you are looking for a hairy beast?" She emphasized hairy beast. "I can't keep track of who knows what sometimes."

"Oh, that." Duh, Loren! She meant the werewolves. "How do you know about them?"

"I overheard Henri and Liam talking at school. I came around a corner at just the right time. They had been arguing about whether a shifter could be a werewolf and went from looking angry to guilty so fast, they couldn't even pretend it was anything else. I wish you could have seen their faces."

I laughed. "Oh, I bet they didn't like that. Connor acted like I needed special clearance when he told me."

"I just bet. And it's a lot to process! I hope you will consider talking to me if you need a listening ear."

The crinoline didn't make it easy, but I leaned forward to hug Kella. "Thank you, I will." And I even meant it.

CHAPTER 17

"I can tackle tonight. This event is going to be fabulous." My reflection in the vanity mirror did not look convinced. Hey, I managed to make some new friends this week, proving I was significantly better at small talk. So tonight shouldn't be a problem. Organizing is easier than socializing any day. I had this! Positive thoughts out into the universe, remember?

Wednesday night with Kella's friends was a blast. I hadn't felt socially awkward at all. When Zoe came back from the bar rolling her eyes, it was easy to jump into the conversation. "You know this town is weird in a lot of ways, but the men here are just as bad as they are everywhere else. That guy asked if I had a Band-Aid because he scraped his knee falling for me."

"Ouch, that's bad." Kella laughed. "What did you tell him?"

Zoe shrugged. "Sorry, no Band-Aids. Maybe the bartender has a first aid kit.'"

"Ouch! Brrr!" Muffled shrieks answered her response. "You didn't!"

"What?" Zoe defended herself. "I answered his question and let him know I wasn't interested. I wasn't nasty about it or anything. Why do I owe him anything other than being civil? I came here to hang out with you all — not spend the evening explaining to a guy I don't want to date him."

"It wasn't that bad of a line."

I think it was Eloise who started it all. "I have heard much worse . . ."

Zoe laughed, "Like what?"

"I got to a guy's house and there was an actual street sign reading 'SPEED HUMP' hanging on his bedroom door."

"Eww, seriously?"

"How about: 'Can I order you at McDonald's because I am lovin' it?' Complete with one of those top-to-bottom elevator looks."

"I've got worse!" I was excited to be able to contribute. "I was taking a forest ecology course, and my lab partner told me we could go back to his place to measure some real wood later."

A chorus of disgust followed my remark. Then, the suggestions started flying fast and furious.

"Can I borrow your phone? I forgot mine, and I need to call my mother to tell her I finally found the girl of my dreams."

"You remind me of my big toe. I am going to bang you on every piece of furniture in my house."

"That is disgusting!"

"There is the old: are you from Tennessee?"

"No! Somebody actually tried to use that one?"

"Yup."

"Is that a mirror in your pocket? Because I can see myself in your pants."

"Ugh! Men are disgusting!"

"Aww, come on. Some pick-up lines are kind of cute." A round of boos met Jolie's defense of the male species.

"Like what?" The challenge was thrown out.

"One guy said he and his friend were arguing about his sweater and asked me to feel it. Then he asked if I thought it was boyfriend material."

There were some groans. "Hey, at least it wasn't flat out asking for sex."

Zoe asked, "Want to hear the worst line ever?"

"You can top those?" I asked. Men were shits if there was anything worse to tell.

She nodded. "The worst is: 'You make me want to be a better person.'"

"But that is so sweet!" another objected. "I would love for a guy to say that to me."

"Exactly!" Zoe said emphatically stabbing the table with her finger. "That is the problem. It worked. And the dick had a fiancée."

The table fell silent except for a couple of murmurs.

"Was this . . .?"

"Yes."

"Well, just because one jerk used it, doesn't make it a bad line. Even total assholes can have good taste in areas outside of morals and personality and whatnot . . . I mean he *did* date you, after all."

I found myself lost in the conversation, but I wasn't about to butt in and ask for details given the pained look on Zoe's face.

Kella looked around the table before setting her wine glass down with a decisive clink. "I refuse to let that man, and I use the term loosely, ruin the evening! So, how about that sportsball team?"

Eloise laughed. "I think you meant to ask about my amazing Halloween party?"

"Yes! Yes, I did." Kella's eyes twinkled even as she pouted dramatically. "Tell us all about how fabulous it will be and rub it in again about how I will be working instead."

Eloise's face fell. "Oh, I forgot about that."

"Oh, sweetie. I was teasing! I would love to be able to make it," she paused to raise her pinky in the air as she lifted her wine glass, "But I will be at the most hoity-toity, swanky, exclusive crush of the season. Hmm, that is an oxymoron, isn't it? Exclusive crush?" She giggled. "Anyway, I meant it. Please do tell us all about it! I imagine yours will go late, and I hope to be able to make it there for some fun before it ends."

Eloise grinned, "Maybe we should all crash your party instead!"

Kella pretended to consider, "Well, we could use some more volunteers on cleaning duty . . ."

Everyone laughed while booing her and a napkin even got thrown her way. I kind of wished now that some of them had volunteered to come help. It would be nice to have friendly faces as part of the crowd tonight. Ugh, perhaps I should rephrase that as friendly faces without expectations.

I considered last night's date with Liam as I tried to get the bobby pins to anchor the floral crown in my hair. It wasn't that Liam was bad company, or that he had done anything wrong . . . In fact, he was pretty great during our time one-on-one. It was just that he was so intent, his enthusiasm and commitment to this wild scheme were overwhelming. When Liam suggested he needed to meet my father and I ought to move in with him, as per the Disney movie, I almost had a panic attack.

Every smile, and even the light that leapt into Liam's eyes, made me feel immense guilt for not being as invested as he was. He was almost maniacally happy about our relationship. I almost hated myself for not being able to return his affection. Although my hormones were only too happy to respond to him anytime, and twice on Sunday.

I sighed and tested my pinning job. Ouch! Apparently, the florist had missed a thorn. It was a relief to have an excuse to frown as the white roses listed drunkenly to one side. I pulled the thorn out of my finger and blotted it on a tissue, sighing. Were there any Band-Aids around here? Could I blame this on the Magic? Another version of Belle's hair always falling out . . . I was going to need some fairy godmother magic to get it to stay in place.

Almost as if the idea conjured her, Millie sailed into the room. She hid a smile when she saw the roses flopping in my face, "I thought you might need some help."

A lock of hair fell out of the chignon and bobbed in front of my eyes. I tried to take the wreath out, but my hair was tangled in the roses. It was so ridiculous, I giggled.

"Thank you! Kella helped me get dressed earlier, and I think I can manage to sit without embarrassing myself now. But if you hadn't come to rescue me, I might have been stuck here for lack of a period appropriate hairstyle."

Millie managed to get the wreath out of my hair with a few gentle tugs. "I am going to start over rather than try to repair this."

"That would be wise," I agreed. "I wasn't sure how long my work would hold."

"It won't move by the time I am done with it." That was quite some threat. By now, all the pins were out and she was brushing my hair. "No wonder you were having issues. I swear your hair has grown several inches since you got here!" Millie exclaimed.

I peered into the mirror confused. It certainly did seem significantly longer, but . . . "That can't be possible. When I went back to Joice for a touchup, I didn't have any roots."

"Hmmm. I would say it is a good sign."

"Huh?"

Millie clucked, "Princesses don't say 'huh.'"

I sighed, but dutifully rephrased, "What is it a sign of?" Princesses probably used better grammar than that too, but Millie let it slide.

"The Magic seems to approve of your 'Beauty and the Beast' approach." What did that have to do with anything? Wait . . .

"You think the Magic changed the color of my hair?"

Millie shrugged, "Why does that surprise you after hearing it made your grandmother sleep for a hundred years?"

I didn't have a response for that. I sat silently, peering intently at my roots as Millie finished. I was fairly certain my hair would now survive a nuclear blast.

Right as she was finishing, my cell phone rang. I checked it. What problem was I going to be asked to resolve now? Was it the caterer? I was shocked to see "Dad" on the caller ID.

I glanced at Millie. She waved at the phone and turned to leave, "Go ahead. I'm done."

I pushed the button to answer while swallowing a lump in my throat. "Hi, Dad."

He cleared his throat. "I thought you should know I proposed to Emilia and she accepted. We are planning to get married on Valentine's Day. I wanted to get it on your calendar."

I straightened in surprise, dropping the phone from where it had been cradled between my head and shoulder. Despite my attempts to grab it, the phone slid down my skirt. I awkwardly leaned sideways, unable to just bend over to pick it up in my corset.

The delay was unfortunately not enough to keep me from saying the wrong thing. "You are marrying Emilia?!"

"I don't know why you are acting like this is a surprise, Loren. Please keep it to yourself for now. She doesn't want it announced until she can tell her family in person when we are there for Christmas."

"What? Wait, does that mean we aren't doing Christmas together?"

"Given your history, I didn't think you would enjoy spending that much time with Emilia. I am sure you are welcome to stay with your grandmother. Besides, I am about as welcome there as you would be here."

"We could do Christmas at —"

"Anyway, that's it. Don't forget: Valentine's Day. I'll make sure you get details about where and when to be there. Goodnight, Loren."

He hung up. I stared at my phone, anger beginning to boil. I didn't get to be told in person like her family? Dropping a bomb like that and following it with dumping me for the holidays? The comment about details made it sound like I wasn't even going to be asked to be in the wedding! Oh, and gee thanks, I'm fine Dad — just the aftermath of a dead body falling on me! Nothing to worry about!

I have always hated that I cry when I get angry. People try to tell me everything will be okay when really I am actively trying to keep from lashing out. The hot prickle of tears was burning my eyes, but my hands were shaking with rage.

I refused to cry. First off, it would ruin my makeup. And as trivial as that was, there wasn't time to fix it. Also, and perhaps more importantly, if I gave in to tears, I would be losing to my father. Ugh, did I really feel we were in a situation where only one of us could win? Great family relations there. I fisted my hands and dug my fingers into my palms. Ouch! Shoot — still needed that Band-Aid.

Deep breaths. My mind whirled. Damn it! I was grounded just moments ago. Oh hell! The Magic . . . I needed to tell Connor.

I picked up my phone and texted him: YOU HERE YET?

A moment passed: JUST PULLED UP.

I responded: I NEED TO TALK TO YOU NOW.

Was that overly dramatic? I decided I pretty much didn't care.

WHERE ARE YOU? came back.

MY ROOM. I ticked off the doorways in the hall mentally, THIRD DOOR ON THE LEFT AT TOP OF THE STAIRS.

WE ARE ON THE WAY.

We? Who was with him? Did he bring a date?

A few moments later there was a knock at the door that startled me. I hadn't moved, not even to put the phone down, I was so deeply absorbed in trying to sort things out. "Come in." I half stood to go to the door, but Liam and Connor walked in before I took two steps.

Why did Liam have to be with him? I didn't need to deal with him now! Oh, damn. Wow. Please don't start drooling, Loren. It wouldn't be dignified, no matter how yummy Liam was in his costume. Oh my god — if Grandmother came along . . .

"Loren, what's wrong!?" Liam asked. "You seem . . ." He paused, "upset." I guess he didn't want to tell me I looked awful since it wouldn't further his agenda. He took my hand and kissed it. "What's this? You've injured yourself!"

It was too much. I started giggling and crying at the same time. "What? Oh, that's nothing. I just got snagged on my hair wreath." I turned to Connor. "I got a call from my Dad. He is engaged, but they aren't announcing it until Christmas," I took a shaky breath. ". . . to which I am not invited."

"You pricked your finger! Shall I kiss you and save the day?" What was Liam babbling about? Kiss me? Oh! Oh. Thank goodness I wasn't in an enchanted slumber! I looked at Connor to see his reaction.

Conner was shaking his head. "I think she would have fallen asleep by now if it was going to be a problem."

If nothing else, Liam's ridiculousness saved me from crying enough to ruin my makeup. I sniffled. Grandmother would be horrified.

Connor noticed. "Liam, perhaps you could find a tissue for Loren?"

Liam searched the room until he found the tissue box, which he brought over and presented with a bow. I managed to pull a third of the box out in a wad. I had to shake the clump to extract a single tissue. I dabbed at my eyes with it. I needed to blow my nose, but I had already broken too many other rules of etiquette tonight to do that in front of the guys. I sniffled into a tissue as delicately as possible.

The gears in Connor's head were visibly turning. "If your father remarries before your story quest is finished, you add a stepmother to the tale. It changes your story arc probabilities — and not for the better. Chances are much higher you will be either Snow White or Cinderella." He paused to let that sink in. "Either way, in many versions of those tales the fathers are dead."

"Wait, are you saying the Magic will kill my father?"

"I don't have enough data. World War II happened right after Snow White came out and it wasn't too long after Cinderella was in theaters. War casualties account for a few missing fathers, but several of the deaths seem highly coincidental. At the very least, I expect somehow your father would become unavailable. It could be that he will travel to a remote location or it could be more emotionally unavailable, which seems to have already started. Your tale needs to finish before the wedding. We are going to have to move our timetable—"

"Loren, we have discussed having gentlemen callers in your room before," Grandmother interrupted from the doorway. So much for hoping she would be too busy to notice. I guess I wasn't going to catch a break tonight. And wow, that was whiny. You can do better, Loren.

"I needed some privacy, all the rental folks and whatnot . . ." I started to say at the same time Connor started in with "Her father is bringing a stepmother into the situation."

Grandmother seemed to deflate a bit. "That man always did know how to cause problems." She stared at me for a moment before walking over to place an arm around my shoulder gently. "Perhaps we should focus on the festivities tonight. We can reevaluate your plan tomorrow. Shall we say brunch at eleven?" She raised an eyebrow at Connor and Liam. It wasn't so much an inquiry as a dare to disagree with her plan.

They were both quick to respond with, "Yes, ma'am!"

"We will figure this out, never doubt that, Loren." Grandmother tapped me under the chin. It's funny how even a show of support from her was also a reminder to have proper posture.

I took a deep breath and composed myself. I wasn't in this alone. Liam alone would happily move a mountain for me. I almost snorted aloud at the thought. Then I almost giggled over how Grandmother and Liam would react to a snort. Wow, I needed to try to find that calm emotional center I kept hearing about.

"After all, Dr. Aatos is on the guest list. I don't want him to have a reason to question my care of you!" I barely caught the "Interfering busybody that he is . . ." she muttered under her breath, as she swept out of the room.

"Shall we?" Liam offered his arm and escorted me to the party. I could feel the crushing weight of his expectations the entire way down the stairs. They were so palpable, I almost caught myself worrying about tripping over them as I placed each foot at the proper fifteen-degree angle on the tread.

CHAPTER 18

Luckily, I was soon too busy to worry about the latest snarl in our plans, or Liam, or Liam's reaction to the news about my father. Liam had given me an antique lapel watch at the beginning of the evening. I tried to decline the gift as being too much, but he insisted so strongly, I would've had to make a scene to refuse it. I checked the time on it now, surprised to find it was already almost eleven o'clock. Only an hour or so to go, although things would probably wind down before then. So far, there had been no major issues, a minor miracle for which I was exceedingly grateful.

I sat in a quiet corner and took a moment to relax, grateful to not be meeting someone else's needs temporarily. I wasn't hiding . . . just following Dr. Aatos' orders.

Liam found me anyway. "I thought you might enjoy a break. Why don't you come out on the patio with me for a few minutes? When we come back in, you can tell me what I can do to help." His charming grin was back.

"I shouldn't . . ." I said, even as I allowed him to help me to my feet. An escape from the noise would be good — I was working up to a splitting headache if I didn't do something about it now. "Let me tell Grandmother first, so she can keep an eye out for any problems."

"Is that necessary . . ." Liam stopped as we rounded the corner and practically walked into Grandmother. Well, that was convenient.

"Grandmother, if you don't mind keeping an eye on things for a few minutes, Liam is going to take me outside for a quick break."

"Please do. Dr. Aatos was giving me some pointed looks earlier as you were rushing around."

"It will be my pleasure," Liam threw the words over his shoulder as he continued to steer me outside.

As Liam opened the door to the patio, I was surprised to see we had it to ourselves. Then I was hit with a fierce gust of wind and understood why no one else was outside. The weather was trying to live up to the holiday. Another gust of wind hit, clearing the cobwebs from my head. This was going to be a glorious storm. Although Grandmother was going to be miffed if it started before her party was over. I decided not to worry — not even the weather would dare disobey her orders.

"Here, I stashed some champagne out here for us to enjoy." Liam held a flute out for me to take.

"That was sweet of you, but I can't drink right now. Remember, it's not safe with the concussion?" Why did I make that a question? Ugh.

"Just a little?" He tried to hand me the glass again.

I took it and set it aside. "No. It can make it take longer for things to get back to normal, or even cause seizures." Dr. Aatos would be proud that I remembered his lectures.

"I would have thought that would all be done by now?"

"Dr. Aatos says most side effects should dissipate within three months, but they can last for years . . . so hopefully not more than another six weeks or so." Even if it meant offending Liam, I wasn't going to do anything to risk continuing the stabbing headaches that were so awful my vision went fuzzy. And the exhaustion, the total exhaustion. I just couldn't go back to that stage.

"Oh. Well, there were sodas around somewhere. Give me a minute and I'll find one."

"I'm fine, really. I don't need a drink."

"But I insist!" He turned with a flair that unfurled the shoulder cape he was wearing. There was no doubt in my mind he practiced the move in front of a mirror. I think he'd chosen his costume to resemble your typical fairy tale Prince Charming as much as possible, while still making a vague attempt at being steampunk. Hence the black leather breeches and high boots with buckles along the side. I had to admit, the outfit was yummy. Definitely better than anything Disney had come up with.

Well, if he wanted to go on a quest for a drink, I wasn't going to fight him. It would let me enjoy the rising storm without distraction.

In physics, I learned you used the same formulas to study the dynamics of water and air. That always seemed weird to me, but tonight I understood. The air was thick with moisture, the scent of roses, and the coming rain. It felt more substantial than usual — its own presence, even without the wind.

I gave a gleeful pirouette, surprisingly graceful in my hoops and bustle. I felt like dancing. I could tell the wind would gladly partner me. I knew the exact pattern to follow in every muscle and sinew, as if we were moving in practiced choreography on a dance floor — the garden inhabitants and I would bend and curl, twining amongst one another. Despite the wildly whipping rose vines, no thorns would catch my hair. We were all poised, quivering in anticipation of the storm.

I skipped to the edge of the patio to better welcome the storm, raising my arms to the rush of the wind against my body. The gardens appeared to be boiling in the wind, and my blood rose as well. If only I could take off and soar with it. We would loop and spiral over the valley, wending between branches as trees waltzed, dos-à-dos with the clouds scudding in front of the moon, then race over the mountain tops. We wouldn't tire despite the rising sun. Perhaps tomorrow we would join wild geese in formation as we continued our journey.

I absorbed it all, elation coursing through my veins. Although I couldn't fly, I would overcome the obstacles before me. I was a part of it all, and we were way too powerful for trivial things like scholarship requirements to deter us for long.

I heard the patio door open. I tucked myself in next to the rose arbor, holding tight to the wild magic for the few extra seconds it would take for Liam to find me.

Wild magic . . . The thought was like a bucket of ice water. If this was the Magic, something big was going to happen and I wasn't sure I was ready. Be calm Loren, you are being fanciful . . . and remember the Magic and overcoming obstacles? Don't let go of that.

But Liam was there, interrupting my wild dance before it even started.

"Here you go, one orange juice for m'lady." Liam presented a wine goblet with a bow and a flourish.

"Thank you." It wasn't what I wanted to say. I wanted to tell Liam to go away, that I already had a partner for this dance. Then I would twirl off into the rain. The wind was a much safer option than him with the Magic about. That thought didn't seem quite right. Maybe I had been pushing things a little too hard?

Liam plucked a red rose to hand to me. "Were you waiting for me here, under the roses? Did you know *sub rosa* — meeting under the rose — was set up by secret societies to signify the meeting should be kept secret? What secrets are we keeping tonight?"

I almost snorted. I fancied the rose vines pulled back in disgust, too. And to think Dad said my thesis wouldn't have any real-world applications . . . I knew Liam was only partially right — secret societies weren't the first to associate silence with roses – that began with a Greek legend when Eros presented a rose to Harpocrates. But I didn't think bringing Eros, the god of love, into this conversation would steer it where I wanted. I settled for a small, hopefully mysterious, smile, and raised an eyebrow slightly.

I took a large swallow of my drink while I frantically tried to come up with a safe response. Something tasted off, like when I was first recovering from my concussion. No need to panic. It was a good thing Dr. Aatos was here. Maybe it was just the aftertaste from the lobster patties not going well with this orange juice? Liam had been rambling on about our budding relationship, and how he hoped to be worthy of me. His speech came complete with theatrical gestures. He didn't seem to need any input on my end, so I tuned him out to focus on keeping calm.

I tried one of the affirmations suggested by Dr. Aatos. *My intention is to bring calm and wellness into my life. My powerful resolve will help with this.* It felt like the idea was imposed from outside my brain. It wasn't working. Fine. *Loren, you will pull your shit together. You will not let the Magic or your grandmother win.* Now take a deep breath and put Liam in his place, so we can get back to the 'event of the season' and blow one more of the ridiculous requirements for the scholarship committee out of the proverbial water. I paused to see if it worked. Right, let's do this. My thoughts broke their mental huddle.

It was time to shut this down. A wave of warmth rushed over my body – a frisson, a moment of exultation. The response let me know I was on the right track. The rose vines swayed in agreement.

"Liam," I interrupted, and took another experimental swallow as I waited to get his attention. Nope, still a soapy, chemically taste. Okay, don't panic. No really, you are done with panic attacks. Remember the good feeling from before, the huddle? Break! Remember?

But a galloping heart, hyperventilation, the constriction in my chest – it surely resembled a panic attack. My vision wavered, and a single rose came into hyper focus. The petals slid, fluttering against each other in pairs before whipping open into tiny wild figures cavorting and leaping from sepal to sepal. I recognized the dance as the one I was going to join moments before. Liam didn't seem to notice the wildlings. One landed on his nose and he didn't even blink.

"I need Dr. Aatos." I managed to gasp. "I'm . . . I'm all . . ." To my horror, my legs became unstable, and I was swaying like the trees in the storm. I started to wilt in such a stereotypical manner, I almost expected to hear someone yelling for my corset strings to be cut.

"Here, sit down." Liam caught me and lowered me onto the nearby bench. I would have managed to be graceful in my collapse if the bustle hadn't gotten in the way. Grandmother would have been proud. Or would she? That thought seemed wrong somehow.

I eventually managed to sit by half collapsing against Liam. He brushed against the rose arbor, and the dancing wildlings tumbled and bounced off him. Each place they touched while pinballing and pinging off his body, a thorn sprouted — piercing his skin and clothes. Why wasn't he flinching? Surely that was painful.

"Take a deep breath." Liam smoothed a hand over my hair. How was he managing to keep his thorns from getting tangled in it? He was good. I heard myself giggle. Ugh! I don't giggle.

"No . . ." I had to take another gasp of air to continue. The smell of his cologne was a physical object forcing its way down my throat, smothering me. "Something . . . wrong." The damn corset wasn't helping. I tugged at the top of my dress trying to loosen it. If I could just get one good breath . . .

Liam knelt in front of me, peering intently. "Breathe in and out. Everything will be fine." Then he got up to sit beside me, pulling me against him. When he folded me into his arms, it was like a shroud being drawn around me. There was a rain of rose petals. I tried to push his arms away, but the air was thick now, impossible to move through. Liam sprouted more thorns where the petals landed. If I didn't look directly at him, something I didn't seem to have much control over anyway, I could almost sense an end goal in the way the thorns were transforming him.

I couldn't grasp the thought. Each inhalation was a Herculean effort taking almost the entirety of my focus. There was an eternity between each laborious heartbeat — the next beat inconceivable. My hand finally completed its odyssey and landed on Liam's arm, my palm stinging as a thorn pierced it. My efforts to push him away weren't effective.

"That's right, just relax." It sounded like Liam was speaking at the other end of a tunnel; as his voice bounced around, it scared the tiny wildlings. Blinking their sparkling dewdrop eyes in consternation, they fled.

Liam finally understood how desperate my situation was, and tried to give me mouth-to-mouth. Even as I waited for breath to fill my lungs, I watched to see what other tricks the roses and the Magic would play. I barely caught sight of one flower as its petals were revealed to be the sails of a ship that deftly rode the current of the wind. Grandmother would approve of the Magic catering to her steampunk theme.

Another breath, but it wasn't because of Liam's CPR efforts. He needed to take that Red Cross class they were always offering. It was almost like he wasn't doing CPR at all ... and he was also fumbling with my bodice ... Was he trying to help me breathe? That was wrong, wasn't it?

My heart finally beat again. Liam's hand was down my corset, lifting my breasts free. That is where he decided this was going? I should have realized earlier ... I was having to find my thoughts as they hid in a thick fog. This was more than a panic attack.

Liam's tongue crawled along the exposed mounds of my breast like a slug crawling across my skin. I still needed to tell him to stop. But I couldn't get enough air in my lungs to whisper, let alone yell. I tried for a primal scream. But the fog muffled it; I couldn't be sure if it even made it out of my head.

My heart beat again. The wildlings in the roses above me morphed into a chorus of Munch's screaming skull witnesses in shades of red and pink.

Oh good, he was stopping. Words echoed, wandering in from disparate directions. "I know you were trying to be a good princess, but I have seen how you look at me. Don't worry. This will be our little secret. I know we should wait — and Loren, you make me want to be a better man — but I am not man enough to resist you." What? The words made no sense. They weren't about panic attacks, breakdowns, or concussions. How was he missing the medical emergency here?

The more I reached for thoughts, the faster they slithered away, until the only solid idea I was able to form was that nothing was working properly. Not a toe or a finger ... I couldn't turn my head. All I could see was the rose vines waving their petals above me. My eyes were watering. My vision was blurring. I badly needed to blink.

"Don't worry about your Dad getting married," he muttered in between slobbery kisses, "It was the prod we needed to take this step. The Magic will make everything right. It means we can be together, sooner." What? No. He was the last person ...

What was I just thinking?

Liam blocked my view of the roses for a second. I heard an echoing grunt and tugs from my skirts and petticoats. As he came back into my line of sight, it finally dawned on me that the petals had turned him into a thorny beast, complete with a mane. That probably meant something . . . something with magic . . .? But what?

Air whooshed into my lungs and slid out again like the tide.

"These damn skirts are ridiculous!" I heard a tearing sound. Right. We need to stop this.

Arm — you need to work. Push.

I heard a tear, felt a strong tug. Kella. Why did she come to mind? Something about the tear would matter to her . . .

Whoosh. Blood slid through my veins.

Maybe if I collected the clues, I would figure it out. I desperately held on to them: the slug kisses on my calf now, the hoop digging into my knee, cloth running over my legs . . . Wait, what was the first thing again?

A metallic clink, then there was an explosion of petals and my tragic chorus of screamers was ripped away by the wind.

"You are so beautiful . . . and, oh yeah, and so tight. I can't wait to be inside you." Hmm, did that matter? The words didn't seem to be connecting. I couldn't actually consider them.

Nothing seemed to be interfacing with my brain.

The roses were being tugged in synchronization with my movements. We were being jostled rhythmically. Were they trying to dance with me? Or maybe they were screaming, too. Liam couldn't seem to hear them either.

All I heard was the blood pulsing in my head.

The jostling knocked the moisture pooling in my eyes loose and a tear trailed down my face. I should wipe it away. It took so much effort. I couldn't seem to remember how to move my arm.

More tears slid down the curve of my cheek.

Thump. The sound of my heart pounding made it hard to hear what Liam was saying. He did something that jostled me enough to knock my head against the trellis with a dull thud. It probably should have been painful, but it wasn't. I just wasn't a person anymore. That was easier.

Words fluttered around me, but they didn't land. "Once we are together, it will all work out for us — like it worked out for your parents when your father did this for your mother. Except it will be better because your grandmother already likes me."

"Young man, you couldn't be more incorrect." Those were different words. A different person? The arrival of a knight in shining armor? The image of my grandmother in a shining suit of armor with a unicorn mount made me think of giggling. But I couldn't remember how.

"What the hell?"

"You cannot do this."

"You know this is the only way to save Loren!"

"You aren't worthy of her!" The thorny monster was going to get slain.

"Who's going to stop me, you?" He sneered, "You practically threw her at me just like you threw Philip at her moth—"

"That's enough! Move away from her. Now!"

Another breath, another heartbeat.

I was bumped. The arbor post was more interesting than the monster. The wood grains were sliding along, each in vaguely Celtic knot patterns. There was a code there, nagging me to decipher it, but breathing took all my effort. The thorny vines pulled away from the arbor to reach toward me. We would dance. I only needed to let them embrace me.

So much effort to force air in and out . . .

Grandmother shouted something, bringing my fading attention back to the conversation floating over my head.

"I don't think so. I am going to finish this. Feel free to watch, though." The words should make sense, but somehow they didn't.

"Get away from her!" The words were starting to come in from further away. Almost floating in . . . maybe the wind was carrying them to me.

A scream, and a thud. Everything froze for a moment, even the vines wrapping around me paused.

I was lifted and Liam loomed large in my field of vision. I was propped upright once more. The vines had better access now.

The wind carried a new voice, "What is going on out here?" The words were granite blocks smashing down. Luckily, they missed my toes.

The rustle of my skirts paused.

Navy-blue words were a whisper on the wind, "No, I swear I heard a scream..."

"I thought it was an elevated sense of smell, not hearing?" The golden words did a little jig in time with laughter. "Come on, it's Halloween. It was probably someone being scared by a plastic spi—"

"Did you see anyone come out here?" The granite words didn't float. They built themselves into a wall. The wall got higher and higher. Surely it would topple soon...

"You heard it, too? Man! My hearing should be better than—" the words got caught in the vines as they trail into the sky. The golden letters attached themselves to the bare rose stems, forming shimmering, translucent blossoms.

"Connor, be quiet." The sharp edges of these words cut my skin to ribbons. Was it good or bad that I could feel again? The green of the letters seeped into my skin and spread soothingly.

Another breath. I had almost given up waiting on it.

A hand. A large hand. Over my mouth when the first words appeared. Blocking my nose, too. Huh, that might be bad. Or would it be easier than living?

My heart beat again. I wondered idly when the next breath would come. I wasn't there anyway, and drowning was supposed to be peaceful.

"Over there!" I tried to hang on as a turret formed on the wall. I wanted to see what the finished castle looked like, but it was swallowed by the waiting darkness and the thorny vines.

CHAPTER 19

I had never realized my grandmother was old. It seemed like a ridiculous oversight in retrospect, but somehow the force of her personality — her will — always overshadowed her physical presence.

The woman lying on the hospital bed shocked me. This wilted person, whose body was so frail I was worried she would collapse from the weight of her blanket, was my grandmother. Each breath she took made her whole body heave. I turned to Henri, uncertain if I really wanted to know.

"Is she okay?"

He wheeled me further into the room until I was close enough to grasp the hand resting on top of the scratchy hospital sheet. Her skin was so thin I almost expected to see muscles and tendons alongside the knobby, blue veins. I cradled her hand gently, for the sake of both our bruises. She stirred slightly but didn't wake.

Henri picked up the clipboard at the end of her bed and flipped through it.

"It looks like the worst of it is a broken hip, no brain trauma associated with the head bump as far as they can tell; otherwise minor scrapes and lacerations. Although, they have her on some pretty strong pain medication . . ." He put the clipboard back with a metallic thump, "And I didn't tell you any of that, because I would like to keep my license."

"What do we need to do about the broken hip? Will they want to put her in therapy? She will need a nurse, won't she?"

Henri walked over and knelt in front of my wheelchair. He looked at me with such gentleness, I had to blink hard to hold back the tears. I couldn't take anyone being too kind to me right now. I turned my head a bit to gaze over his shoulder at the hand again. The age spots reminded me of the pattern on the linoleum tiles. I had been paying a lot of attention to the floor, too.

"Loren, I know you are worried about her, but she has a whole team of people here who will take care of her. Ms. Millie and Stanley are on their way. Right now, we need to focus on getting you taken care of."

Frowning sent another wave of pain through my head. We were back to that again. I knew something was deeply wrong, even before I fully regained consciousness. Fear and an antiseptic smell, which couldn't be mistaken for anything but a hospital, lodged in my throat making it hard to breathe. I would have hidden away in the blackness if I hadn't desperately needed something to drink. It still tasted like something had died in my mouth, but they wouldn't let me brush my teeth. I ran my tongue across my teeth hoping it would help.

"Now that you have seen your grandmother, we need you to make some decisions." My thoughts shied away from what those decisions might entail. It was easier to focus on the skin stretched across Grandmother's metacarpals, like the strands of a spider web.

His voice kept getting softer, "It is your decision as to whether or not the nurse does an exam, but doing it now will gather the best evidence if there is a chance you might want to press charges. It leaves your options open." The pain in his voice broke my concentration.

I turned my head to focus on him in time to catch a tear slipping from his downcast eyes. There was something mesmerizing about the display of emotion from such a physically strong person. Strong people aren't supposed to be able to be hurt.

"Loren, I am so sorry. I can't believe . . ." He didn't seem to know how to finish the sentence. My hand floated up to wipe his tear away before I realized it was happening.

A throat cleared from behind us. "Henri, we need to talk to Loren before you do." Chief Duncan's voice lacked its usual snap. He seemed beyond exhausted. I turned my head a fraction to see him at the door.

"Right . . . right. Sorry."

Chief Duncan cleared his throat. I saw him shift his weight from foot to foot in my peripheral vision. "I don't mean to pressure you in any way, but the nurse is available to do a rape kit, if that is what you decide you want."

There was that word. I had avoided even thinking it. Had I been raped? I mean, he had done . . . stuff, but how far had it gone? Everything surrounding those memories was muzzy.

I hadn't been able to remember anything at first, but the fog was lifting slowly. I could recall odd fragments, but there was no cohesiveness, no order to it all. What I remembered was awful, but the idea of him thrusting into me was vile on a whole other level. My stomach rebelled against the thought. Not knowing wasn't going to put my mental health in a good place if I let myself think about it — any of it.

Chief Duncan continued, "You don't have to do the kit to press charges, but the DNA result may change what we can charge him with."

Henri was with me when I woke, but he had struggled to talk to me about what happened. The nurse interrupted before he finished telling me about how he, Connor, and Chief Duncan came outside to find Liam with both Grandmother and me unconscious. Liam's plan had been fairly obvious — my rumpled skirts hiked up, torn and flung underwear, his pants unzipped.

Henri rode to the hospital with Grandmother while Chief Duncan came with me, Henri updating both sets of EMTs en route. Chief Duncan had Liam arrested. Connor had stayed to give a statement and help wrap up the party and make excuses for the hostesses being absent. Kella promised to help too, although she was angry about there not being enough space in the ambulances for her to come, too. She made Henri promise to tell me she would come as soon as she kicked the last guest out.

Worrying about the party didn't even occur to me until I was reassured it was taken care of. I didn't even remember it was going on until it was mentioned. Those concerns joined the thoughts circling my head like vultures. I needed to know what happened. But did I really *want* to know? A dizzy spell hit, and the pressing lack of oxygen forced me to concentrate on breathing. But the hospital smell I drew in with each breath wasn't helping. Come on Loren, passing out again won't accomplish anything!

When I caught my breath I asked, "Would the tests help tell how far . . . things . . . went?" I couldn't bear to say the word 'penetrate,' and I didn't know who to direct the question toward. I just hoped one of them knew.

Chief Duncan answered, his voice carefully even. "There is no guarantee, but the nurse can swab you and the DNA tests can tell fairly accurately if there are any cells with Y-chromosomes present." But could it tell from what kind of cells, like from skin or . . . or . . . the other kind? I should know if those cells were different from skin cells if you put them under a microscope. Hell, I had drawn them for a class exercise. Why couldn't I remember?

Henri added, "It may help you know what happened."

The need to know was building to an unbearable pressure, causing my head to throb and my hands to shake. I swallowed twice before I got it out. "Let's get it over with, then."

"Loren, is there someone you want to stay with you? I will get them for you. Or if you want, I will stay with you . . .?" Henri suggested hesitantly.

I shook my head slowly while considering. I wasn't sure if there was anyone I would be comfortable with. Grandmother wasn't available and she needed Millie, not that I wanted them there anyway. It was too horrible to put them through and too embarrassing. And princesses don't do that kind of thing. I wanted to ask for Kella, but I didn't want to wait for her to get there. I wanted this all done. Also, I didn't want anyone else to know about this. I didn't want anyone else around me to treat me like I was broken, even if I was. And kind of had been for a while.

"Loren?" Henri's gentle tone brought me back to the question at hand. Umm, decision time. Well, being alone didn't sound good, and I didn't want anyone else involved. That made him the only option.

"Could you not watch?" Ugh! That quaver in my voice sounded pathetic.

"Whatever you need."

The tears started again, and I couldn't seem to make them stop.

CHAPTER 20

Everything spun as I jerked upright. I was forced to raise trembling hands to my forehead to bring all the circling loops of my vision back into alignment. Whatever woke me was loud. My ears were still ringing.

As the adrenaline surge faded, I became aware of my surroundings. Namely, that I wasn't in my room. How did I get here? Why didn't I remember? I was so tired of these setbacks. I would have to see Dr. Aatos again. Perhaps he could figure me out.

A furious bellow interrupted my thoughts. What *was* that? It certainly wasn't helping my transition into wakefulness. I hadn't slept well, and if I prodded, I would remember the dreams that made my sleep so restless. I was perfectly happy not to remember them though. I pulled the pillow over my head. I let the dream fragments evaporate, carefully monitoring the process without getting too close.

I could stay here — hide out in this room. It was an appealing idea. But chances were the roaring was related to me. I didn't have enough information as it was: too much I didn't remember, too many secrets, too much I didn't know.

I wasn't sure I could take not knowing one more thing. With a sigh, I dragged myself out of bed. I wasn't going to be sneaking up on anyone with how stiff I was. My popping joints and creaky body would surely give me away.

Hmm, that was my bag. I didn't remember packing it though. Ugh, maybe I hadn't . . . Why were there only princess clothes? I wanted my cozy clothes. The ridiculous bathrobe that matched the lacey nightgown I was wearing would have to do. At least my legs would be covered.

I took the time to tie all three of the bows lacing the bodice. The gauzy layers weren't substantial enough armor to face the world. Knights got iron and steel, but princesses have to rely on silks and lace. Weren't knights supposed to be the brave ones? Talk about a rigged system.

I cracked the door and peeked out. The roaring seemed to be off in another part of the house, but there was no reason to be careless.

As I crept through the halls toward the snarls — the angry noises started forming muffled words – that was a good sign, right? I was a bit distracted by the art deco styling. Whose home was this?

I stopped outside the room the growls were emanating from. I leaned in to listen, and almost knocked a framed print of a nude woman reclining on a crescent moon off the wall. Was that Henri speaking? Was this his house? I would have imagined his décor would be more along the lines of an English hunting lodge – heavy leather chairs, dark wood, deep masculine colors . . .

My ear wasn't quite pressed against the door, so it didn't count as eavesdropping, right?

"Don't you tell me to calm down! This is a fucking mess!"

There was a brief pause in the bellowing.

"What is wrong with you? Of course, I am involved! What did you expect? I was there, holding her hand last night at the hospital because there wasn't anyone better. That procedure was awful. And she didn't complain once, but the whole time, tears were dripping down her cheeks." I heard a pounding noise followed almost immediately by a cracking noise. "I couldn't do a damned thing to help. If you can tell me you wouldn't get emotionally involved, then you are almost as big of a dick as he is!"

Okay, that was Henri doing the yelling. From the one-sided conversation, I could guess he was on the phone. He mentioned a hospital. Had something happened to me? No — wait . . . Did something happen to Grandmother? Why couldn't I remember? My blood started pounding in my ears, making it hard to make out Henri's yelling.

"No, this was what you planned from the start."

. . .

"You aren't as clever as you think you are. You had better get over here. You are going to help me deal with this mess."

. . .

"Shit, what am I going to tell Dad? This is going to kill him!"

. . .

"I will expect you here within the nex—"

"You must be Loren." I nearly jumped out of my own skin, but still managed to spin around to see who had crept up behind me, clutching my robe as protection.

"Oops! Sorry, I didn't mean to startle you. I'm Henri's friend, Paulo."

Another great looking guy — didn't this town do anything normally? The sides of his dark hair were undercut, and the longer middle hair was tempted to curl. His long lashes swept over warm brown eyes. This might have made him appear soft and vulnerable, but a slight crook in his nose saved him from that. The muscles peeking out from the rolled-up sleeves of his oxford shirt didn't hurt, either. It was all enough to make me take a step back. The easy grin fell off his lips, and he casually withdrew the hand he held out for me to shake. I appreciated that he was trying not to make me feel awkward, but I couldn't seem to find my social graces anywhere.

"I really am sorry. I'm a veterinarian and I've gotten in the habit of moving carefully so I don't startle the animals I work with. It does mean I tend to startle people, though." His self-deprecating smile invited me to be disgruntled with him, instead of with myself.

"What do you say to some breakfast? I stopped by to see if I could help this morning after Henri canceled on me, and so far, food is the only thing I have been able to think of, so I hope you are prepared to be stuffed. What would you like? I could do French toast? An omelet? Henri has a waffle maker somewhere . . . Shall we see if we can pry Henri out of his office for some breakfast?"

Somehow, even the idea of food was far too much for me to consider.

He didn't wait for me to answer but turned and barged right on into the library. I lingered in the doorway, distracted by the rows of books. I was just reaching for the light switch when Paulo let out a high-pitched yelp, similar to what his furry patients might make if you stepped on their tail. "Oh my . . . You weren't exaggerating."

Henri growled, "Fifteen minutes, Connor!" I peeked around the doorframe. He was sitting behind a desk in a swivel chair, and his back was to me. His shadowy bulk leaned forward as he slammed the old-fashioned phone back on its cradle with a bang.

Paulo hadn't moved, and now Henri slowly swiveled toward him.

"If anything, I would say I understated the issue." The words were said calmly, but there were underlying notes of despair, rage, and frustration. "Have you warned Loren, yet?"

"Umm . . . no. To be honest, I didn't think it could be as bad as you said it was." Paulo deflated — gone was the bonhomie, replaced by a tightly strung fragility that made my emotional status seem robust. We were a mess over here. I knew what my problem was. It was nice to have a concussion to blame things on, but what was wrong with the guys?

Henri sighed, "Loren, how much did Connor tell you about my family's, umm, peculiarities?"

"Umm . . ." I racked my brain, trying to figure out what he was referring to. We had hardly talked about his family. Most of what I knew was from Liam. I wasn't sure I trusted any of it now. Why was that? I tried to smooth the cringe off my face. Maybe there was something to that social mask my grandmother always talked about. I leaned my forehead against the doorframe trying to recover.

"Do you want me to tell her?" Paulo asked.

There was a vague wave from the Henri shadow.

Paulo turned back toward me. "Why don't you come sit with me, here." He led me over to a couch near the window. Sun poured from the window over the couch. The beams of light felt like a spotlight given the stark contrast to the rest of the room. I tried not to flinch when Paulo touched my elbow. I was twitchy this morning.

After settling me, Paulo sat and turned toward me, every line of his body showing he was engaged and ready for a cozy chat. He was good — I found myself relaxing the muscles that had been trying to pull my body into a ball. I bet even the most direly wounded animals trusted him.

"Well, as you know, fairy tales are real. Some of the critters in those tales are also real." He paused for me to react.

"Oh that. Yes, I knew about the werewolves. Connor told me because of Liam." I stuttered when I said Liam's name. There was something there. I gingerly circled the idea in my head. A grimace wrinkled Paulo's forehead.

"Right. Well, did Connor tell you it was an x-linked inherited trait?"

"What?" I knew this stuff, but I was having trouble processing the connections. Did everything go back to genetics around here?

"It means being a werewolf will run in a family — more specifically through the women in the family. Liam is a werewolf and his mother and Henri's mother are sisters. So, Henri has hypertrichosis just like Liam."

"Oh. Right." I swallowed and nodded. I needed to carry that family tree of Connor's around with me to keep track of all this. "So Henri is a prince *and* a werewolf? He got screwed by genetics from both sides? That doesn't seem fair."

"It really isn't," Henri muttered. "You'd think the Magic wouldn't have allowed it. I mean it was supposed to be a fifty-fifty chance on the hair."

Paulo ignored the tone in Henri's voice. "It is commonly thought hypertrichosis shows up in the strongest of the wolves as an indication of who the next leaders will be. Kind of like the wolf is so strong it shows through even in the human form, and while that's great and all, it does create some problems outside the Pack. Nowadays, those born with it generally have their hair removed to make life easier, and to help keep our secret."

"That makes sense. What I don't understand is why we are discussing it . . ." And how Paulo knew all of this. Where did he fit into everything?

"Well, do you remember when you were basically forced to stay with Henri last night?"

Not really, no . . .

I was about to answer when the doorbell rang. Paulo popped up, "Be right back. Somebody needs to get that, might as well be me! Won't be but a minute."

A deep sigh came from the shadows around Henri's chair. "Well, he's not taking this well."

"What about you? Are you okay? What's wrong?" I wasn't sure if I was asking about him, or myself.

"It's . . ." he heaved another sigh and then paused. The pause stretched long enough I was tempted to go hug him or prod for what I could do to help. He responded before I decided what to do. "Let's just say the Magic is making me regret wishing things were different. They were actually amazing."

Paulo breezed into the room. "Look who the cat dragged in . . ."

My father followed him. He must have come after hearing about the hospital stuff last night, after hearing about Grandmother. It was astounding he dropped everything to come, given how tense our relationship was recently. He hadn't even come for my first accident which was on my birthday.

I jumped up and raced over to him. "Dad! You came!"

It wasn't until I threw my arms around him and hugged him that I saw Emilia was with him. Ugh! She was wearing a bubblegum pink sweater. No way that was an accident.

My father tolerated my hug for only a few seconds before stepping back. Emilia pasted on a huge smile. "Loren, how nice to see you!" Emilia hugged my stiff body more tightly than my dad. Right, not buying it. Remember when you threatened to quit if you had to work with me? The Magic arranged for exactly the right person to be an evil stepmother. I wasn't going to trust her act for a second.

"It was such a beautiful drive to get here! The trees and the leaves, oh my! Simply gorgeous! I am so glad Philip suggested a visit! And we stopped at the cutest little antique mall and roadside stand on the way here."

Huh, they stopped to shop instead of coming straight here?

She paused for someone to comment but when there was no gushing back, she plowed right on into the awkward silence. "Oh, I almost forgot! I got you something." Almost forgot? She had been holding the white bag the entire time, and had, in fact, thumped it against my barely healed ribs while hugging me. Now she was thrusting it toward my right hand like she couldn't see the brace on it. I just got my left hand wrapped around the handle when she announced, "They are local organic apples!"

I snatched my hand back so quickly the bag handle ripped, and apples went flying everywhere.

Emilia's mouth formed an almost comically round 'O' in her shock before she shrieked, "What is wrong with you?" Um, yup. Those are the true colors I was expecting.

Paulo jumped forward to help gather the apples. Meanwhile, I stood gaping at her trying to invent a plausible reason for freaking out about apples. How do you explain to someone that you suspect she is an evil bitch — oops, I meant witch, really I did — out to get you, and perhaps the apples she gave you are poisonous? I mean, without sounding like a lunatic, that is.

Henri stepped in, "I guess you didn't know Loren is allergic to apples." I almost laughed, of course she didn't know. What a way to phrase it. It was as good a cover as any . . .

I threw Henri a grateful glance for his quick thinking.

Dad wasn't having any of it, "Since when?!"

"It's a recent thing," I said weakly. Recent as in the last two minutes. "I'm—"

"Loren, you need to apologize to Emilia." The words were already on my lips, but now that he was ordering me to . . .

"What?"

"You heard me. I see exactly what is going on. I won't be made into a villain again!"

Again? "Dad, what in the world are you talking about?"

Before my father responded, the distant chime of the doorbell sounded again.

Paulo popped the last of the apples into the torn bag. "Wow, it's like Grand Central Station around here today! Why don't I go see who that is? Be back in a jiff."

Henri saved the day yet again by breaking the suffocating tension. "So, what brings you here, Mr. Hughes?"

"Oh please, call me Philip! Mr. Hughes makes me feel old. I'm here to meet Loren's fiancé of course!" He glanced around like he expected someone to pop out of the woodwork. "So, where is the lucky man?"

Huh? I needed someone to trade a confused look with. I couldn't see Henri well enough to do that.

"Can't wait to meet him. I like a man that is willing to take charge and make things happen. Sounds like he will be a perfect match for you, Doodle. Opposites attract and all that. Sounded solid — it will help balance you out. Plus, you can tag along while he works! He can hunt his beasties while you hunt plants for your little drawings."

I was too bewildered to say anything. I sat abruptly on the chair behind me. My fiancé? What the hell? How did I get engaged without knowing about it?

Henri cleared his throat, "Am I to understand Liam called you?"

WHAT! Liam, my fiancé?

"Sure did. Wanted to ask for my blessing. Is he here?" He turned toward me. "Speaking of which, why are you here? You ought to answer your cell phone! You were impossible to track down. That prune-faced maid of your grandmother would only say the last time she saw you was at the hospital. I had to raise hell at the hospital to get someone there to tell me where you were."

I hadn't felt great when I woke up, and my father wasn't helping. A vise tightened at my temples with every word that flew out of his mouth. The headache was getting so bad I wasn't sure I could make it through the entire conversation without vomiting on Henri's oriental rug.

"Mr. Hughes, er, Philip — last night . . . Well, there was an . . . incident last night."

"An incident?" My father's eyes narrowed, and he turned a suspicious look toward me.

Paulo came back into the room with Chief Duncan.

Dad saw the uniform and jumped to all sorts of conclusions. "What sort of mess have you gotten yourself into now, young lady?" The words were practically spat at me.

Emilia snorted. "You just can't stay out of trouble, can you?"

The accusations were so unfair — at least I felt they were — and yet, I didn't know why I would expect anything else from Dad.

"Ms. Hughes is not in any sort of trouble with the law." Chief Duncan was frowning fiercely as he addressed my father and Emilia. "I only need to have a few words and get a statement from her."

"Did you need to talk to me now, Chief Duncan?" Please say yes, please say yes.

"Whenever it is con—"

"Duncan, huh? I should have known you would be mixed up in this somehow!"

Whoa! The looks those two were giving each other . . . I was glad I wasn't standing between them! They seemed as pissed off as I was, hearing there was a fiancé I didn't know about.

Did I dare try to diffuse the situation? I stood and walked over to stand next to the chief — not between the two of them, but close enough to break their stare down. "I am free now. Henri, do you have somewhere we could talk?"

"We just got here! I'm sure whatever it is can wait. We'll have Loren give you a call later in the week. We have lunch plans."

We did? Did he plan that with Liam, too? Something inside me snapped. "Actually Dad, I would like to get this over with. Then I need a nap. I am exhausted."

My father grabbed me by the arm and yanked me to his side. I shrieked as stabbing pains shot up my not-quite-healed arm. "Don't use that tone with me, young lady!" He was turning red, and the vein in his forehead was bulging as he hissed at me. "Partying all night and being hungover is no excuse for such disrespectful behavior."

His grip tightened. "Dad, you are hurting me!" I started pulling at his hand.

Chief Duncan was suddenly there, grabbing Dad's wrist. "I suggest you let go." His tone was closer to a growl than a voice, it was so menacing.

"Who are you to tell me how to behave?"

"I'm the Chief of Police. That's who. Now you can let go, or I will be happy to charge you with every last thing I can think of including assault, disturbing the peace, and I am just itching for a reason to charge you with your crimes from twenty-five years ago. The ONLY reason I haven't arrested you before now is that Aurora begged me not to. She's dead. Don't. Tempt. Me." The last three clipped words rang, each their own distinct sentence. There was something big floating right out of reach, but I was too tired and upset to get it to coalesce.

Dad stepped back, surprised anyone would challenge him. He usually had better command of a situation. "What? You can't charge me now!"

"Under North Carolina law, there isn't any statute of limitations for rape. You can research the matter if you don't believe me — under Chapter 15."

Oh my god. Fragments from the last twenty-four hours fell into place and my knees gave out. I sank into a crouch and buried my head in my knees. It didn't shut the noise out though. I couldn't process the images slamming into my mind.

"Oh please," he scoffed, "Everyone will say you are a sore loser because I stole your girl! I will sue you for defamation and maligning my character! It will be your word against mine."

"It won't. Roselle Dalton is willing to testify. Loren's rape last night made Mrs. Dalton reconsider her position."

The chief's words sat there, swallowing all the oxygen in the room, and stalling the conversation. Liam's atrocious, no that wasn't right – abominable? Appalling? Deplorable? Dreadful? Horrific? It was impossible to find an awful enough word for it. I couldn't raise my gaze, couldn't handle seeing anyone's reaction.

"Shit!" Dad drew the word out into two incredulous syllables. "Is that what all this is about? You realize you are likely blowing some drunken misunderstanding out of proportion."

I heard a meaty crack.

"Don't even think about opening your mouth again." That was Henri. I hadn't heard him move, and it startled me enough that I jerked my head up. Henri's back blocked most of my view, but I could still see the look of total shock on my father's face as he held his hands over his nose.

"What the fu– "

Henri punched my father in the stomach. Chief Duncan stood impassively by, examining his nails. "So . . . Paulo, what color did you decide to paint the clinic van?"

"We decided on yellow. It's not the most aesthetic color choice. But safety first . . . it will be useful when we are on the side of the road like when with the horse that got hit by a car near the riding trails."

There were a few sucking gulps and then, shockingly, I heard my dad laugh.

"That's the way of it, is it?"

Dad walked over to a table in the hall while cradling his jaw. He grabbed a rose out of the flower arrangement, pulling half the other flowers out of the vase as he did so. What? Flowers?

He came back into the room and flung it at Henri. "There. She's all yours. Good luck with that. God knows I am done with her." Dad grabbed a gaping, stuttering Emilia and dragged her from the room.

Everyone that remained turned to look at me to see my reaction, including Henri. That is when I saw he was absolutely covered in hair.

Oh my.

CHAPTER
21

"You will need a Lumière and Cogsworth of course." Paulo was chatting merrily away as he flipped pancakes. "That's where I come in. I get to be Lumière . . ." He performed a fancy bow, complete with a sword salute done with his spatula. "And fuss britches over there," a spatula gesture at Connor, "can play Cogsworth."

The grin he gave Connor was edging out of the mischievous range and toward evil. I sat perched on a stool at the kitchen island, toying with my vintage, cut-crystal juice glass while Connor and Paulo twittered at each other like territorial songbirds.

Paulo slid pancakes onto a plate, added butter, and a small lake of syrup, and put them in front of me. I stared at the plate. He didn't expect me to eat after that scene, did he? I picked up my fork, but I couldn't make myself take a bite. The sweet smell of the syrup hit my nose and I swallowed convulsively. Learning my father raped my mother left me so nauseated I wasn't sure I would ever eat again.

Apparently, Henri was the person Connor originally planned for the role of Beast. Their current theory was that when I was forced to stay with him because no one at the hospital would approve my discharge if I was staying at Grandmother's on my own, it was enough for the Magic to latch onto the

'Beauty and the Beast' tale. We needed a beast, so the Magic regrew all the hair Henri removed years ago.

I wasn't convinced. It was a bit tumbled about from either the classic or Disney retelling of the story. But I wasn't in any mental state to form a coherent argument or counterplan. Instead, I was sitting there, allowing myself to be numb. And nauseated — how was it possible to be both?

Paulo eventually broke off bickering with Connor when he noticed my full plate. "You aren't eating. Are the pancakes okay? I can make you something else instead. French toast? Crèpes? An omelet?"

I forced myself into action, pushing the plate ever so slightly away. "I'm sorry, Paulo. I don't think I can eat anything. I am just so tired."

Connor looked me over with a critical eye, making me realize I was still in my nightgown. Did I really meet with my father, Emilia, and the chief in it? Ugh.

"Maybe a nap . . .?"

It would be easier than trying to be social, so I nodded. "Yes. I'm going back to bed. Thank you for the pancakes, Paulo. Maybe I can finish them later?"

"You let me know when you are hungry, and I'll prepare a culinary cabaret. I am going to go brush up on the lyrics of "Be Our Guest" while I am at it. See what I can do about locating some dancing flatware." He smiled at me and I dredged up a weak grin for him as I slid off the stool.

"Thank you."

I heard whispers and a scuffle behind me. When I paused by the kitchen door to look back, the three guys straightened and gave me angelic smiles. Paulo put his elbow into Henri's ribs, not indelicately from the grunt that followed.

"Loren, would you join me for dinner?" Henri managed to appear sullen and vulnerable at the same time. Quite a feat with his ultimately masculine face covered with fine dark hair. Paulo nudged him in the ribs again. "Please?"

Then it hit me — I was going to have to stay here. I was trapped by the Magic, and it had chosen my future spouse for me. The blood drained from my face and the edges of my vision started to fill in with oscillating black spots. I grabbed the door frame for support.

Shit, what was my line? Was I supposed to agree and not show up later, or refuse? I couldn't remember. It was like the time I tried to be in our high school's Shakespeare performance and had nightmares about forgetting what came in Act 5. All I could remember was "A horse! A horse! My kingdom for a horse!" which wasn't even my line.

I didn't want to hurt Henri. I didn't object to him so much as being forced into this situation. Would he think I was rejecting him, or would he realize I was just playing the part? I wanted to get away to process it all without anyone watching. But now I'd waited too long to say something. Awkward.

Without prompting, Grandmother's voice floated through my head. "If you can't say something appropriate, it is sometimes better not to say anything at all." I had laughed at the time, as she didn't know she was modifying what had become an adage. I mulled the idea over for a second and decided it fit the situation. What a simple solution. I turned away and walked back to my room.

I wandered down the hall – a bit like an aimless spirit in my old-fashioned nightgown. I hated feeling so lost. "This simply won't do." Another bit of grandmotherly wisdom, also true.

I needed to find direction, take charge in some way. Perhaps a list? When I am overwhelmed, I like to make lists. I find they create order out of chaos. The thought alone had me straightening my spine.

Maybe I needed two lists. Things I could do something about, and things I couldn't yet do anything about. I needed to remember "yet" was the key word there, and stop fretting about anything on that list until "yet" got here.

New business or old business first? How about having a mental breakdown — that seemed fair. Ugh. Not helpful, Loren. Try again. How about we start with something easy? Okay. Let's see . . .

Item 1: Get dressed. Being in actual clothes would help me feel like less of an invalid, less breakable. It would be a good start. Plus, it was a very doable task.

Maybe with armor on I would be able to tackle something a bit harder. Something with a deadline even . . .

Item 2: Read over the statement the chief left with me and sign it. Correct as necessary.

It was bad enough telling everything to the chief the first time. I didn't want to have to read through it all, perhaps relive it. I also didn't want the task hanging over me for the next couple of days. Better get it over with, assuming I could manage it.

The statement was ostensibly why the chief stopped by. He brought Henri his statement as well. Despite that, it felt like an excuse to check in on me. Which was kind, given the rest of our history and all. Does that mean he doesn't suspect me of murder any longer? I mulled over the information he had provided. If I was lucky, the DNA evidence collected the night before might be ready in about 8 months, although 2 years was more likely. It was stunning that I went through all of that and it might not even matter. The case against Liam was pretty solid though, given there were plenty of witnesses.

They would apparently be prosecuting Liam with or without my testimony. Another thing to consider – how involved did I want to get with the trial? Would that count as 1A? Maybe I needed to give myself time to think about it. Otherwise, it might be a while before I got to the second item on my list.

Speaking of a second item, how about the stuff that happened while Chief Duncan was here?

Item 3: Freak out about the family history revealed today. Get details.

I mean, holy shit! The chief and my mom? I gently prodded the idea. Dad raped Mom? Ugh, that was too hard to unpack right now. For multiple reasons. Why did they stay together? It was incomprehensible.

Getting details was going to be tricky. People who might know those details: my father, my grandmother, the chief, and . . . who else? My father didn't seem like he would give me the full, unbiased story. Grandmother and the chief likely had some painful personal memories involved. Was I comfortable pushing? I mulled it over. I would prefer an alternative . . . Maybe Connor knew? He collected everyone's stories after all. Connor would have to do as a starting point.

What else did I need to do? No, not freaking out. That wasn't going on the list, remember? Maybe some research, now that we were full tilt into a tale. It didn't seem at all questionable now.

Item 4: Watch Disney's "Beauty and the Beast" again . . .

I was going to have the movie memorized pretty soon, but it felt necessary. Perhaps it would help with finding a way forward. That should go on the list. It would also be a little bit of fun. Maybe I could get Henri and Paulo to join me in a sing-a-long. I bet Paulo makes fancy popcorn too, sprinkled with cheese or caramel.

Item 5: Decide how to react to the decisions the Magic made. Consider talking to Connor about whether any changes could be made, and what I would have to do to make that happen.

Was it too late for Henri to back out?

I gave a mental snort. I just loved how I was acting like I had any choice in the matter.

And next on the list . . . Ugh, fine, Loren. Honestly, a good cry was reasonable given the situation. The situations even. I was scared it would be hard to stop once I got started. But realistically, it was all going to hit me at some point. I couldn't stay numb forever. Better make time for it.

Item 6: Get dark chocolate. And chips — the cheddar and sour cream ones.

Hmmm. And Millie's chocolate croissants, if she had time to make them. Would comfort food help? Wasn't that the standard? Drawing always worked in the past, so I hadn't tried the whole pint-of-ice-cream-and-a-spoon thing. But drawing wasn't an option now. I needed to figure out something to look forward to. Some bright spots in my days . . .

At that point, I reached the guest room. I couldn't be trusted to remember my list without writing it down. Especially since there were more things to add. Getting real clothes for instance. I needed some paper and a pen.

I sat on the bed to check the nightstand and tiredness hit. It was almost like a physical blow. Not enough sleep last night for sure. That, or I was about to become Sleeping Beauty. I almost didn't care; at least then I wouldn't have to figure anything else out immediately.

Maybe sleep needed to come before everything else. Everything on the list could move down a spot to make way for Item 1: Take a nap.

CHAPTER 22

I woke later to a quiet knock on the door. I glanced at the clock even as I said, "Come in."

Whoa! Some nap! The light outside my window was fading in the late afternoon.

"Loren?" It was Miss Millie. "Hi, sweetheart." She came in, carefully balancing a tray that she set on my bedside table. Fragrant herbal steam rushed toward me as Millie leaned in to give me a hug. "I was so worried about you. I went to the hospital yesterday morning after dealing with your dad, and couldn't believe you were gone. I would have come sooner, but your grandmother needed me. Henri said you were still asleep, anyway."

"Yesterday?" Wait, how long had I slept?

Millie shrugged philosophically. "Sleep is healing. Your body needed the rest."

The rest of what Millie said filtered through. "Is Grandmother okay?"

"She is a little shaky, but the doctors say she will recover. She is going to need help until she can walk again. This afternoon I am going to try to find a nurse she won't be able to cow before the introductions are completed."

"Good luck!" I couldn't picture it happening. "Maybe you can find a retired drill sergeant? He can order her to relax. I am not sure who I would feel sorrier for!"

Millie laughed, shaking her head at me. "Probably the drill sergeant."

She cleared her throat, "On a more serious note Loren . . ." A long pause while Millie picked at the bedspread. I wasn't going to like this, was I? "Henri said the nurse at the hospital didn't get a chance to talk to you about a prescription before you left, just in case . . ."

A prescription? "I told them I wanted to wait for test results before taking any antibiotics." I'd been over this already . . . they inevitably upset my stomach.

Ms. Millie shook her head. "No, you need to decide within another day or so on this, sweetie." She was staring at me expectantly, waiting for the light bulb. I shook my head and shrugged. I knew the blank look was still on my face.

"Unless you maybe wanted to keep it."

It?

She raised her eyebrows at me. It?

Shit.

IT!

Fuck.

Was I *pregnant*? It had never occurred to me. What the hell was wrong with me?

Connor's damn wall chart flashed into my mind: seventh sons, my promise to myself to be redundant . . . This was beyond bad.

"Oh my god!" How would that change things? If I was pregnant, would I have to marry him? After *that*?!

There was no way. The Magic could do whatever the hell it wanted. Not a chance.

"I have some tea." She held it out in both hands, an offering. "It will take care of anything if that is what you want . . . But you would need to decide soon."

I couldn't do it. I couldn't raise his child — having parts of him inside me for nine months! The possibility alone made me want to vomit.

But what if my mom had made the same decision? Shit — my mom went through this, too! Was that why she and Dad stayed together? Because of me? I wish she could be here now.

I wasn't ready to be a parent. I couldn't take good care of myself recently! Adoption was an option — but what about the Magic? Would adoption mean I was trying to escape destiny and qualify this as a fate tale? I was pretty sure as far as the Magic was concerned, having a baby would tie me to him. I couldn't do it. I didn't want to see him ever again. Shit!

I cleared my parched throat. "Is Connor around?"

Millie blinked owlishly. "Connor?"

"Yes, I need to ask him about the Magic."

"Oh. We could call him?" I nodded. "I'll go get the phone for you. You drink this in the meantime. It is good for stress." She rearranged the cups on the tray to give me the other option.

I wrapped my hands around the cup and inhaled its scent. "What's in it? It smells good."

Millie paused in the doorway, "Mostly chamomile, lemon balm, peppermint, lavender, and honey. I'll be right back!"

I sipped the tea while I waited. I didn't have the energy to rail against the Magic. I wanted to, but I was too tired. Why couldn't I remember how far things went? Knowing would settle a lot of this. Perhaps someone could ask him. No, we wouldn't be able to trust his answer. Asking wouldn't help.

How would this play out if it was a fate tale? The thing you were trying to avoid happened anyway, right? So, would I have anything to lose if I tried to avoid it? The worst that would happen is expended effort, right? Could anything get twisted to make it worse? Everyone seemed to think the Magic latched onto Henri instead. So, wouldn't that mean Liam was out of the picture? And if that was the case, I shouldn't be pregnant . . .

Okay, let's set the Magic aside for a minute. What did I want? I didn't know how I would raise a child without being resentful every day of the choices made *for* me, instead of *by* me. I mean, I might want to consider being a mother someday, maybe, but not like this. Not now. I put the tea down while I considered.

Did I owe Liam's cells the right to live in me for nine months? I mean, technically the baby was innocent, but could I handle being pregnant? I tried to imagine it. It would be a daily reminder. All the appointments and strangers touching me, having to go through birth – it would be another way of having my body taken without my consent. The weight of it crushed the air out of my lungs. Just like that night. Oh god . . . My heart was hammering its way through my ribcage. I couldn't get enough air into my lungs. Liam's hand was over my face. I was drowning again. I clutched at the blanket so I wouldn't fall over.

I CLUTCHED the blankets. I wasn't frozen.

I wasn't being raped.

I could move.

I flexed my fingers again and clenched my toes.

Dr. Aatos' lecture flashed through my brain. Anxiety and hyperventilating are linked in both directions. "Control your breathing, control the anxiety." I forced myself to take a deep breath. I practically choked, but I made myself do it again. And again. I forced myself to unclench, working toward relaxing my body. A high-pitched ringing started in my left ear.

Breathe in, 2, 3, 4. Hold . . . And now out 2, 3, 4.

Breathe in, 2, 3, 4. Hold . . . And now out 2, 3, 4.

Breathe in, 2, 3, 4. Hold . . . And now out 2, 3, 4.

And again. And again.

After a minute, I was able to lay back on the bed. My body was coated in a film of congealed sweat.

Did I have the energy to shower? It would require moving. Huh . . . Maybe in a minute I would find the energy.

I woke up when I heard voices coming down the hall. Darkness had taken over the room while I slept.

"Loren, dear?" Millie was knocking on my door.

"Yes?"

Millie cracked the door and light spilled across the floor. "Loren? Connor is here. We thought we could get together to update everyone and discuss options."

I leaned over to my nightstand and turned on the light. A frown flickered across Millie's face and settled in as a furrowed brow. "Maybe a shower and some clothes would be good first?"

I must look rough. I almost laughed. "I do want a shower. I'll try to be there soon."

Millie seemed like she wanted to straighten something on me, but managed to resist. "All right, let us know if you need anything."

I watched Millie leave the room before getting up. I had apparently been fighting with the bedding in my sleep. Looked like the blankets won. I wrestled myself out of the tangled pile, nightgown hitching up in the process. There was no way to be modest — or graceful, apparently. I fell out of bed more than stood. I hadn't entirely managed to get the sheet unwrapped from my ankle. Grandmother would not have been impressed.

Even two days ago, I wouldn't have believed it possible to miss her fussing over my lack of poise. Tears pooled in my eyes.

I found a tissue and blew my nose. Right, focus. I was supposed to be doing something. Something about Millie . . . Right! The meeting. A shower. A shower sounded good anyway. Heading to the shower.

The first wafts of steam in the shower amplified the stink of my own sweat, but there was something else . . . Oh god, I also smelled Liam's cologne.

My "quick shower" turned into a thorough scalding scrub that ended only with the capacity of Henri's hot water tank.

After the shower, I managed to make it to the meeting. My hair was still damp, and I wasn't wearing any makeup. I couldn't bring myself to care. Looking nice for others wasn't on my list of things to worry about right now. Leaving my room had been difficult. But once I realized everyone was sitting around deciding things, it was enough to propel me out the doorway, down the hall, and into the living room.

I shouldn't have worried about everyone making decisions for me without my being there . . . They were happy to do it while I was there, too.

While I waited for a chance to ask what we were currently arguing about, I blessed whoever had decorated the living room. It was well done, but so different and barely shy of over-the-top, it gave me plenty to contemplate as those around me bickered.

Trying to figure out the wall behind me took a full ten minutes. I was forced to interpret it through its reflection on the mercury glass surface of the coffee table. The yellow Cymbidium orchid on the table kept blocking my view. I moved it to the end table next to me. Then I was finally able to determine the wall was actually button tufted, with more padding than the chaise I was seated on. Eventually, I also decided it was four color tones, and not the two I originally assumed — the colors were a bit wonky in the glass reflection: cream, dove gray, a light turquoise, and a pale viridian hue. It must be a real pain in the ass to keep dust-free.

The furniture continued the art deco theme I noted previously in the hall. The curved lines helped offset the strong geometry of the tufted wall and the woven pattern reminiscent of a compass rose in the rug. Compass rose . . . *sub rosa* . . . Liam. NO! We aren't going there. Deep breaths. Focus on . . . anything else. The room. Yes. Any distraction.

Millie — she looked like a Vermeer.

Millie sat folded into an armchair, hands clasped in front of her midsection. Something about the way the credenza, curtains, and arcing palm plants were arranged behind her made it seem like she was in a Vermeer painting. Maybe it was in how the light was falling from a nearby window. Or maybe it was the sheen of the curtain? She, too, seemed to be waiting for a chance to speak. Unlike me, she didn't seem to mind.

Connor was also in an armchair, leaning forward, his weight resting awkwardly on the swirled wooden arms. He was arguing with Henri and Paulo, who were sharing a curved sofa. How would Vermeer have handled all of Henri's hair? Something to do with the light creating a nimbus in it probably . . . The fluffy style of Degas would probably be better for his portrait.

I was watching the different ways the light reflected off Connor's stubble while he shook his head in disagreement. I should care about this, shouldn't I? I tried to check back into the conversation.

"I know your rules, but someone better check in with Chief Duncan. He is going to be apoplectic if he figures it out himself. He could help keep the issue from becoming public. He might help us figure out an alternative!"

"He isn't going to break the law for us, Connor!" Henri hissed. "Excuse me, do you mind if we borrow your prisoner?" Henri made a theatrical gesture to go with the sing-song voice he was using to illustrate how ridiculous Connor was being. "You see, it's just he might have trouble not turning into a wolf during the full moon. That might be a tad awkward. What, a courtroom trial? Oh, don't be silly — I promise we will dispense our own archaic form of justice. A trial simply won't be necessary."

For a moment I thought Connor was going to growl. Henri stopped him. "It's not my decision. I'm not on the Council. I'm not even being told what they plan to do about this."

"You could try to convince your father — he leads the Council aft–"

"No. I'm not going to push him on this now. Connor . . ." He threw his hands up in exasperation. "Look. I just had to tell my dad Liam tried to rape Loren." I flinched at the black-and-white harshness of his word choice. "That there were no questions as to his intention, or for that matter, *any* chance of it being honorable. Now he has to help decide Liam's fate. Any sort of changing the rules now will look like he is asking for special treatment for someone he considers his son. He can't do it, and I will not ask him to do it. So drop it. Let's please focus on what we *can* do." Henri turned deliberately to me.

I was glad I was paying attention, but I still didn't know what to say. "Ummm..?"

"Okay." Connor switched gears faster than I could. "We need to figure out what we are going to do about your story Loren, try to determine what the Magic's current plot is, and if we want to change it in any way."

"It is rather obvious what the Magic has in mind, isn't it?" Paulo accompanied the statement with a full arm gesture at Henri and his hair.

"But it doesn't make any sense. There is no template for it happening this way in any of the tales!"

"Wow Connor," Paulo snapped. "You sound more upset that you don't understand what is happening than you did about what happened to Loren and Henri!"

"Because I can't help them if I don't understand! I can't keep you all from getting hurt!"

Did everyone else miss it? Connor had been gently guiding before, but with his last statement, he stepped over the line into the role of air traffic controller. There was a problem there. "Umm, doesn't that seem like we are setting ourselves up for a fate tale rather than a supernatural husband-type tale?" Everyone stopped to stare at me.

Paulo broke the silence by bursting into almost hysterical laughter. "Well shit," he gasped. "That is just too perfect. You really *are* Cogsworth."

"Wait . . . But . . . I'm not!" Paulo had managed to fluster Connor.

I cleared my throat. I was too tired for the existential physics I knew Connor was about to launch into. Time to redirect the conversation. "I hate to interrupt. But right now, the main thing I want to know is how to keep from having the Magic latch onto the idea that I belong with Liam. In fairy tales, what he did was usually enough to seal the deal."

"You poor things. I am so glad you have me to straighten things out for you." Paulo was annoyingly smug as he rolled his eyes at us. "Remember after Belle has been trapped in the enchanted castle for a while? Right, then she runs away and tries to escape her fate. You with me so far?" We all nodded. "What happens next?"

I racked my brain. Let's see, she rides off on her horse, the woods are all creepy, and then . . . Oh. Seriously?! Either Paulo was finding a clever way to spin the events, or the Magic was twisting the tale in a sadistic way.

Henri beat me to it, saying with a groan, "She was attacked by wolves. The Beast ends up rescuing her."

"Hmmm, I have said all along you had a much higher probability of landing the role of Beast. You are like the prince of the local werewolves . . ." Connor trailed off when he saw the glare directed his way by Paulo.

"That is because you are an idiot who can't see what is right in front of you." Paulo's face twisted into a grimace and he turned toward Henri. Henri frowned at him. What was going on there?

"Right," Paulo said. "I can tell where I'm not wanted. I can't take listening to you all trying to orchestrate this mess for a second longer, anyway." Paulo whirled with a false smile plastered across his face. "Loren, you haven't eaten recently, have you? I am going to go put something together for you. Any requests?"

Why did that feel like a loaded question? "Umm, how about I trust you to pick something out?"

"I already did, doll. I guess we are going to see what you think of it."

Umm, okay?

He flitted out of the room, leaving us all in silence.

"So, does this mean the Magic isn't going to push me at Liam? That I'm not likely to be pregnant?" I asked.

Connor's eyes widened in panic. "I don't think we should assume anything like that. I'd prefer to be sure. Millie, didn't you talk to her?"

"She had questions." Millie's shrug was very Gallic.

"Loren . . ." Connor started, then trailed off, "I don't want to tell you what to do, but the laws surrounding rape are complete shit. I couldn't believe how bad they were when we were researching options. At this point, I can't help but believe Liam will take full advantage of them in any way he can. For instance, if you are pregnant, Liam can sue for custody or visitation rights unless he is convicted." What the hell! That was ludicrous.

"He won't get the chance to," Henri spoke up. "I am willing to claim the baby as mine to create a legal barrier. He would have to sue to have paternity testing performed. Liam won't be around long enough for results to get back. The Pack isn't going to allow it." I could have kissed Henri for saying that. He managed to calm the swell of panic beginning to take over. "That way, it is your choice. You can choose what to do."

"I appreciate the offer, Henri." I took a deep, shaky inhale. "I can't handle having a baby right now, though."

"That's probably for the be–" Connor was cut off.

"I will go make the tea for you." Ms. Millie glared at Connor as she left the room.

"Wow. You are really managing to win friends and influence people tonight, Connor." Ouch, I was glad Henri's venom wasn't directed at me.

"What'd I do?" Connor demanded.

Henri sighed and put his hands up to his forehead. Then he felt the hair there and jerked them away.

"How about it's a complicated and personal decision Loren had to share with the group. Your high-handed approval of her falling in line with what you think best was a bit indelicate. It would have been better left unsaid."

Umm, and that wasn't at all awkward either. Sheesh.

"But –" Connor spluttered.

"Please just stop." Henri was terse, biting each word off. "I don't have a lot of patience left after the last forty-eight hours, and I'm trying hard not to say anything ugly. Please, just take a break. We can talk about it later if you still feel the need."

Connor swallowed visibly and nodded. "I'm sorry Loren, I didn't mean to be insensitive in any way."

"Thank you for the apology, Connor. So . . ." I tried to move us past the tense moment. "Are we thinking Paulo is right? What does that mean?"

Connor glanced at Henri before speaking, "It is a reasonable interpretation. It would also be mutually beneficial. I mean Loren, it would help steer your story quest the way we want. Henri, well, Uncle Nick has been after you to marry so you can join the Council. It would benefit you, too."

Henri rubbed the bridge of his nose. I swear I heard him mutter a cuss word under his breath. "Fine. That's great." He didn't mean it at all. "But you know what, I get to help steer the direction this goes, too."

He stood and made a dramatic, flourishing bow that ended with him before me on one knee.

Umm, what the hell? He stretched a hand out toward me, "Loren Roselle Hughes, will you marry me?"

What?! My mouth was hanging open. I snapped it closed. I glanced at Connor to see his reaction. He looked as surprised as I was. Right, on my own here.

"Umm . . . this seems a little sudden?" Did that sound like a question? Argh! How do I say this kindly while also conveying a firm no? Why didn't Grandmother teach me the social script for this? "I don't . . ." Henri stopped me with a hand wave.

"I understand. But we both have our roles to play." He smiled rakishly, but it didn't reach his eyes. I don't know what caused the pain there, but it was breaking my heart. Then he leaned in and whispered, "Plus, this is going to tick Connor off, and right now that is appealing." He winked, stood, and left the room.

Connor broke my confused daze with his muttering, "Interesting, he's going with a traditional version. I wonder if he is thinking of Lang or Villeneuve? This changes the probabilities . . ." He stood and started pacing. "And if he is able to control things, then is he getting sucked into Loren's tale, or is Henri going through his own tale that is running parallel, or overlapping somehow? Can there be two tales at once? Oh, man! And if he is only just sucked into her tale now, does that have any bearing on whether or not he will have his own tale later?"

Why did I get the feeling that Connor had completely forgotten my existence? I'm right here — remember? Seriously? Maybe I should rethink the option of the whole town being delusional.

Connor grabbed his notebook off his chair and plopped on the couch. The formulas he frantically scribbled weren't anything I could comprehend. Great, that was another migraine level headache coming on. Time to leave.

"Loren, before you go . . ." I heard Connor say from behind me. Then I was grabbed. Panic arced through my body, a lightning current that froze every muscle. Only it didn't. The realization dawned because my heart was still beating. In fact, it was racing — threatening to pound out of my chest. The realization loosened the bands clamped around my rib cage enough that I managed a small gasp of air. And another.

". . . Loren, what's wrong?!" It was Connor. Connor touched me. Not Liam. NOT Liam. Muscles that were clenched released suddenly, and I would have fallen over except Connor still had a hold of me. I felt disconnected from my extremities. My consciousness, and even all the heat in my body, coalesced into a single point floating a few inches above and behind my head.

I jerked my arm away from Connor's grasp, perhaps a poor choice given my lack of coordination. But I managed to stay on my feet. "Don't touch me." It was almost a shriek. "Please. I'm sorry . . ."

Connor jerked his hand back. He took a step away, hands up defensively. "I'm so sorry. I wasn't thinking. Loren, I didn't mean to –" His apology was interrupted as Paulo skidded into the room — he was running so fast he had to grab the doorframe to slow himself down.

Then Paulo lobbed a verbal grenade: "Liam has escaped! Where is Henri? He needs to know!"

His words unplugged something in me. I watched from outside myself as everything froze, and I shut down.

"What? How did that happen?" Paulo didn't answer Connor's question, because he had already turned and sprinted away. I could hear his footsteps retreating, and my vision tied into what I was hearing. I was having some weird tunnel vision where everything was moving farther and farther away. Like the footsteps were a soundtrack, and I was the one moving away from myself . . . or maybe my brain was slipping to the side.

I stumbled. Connor reached out to help, but jerked his hands back before he touched me. "– you should . . . seizure or some– . . . Millie!" Wow, he was loud. "Millie!"

CHAPTER 23

If I stayed here another minute, I was going to have the wood grain from the door embedded in my forehead. I'd already memorized the grooves and dips in the few square inches of wood I could see. All I had to do was turn the knob. I could do this. I could. I wasn't going to let this ruin me.

Except it was easier to be strong here, in my room. No hint of a panic attack. There was no one walking on eggshells around me.

If everyone would just stop treating me like I was broken! Even if maybe I was . . . it made it impossible to be anything else.

Facing everyone, maybe getting more news. All my problems were waiting there, lurking just on the other side of the door. I couldn't do it.

Except I had to do this. I needed to go do something about at least one of my problems, or I wouldn't be able to have any self-respect ever again. NO CHOICE, Loren. TURN THE KNOB.

My fingers clenched so hard they started to cramp around the knob.

I sighed and gently banged my head against the door.

It must have jarred a thought loose. Facing everything was too overwhelming. But maybe that was okay. Maybe I just needed to pick one thing, and take a baby step forward.

Right, a plan of action . . . That sounded good. But which problem should we tackle? Okay. A list. I can do this.

Loren's problems.

Number 1: post-concussive syndrome. Except that won't work. I'm not supposed to do anything interesting with my brain. But inaction is not helping me feel like I am taking control. Although, maybe I could give myself points for it anyway. Sure, let's do that — maybe call them bonus points for after you find something that can be accomplished.

Hey, I was getting better at this pep talk stuff.

Okay, problem number 2: finishing my thesis requirements. I was so ready to be done with it all! It was the roadblock keeping me from moving forward with the rest of my life. But I can't do anything yet. Refer back to problem one. Again, not at all helpful in moving forward. Although, maybe I could do some less brain-using things like finding a gallery to host my show. I would need to talk to people. People like my grandmother. Hmm, I wasn't ready for that yet. Right, what else was on the list?

Number 3: I was suspected of murder. No, scratch that — not my problem. That was the chief's problem. He had it all wrong. He didn't seem the type to manufacture evidence though, so I should be safe. Besides, assuming it was murder and not a land shark — yeah, I know, ridiculous — it's not like I could solve a murder mystery.

I wasn't going to worry about that. Okay, maybe a little. But I am kicking it off the list. Got it, Loren? Find a new number three — shouldn't be hard to find something.

All right, new problem number 3: fairy tale bullshit. Ugh. Maybe we could come back to this one? But that really only left problem 4 (dealing with my father), or problem 5 (the recent incident I wasn't ready to examine too closely yet). Door number three it was.

Right. Fairy tale bullshit. I shifted so I was leaning with my back to the door instead. I rubbed my forehead. I had stalled too long; there were ridges embedded in it. Where were we with my tale? Back to the *"Belle et la Bête"* traditional version, or were we doing the Disney version? Heck, were we controlling anything, anymore?

If Connor's quest was turning this all into a tale of attempting to escape one's fate . . . We managed to sidestep the topic last night, but it needed to be discussed. Was Connor coming back over here this morning? Didn't he ever have to work?

What else was going on with the tale? Right, Henri's proposal from out of the blue. What was he up to? Hmm, Henri was stuck in this, too. I allowed the idea to roll around in my head. Maybe I needed to go discuss things with him.

Something I could handle. I think. I brightened as I realized no one else was likely to be around this morning . . . At least I assumed they all had jobs they needed to get back to.

I turned around and faced the door again. Just breathe. I concentrated on the cool air coming in through my nostrils, then let it flow out past my lips. My heart was pounding, but I managed to reach out and turn the doorknob.

Go, Loren! Look, you made it through the door. And no one is in sight. That wasn't so bad!

Now, where would I find Henri? I slipped silently along the hall, the plush carpet runner making me practically silent. A sense of déjà vu hit as I realized Henri was on the phone in the library again. I slipped past the lady reclining on the moon and peeked around the doorframe.

I checked behind me; I didn't want to get caught lurking in the door again by Paulo.

". . . I need to run.

. . .

Right. I will call you back with those details as soon as I can.

. . .

Thanks. Bye."

He swiveled his chair around to face me, "Hi Loren! I wondered when you would make it down." He smiled warmly — curiosity, not criticism.

I hadn't expected him to notice me yet. Now that I was here, I didn't know where to start. I would have to plan a few further steps ahead next time.

I sidled over to the couch like my slinking would somehow make him less aware of my intrusion. Are you considered *more* unbalanced when you are aware you are being irrational and can't snap out of it?

He came over and sat on the loveseat set perpendicularly to the couch.

Henri is a bit unnerving. Most people don't pay complete attention during a discussion; their minds wander, or they are worrying about what to say next and miss things. Henri has this kind of intense focus. He manages to be one hundred percent there in the moment, noticing everything. That focus was now entirely on me.

I was going to have to work hard to hold it all together under his scrutiny. I stared at him. It was surprising how much of his bone structure I could make out under his hair. He wasn't monstrous at all. Did he even qualify as a beast? We needed to talk about this. How was I going to get a conversation started? Calling his proposal ludicrous wasn't exactly kind – to either of us. The thought made me grin a little.

Henri beat me to getting the conversation rolling.

"You know Loren, I don't know if anyone has told you this, but you are an amazing woman. You have survived so much recently. I wanted to make sure you remembered that. Also, I feel honored you trusted me enough to let me be there with you for support. I hope you will let me know if there is anything else I can do."

The brave face I was putting on crumpled. To my horror, it didn't stop there. There was a black hole in my center, and everything collapsed into it. I pulled my feet up and tucked into a ball, sobbing.

Maybe I was the only one who saw myself as fragile? Was that a self-fulfilling prophecy? Maybe I could let others tell my story for a little bit, just until I got my internal narrative rebuilt. Did it work that way? Hell, wasn't that what this was all about? Did the Magic break me so I would be okay with it telling my story?

I hadn't seen Henri move, but his hand was on my shoulder. He was kneeling in front of me, offering me tissues. "I'm sorry. I shouldn't have said anything."

"No," I hiccupped, between shuddering sobs. "It was the perfect thing to say. Thank you."

Confusion was written all over Henri's face. The deep furrow in his forehead was making his hair stick straight out in a crest. Not a terribly scary Beast — in fact, it was so comical, my sobs were transforming into giggles. This deepened the furrow, creating furry spikes.

"I am a bit confusing, aren't I? Sorry –" a hiccup interrupted my apology "'bout that." I took a deep breath. It was only a little shaky. Might as well keep going. "I am also sorry you got caught up in all this. I didn't mean for you to go all furry."

"It's not your fault, Loren. No, really." I had to stop shaking my head as he raised my chin gently with a finger. That intense gaze again . . . "I don't blame you for any of this. I might consider being upset with the Magic, our ancestors, and maybe even Connor. Liam — well, I cannot begin to express how enraged I am with Liam. But I'm not upset with you." He was sitting on the couch next to me now. He bopped my shoulder with his. "Hey, we are in this together."

"But if I hadn't tried to control where things were going, or let Liam try to be the Beast, or maybe if I told him 'no' earlier . . . perhaps you wouldn't have gotten sucked into this."

"You are *not* responsible for what Liam did. That is entirely on him."

"Hmm." I did know that, but my heart was still coming up with a million *what if, maybe,* and *if only* thoughts.

Henri shook his head at me. "I repeat. This is not. Your. Fault." My doubt persevered. He cocked his head a bit and leaned back into the cushion. "Not a single bit of this is your responsibility. I know how you feel, though. I can't help but think that if I had called him out when I saw him being a jerk in the past, maybe this wouldn't have happened. It was just . . ." he paused considering word choices, and settled with a sigh, "*complicated* with family politics. I suspect that is part of the reason I got pulled into this. The sin I am being transformed for. Of course, there are others, too."

"I can't imagine you doing anything as awful as the prince in the tale. I mean, you have been nothing but kind to me."

Henri grimaced. "Recently, someone pointed out to me that I wear a metaphorical mask, and hide large parts of myself. Maybe the Magic actualized that, and now I have to hide myself away. Perhaps this is the story I was creating for myself."

"Oh." I didn't know what to say. Asking about what he was hiding seemed too personal. I mean if he wanted people to know . . . At the same time, after all he had offered to do for me . . . "I don't mean to pry, but if you want to talk to someone about it, I'm happy to listen."

Henri started to shake his head in negation but stopped midway through the motion. He looked at me, but for the first time in the conversation, he wasn't completely present. He was obviously thinking hard. He got up and prowled back and forth across the room. He was starting to make me nervous. What could he possibly have in his background that was so awful? I ran through the options. If this was sticking to the fairy tale version: not letting someone in out of bad weather, or failing to be seduced by a fairy. Nothing appropriate to this level of agitation.

He dug his hands into his hair and sighed. "I should tell you everything, but . . ."

"Please don't feel pressured – I was trying to help, not make the situation worse."

"No, you deserve to know what kind of a mess you are taking on here." He paused, "Or most of it, at least."

He flopped down in a way that would have gotten him lectured by Grandmother. He sighed; he was dancing around the edges of something. "It's nothing personal, but you aren't the kind of person I would usually date." He realized what he said, and horror washed over his face. Then the back peddling started, "I mean you are beautiful, and talented, and smart, and so brave. I mean, shit — you are the kind of person I should date. It's just . . ."

He was so agitated. I tried hard, but I couldn't help but laugh. "Are you about to ask me if we can still be friends?"

"What? No! You are exactly the kind of person I *need* to date — to marry, even. I need someone the Council will approve of. I'm not sure my heart is in it, but I am going to try." Well, that was romantic. But who was I to judge? My heart wasn't in it either.

"The Council, do you mean the werewolf Council?"

"Yes. You have to be mated before you can join the Council –"

Mated? "Huh? Why is that?"

"I'm not exactly sure. I believe it's mostly tradition at this point. I think it might be a carryover from the wild. Most Packs are family groupings with a mated couple leading. Unmated adults are generally under a parent or lone wolves. I've petitioned to have Council membership requirements changed, but I'm not making any progress."

"What does mating mean? Married with kids?" That kid thing again. I hadn't signed on for kids!

"Not always. I can't figure out where the line is. Kids aren't necessary — it's not even married, always. On the other hand, I have seen where getting married didn't cut it — that was ugly. It is like a switch getting flipped. Your scent changes, and everyone in the Pack just *knows*. They don't have to be told or introduced to the mate."

Scent. Umm, I guess we never discussed if werewolves had heightened senses in human form, or was he talking about wolf form? I hope I didn't stink to him. I was going to have to quiz him later. Focus, Loren, Henri's sharing his troubles with you. "Is that some sort of special Pack magic?"

"Perhaps. I'm not sure. No one I've dated has apparently met the Council's requirements. My father wants to retire as the leader of the Council, but he won't until he can hand the position over to me. He won't do that if I'm not on the Council. With everything that's happened recently . . . I mean, the stuff with Liam — I thought he was going to have a heart attack. I just can't disappoint him, too."

"Umm, are you sure I will meet the Council's requirements?"

"The Magic wouldn't pick you out for me if you didn't. I can't have a happily ever after without being a part of the Pack, without being on the Council. They are my family."

I considered the idea. It was easy for me to question his goals. To wonder if the Magic didn't have an alternative option that would also make him happy.

But if that applied to him, it also applied to me. I was pissed at the Magic for derailing my goals and trying to substitute alternatives. How did I phrase this gently?

"Are you sure? The Magic seems to have its own ideas about what would make me happy."

"The Magic can't ignore this. Everyone's safety is at stake — there aren't many strong leaders in our generation. We have always followed the Council. We work under the collective leadership of mated pairs that are also family leaders, just like how real wolves are led by an elder mated pair. But now there are all sorts of ridiculousness about alphas and strict hierarchies in pop culture . . . The Magic is twisting our Pack to fit. If I don't stay with the Pack and become the leader, there isn't any other viable option. I used to think Liam might be a possibility, although I worried he would enjoy the power granted by the position while ignoring the duties that came with it.

"The last person I was dating broke up with me over this." Henri's head drooped. He was sniffling, "Said the Pack had to come before our relationship — that I would eventually hate myself for turning my back on the Pack for love. I don't know why our love wasn't enough, why the Magic chose me to be the Beast instead. I have to believe it is because a relationship with you will fix everything."

Wow. No pressure or anything . . .

I put my arm around Henri and took my turn offering the box of tissues. He wasn't a messy crier like I was, but it was something I could do at least. I scrounged around for the right thing to say. Nothing came but the truth. "I'm sorry. That sucks."

"It really does."

"Wow. We are just a mess here."

"That is certainly an accurate statement," he replied.

"So, our current plan is basically to hang out and hope we start to love each other because it will fix things?" That was entirely unsatisfying — like we would be letting the Magic win. Did the Magic make problems to force us into a certain solution to fix them? How was that magical?

Henri laughed. Well, glad I could cheer you up. I rolled my eyes at him.

He teased, "You don't have to sound so disgusted by it."

"It's just . . . Well, I was hoping for something I could do to feel like I was a bit more in control."

"How's that working out for you? Didn't we decide that was playing with fire last night?"

He wasn't wrong. I shook my head. "I don't know."

"We are both pretty decent people. The Magic seems to be pushing us together. I think we could find some common interests. Would you please consider giving it a try?"

I hesitated too long before answering. Henri pressed his case, "If we try, and it works out, we both live happily ever after. Not so bad, right?" At this point, I couldn't picture what happily ever after might look like — with or without him. "I promise to help you get through your thesis requirements while we try. Then, even if things don't work out between us, you will have one less problem to tackle afterward."

I thought it through and sighed. "You don't have to bribe me. I just don't want to marry someone who doesn't love me. Especially if they still love someone else. You have to promise to be honest about your emotions."

"You have my word."

I couldn't think of any other objections, besides the logical one: this was all absurd.

"All right. We can try."

Please don't let me regret this.

CHAPTER 24

I eyed Henri with disbelief as he lounged. How was it possible for him to look so blissful with everything going on? His front paws hung over the gunwale of the sailboat. His tongue lolled out of his snout, his fur spiked blown every which way. To top it off, a strand of dried algae was plastered to the fur on his forehead. Did you call it a forehead on a dog?

I still couldn't believe we were playing hooky like this. I mean, I appreciated the guys trying to cheer me up about missing Kella's play, but wasn't someone going to notice us taking the biggest "dog" ever for a joyride? I shook my head as he turned and grinned at me. At least I think it was a grin — I wasn't good at reading canine facial expressions. Who knew my parents were denying me valuable life skills by saying "no" to my request for a puppy?

Of course, I lacked knowledge of werewolves, too. I didn't realize they could be out during the day or switch forms at will. Henri's wolf side made for the perfect way to escape the house without having to worry about bigfoot stories getting around, but it did make communicating a bit hard.

Henri stood and turned around to rest his head in my lap. He had to lean over to do it. He was huge. He rolled his eyes to stare at me pleadingly.

"Ugh, Henri! You're all wet!" I laughingly pushed him away and wiped fur off my pants. Why did Belle have to wear white? The blue chinos I was wearing might survive this trip, but my white blouse was done for. Everything that wasn't covered by a life vest was grimy already. I was not pulling off looking like a princess today, but I was enjoying myself. Paulo and Henri were good company, even if Henri couldn't talk.

Henri settled in against me. The cold spray had already drenched me, or I would have protested more. It was a good thing it was a warm day. Henri rubbed his head against my torso.

"He wants you to scratch him behind his ears." Paulo wasn't trying to hide the laughter in his voice.

"I'll just bet he does," I muttered.

"Algae gets itchy when it dries in your fur."

I sighed and obliged Henri. I was going to have to pick algae out from under my nails later. I must have made a face because Paulo started laughing at me. Henri closed his eyes and lolled against me in ecstasy.

Paulo laughed at Henri's behavior. "You must give good skritches."

"I'm stopping if you start thumping a leg," I warned Henri. His eyes popped open and this time I was sure he was grinning at me. I finished and gave him a pat on the head.

Paulo choked back a laugh, and when I glanced over at him, searched frantically for something to change the topic. "So, Loren . . . How are you liking Lointaine so far?" I caught Henri rolling his eyes at Paulo's conversational gambit. I thought back to what Connor had said on the way to the theater and had to chuckle myself. Paulo pretended to glare at us, but he was obviously waiting for a reply. Boo!

"It's a lot to get used to, and the rules keep changing on me. It's like . . ." How did I explain this? "Have you ever been driving on the highway in torrential rain, but somehow when you look out the windows, all you see are blue skies and spires of puffy white clouds? You can't figure out where the hell the rain is coming from? It's surreal like that. I'm in the middle of an 'idyllic and peaceful' town, and my life has never been more complicated and stressful."

"Oh man, I remember those days. It is a big shock."

"Didn't you grow up knowing about the Magic?"

"No, I wasn't aware of the Magic until I was in my mid-twenties, when I became a werewolf."

"Oh." Henri rubbed against my side again, trying to get rid of a piece of lake weed that had dried and matted in his fur. I pulled it off for him. "I thought you grew up in Lointaine? Am I wrong?"

"I did. But not everyone in town knows about the Magic. In certain families, it is a well-known secret. Is that an oxymoron, a 'well-known secret'? Louis's descendants know about the Magic as a general rule, the werewolves know about werewolves, and everyone else pretty much ignores or explains away anything that doesn't fit their expectations. No generational secrets in my family, no princely quest to worry about. I was just one of the poor townsfolk growing up."

Poor townsfolk, huh? It was hard to picture him that way with his current flair. I grinned at him; Paulo had sided with me to get Henri to watch *The Princess Bride* two nights ago. "'Poor and perfect, eyes like the sea after a storm'? Are you the Dread Veterinarian Paulo, then?"

"I'm sure some of my patients think so," he muttered.

"I understand why someone would come back if they didn't know about the Magic. It is picturesque."

Paulo shrugged. "I didn't mean to come back — it was just supposed to be for my internship. My plan was to get a job at a zoo with a conservation focus. I considered the zoo near the vet school because Roanoke is bigger than Lointaine."

"Couldn't you still do that?"

Paulo's face hardened. "It's not allowed by the Pack."

"What? Why not?"

"To protect the Pack's secret. It's hard enough with everyone contained here. The Council has members working in strategic positions. People in emergency dispatch to catch calls. Someone at the hospital who knows when to call our doctors. A CSI tech to make sure no evidence of werewolves gets collected. You get the idea. Could you imagine if we spread out across the country? It would be . . . impossible."

I caught myself chewing on my lip. Grandmother would fuss at me for that . . . Connor, too.

Paulo sighed. "Go ahead and ask whatever is bugging you. I hope you'll come to me if you have any questions in the future, too."

"Well, I just don't understand why you became a werewolf. Was it worth the sacrifice?"

There was a pause before he answered. "I didn't feel like I had a choice. Has Henri explained how werewolves can heal almost any injury by shifting?"

I shook my head. Paulo glared at Henri, who dropped his head down onto his paws.

"Well, they — I mean we — can. Shifting is like a factory reset for your body. No flu, no cancer. It even gets rid of moles, freckles, and acne. Our bodies produce extra relaxin hormones, just like pregnant women, to facilitate muscles and ligaments moving during the change. Even ajinxt scientists have caught on to relaxin's healing abilities. They are looking at using it to help with heart failure, high blood pressure, and musculoskeletal diseases. But those high relaxin levels lead to joint pain and make us clumsy.

"Anyway," he continued, "I got kicked in the abdomen by a horse, which ruptured my spleen and damaged my intestines. When I collapsed, the horse stepped on me, crushing my right hand. No spleen meant a compromised immune system, and nerve damage in my right hand meant I wouldn't have the fine motor skills to perform surgery." Henri whined. Paulo glanced his way, "You had your chance to share. Now you'll just have to deal with how I am telling the story.

"So, when I was offered the chance to join the Pack, it was the only option that allowed me to be a veterinarian. I didn't know what else to do with myself, or how I would pay my student loans."

I groaned, "Ugh! I know all about that. If I don't get my scholarship committee's thesis requirements taken care of, I will never, ever, pay mine off. I'm glad you found a way forward, even if it wasn't exactly what you wanted."

"Don't worry, you'll find a solution, too. You've got lots of help."

"You included?"

"But of course!" He said it with a bad French accent. "It is my sacred duty while playing the role of Lumière. Henri, I see you rolling your eyes at me! Where would you be today without me entertaining you? At home, in your gloomy castle! Don't judge me!"

I couldn't help but laugh at them; it was the first belly laugh I'd had since . . . well, in days at least.

"I see lots of sailing in your future. Would you like to learn how to steer?" Paulo asked.

I eyed all the lines of the boat wearily. I would have been happy to just sit there and enjoy the sun, but sailing was one of Henri's favorite ways to spend his time. I should try to figure that all out if there was any possibility of us ending up together. Especially since I had no intention of getting into fishing — unless it was to draw the fish, maybe? Nope, not even then.

"Sure, I'd love to learn," I said with forced cheer. "Umm, where do I need to sit?" He patted the wood next to him, so I carefully scooted across the deck to change places with him. I didn't have to go far on the tiny boat; we were practically on top of each other already.

"So, when you are sailing, you can't go straight into the wind because then the wind can't fill your sails. You go into it at an angle. That means you make a zig-zag across the water. It's called tacking. This is the tiller. You use it to steer. The boat goes in the opposite direction you turn the handle."

"Okay."

"Right now, we are on a starboard tack. For now, keep the tiller the same way I have it. In a little bit, we will come about, so we are on a port tack. That keeps us heading in the general direction we want. We are going to steer into and across the flow of the wind. The sail will switch from being filled by the wind on this side to being empty, and then swing across the boat, to be filled by wind on the other side — like the times I told you to duck."

"Umm. Are you sure I am ready for this?"

"Nope."

"What?!" I squeaked and turned around to look at Paulo. Unfortunately, I swung the tiller around as well. Paulo laughed at me while pushing my head under the boom as the sail responded by swinging across the boat.

"Okay, turn the helm into the wind now. Don't stop, or we will stall out. You want the tiller right about here." He helped me get pointed in the right direction and, to my great relief, the wind caught the sail and filled it with a snap. "See, you did it!"

"Only because you fixed my mistake," I grumbled.

"Next time it'll be all you." Henri thumped his tail in encouraging agreement.

He was right. I did complete the next tack successfully, although he talked me through the whole thing. After about thirty minutes, I was beginning to get the hang of it. I had tacked, intentionally even, five times. I'm not sure they had all been necessary; it seemed more likely Paulo was trying to help me be comfortable with the maneuver.

I could appreciate why Henri loved sailing so much. It was breathtaking. It felt like flying. I was having flashbacks to Halloween, but the good parts this time — where I danced with the wind. The wind, the water, and I were dancing now. And since the wind was connected to the branches of the trees, and was driving the waves to the shore, and on and on . . . I was linked to the whole world in an ever-widening spiral. It was one of those rare moments that hang suspended in golden perfection. I almost saw flashes of green and gold move through the spiral in response to my actions. Those golden fragments were being blown into me by the wind, infusing every part of me, down to the last tiny cell. It was euphoric and magical. And yet, the last time this happened . . .

The thought brought the experience to a crashing halt. Was this the Magic? Was it a portent of an important moment in my tale? Or a sign trying to tell me I was with a potential spouse? Except that would mean Liam was . . . No, it couldn't be that. Would I ever be able to enjoy a breeze again without thinking about Liam and what he did?

Were there any fairy tales where the wind was important? I racked my brain. There was "East of the Sun, West of the Moon," or the one where the wind and the sun argue about who can make a man take his coat off first. I would volunteer for some ruffled hair and a little sunburn over the current plan, but I didn't think that was where this was headed. It seemed like the tale needed to be something popular, and neither fit the bill. But who knew at this point? Probably Connor. I mentally stuck out my tongue at him.

The wind grew stronger, and I struggled to keep everything in the right place. Without the connection guiding the dance, I couldn't just react instinctually; it took a lot of planning ahead to do things that took strength from my good arm. Despite that, it was still thrilling. We surged over the lake's surface.

"Want me to take over for a bit?" Paulo offered. "It's getting a bit windy."

Henri whimpered and nudged my arm.

"Sure, I don't want to overdo it. I'll get yelled at by all my doctors." I grinned and looked at Henri. He was nodding his head. That was a sage expression for a dog whose hair was sticking up in wild spikes. I couldn't help but giggle. Hopefully, it wouldn't hurt his feelings that I was laughing at him. He stopped panting and gave a doggy smile. Apparently, we were good.

I reached out and ruffled his fur. He took it as an excuse to scoot over for another round of scratching. I obliged. He settled in against my leg in contentment. If I married him, we could sail together. It wasn't reason enough alone, but it deserved a spot in the 'pro' column of my considerations. Did he like art museums? Would we be able to find enough common interests to make things work?

"Seemed like you were enjoying yourself. Careful, it's easy to get addicted to," Paulo teased.

"I can see that. Don't worry, I'm not going to crawl up to the front of the boat and fling my arms open à la Rose from *Titanic* or anything."

"Oh, please don't. That is the last thing we need the Magic to latch onto!"

Henri's head flew up from my knee, and banged into my elbow, sending ripples of tingling pain all the way to my shoulder. I checked to see if he was hurt, but he barely noticed the impact. His whole body was alert and focused, from the tip of his tail to his perked ears. He sniffed the air over the edge of the boat and growled at the water. Paulo turned to look, too.

A sudden, strong gust of wind ripped across the lake. The sail whipped around, and the whole boat rolled right over. As the sky and water tumbled past, I had the inane thought that this kind of thing must be why Paulo insisted on life vests for all of us, even Henri. Not at all a useful thing to occupy yourself with, Loren! How about figuring out where the boat was? I gasped involuntarily as momentum drove me under the surface of the frigid water.

I hung momentarily, suspended in the frigid pale-green water, stunned. Belle's silly blue bow must have come loose from my ponytail. My hair was now floating in a nimbus around me. I fought it out of my face as my life jacket started to pull me upwards. I kicked my legs to help propel myself back to the surface and was surprised when I met resistance.

Something was wrapped around my ankle. Despite my lifejacket, I was being yanked downward. What was going on? I peered through the murky lake water. Was that some sort of lake weed?

Then Henri was there, snapping at the weeds, pawing at them. The tightness around my ankle relaxed, and I kicked hard. I popped up into the air and gratefully drew in a deep, gasping lungful.

Henri was there a second later, licking my face worriedly as he paddled. "Henri!" I gently pushed him away so he would stop bumping into me. "Stop it, you are making it hard to swim!"

"Loren!" Paulo yelled. I thrashed my arms so I spun around in a circle until I was facing him. "There you are. Thank goodness!" He swam over with a graceful lifeguard stroke and helped push away the sails I was close to being tangled in. Holy moly, the water was cold!

Paulo got right in front of me. "Loren, I need you to listen. It's important we get the boat upright before it goes over entirely and turtles on us. I need you to hang on right here." He positioned my hands and made several other adjustments to various ropes as he continued. "After I uncleat the mainsail, I am going to go around to the other side and pull. I need you to kick up out of the water and pull yourself into the boat when that happens. Once you are in, I need you to come right away to help me in, on the other side. Think you can do that?"

I nodded and clenched my shivering teeth so I could answer, "Yes." I wasn't actually sure, but it sounded like I better manage.

Paulo disappeared around the boat, and I noticed Henri paddling nearby. His head was continuously swiveling, watching all around us.

"You ready?" I heard faintly from the other side of the boat.

"Yes," I called back. It came out as two syllables because of my chattering teeth.

The boat heaved, and I kicked and pulled. It was almost like I got scooped into the boat as it righted. I flopped like a beached marine mammal, flat on my stomach across the boat. I was so tired, but there was something I needed to do. Paulo. Right! I forced myself to gather my feet under me and used them to push myself to the edge. Where was Paulo?

There! I leaned over and helped pull him in as he kicked himself up out of the water. Oh, that hurt. My wrist sent fierce twinges up my arm.

"Where's Henri?" He asked.

"Over there." I pointed. It wasn't much warmer out of the cold water; my muscles were clenching in an attempt to pull everything toward my core, and my chest ached.

"Henri!" Paulo called. Henri paddled over closer to the boat, and Paulo pulled him into the boat, too. He shook himself and water went flying everywhere. Then he came over and crawled into my lap and leaned against me.

"Henri!" I started to protest, but I stopped when I realized how warm he was. Heat was radiating off of him — it was the most wonderful thing I ever felt. I wrapped my arms around him and hugged him to me.

Paulo was rummaging around in the tiny storage space under the front of the boat. He pulled out a bucket and made quick work of bailing. Luckily there wasn't a lot of water. He talked as he bailed. "Loren, we need to get you warmed up. First step is getting you out of your wet clothes. I've got a blanket in here we can wrap you in."

It sounded so cliché, I couldn't help but giggle. "That is the worst, most overused line ever, Paulo." He gave me a look. "I know, sheesh, pass the damn blanket."

I gently moved Henri off my lap so I could undress.

"Why don't you dry off with this first?" I turned around and saw he was patiently holding a nubby wool blanket for me over his shoulder. It was old and full of holes, and I didn't care at all. I took it, and I was grateful to wrap up in it. Cutting the wind made me feel significantly warmer.

Henri and Paulo politely looked in the opposite direction. I turned my back on them anyway. My hands shook so badly, it was hard to undo the life vest clips. The buttons on my blouse were harder. The fabric of my pants clung to my skin and was almost impossible to push down my legs. The wind hit my bare skin. It didn't seem possible, but my goose bumps got bigger.

"You ready?" Paulo asked. "I found some old clothes in here."

"Thanks." While I was rubbing myself dry, Paulo started to undress. He crossed his arms and pulled his t-shirt off. It made an undignified slurping sound as his marvelous abs were revealed. I turned to Henri, who was draped in a towel, to share my amusement. He gave a chuffing sneeze that sounded like a laugh and I couldn't help but to laugh myself. Soon we were all howling. Henri's laughs sounded a lot like panting.

Paulo was still chuckling as he passed me a cream-colored fisherman's sweater, obviously bought for a man much larger than I. I turned my back and let the blanket fall to my waist to pull it on. I pulled the round collar up to get all snuggly and sighed as blissful warmth enveloped me.

"I don't suppose you have any pants?"

"Unfortunately, only shorts."

"Better than nothing, I guess."

"I bet you will never guess what color they are." Paulo teased.

Yup, they were blue, and also for a larger man. I groaned, but pulled them on and tightened the drawstring as much as possible, before wrapping myself in my blanket.

I kept my back to the boat to give Paulo as much privacy as possible in the small space as he finished changing. Henri came over trailing his towel. He plopped his back end on my feet and looked at me with big, beseeching puppy eyes.

"I'm not exactly sure what you want, but I do know I am not snuggling you again until you are a bit drier, so why don't we start with that?" He thumped his tail back and forth into the side of the boat. I chuckled and grabbed the towel to rub him down.

"Well, I wasn't expecting *that*," Paulo said, as I heard him adjusting ropes and sails. He reached past me and grabbed the tiller. I took that to mean it was safe for me to turn around. Henri crawled into my lap and I pulled the blanket around both of us so just his head was sticking out.

"Which part?" I asked, "Where we almost froze, or where we all sounded like hyenas? Or where the perfect wardrobe was stashed in the boat? I am not sure Kella would approve, though."

He chuckled again. "I meant the capsizing part. I haven't done that in a long time. I usually would have handled a gust like that better, but I was a bit distracted."

Henri whined and put his head on his paws, pulling the blanket open.

Paulo sighed. "Don't do that. You should know I'm not upset — and it was a good thing you noticed the grindylows were about. I'm more irritated with myself. It was a bit cocky of me to head out today. I know the weather seemed perfect for it, but the water temp was in the low sixties. That can get dangerous fast, and we didn't dress or pack appropriately for it." Paulo continued to address Henri, but I was still stuck on the first thing he said. Why did it sound familiar?

"Grindylows?"

"Yes, Grindylows. They are from the folk tales of England or Ireland — I can't remember which."

Right, that wasn't seaweed accidentally trapping me, they were slimy fingers, intentionally wrapping around my ankle to drown me. No big deal, right? A shudder ran through me.

"Oh. Are they usually dangerous?"

"Not generally; they were unusually aggressive today. They may have helped turn the boat over, but it could have been the wind and my distraction. It's hard to say. We didn't have too many in the past, but they have started to be a problem since the Harry Potter movies came out."

"The movies control what kind of creatures are around?"

"I don't think the movies create the creatures or anything. They are already around and attracted to Lointaine because of how much magic there is here. Pop culture seems to affect population numbers, and maybe characteristics. I should probably add grindylows to the species I am tracking to study that. But, you probably don't want to hear all about that . . ."

I smiled. "It's better than thinking about how cold I am. For instance, have you ever seen a unicorn or a dragon?"

"Oh, I wish! So far no dragons, and . . ." He turned to me with a devilish grin, "I'm not the kind of guy that unicorns hang out with. But we will be back at the marina in just a few minutes, where we can warm you up and get something to eat."

The mention of food made me realize I was ravenously hungry.

"That sounds amazing. Can we have soup?"

"You and your food!" Paulo laughed at me. "You are fun to feed. I know the perfect place. It's on the way home. They have great clam chowder, and make the best calamari in town — and I would say that even if they weren't the only place in town that serves squid. It's divine." He grinned, teasing me with his word choice. "Additionally, they have a patio that allows dogs. They will even bring Henri a burger."

"I am going to need to eat outside, myself," I said ruefully, looking down at my outfit.

Paulo shrugged. "It doesn't look that bad. Now your hair . . . well, I have a brush back in my truck. We should be able to make you presentable. If not, we can call ahead and get food to go and head home."

I rolled my eyes and stuck my tongue out at him playfully. Henri gave a little yip of agreement. I wasn't sure which side he was agreeing with, though.

"Do you guys do this often? Take each other out in wolf form?"

"Not usually. There generally isn't a need for it." He paused, considering. "Transforming is kind of like sleep. It's something your body *needs* to do, and there are times when you are more likely to do it — mainly around the full moon. But just like you can take naps when you don't need to sleep, we can change other times too. You can only resist changing for so long, and it's harder to *not* change during the full moon."

"Huh. Thank you for sharing that with me." I considered. "It clarifies what you meant about Liam and jail. So, if he can't go to jail, what will happen to him?"

Paulo frowned. "Werewolf justice is harsh — it is a matter of protecting the Pack and our secrets. No one wants to be a lab experiment. If they can catch him, the Council will vote on his punishment. At this point, I suspect he will be executed."

"Oh. Um, okay." I wasn't entirely sure how I felt about Liam being killed. At least a small part of me relished the idea. I wasn't sure I was okay with that. Forget the fussy manners and magic sparkles — fairy tales were dark. Dark and dangerous. "Speaking of things we don't know . . . Are there other fairy tale creatures I should maybe be aware of?"

"Well, that is a bit hard to say. I'm not sure of everything that might be around. Although, I suspect we have a brownie or hob at the house." Henri nodded his head in agreement. "It would go along with the idea of invisible servants in the original 'Beauty and the Beast' pretty well. I've been leaving out milk, fresh bread, and honey to cover all our bases. It disappears nightly in any case. You wouldn't know anything about that would you?" Paulo addressed the last to Henri.

Henri raised his eyebrows and did his best to appear innocent. "Hmmm," Paulo said narrowing his eyes. "Well, in any case, it's supposed to be for the hob."

I suddenly realized Paulo was dressed in shorts and a t-shirt. "Oh gosh, are you warm enough?" I felt guilty for hogging the blanket. "I can share the blanket?"

"I'll be fine. Werewolves are pretty tough and tend to run warm. I would prefer to be a bit more dressed, but I'm only a bit chilly. You, on the other hand, are at risk for mild hypothermia if we don't get your temperature back to normal soon. I suspect that is why Henri is acting as a space heater."

Henri's belly growled loudly interrupting the conversation. Paulo laughed. "I'm not sure which of you that was, but I promise to feed both of you soon. Be patient, we should be on shore in about ten minutes."

Just enough time for me to fret about how many creatures I was around every day that I never saw.

CHAPTER 25

"I'm just saying, you guys got to pick where we ate dinner, so I should get to pick what we do tonight." I turned and pretended to glare at Henri where he sat in the back seat of the car. "Besides, you cheated last night." He had snuck a card, which asked me to marry him, into the trivia game we were playing. When I turned him down, he told me I lost the rest of my turn for giving the wrong answer.

Henri had decided it was safe enough for him to ride home as a human, given the twilight shadows. To be extra cautious, he was wearing a cap, big sunglasses, and his sweatshirt hood was up. It wasn't at all suspicious. Really.

I heard a theatrical sigh from the back seat. "That wasn't cheating, it was romance!"

Paulo had stayed out of the debate, concentrating on driving through the dark and twisty roads, but at that, he snorted and then burst out laughing.

"Hah! See Paulo agrees with me. Honestly, I'm too tired for games. And you need to be educated. I can't believe you haven't seen *Firefly*! We can all snuggle on the couch, wrapped in warm blankets, with popcorn and some of Paulo's spiked hot apple cider. Doesn't that sound amazing?" I sighed contentedly picturing the evening ahead. But there was silence in the car — awkward silence. That was unexpected.

". . . Loren, maybe you and Henri should spend some time together, alone."

"Oh, right." Mentally, they came as a set, and I considered them both my friends. I didn't know how I was going to do this marriage thing with Henri. I loved him, but I didn't *love* him. I felt hot pricks of frustration trying to manifest as tears.

Thank goodness we were almost home. We were just around the bend, actually. I turned to look out the side window and tried not to snuffle.

"Uh, oh. Busted." Paulo said.

"What? Oh, no." Henri said from the back seat. I discreetly wiped my eyes as I turned around to see what they were talking about.

Connor's car was in the courtyard, and he was sitting on the front steps. He was backlit by the porch light, so his face wasn't visible, but every line of his body was radiating disapproval.

Paulo parked the car. The guys got out reluctantly, like little boys heading in to be punished. Did I miss something?

"Where have you all been? Why haven't you been answering my calls?"

Paulo shrugged, "My phone got dunked in the lake. It is currently not working."

"The lake! What?! Didn't anyone else have their phone? I called all three of you."

"I'm sorry. Mine's in the trunk. I didn't remember to grab it when I shifted back," Henri explained.

"I left mine here. I didn't want it to get wet on the boat or stolen from the car." Why did Connor sound so mad?

Connor was so worked up, he sputtered a full minute before getting any actual words out. "You went boating on the lake? What were you thinking? What if someone saw you?"

"Henri went in his wolf form so it wouldn't matter if we were seen!" I defended our actions to Connor.

All three of the guys groaned, Connor in disbelief, and Henri and Paulo in a more I-can't-believe-you-said-that-and-gave-us-up kind of way. Was it supposed to be a secret?

Paulo started walking inside. He grabbed Connor's arm in one hand and mine in the other and towed us along. "I simply arranged a romantic outing on the lake in my capacity as Lumière." He stopped and spread his hands wide and gave a broad smile that turned impish. "Now it is your turn to disapprove as Cogsworth."

Connor spluttered.

"*Sacré bleu!*" Paulo threw his hands up in comic amazement. "That's perfect! You really have the hang of his character. I can light your hand on fire if it will help you get further into the role?" Paulo's professed concern almost had me giggling. I felt bad for laughing at Connor, though I appreciated his help. My suppressed giggle came out as a snort.

Connor glared at me. His gaze swept from my squelching shoes to my too-big shorts covered in dog hair and then up to the oversized sweater sagging off one shoulder. Algae stuck to the sweater as well, probably deposited by Henri. My hair stood out in snarls around my face — we couldn't find Paulo's hairbrush. Unfortunately, I couldn't blame this mess on the fact that Belle's hair was always falling out of place.

"Blargh!" He sputtered once he took it all in. "You need to be a princess. Princesses are serene, graceful, and elegant. For Belle, we can add curious and intelligent if we are going with Disney. Right now, the kindest description I can use for you is grubby! You are risking your story! Do you want to turn this into Cinderella? Cinderella gets dirty! Belle doesn't." His voice was rising. He looked like he wanted to stomp his foot. Tears burned as I blinked them back. I didn't mean to end up this way, it was disgusting. The messes always just seemed to happen.

"Belle is also kind, brave, and accepting," Henri said softly, but firmly. "Loren managed to be all of those things today." He wrapped his arm around me, taking sides while also asking for understanding from Connor with his tone.

"Disney's Belle is stubborn, outspoken, and independent," Paulo said. He wasn't placating, he was goading. "You can't expect her to follow your rules without any pushback."

"I'm not done," Connor said. He pointed at Henri. "You are supposed to be protective and reclusive, no matter which version of 'Beauty and the Beast' you are trying to force. What you did today didn't further either version!" Henri visibly deflated.

Paulo noticed and started to speak, "But..."

Connor cut him off, "Paulo, you are doing too good of a job of being Lumière. Play the part, don't let it consume you. I am not the bad guy here, remember? Also, you three need to get on the same page. Which version are you working toward?"

"Why don't we head inside?" Henri suggested. "Connor, perhaps you can calmly tell us exactly what the rules are, and why."

Paulo opened the door and we all filed into the house. Well, Connor filed. Henri ushered me in like he was leading me through a dance move. I squelched in my wet sneakers, almost falling over as I toed them off to avoid leaving muddy shoe prints across the hall runner. And Paulo... well, Paulo seemed like he was managing to propel himself through the power of his glare alone. Fiery glare jet propulsion. I muffled a giggle at the thought as I followed everyone into the house.

Paulo turned the lights on in the living room. I eyed the furniture and the carpet. Was I clean enough to sit on either? Definitely not the white chaise I sat on during our last meeting. I considered the dark viridian chair, except it was velvet and would be hard to clean...

Henri saw me eyeing the armchair. He grabbed a throw from inside a decorative chest and draped it over the chair. He drew it back a few inches as if he was holding it for me. "My lady..."

Sitting was easier than arguing.

Connor waited until Henri sat before launching into conversation.

"You two need to stay here, in this house, or on Henri's grounds, if you want this story to work. We don't know what the rules are yet, let alone how far we can bend them. Also, no visitors! The only exception is if you are doing the Disney version of the tale, and the guests are here to clean or take on the role of a servant in some way."

Oh. Yikes. I didn't mind staying here so much — I was an introvert and in need of recharging. Being told to hermit myself was not a sacrifice, but Henri was an extrovert. The last couple of days, he lit up whenever we had guests, even when it was just Paulo. Henri was going to have major cabin fever. I glanced over at him with concern and caught Paulo and Connor looking at him, too. I guess I was right to be worried.

And wait! What about my neurologist appointments, physical therapy, the trauma counselor, scholarship and etiquette classes . . .? I couldn't skip any of those. But maybe I would wait to bring those up later, once Connor was calmer.

Almost as if he sensed my rebellious thoughts, Connor swung around to me. "Loren, you are not to do any cooking or cleaning."

I held my hands up, "No arguments here!" Except who would do the work?

Paulo cleared his throat. "We will need to make sure to leave extra treats for the hob in that case. I will do what I can, too. What I am concerned about is safety. Liam knows where Beauty is, unlike Gaston. Being out of the house seemed safer."

"Maybe the Council could help with that?" Connor asked. He continued, "If they want to find him, they should keep an eye on Loren."

Henri sighed, "Maybe we should schedule a meeting with the Council. Am I allowed to go to that? It seems like ensuring Loren's safety is worth the risk."

Connor spread his hands, "I don't know the rules. This is all guesswork. Educated guesses, but I can't promise anything. I can tell you what I think is best, but you and Loren need to decide how closely you want to align your lives to the story, to help it fall into place."

Henri heaved a sigh that made his forehead fur floof up. He looked so depressed I wasn't the tiniest bit tempted to giggle.

"I might as well stay here." Henri was practically growling. "I can't get rid of my hair — it grows right back no matter how I try to remove it! You can practically see it happening like a time-lapse video."

"That might be a good thing." Connor offered. "It is evidence the Magic wants you locked into the role of Beast."

"Right. That's good news." Henri's tone was clearly skeptical.

"Why don't we all go get showers and change? It's been a long day. You two should take a break tonight. Henri, let Loren introduce you to *Firefly*. I'll make snacks for you. Then we can talk again tomorrow?" I wanted to protest Paulo's plan since it put off the discussion that needed to happen, but I was so tired that procrastinating held major appeal.

"That's the way to get into the spirit of Lumière!" Connor cheered on Paulo's efforts at the worst possible moment. "And *Firefly* is great! You'll love it!"

We all groaned and got up – leaving him alone in the living room.

"Wait! What did I do this time?" Connor hollered after us.

CHAPTER 26

"Isn't Connor supposed to be here?" Henri paused to ask the question as he entered the living room. I admired the lines his body made as he leaned against the door frame. It was a shame that I could appreciate him artistically, but I felt no chemistry. Although, Beauty's love for the Beast grew over time . . . Perhaps it was supposed to be this way for now?

Paulo answered without looking away from the sheets Connor had taped to the walls, "He got a work call and stepped outside. He said he'd only be a minute . . ." he looked down at his watch. "Although, that was ten minutes ago."

Henri joined us. "What's all this?"

"Plot point checklists filled out for Loren. Connor wanted to explain them to us." That was convenient because I had a LOT of questions — starting with why so many boxes were checked on the Sleeping Beauty list: baptism problems, enchanted sleep (with a question mark next to it), and rape/true love's kiss. Left unchecked were: wished-for-child, pricked finger/splinter, giving birth, ogre mother-in-law (optional), and attempted cooking of children (optional). I had almost forgotten about Perrault's lovely version with its jealous, hungry mother-in-law. While researching, I was mildly disgusted by the misogyny in Perrault's versions of the tales, but those feelings had grown into loathing. I needed to review the other lists too, but I was worried I would forget my questions.

Henri had no such problems and skimmed his way along the wall. "These are gruesome! Cannibalism? Birds pecking eyes out? Cutting tongues out?"

"Henri, didn't you read these as a kid?" Paulo asked.

"The original tales are *awful*," I added.

"I did read fairy tales — how else would I have known about the version where the Beast proposes? But I don't remember them being this bad. Damn!" He physically recoiled from the board. That made me nervous, so I got up to see which checklist had bothered him. "This is making me uncomfortable in my role as Beast."

Paulo's mouth dropped open. "You are just now uncomfortable playing the role of a man who locks up a woman, doesn't accept 'no,' and pesters her to marry him daily? Henri, I love you, but you are occasionally painfully dense. I believed we were all just making the best of a bad situation, not that you didn't realize it *was* a bad situation."

Apparently 'Little Red Riding Hood' had made Henri uncomfortable . . . It had sick grandmother, wolf, and rape (optional) checked off.

I kept reading. Optional variants of punishments for the wolf included drowning, burning, boiling, and being chopped open. And then Perrault had his version where there was no punishment because Red isn't rescued. Fucking Perrault, ensuring bad little girls everywhere know they will be abandoned by society. I didn't bother stopping myself from rolling my eyes. At least Connor had also listed the earlier version, where Red escaped on her own, as an option. It wasn't a popular version of the tale though. It was a shame Connor seemed to believe that mattered.

"I meant *more* uncomfortable," Henri grumbled. "Although now, I wish I hadn't started with the proposals to bug Connor." Well, that made two of us.

As if the mention conjured him, Connor returned. He held up two brown paper grocery sacks, "Sorry, I forgot these in the car. And there were questions about data from a coworker."

"Whoa, that's so strange. I am actually jealous of you. I miss work." Henri seemed surprised he felt such a sentiment. "And it's not just guilt for the extra workload I've created for my partners."

"A break will be good for you," Paulo reminded Henri.

Connor responded at the same time, "You hate lying."

"Lying?" I asked.

"I told them I'm on an emergency trip for Doctors Without Borders," Henri explained. "Everyone is going to have questions, and want to see pictures when I get back."

Yikes — lots of guilt there, and lying was a bad idea when the Magic was around. "Could you tell them what is really happening? We are acting like we can't tell anyone about the Magic. Is that true?"

"It's not that we can't tell people. It just doesn't tend to go well, in my experience. I might get them to believe this," Henri swept a hand down his body, "although it might cause an invasive examination. But they wouldn't understand why I cannot work. It's just a cosmetic problem after all — extra hair doesn't require staying home. And the longer this goes on, the more they would wonder why I didn't just remove it, instead of going without a salary, and asking them to handle my patients."

"I meant to ask you about that," Connor pushed his glasses up the bridge of his nose. "I don't mean to pry, but can you afford the break? Do you need money?"

"Thank you for the offer, but I'm okay. I had extra savings for my next charity trip, which I have to postpone anyway."

"Let me know if that changes?" Connor requested.

"Sure, but why don't we move on to the plot lists? I have questions."

"Why don't you give me those bags first?" Paulo asked.

Connor looked down at the bags, seeming confused that he was holding them. A wry expression washed over his face. "Right. There are some flowers that need to be put in water. I hoped they would cheer things up."

I suppressed a giggle at Connor, in all his glory of awkward angles and intersecting lines, as he tried to pass the bags to Paulo. It was a mess artistically, and yet so much more appealing than Henri's detached perfection.

Paulo lifted a bouquet of sunflowers out of the indicated bag, raising an eyebrow at Connor. "Can I just dump everything else in the kitchen for now?"

"I also got dessert . . ." Henri perked up. It was sweet that Connor knew how to cheer up his cousin. "It should go in the fridge."

"Got it. Don't say anything important while I'm gone."

Henri waited a moment and then said, "Anything important." I shook my head. Henri chuckled, "Sorry, I couldn't resist."

"I heard that!" Paulo hollered from down the hall.

It was Connor's turn to shake his head, "Werewolves! I always forget how good their hearing is." Wow. I made a mental note not to have any private conversations in the house with Paulo or Henri around.

Paulo was back a minute later. He'd put the sunflowers in a cobalt blue pitcher, which he set on the coffee table. "Did you get these from the Brinkleys?" he asked Connor. "I haven't seen the heirloom varieties with these rust colors anywhere else in town."

"I did. I stopped by the farmer's market on the way over, before hitting up the bakery. Mrs. Baxter asked me to pass along a greeting with the scones."

Scones! Yum. I had been missing all the treats Ms. Millie plied me with when I was at Grandmother's house.

"Okay," Connor shifted gears as he turned to the wall of papers. "So, when one of Louis's descendants is born, their tale possibilities are unlimited — they could end up playing a role in *any* story. As time goes on, those possibilities collapse. For instance, if you don't get locked away in a tower, you cannot end up as Rapunzel. Each tale has several major elements that need to occur, and tracking those variables should allow me to determine where we will end up, once the function has fully collapsed. Loren's story still has quite a few options open, but the probability numbers are highest for 'Beauty and the Beast' right now."

"Wait," Paulo interrupted. "How are we not *undeniably* Beauty and Beast already? I mean, look at Henri."

"Henri could be having his own tale at the same time Loren is having hers. For instance, if Loren's father were to elope, we might shift into Cinderella or Snow White. I'm not sure which plot points are flexible — is Loren too old to be Snow White? What if she doesn't have stepsisters — does that make

Cinderella impossible? I would have presumed so, but Disney got rid of all the siblings in 'Beauty and the Beast,' so who knows!"

"Wait, if she's not my Beauty, I may be stuck this way for years?" Henri looked about ready to panic.

Connor's eyebrows scrunched, "Well, that is the way the story goes." Even with all the hair, I saw Henri's face blanch. He collapsed into a seat.

"But we were controlling the Magic," Paulo said. "You make it sound like we are just tracking it."

"It's more like we are trying to help steer it in a direction." Connor struggled for a better description. "We are creating a path of least resistance, to make it easy for the Magic to follow a specific tale. Like a lightning rod in a storm, or digging a channel for a stream of water to follow. As the tale starts, the possibilities are too big for a single fairy tale channel. We want to help the Magic settle into the channel we chose, make it the best fit. However, if the Magic is determined on a course, I'm not sure that we can do anything about it. That is why I got upset when you all left the house. You expanded the options to include water tales, like *The Little Mermaid*, instead of narrowing them. But, I didn't explain things well before, so you didn't understand what was at stake, and that's on me. I should just be offering options, and my best guess at outcomes — not trying to control your lives."

Henri shrugged, "No worries, you were right — it was a bad decision. Dad would yell at me, too, if he found out — even if we weren't also dealing with the Magic."

"I just don't want you stuck as the Beast for years," Connor said. "That would certainly be a grim situation."

I wanted to crack a joke that it wasn't grim, it was actually a D'Aulnoy situation since she was the one that had cursed Louis's descendants and all . . . but nobody was likely to get the pun on Grimm/grim. Well, maybe Connor would. I stated the obvious, instead. "If we had been in control, Liam wouldn't have happened."

"Wait, I understood that Liam was Gaston. Handsome on the outside, putrid on the inside . . . Didn't something along those lines *need* to happen?" Paulo asked.

"But he wanted to be the Beast," Henri said.

"Well, he never looked the part . . ." Paulo's eye twitched like he was trying hard not to roll it.

"I think he was fixated on the role of a dashing prince," Connor responded. "He didn't want to listen to me about the specifics of *Beauty and the Beast*. That said, Liam's actions do seem to be in line with Gaston."

"So, everything that happened fits *Beauty and the Beast*?" I asked. How was I supposed to choose a tale to follow if getting . . . well, having *that* happen, was a possibility, even if it wasn't in the story?

"Yes, because Gaston was definitely willing to force the issue despite Belle's protests. But remember, this isn't in any way settled. Multiple options are still open. The Magic can switch to another tale. It is perhaps even more likely if we are trying to pull it away from a path it was already following. A good analogy might be lightning following the path of least resistance to reach the ground. Our job is to make *Beauty and the Beast* the lightning rod, and hope the Magic follows."

"Wait, you *hope* this works?" Henri did not sound pleased. "You aren't certain it will?"

Connor's shoulders hunched in a shrug. "I don't have enough data to be sure of the model's accuracy yet. So it's all guesses — educated guesses, but guesses nonetheless. It's part of the reason I regret getting frustrated last night. This might all be for nothing. I need to respect whatever decisions you and Loren make."

"I consider myself locked into the 'Beauty and the Beast' tale at this point," Henri tugged on his fur as he said it.

Everyone turned to look at me. What, like I had a choice? "I can't come up with a better tale."

Connor nodded. "I haven't been able to, either. I'm hoping you will let me stay involved though, so I can fine-tune the model to be more useful for the next princess affected by the Magic."

Henri answered readily, "I'm happy to have you involved. Why don't you stay for dinner, so we can discuss options? I can help get everything ready, Paulo."

"Thank you for the invitation. I've heard Paulo is an amazing chef. I'd love to stay." Connor glowed. I suppose it was nice for him to have worked things out with his cousin.

"You can set the table. Stay out of my kitchen," Paulo grumbled at Henri.

Henri laughed. "Aren't you supposed to be the character pushing us to be 'hospitable?'"

Paulo gave Henri a look before turning to us, "Give us fifteen minutes, and we'll have a culinary cabaret laid out. I can't promise dancing forks, though."

After Henri and Paulo cleared the room, Connor turned to me. "It didn't escape my attention that you still haven't answered. Are you okay with my involvement in this?"

"Why is it so important to you?"

"Well, that's complicated, and it involves people I'm guessing you'd rather not talk about right now."

He meant Liam. I knew from the way his concerned gaze settled on me.

"I think I need to understand."

Connor nodded. His gaze lost its focus, as he gathered his thoughts. "When we were kids, we played at being heroes in the forest. We fought monsters with stick swords. We went on epic quests for magical ingredients that were the last item needed for a healing potion.

"Liam tried to push one of us to play the princess being rescued. Our job was gushing about how brave he was, but no one ever wanted that part. Something about the fact that everyone disliked being the princess, that we often skipped having the role filled, bothered me. It finally hit me that in order for there to be a hero, a person had to need rescuing. My longing to be a hero also meant longing for someone else to be in trouble. I couldn't wait to grow up and for there to be a damsel in distress — but she was just a prop, not a real person.

"I didn't enjoy the games anymore. When I tried to explain, Liam got angry, and said being a Prince was wasted on me. Henri said people will always need help, and it was right to want to help. He wasn't wrong, but he didn't understand me, either. I ended up talking to my mother about it. She suggested considering a way to be a hero that didn't require someone else to be in danger. And so far, the only thing I've been able to come up with is to stop the danger before it starts — to keep the damsel from needing to be saved in the first place."

Perrault would hate him. I was feeling quite the opposite.

"Since the Magic was going to force me to go on a quest, it seemed logical to save the princesses from needing to be saved."

Wow, talk about an upgrade in difficulty. I teased, "So you decided that instead of rescuing one woman, you would rescue them all?"

Connor's eyes widened in surprise before he laughed. "Well, so far, it doesn't seem like I have made any progress." He sobered. "In fact, I worry I am only causing problems for you. I'm not sure everything would have happened with Liam if I wasn't involved."

"Liam is the only one responsible for his actions," I repeated the same tired phrase everyone had been saying to me and hoped it helped him. I wasn't having much luck with the idea yet. "Besides, you are taking on hundreds of years of misogyny, ingrained into our collective unconsciousness — things woven into our worldview, from a very young age. That is way harder to fight than an ogre or dragon."

"That's an interesting way of looking at it. I was thinking of it more as taking on the Magic, than the collective unconsciousness."

I shrugged, "There is some chicken/egg stuff going on there."

"No, that's an interesting perspective. I need to consider the implications. Thank you."

"You're welcome. Oh, speaking of thanks, I appreciate you bringing the flowers. Sunflowers are one of my favorites."

Connor lit up, "Me too! They are one of the first things that blew my mind about math. The seeds grow in spirals related to the Fibonacci sequence!"

I nodded. "It is fascinating. We studied the golden ratio in art — Leonardo da Vinci used it a lot."

"I didn't know that artists studied math." He ran a finger along a petal. "I should have realized — it makes sense with how much Da Vinci studied anatomy and structure. Lots of examples of the golden ratio there. Do you like sunflowers because of the colors? I've noticed you like saturated colors."

"I actually like them because they turn toward the sun. If it isn't sunny, they turn toward each other, and I've always felt like there is something to learn from that. Not that we need to be positive all the time, or anything fake like that. It's more that we can draw energy from the good parts of life, and know that there are others there to help, even when nothing good is in sight."

It was a lesson I was still learning. I was surprised by the number of people who had been there for me this last week, and by the people currently here.

I smiled at Connor, one of the people I had learned I could turn to. "I've been meaning to thank you –" I was interrupted by singing from down the hall.

Apparently, we were trying for the whole dinner and dancing scene again. I laughed. Paulo might be a good dancer, but we needed to get him singing lessons.

CHAPTER 27

I stared at the closet, at all the clothes somebody else had unpacked. Was it Paulo or was it the hob? Did it matter? I knew it was supposed to be helpful, but that didn't make it less of an invasion. Would complaining chase the hob away and affect my tale? And was I actually grateful to Grandmother, because most of my underthings were pretty and new, instead of comfy and wicking? Ugh, why did everything have to be so complicated?

I inventoried the shelves. Right — none of my old clothes were included. It was for the best. Keep telling yourself that, Loren. I sighed. Oh wait, my hiking backpack was there. Yay! Anything else not princessy?

I looked around the room. Several of my sketchbooks were on the desk. Maybe Millie sent my class books and thesis notes over, too? I walked over to peek in the desk drawers. Let's see — top drawer: address book, pencil case . . . Second drawer — I slammed it shut almost as soon as I opened it. I propelled myself backward and put out a hand to catch myself on the bed frame. Deep breaths. They are only colored pencils, Loren. They won't hurt you. It doesn't matter who gave them to you. It doesn't. They were still just nice colored pencils.

You know what? Fuck that! It *did* matter. Anger welled up inside me, rose from my bones, and collected in a solid ball in the center of my chest. It pulsed forcefully, pushing against my skin. I walked across the room and yanked the drawer open. I snatched the pencil case out of the drawer and threw it across the room. Where was the rest of it? I tore open each drawer in the desk, ransacking them. It wasn't as satisfying to throw the sketchpad — too much air resistance. It wasn't enough.

Henri knocked on the door. "Loren, everything okay? It sounded like you fell or something?"

I opened the door and went back to picking up the items strewn across the room.

"Nope, just taking out some garbage."

"Garbage?" Henri bent down and picked up my sketchpad. He straightened its pages and set it on my desk.

"Yes. Garbage." I marched out the door.

"Loren? Where are you going?" He was scurrying to catch up. It was usually the other way around. The role reversal sent a jolt of power through me. He was peering over my shoulder. "You've walked by several trash cans . . . You aren't destroying your artwork, are you?" He sounded horrified. Another time it would have made me giggle. "It will all work out! You don't have to give up on your art."

He reached out and physically stopped me so I would face him.

I didn't want him touching me or stopping me.

"No." I didn't yell, but it was more than firm. I forced him to drop his hands by shoving through him with my shoulder; it was not a gentle shove, either. For all my pushiness, I was aware that Henri was allowing me to do it. And that pissed me off. I stomped past him.

"I'm not throwing my art out or giving up," I bit the words off. Neither the Magic nor Liam could take my art from me. In fact, once I finished this, I was going to go find new supplies, come home, and paint. "I just don't want this anywhere near me. In fact," the realization of where I was headed dawned, "I need to burn this shit, or throw it in the lake."

"I'm not going to stop you, but I am curious why . . ."

"Because Liam gave it to me."

"Oh." Great, he understood. "Want some help? Here let me get the door."

"Doors are great, but I need to do the rest myself."

"I can respect that. Want company?"

"Sure."

He held open the door that led from the kitchen to the side yard. I paused briefly, fire or water? I would have to wait for the logs to catch in the fire pit. That settled it — lake it was. I stomped across the patio and along the trail through the woods until I reached the lake's edge. Crushing the crunchy leaves littering the path was therapeutic. It seemed to take less time than usual to reach the lake.

The lake was as still as I had ever seen it. The light skipping over the water's surface implied movement more than the surface of the water itself did.

My firm stride echoed under the small dock — the pounding noise fit my mood. I paused only for a second at the dock's end before thrusting everything I held away violently. The pencils, the tubes of paint. The pad of paper. They all went plopping into the water. Some sank right away, and others floated. The waves I created on the smooth surface were satisfying. I took a second to admire the effect.

Part of me wanted to sit at the end of the dock and process the moment for a while, but I wasn't going to give Liam a second more of my time. I mean, it would happen at some point; I wasn't superwoman. I would probably have another panic attack in the future. But now, while I had control of the situation? Nope — not happening. I whipped around. I wasn't even going to stick around to see if the rest sank.

I laughed. "I just littered. I never litter. What would Connor say about a princess littering? I don't think I am going to get any cute bird or mice companions now." Oh well. "God, that felt good!"

I started back up the hill. On to the art store. Hmm, that might be a problem. Not being able to drive sucked. I turned around to address Henri. He was grinning like a madman.

"Henri, is Paulo around? I *need* new art supplies."

"He is not. If you make a list, we could have them delivered . . ."

But . . . I wilted.

Wait. Why did I care about the Magic's boundaries? My own boundaries weren't being respected. Not okay.

"No. I know it doesn't seem logical, but I need to go now." I mean it was logical if you take my mental health into account. Surely that counted for something? Did Lointaine have any taxis?

"Hmm . . ." Henri was rubbing his neck absentmindedly. He was now apparently used to the fur; he didn't jerk his hand away as he had in the past. "I think I can work something out. I'll make a call as soon as we get back inside."

I fell a smidge in love with him for not questioning my need to go now. Maybe this would be a bonding experience that sparked something between us? Wait, would that mean the Magic set up this whole thing, and it wasn't me taking charge? Ugh! All this second-guessing myself! No. Enough. The Magic couldn't have my art. It was mine.

CHAPTER 28

I eyed the trunk of the car with disbelief. How could the contents of two medium bags and one box cost $573.27? I mean, I know good art supplies are expensive, but I'd only ever bought a few items at a time. I'd never had to outfit myself from scratch. Take a breath, Loren. You aren't going to regret this. Not one penny of it. You needed that easel, and the acrylics will be good if you want to try something different for a while.

I mentally reviewed my purchases. Did I forget anything? I wish I had taken the time to make a list.

I peeked in the bags: three different types and sizes of paper, two pre-stretched canvases, graphite pencils, colored pencils, some new brushes, watercolors (phthalo blue and green, new gamboge, raw umber, cadmium red, alizarin crimson, red oxide, indanthrene blue), a basic set of acrylics, kneaded eraser, pastels, fine-tipped markers, paint palette, brush holder, scissors, art tape, easel . . . It should be more than enough to get started.

I prayed my skills were back. I needed to complete a commission or two and get paid. Having my bank account this low was scary.

Henri closed the trunk and I gave him a hug. "Thank you for driving me." I paused. "And for getting them to close the shop so we could sneak in without being seen by anyone. It felt like we were on a secret mission."

"I hope it does stay a secret. Can we agree not to tell Connor about this? Or do we beg forgiveness?"

I mulled the question over. "I don't know. Do you think it will matter to his calculations?"

Henri shrugged before getting in the car. "I was hoping I could tell him it was the equivalent of giving you a library."

"Umm." I giggled, "You would go broke if you walked into an art store and said, 'This is all yours.' Would you ask me to close my eyes as we walked in, too?" Henri rolled his eyes at me. "I appreciate the thought, but . . ." How did I say this tactfully? Huh, maybe I didn't worry about being tactful. "I needed to do that for myself." It was good that I hadn't let him pay. Really. It was important that I didn't associate this bit of pulling my pieces back together with anyone else.

"I can respect that. I'll have to figure something else out to do later."

I groaned. "Why does that sound dangerous?"

"Oh, ye of little faith. Don't you trust me to make grand romantic gestures?"

"You do them a little too well." I laughed. "Seriously, you don't have to do all of that."

"It's fun, but I'm hearing it makes you uncomfortable?" He glanced away from the road to see my reaction.

"It's just . . ." I shook my head, not to say it didn't make me uncomfortable, but to say that I didn't know how to explain it. "I don't know how to say this without hurting your feelings."

"Go ahead and say it anyway. This won't work if we are so careful of each that other we don't talk about an issue."

"All right." Deep breath, this was Henri — he wasn't going to be a jerk about this. "I'm sorry, but it doesn't seem like our relationship is worth grand gestures yet. It's as if you are being romantic to be romantic, not because you love me and it drives you to romantic displays. I guess it doesn't seem genuine in some way."

Henri mulled it over for a minute. He was concentrating on the road as one would hope your driver would, so I couldn't read his face. Not that it would be easy with his sunglasses and hat anyway.

"Do you remember when we talked before about how I needed this as much as you? Well, that isn't accurate." My heart dropped. Was he going to quit this whole experiment? Would that be a bad thing? "I may need this more than you."

"Huh?"

What?

We were on the single lane dirt road on his own property, but Henri still pulled slightly to one side and put the car in park before turning toward me.

The sun was shining through the ochre and bronze leaves, transforming the woods into a cathedral of stained glass. It was entrancing; I almost missed what Henri was saying.

". . . you to swear not to tell anyone."

Huh? I whipped my head around. Fairy tale oaths were serious things. What if the secret was something dreadful and it needed to be shared? Henri wasn't meeting my gaze. He was wiping his hands distractedly over his thighs and staring out the window.

"Umm, I don't know if I am comfortable with that. What if I swear I won't tell unless I think keeping the secret will harm someone?"

He licked his lips and swallowed, considering a moment before answering, "I can live with that. It's not that kind of a secret."

"In that case, I promise."

He took a deep breath and the words spilled out, "Loren, I'm gay."

"Seriously? That's it?!" The words popped out before I could stop them. "I thought you were going to tell me you murdered someone or something!" Umm, yeah, the chief accusing me of murder wasn't bothering me or anything.

Wait. Hold on a minute, why was he trying to date me if he was gay? My brain made a couple of the non-linear leaps it favored recently. "Wait! You and Paulo!? Why the hell did you propose to me?"

I had never seen Henri at a loss for words, but he was fumbling them horribly now. "I . . . we . . . well, I can't let it get out that I am gay. It would destroy my father, especially after . . . well, you know." He waved his hand vaguely, and I did know. "He's been on this kick about me settling down and having kids so we can continue the Pack and the family line."

"I don't mean to sound insensitive . . . but has he said anything against gay people? I mean, couldn't you use a surrogate to have kids? That's not a reason to not be with Paulo."

". . . I guess. I wonder if we . . ." He brightened momentarily, but then his shoulders slumped. "It's a little more complicated than that. Dad wants me to take over as the Council leader. But my relationship with Paulo apparently isn't qualifying me to join the Council, which I don't understand!" He pounded the steering wheel. "Best I can guess is that . . . well, the Pack has certain prejudices, and even if Paulo were a woman, those alone would make my appointment controversial if we were mated."

"You mean the werewolves are racist?"

"What? No!" He shook his head. "Well, maybe some members are, but it's not that. I should have explained this to you before now. . . . Okay, I'll try to avoid all the special terms we have for it. Basically, it boils down to this: there are those who are *born* werewolves, and there are those who are turned *into* werewolves. Werewolf society considers made werewolves like old money considers the nouveau riche. Better than not having money at all, possibly important for keeping things from stagnating, but also lacking in taste and culture."

"And Paulo is a made werewolf."

"Yes."

"If Paulo's not an option, how am I being considered?"

"Frankly, because no one would dare to argue with the Magic. It called the wolf out of me, remember?" The last was dryly delivered.

"Oh."

"As far as they are concerned, you are putting me more fully in touch with my wolf side. So obviously, you would be good for the Pack."

"But, what about Paulo? Don't you love him?" It was so obvious to me in retrospect.

"I do." Henri put his head in his hands and let out a single sob. "He broke up with me. He said I had to try this — that he just wanted me to be happy. He wasn't ever happy hiding things. He only did it for me. It was slowly killing him to keep things a secret. He said we were obliged to consider the Pack's needs, too. I told you about that already."

It still sucked, and poor Paulo! I rubbed Henri's back. What could I say to help make any of it better? I settled for the truth. "That sucks."

Perhaps it was time to show the Pack they were wrong? It was ridiculous to think of Paulo as lesser. Given that Henri had been entrenched in the Pack his whole life, it might take time to get him to see that.

I considered Paulo — how was he managing to help with my fairy tale? Hell, I strongly suspected he was responsible for several of Henri's grand romantic gestures. Henri only had to walk in and pop the question. Which brought me back full circle to the start of the discussion. Once Henri regained his composure, I asked, "I'm sorry, but I'm confused. What does being gay have to do with the grand romantic gestures?"

"Right. Until the Magic kicks in, I don't think I can be romantically attracted to you."

Wow, that gave me all sorts of warm fuzzy feelings. Hmm. "Shouldn't the Magic have already started to work?"

"I don't know. I know what I think a successful relationship looks like. The best I can do is try to mimic that until it works."

"Fake it till you make it, huh?"

He shuddered. "It sounds so vile that way, but yes."

It was what we agreed to earlier, but the scale of the problem felt larger than before. I wasn't sure I wanted to be a part of this anymore.

"If it is making you uncomfortable, I can stop. I don't want to do anything to hurt you." He looked miserable.

I sighed, "I don't know what to do, Henri. Do you actually trust the Magic? I don't have such a great track record with it. It doesn't sound like it did great things for my mom, either."

"I wish you knew my parents. They are why I trust the Magic. Maybe you could ask them or your grandmother about it? I bet Connor has a list of people you could talk to?"

I thought about my grandmother and the chair she couldn't let go of in her library.

Henri prompted gently, "You seem to have faith that the Magic caused the bad things in your life . . . Do you think you could have faith that it can change things for the better, too?"

This was ridiculous. But how much choice did I have? It's not like I wanted to move out of Henri's house with Liam still around. Even if I didn't believe in the Magic, would I do anything differently? I might fight harder to finish my thesis and get my art back. But there wasn't anything stopping me from doing that now on our current path.

Beauty and the Beast was bad enough when it was about Belle changing the Beast. I wasn't sure if the Beast not being happy with himself made the story better or worse. Changing because you wanted to change was better than outside forces telling you that you weren't good enough. But Henri not liking himself, well, that made me sad.

"I honestly don't know, Henri. I'm willing to keep trying, but I'm having trouble trusting our relationship. Could you stick to things you genuinely mean for now? Not where you wish things were? I want to marry someone who loves me, not only hopes to someday."

Henri blew out a big breath. "That's fair. I will tone it down. I think I have to keep proposing every day, though. I'll ask Connor and stop that too if it is safe."

"Thank you."

"I just want everyone to be happy, to live happily ever after."

"I know, Henri. Me too. I just hope the Magic and I are on the same page about what that looks like."

CHAPTER 29

"How could you say 'No'?" Kella shrieked. She gestured with her fork as she continued. "I mean I know *how*, but still! Damn! You are a stronger woman than I am!"

I struggled with what to say. I needed to explain the dilemma to Kella without breaking Henri's trust. I played with my napkin, twisting it between my fingers.

"I guess it comes down to the fact that I don't love him. There isn't any chemistry."

"Yet?" Kella pried gently, "It seems like it *could* happen. I mean, especially with the Magic involved? Isn't that what it is supposed to do? I mean, Stockholm syndrome is kind of a traditional part of *Beauty and the Beast*, isn't it?" She sipped her coffee.

"I don't want to count on the Magic making us fall in love. I think we could be good friends, he is a nice guy." But he was trying so hard. Would that change after we were together? Would one of us end up resenting the other? "For us to move forward, I would have to decide I am all right being married to someone who is just a friend."

"I'm sorry. That's hard. Especially since he is going to ruin you for anyone else at this rate. Tell me about the other times! I am going to enjoy it vicariously."

I sighed. The daily proposals were torture. "He has a lot of free time to plan since he doesn't get to leave the house much. Let's see." I rolled my eyes to the ceiling, and ticked the proposals on my fingers, "There were the rose petals and hot chocolate bar near the fire pit; leaves raked into a heart shape on the misty lake shore; candlelight and romantic dance music in the living room; pancakes with 'marry me' written in syrup and delivered in bed; a treasure hunt that ended with an engagement ring; a romantic champagne picnic; and asking while we watched a meteor shower." I frowned. That was only about a week's worth of proposals.

"Ugh, I can't remember the others. Oh, wait! Out in the rowboat on the lake. The bow was decorated with flowers and everything, but his knee got soaked." I giggled remembering. "I'm still forgetting four or five others, though. That is part of the problem. I don't trust my brain. I can't trust my memory or my feelings. It seems like a horrible idea to make a big decision right now."

Kella made a comforting noise. "I can see why that would make it more complicated. Not to mention everything else. Speaking of which, I have been meaning to ask — what did your committee decide about classes?"

"I think Henri bribed them somehow," I said as blandly as possible. It was nice of him to help. Though it felt a bit like I was being managed again, I was pretty sure that was my hang-up. "He is giving me private ballroom dance classes, and they are counting as make-up classes."

"Oooh! He is a good dancer! I practically melted in his arms during the last Solstice Ball." Kella fanned herself. "That, at least, is an easy fix."

"Um, yeah." He was a good dancer. It was kind of a problem.

"You don't sound happy?"

"It's, um, it is still hard . . ." My eyes burned, which pissed me off. "Sometimes I can't handle having him touch me. He is so kind when that happens. And then *that* makes it hard for me to tell him 'no' when he proposes."

"Hmm," Kella frowned at her croissant. "In any other situation, I would tell you he was acting like an ass for pushing you. But . . ." And that was exactly my problem. All the 'buts.' She sighed and glanced at the clock. "Oh wow! Henri and Paulo will be back soon. Umm, I need to talk to you about Liam." She took a breath. "I am sorry I didn't say anything. I should have told you how much of a dick he was. I figured he would turn into Gaston though, and you needed a dick for that. The Magic was supposed to work it all out; I didn't realize how far he would take things."

"Nobody did, Kella. It's not your fault. It's nobody's fault but his." It was my mantra recently. I almost believed it some days.

"I still feel guilty. Do you want to talk about it?" She waved her croissant. "I mean him . . . or it . . . or, would you rather move on . . .?"

I searched for words while reducing my last bite to crumbs between my fingers. "I wish they would find him. And it's not just that he might be after me." I struggled to explain, "I thought I was stronger than this. I am scared all the time — and jumpy. I hate it. Henri does something amazing, and I don't have the emotional capacity for happy feelings. And since I am stuck here, I can't get any space to think about the situation and figure out how I feel about Henri."

I took a deep breath. "I need another option, but nowhere is safe enough. At least not in town, and the police still don't want me to leave." Not to mention the last time I seriously considered it, I had a panic attack. I needed to get that under control. It's not like I could marry Henri to feel safe. That wouldn't be fair to either of us.

"Chief Duncan is still going on about that?"

I nodded. "I don't think he believes I did it anymore." Things had changed between us — first with the revelations about him and my mother, and then the incident with Liam. It was hard to put into words, and the part about him and my mother felt oddly personal. "But he also doesn't have any better options, so he can't just let me go. I honestly don't know where I stand with him."

"Huh. Seems like he's going to have to let you off the hook soon if he doesn't find some way to pin it all on you. You know, you could come stay with me." I blinked, trying to keep up with the rapid switches in topic.

Her offer was touching, especially considering the potential magical fallout. I blinked away the tears trying to form. "Thank you, I really appreciate it. But I'm going to have to find a way to get some mental clarity while I'm here because I don't know what would happen to the tale if I left now. Connor was so upset the last time we left the house. I'm not supposed to have guests, either. You only got to come because I suggested someone needed to fill the role of the enchanted wardrobe."

"You did not!" She feigned indignance as we both laughed.

"I did. I'm sorry, but Disney didn't give you a cute French name. That was almost a sticking point with Connor. He was talking about making you wear a feathered boa to fit the role. I saved you from that at least!"

"Hmph. This is what I get for bringing you new colors to wear." She smiled as she said it. "Well, despite all that, the offer is open, if you change your mind."

"Can you imagine what Disney sequels would have to say about Belle and the wardrobe running off to live together?"

Kella threw her head back and laughed. "Sounds more like a XXX film than a PG one."

"Did I ever tell you about how when I was in the hospital the first time, I overheard this weird discussion? There were a couple of teenage boys debating which Disney princesses were virgins when they got married. I had to work it out because I came in partway through the conversation. 'Does it count if Ariel was in fish form?'" I mimicked a deeper male voice. "'Not Snow White, unless it was with a dwarf, and you know if it was with one, it was with all of them.' It makes sense now that I know about this town and fairy tales, but at the time, I wasn't sure I wasn't having a hallucination. I mean what sort of teenage boys talk about Disney princesses?"

Kella said through laughter, "Well, sex was involved. Those youngsters would surely win the bad pickup line competition. I can just imagine it," she paused and wiped her eyes. "It would be like, 'I can take you on a magic carpet ride,' or 'I must be Pinocchio 'cause I have some magically growing wood.'"

"Eww! Those are awful!" We were both laughing hysterically. We had barely collected ourselves before we heard the guys come into the house.

"Uh oh, they don't sound happy." Kella was right, and their displeasure was more obvious the closer they got to the kitchen.

"How can you be surprised, given everything that has happened?" I had never heard Paulo be so sharp with Henri. They seemed to pause down the hall as the conversation escalated.

Henri defended himself, "But this puts us all at risk! It's a whole new level of selfish."

"Damnit, Henri — it's just Liam being Liam. He has ALWAYS been selfish. He takes what he wants, and has NEVER cared how it affects anyone else. This isn't new."

Henri said something quietly.

"Fuck, Henri — he raped Loren. She isn't the first person I've heard about, either! Get over the fact he is risking your secret."

"Why didn't you say anything?"

"You wouldn't have believed me. You *still* don't believe me about how awful he is. Why should I think anyone else would listen if you won't?"

I glanced at Kella and found her looking as stunned as I felt.

"I'm so sorry. I've failed you. I don't know what else to say . . . You're right." Henri's words barely reached us. I expected to hear something else from Paulo, but instead, he stalked into the kitchen.

There was an awkward pause as Paulo realized we must have overheard the argument. Kella was braver than I was and broke the silence. "So, um, how did the Pack meeting go?"

Paulo had recovered from his initial shock and was now costumed in a brittle smile. "Well, we figured out how Liam escaped. It seems when the van transporting him arrived at the prison, they opened the door and there was only a," he made air quotes, "'large dog' in the back. They called animal control for the 'dog,' and put together a manhunt for Liam. The 'dog' was taken to the local shelter and checked in. But, shockingly," he pretended to be surprised, forming his mouth into a round O with his hands on either side, "the 'dog' wasn't there in the cage the next day."

Henri must have walked in while we were absorbed in Paulo's story. "He risked exposing all of us so he could escape. The Council is displeased, and wants him found." He sounded tired.

"Displeased?" Paulo gave a sharp laugh before continuing, "They are beyond pissed! I can't say I disagree with them." I was on Paulo's side. I mean, besides Liam, was there anyone who didn't want him caught?

"You think he stayed in town? Surely even Liam has enough common sense to leave?" Kella asked. "Wait, I can't believe I said that. Of course he didn't."

"Did everyone besides me know how awful Liam was?" Kella and I both flinched at the anguish in Henri's voice. He didn't wait for an answer. "Connor said he will probably try to get to Loren. Liam probably thinks he can fix things if the two of them are together."

Paulo was nodding, "Liam does like an easy fix."

Okay, breathe. It won't happen. Henri and Paulo are both here. They won't let anything happen. I leaned over to put my head on my knees.

"Wait, how did Connor get involved in this?" Kella sounded as confused as I felt. I appreciated that. "He isn't a part of the Pack, is he?"

"No, but the Council actually brought in some outsiders this time. They are extremely concerned about their secret becoming public — well, *more* public I guess. Nobody has ever avoided them for two weeks before." Paulo still sounded peeved, but there was a tinge of awe as he continued, "They invited Chief Duncan."

And another deep breath, all the way into the diaphragm. And let it out now. I sat back up slowly.

Kella made a little moue, "Wow! They shared their precious secret with someone? From the way they acted when I found out . . . I feel like I need to overnight Satan some ice skates." Kella rolled her eyes.

Paulo chuckled, "You should have been there, Kella! The whole werewolf revelation blew his mind. I thought his head was going to implode and bitty bits of brain were going to rain down on us all. Someone had to transform to get him to believe it."

Panic was turning into rage.

"You all can laugh," Henri said, "But I suspect the chief is back at the station going through all his unsolved case files right now. Seeing if this information changes anything. We are going to have to walk a delicate balance with him."

I just couldn't let it go. "Why would Liam think he has any chance with me? That's ridiculous!" Oh gosh, I was yelling. And yup, everyone was staring at me. Great.

"Don't worry, Loren. That's part of what we discussed. We set up a guard rotation to keep an eye on the house. We will know if Liam tries anything."

Paulo was trying to help, but the fact I needed surveillance because Liam wasn't checking into reality was maddening. Plus . . . "Wait, so now I am bait? That is not okay." I realized that wasn't fair, even as I was saying it. The Council wasn't putting me in danger. That was Liam. Again.

Henri responded, "I'm not thrilled with the lack of privacy, but the Council overruled my objections. Honestly, if Liam is targeting you, I'll feel better knowing there is backup."

Kella was frowning at her watch. "I can't believe I have to leave in the middle of all of this, but if I don't, I am going to be late for the brush-up rehearsal. Will you please call me later and let me know if there is anything I can do to help?" She paused a second, "Or anything else I need to know?"

I instantly felt guilty we hadn't gotten around to talking about the theatre or Kella's logistical problems. She was adjusting the theatre's schedule to fit performances for *The Tempest*, while also rehearsing *Pirates of Penzance*. I was still pissed I wasn't going to be allowed to leave the house to see either show.

"I mean it. Anything." I apparently took too long to respond, since Kella was verbally prodding me.

"I promise. Thank you for babysitting me this morning." I grinned at her and she laughed as she hugged me. "I hope we can visit again soon!" I promised myself I'd be a better friend, and make sure to listen to her problems next time.

"You bet!" Kella agreed. "Bye, boys!" She waved over her shoulder.

Henri and Paulo waved goodbye obediently until the door closed behind her. There was a pause while we all floundered with how to start the conversation back up again.

Henri chose to retreat. "I have to plan the guard rotations. I should be done in about an hour. We could eat lunch then?"

"Sure," I mumbled.

"We can do that. Any requests, or should I whip up something from whatever's around?" Paulo asked.

"I'll be happy to eat whatever you make."

Paulo nodded to Henri's back and then watched as Henri wandered off toward his office.

"Right." Paulo turned to me with a cheer that seemed forced. "Any preferences for lunch?"

"Hmm, something easy?" It felt awkward to accept lunch, given that he had already handed over Henri on a platter. "I don't want to cause you any trouble."

He gave me a more genuine smile. "It's no trouble. I love to cook for people."

"What about some soup then?" It was a typically dreary mid-November day, and something warm sounded good.

"You and your soup." He smiled, "I have some butternut squash leftovers that need to be eaten. Soup and salad?"

"Sure! That sounds yummy. What can I do to help?"

"You can keep me company if you like?" He gave me a devilish grin. "Or I can give an impromptu performance."

I laughed, and he took it as an invitation. His voice went off-key as he sang Lumière's song from the Disney movie. He even did a little pirouette as he pulled ingredients out of the fridge.

"Oh no, that's *really* okay," I said through giggles.

"You don't like my singing?" He wasn't at all offended, although he was pretending to be.

"It's not that, I just don't want you to have to go through all the extra effort," I played along with the charade.

"Hmmm. I don't believe you." Then, in a lightning switch of topics, "You like bacon, right? Who doesn't like bacon?"

"I love bacon."

"Good. I'll make a fried green tomato, goat cheese, and bacon salad." I suddenly couldn't wait to eat lunch.

"Do we have to wait for Henri?"

Paulo laughed. "It will take me a little while to get everything made, but let's just say he better not take any longer than he said he would." He winked at me.

He was being so kind! I took a deep breath.

"Paulo, I have to ask. How in the world are you doing this? How can you be so nice to me? I would hate my guts!" You couldn't have made that a little clearer, Loren? Ugh! Your big chance to discuss this, and you are unintelligible.

"Oh sweetie," his words were so full of compassion. "I don't hate you. If I was mad at someone it would be Henri. But I love him." He cocked his head a bit, "And I understand where he is coming from, even if I know he is wrong."

Hmm . . . interesting.

Paulo continued after a short pause, "I realized that if he can't accept himself for who he is, he won't be able to believe I love him." He rolled his eyes at Henri's ridiculousness. "He is way more worried about his parents and the Pack than he needs to be. We broke up because I didn't want to hide our relationship. I came out to the Pack to prove being gay wasn't an issue. Henri seemed to be coming around to the idea, but then the Magic turned him all hairy. If Henri didn't try to work it out with you, he would wonder for the rest of his life if he could have been in a conventional relationship. That would have broken us, and caused resentment. This way, there is a chance of saving our relationship — or at least ending up friends."

His eyes flickered back down at the tomatoes he was slicing. "I'm embarrassed to say I considered asking you to marry him in name only. But I'm selfish. I want to be with him in the spotlight for his special moments. I'm not willing to settle for hoping to make eye contact from the sidelines."

I considered the potential solution. It didn't sound ideal for anyone.

"Hmm." I responded, "It still seems like it must be hard to watch this."

"Of course it is. But it was building to this, way before you got here. I'm realizing I can't hide in the shadows anymore. Not with so many other big secrets to keep all the time, too."

Right — the fur, the whole werewolf thing. Paulo finished slicing the tomatoes while I considered what he had said. Tension was building in the room, but I couldn't say why. Paulo carefully washed the cutting board and knife and put them in the dish rack.

Then he came and stood directly across from me. He braced his hands on the counter before looking me in the eye.

"I owe you an apology." Huh? He swallowed audibly before continuing in a rush, "I knew how awful Liam was and I didn't do anything about it because he was blackmailing me — threatening to tell everyone about Henri and me if I didn't do as he asked."

Whoa.

"If I had known he would try to do that to you I swear . . ." He choked up and took a moment to collect himself. "I would have said something, no matter the cost. No one should have to go through that." The last few words were raw. I truly believed he knew the level of pain I experienced.

I reached across the counter to hold one of Paulo's hands. He let me, intertwining his fingers with mine.

"Paulo, did Liam do something to you too? Or someone else . . .?"

Paulo collapsed, sobbing onto the counter. He pulled his hand away from mine to bury his face in both of them.

"I didn't think anyone would believe me. He never showed any interest in men before." It was hard to catch his words, blocked and muffled as they were by his hands. "I should have said something, though. I am so sorry."

Wow. All I'd learned in the previous weeks about the court system spiraled through my brain. I spent the majority of my time being afraid, rehashing what Liam did to me — tumbling the options and the what-ifs countless times. I had to carve out space to think about anything else, even the important things like the Magic and my thesis. Liam invaded so much more than my body with his actions. One of the things I considered was whether or not pressing charges would make me responsible for Liam's future victims. I wouldn't have thought I could be grateful for the mental energy given over to the topic, but it let me respond to Paulo without needing time to consider the question.

"Paulo, what Liam did to me is not your fault."

"But I could have stopped it."

"No," I insisted, "Suppose you had reported him to the police. That they believed you, and there was lots of proof."

He was shaking his head, "But I didn't have any—" I plowed forward because it didn't matter.

I repeated, "That you had proof."

"That he was then magically convicted . . ." Because magic is apparently what it would take, given the statistics I found.

"Even with all of that, Liam wouldn't have been in jail for long before getting out. There would be nothing to stop him from going somewhere else and doing the same thing. Hell, there's not much to stop him from doing it here, again. Sure, some people would believe you, but no one wants to believe someone they like is a monster. It's not part of their story about Liam, so they would explain it away somehow."

They get irritated with you for causing their mental dissonance, and then that turns into victim blaming. At least, that is what I was telling myself had happened with my father.

I honestly wasn't sure if I was working so hard to convince Paulo, or myself, at this point. I talked all this through with my therapist several times. Eventually, I would believe what I knew to be true.

"It is *absolutely* not your fault Liam did that to you, *or* to me." I added as an afterthought, "It's not my fault either."

Paulo shook his head and wiped his face on his sleeve. I got up and walked around the counter to hug him. He sobbed in my arms. "I couldn't do it to Henri. I didn't know how his father could ever accept me if I said anything about Liam. It was selfish, though."

The extent of Paulo's quandary became clear. I realized with horror that Paulo would have seen Liam at every family holiday if he and Henri were a couple. Damn! If things worked out with Henri, I might be in the same boat.

"Liam is . . . is . . ." I was spluttering. "Well, shit! I can't think of anything bad enough to call him. I mean, even pond scum and dirt balls are useful, ecologically." Why didn't we have better words for this — did we think by naming it, we would conjure it into existence? Is that why we didn't talk about rape?

"He is a fucking dick." Paulo agreed with me through snuffles, before blowing his nose on a paper towel. "Thank you for believing me, Loren." He sniffed experimentally, reaching for another paper towel. "I haven't –" He paused mid-sentence and sniffed again. Then with a gasp, he whirled around and rushed over to the stove.

The soup had boiled over the edges of its pot, and wafts of smoke were rising from the burner. I hurried over to help. Paulo surveyed the mess with wide eyes and fisted his fingers in his hair.

"Well," I said, refusing to let this become a disaster; in the scheme of things, it was so small compared to the mess we were discussing. "Looks like we're down to just salad for lunch." Paulo relaxed fractionally.

"We are going to need to leave out a whole bakery's worth of bread for the hob to take care of this mess."

I couldn't help but giggle at the absurdity of the pronouncement. Paulo started laughing too. The next thing I knew, we were on the floor gasping and howling with laughter.

We could still laugh. Maybe things really would be all right.

CHAPTER
30

And that is how Henri found us when he walked into the kitchen — in a giggling heap on the floor, next to the burned soup. The fire alarm gave an indignant beep overhead as he stared at us.

"No wonder you guys missed the phone call. Paulo — could you call the chief? He had some questions you might be able to answer about the vets in town."

Paulo looked around the kitchen at the mess.

"Don't worry, I've got this." I volunteered. Henri glared at me. What was that for?

"Hmm, let me think about this, dishes or phone call . . ." Paulo made weighing motions with his hands. He still seemed a bit brittle around the edges, but for now, he was holding the pieces together. "Do you have the number?"

Henri held out a slip of paper.

"Great, thanks." Paulo levered himself up off the floor and took it. He pulled his cell phone out and dialed the number. "Hi, this is Dr. Martín returning a call from Chief Duncan."

Henri held out a hand to me and helped me off the floor. I reached for the pot on the stovetop. It needed to soak in hot water, or it would be impossible to clean. Henri frowned at me, "Don't you dare!"

"Huh?" I'm so eloquent.

Henri heaved a sigh and gently took me by the shoulders, turned me around, and gently pushed me over onto a kitchen stool. "Are you trying to turn into Cinderella?"

Oh right. I could feel my eyes get big. I shook my head as Paulo started talking again. I didn't want to interrupt.

"Chef Duncan! I hear I can be of help?" Paulo sounded as puzzled as I was. A moment later a polite smile twitched across his face, and he gave a half-hearted laugh.

"Oh. Nickolaus Randolph said that, did he? Well, of course, I'll help in any way possible."

Henri and I exchanged looks, what did his father have to do with this?

"You are right. It is better to keep the circle of people who know everything as small as possible."

I waited to hear what he would say next.

"What do you mean by 'exotic'?"

Henri took the pot off the stove and over to the sink. I wasn't even trying to pretend like I wasn't listening in on Paulo's phone call.

"Well, for the lizards, just my clinic. No one else in town does reptiles. Most offices only handle cats and dogs. Several handle farm animals. I do all the exotics, like lizards and birds. I don't know of anyone locally that does aquarium animals. Not much demand for it around here."

A short pause, "Like the small, freshwater kind?"

Paulo was shaking his head. "Two and a half centimeters long? No, nothing like that around here. You would need an aquarium that was at least twenty feet long for a shark with teeth that size. I'm pretty confident I would have heard about anything like that in town. Closest thing would be the aquarium in Hendersonville."

Another brief pause; I wished I could hear the chief's side of the call. Asking Paulo to put the call on speakerphone would be too much, right?

"Squid? Umm, this must be some case you are working on. I don't know of anyone with pet squid. They do extremely poorly in aquariums. The large public aquariums don't even try to keep them."

Squid? I mouthed the word at Paulo. He responded with an exaggeratedly perplexed face and shrugged.

"I can ask around, but I don't think so. You should check with the aquarium folks in Hendersonville. Maybe they could tell you about aquarium cleaning services and then you could ask them about their clients?"

. . .

"Snakes? Yes."

. . .

"Do you mean venomous? Poisonous means . . . never mind. No. I don't have any venomous snakes coming through the clinic."

. . .

"Yes, I'm sure. It's office policy. Our insurance company won't let me — liability is a mess. I don't know if anyone around here keeps venomous snakes, anyway. I mean, you hear occasionally about those snake handling churches, but I don't know anyone that specifically has one."

Henri had stopped cleaning, the sponge dangling from his hand, and was staring at Paulo too.

"Well, I can't know for sure, but offices that would be likely to have it are: Tails Wag Animal Clinic, Pet's Vet, Healthy Paws, Lointaine Animal Care, Creatures Great and Small Vet Care, Main Street Animal Hospital, Puppy Comfy Clinic, Black's Family Pet Care . . ." He kept going through about fifteen names, ending with ". . . and of course, my own office."

Paulo listened for a moment and shrugged, though the chief wouldn't be able to see it. "Well, most vets spend about a third of their time in surgery. Ketamine is used as an anesthetic for short procedures on animals. Most of the offices in town would have it on hand."

. . .

"One final question? Sure."

Paulo's jaw dropped and he swallowed. Henri was shaking his head, but he didn't look nearly as worried as Paulo did.

"No sir, I don't know of any werewolf with a scar like that on its paw."

. . .

"Yes, I am the Pack doctor, but –"

Well, that was news to me. Pack doctor?

"Look, I'm not saying there isn't someone with a scar like that. But no one has come to me with deep puncture injuries." Paulo thought for a second, "Werewolves are quick healers and don't tend to scar. Any chance this is something else — maybe there was something stuck to the ground, or the paw, that affected the track?" Paulo frowned briefly and shrugged. "I'm sorry, I can't be of any help there."

. . .

"No, I don't think the Council would agree to having everyone printed."

Henri and Paulo exchanged glances.

"No, that's not how it works. I honestly don't know how the Council would feel about your request. They have an almost overdeveloped sense of justice to help protect the Pack, but you are asking for a registry. You are going to have to talk to the Council to see what you can work out. Maybe we could find another way to help."

Paulo paced while he listened to the chief's response.

"I don't know. You said the print was on a blanket? Maybe you could let one of us smell it? How old is the track?"

. . .

Paulo explained, "Werewolves have an excellent sense of smell, just like a dog. We would likely be able to say who it is by scenting the track, at least, if it isn't too old."

. . .

"Umm, I'm not sure. It can depend on a lot of factors." Paulo sounded uncertain. "Was it sealed in plastic? It could be longer than months if it has been wrapped tightly or sealed in a cool place. If it was hot or wet, not such a good chance."

. . .

"Well, no promises, but I suspect they would prefer it to trying to corral everyone into getting printed – nose or paw. I can check with them."

. . .

"Right. That would probably be better. Good luck with that."

. . .

"You're welcome. Goodbye."

Paulo hit the button that ended his call and whooshed out a long sigh before turning to face Henri. "Go ahead. I know you are dying to say it."

A grin briefly flitted across Henri's face. "All right . . . Told you so."

"You sure called that one."

"I wish I was wrong."

"Me, too. He has done his research, Henri. Did you know dog paw prints aren't unique like fingerprints but nose prints are?"

"Oh, Dad's going to love that." Henri grimaced as he said it.

"Man, he works quickly!" I said. Once I learned about werewolves, it still took me a week to make the connection that one likely made the paw prints on my blanket. The chief did it in less than twenty-four hours.

"Do you think he actually needed to know all that stuff about sharks and squid?" Henri asked. "Or was it all a lead-up to the werewolf stuff?"

My brain replayed the discussion the chief had with his hapless staff person about the serrated pleurodont teeth and Officer Ramos's notes about sharks.

Paulo shrugged. "Who knows?" He wandered over and sat on the stool next to mine.

I spoke up. "He probably was curious. Remember Charles Gifford, you know — the guy the chief thinks I had an affair with before I murdered him?"

The guys both nodded.

"He was apparently bitten by something with serrated pleurodont teeth. The guy talking to the chief said sharks have that kind of teeth." I remembered the rest of the discussion. "In fact, they also said something about snake venom."

Henri raised his eyebrows. "That's a bad day," he said.

Paulo, on the other hand, looked like he was turning into his own ghost, he was so pale. I'd never seen anyone so desolate. "Oh no. No, no, no."

I reached out to steady him — I wasn't sure he wasn't going to fall out of his chair.

"Paulo, what's wrong — what is it?" A thread of desperation was weaving its way through Henri's voice. He took over supporting Paulo, and Paulo leaned into him, sobbing. Henri and I exchanged helpless glances over Paulo's head.

"It's Liam again."

"How?" I asked gently.

"The teeth and the venom, I know what it is from: a dragon. Liam has dragons."

What. The. Hell. Dragons?! That was just too much. Seriously? And wait – Liam knew all along about what was going on with the murder and let the police breathe down my neck? How could I still manage to be surprised by how much of a dick he was?

"You lost me there," Henri said it lovingly as he knelt in front of Paulo. He gently tilted Paulo's chin up with a finger. "You are going to have to start from the beginning." He gazed into Paulo's face. Waiting.

"You know how sometimes Liam's clients want a canned hunt?" Paulo asked.

Henri's lips tightened as he nodded. I didn't know what a canned hunt was, but Henri didn't approve.

"Well, he sometimes brought me in when the animals needed a vet. Some of the animals weren't legal to have here. Hell, most weren't. Liam blackmailed me so I wouldn't say anything. He forced me to train some of the animals to fall over and hold still when they heard a gunshot, so he could get away with using them multiple times."

Paulo started crying. He looked gorgeous doing it. It was totally unfair. His damp lashes stuck together in long clumps that not even the best mascara could achieve, and his eyes were dewy. He wasn't at all red or snotty as tears traced delicate trails over his high cheekbones.

"God, I should have said something."

"Shh, it's going to be okay." Henri pulled Paulo into a hug. I would have disappeared if I could have. As much as I wanted to know what was going on, this was too intimate for me to witness.

Ooh, or not. Henri turned his head toward me. The look on his face — I never imagined he could contain that much rage. Liam was lucky he wasn't here in the kitchen with us. I wouldn't lay high odds on him surviving an encounter with Henri.

"We'll figure it out, but I need you to tell me the rest." Henri's voice was so soothing, I bet Paulo had no idea how much rage he was restraining. Henri must have an amazing bedside manner.

Paulo snuffled delicately and pushed away from Henri. He straightened his spine. "Right. Well, remember how they couldn't figure out why Gifford was in town — it was weird because nothing was in season?" I nodded. "Well, I'm pretty sure he was here for one of Liam's canned hunts. Only it wasn't boar or deer . . . He was hunting a Komodo dragon. They have serrated pleurodont teeth and are venomous. If Charles Gifford was bitten by one, he would have likely died from it within hours without intensive medical care."

Oooh. Huh, maybe that is where the idea of dragons came from originally. That made a heck of a lot more sense than a fire-breathing lizard. Although it didn't explain the burns — maybe a campfire? Come on — focus, Loren! You are turning into Connor!

Henri managed to stay focused. "Well . . . damn. I think we are going to have to hope this one stays in the unsolved case files for the police department. Where the hell did he get Komodo dragons? It's not like you can order them from a catalog."

"I'm pretty sure he had animals, both dead and alive, smuggled into the country for his hunters on a regular basis."

Wow, he really was Gaston. How had I ever agreed to date someone so vile? I had been drawn to him. I had thought he was handsome! No, you know what, I was absolutely going to blame that on the Magic. I could reconsider my standards for guys later, assuming I ever had a choice about who to date again.

"I didn't know him at all." Henri pulled out the third stool at the kitchen island and sat down dejectedly. Now Paulo and I were exchanging concerned glances. Henri rubbed his face. "You said he was blackmailing you . . .?"

I knew what was coming. I was guessing Henri did, too.

"He said he would tell everyone we were together if I told anyone about the animals. I knew you would be upset, and I didn't want to lose you."

But he did anyway. The unspoken thought hung heavy in the kitchen air. Henri pressed his lips together and closed his eyes, head lowered. He looked like he was trying not to cry; I was close to tears myself.

"It's okay. It's better this way. I'm glad you are with Loren." He swallowed and gave a wobbly smile. "I couldn't deal with all the truths I wasn't speaking for much longer, even if the Magic hadn't interceded. This is better for the Pack. Maybe now, if they catch Liam, it won't matter what he says about you — about us. No one will believe him, now that you two are together."

Damn. No pressure or anything. This relationship was so screwed.

CHAPTER 31

"You still don't love me." The constant proposals were wearing me down. Even if they weren't, who could resist a snowman holding a ring on one of its twiggy fingers? Maybe it was a good thing I had plenty of practice refusing Henri's proposals. It was almost automatic now after thirty-two of them. Not that I was counting . . . Or wait, could I count the time he tried to recreate the balcony scene from *Romeo and Juliet* by climbing the side of the house? I hadn't answered, just walked away shaking my head at his ridiculousness. I also didn't say "no" the day he dressed up like Wesley from *The Princess Bride* and followed me around saying "As you wish!" I just commented that there was never a convenient hill when you needed one. So, technically, there were only thirty refusals.

"But I do love you." That was news. I raised a questioning eyebrow. "I care about you. I respect you. I enjoy spending time with you. You are beautiful, inside and out. I appreciate all your quirks, like how you are so not a morning person." I laughed at this, and he continued, "I enjoy laughing with you. I love your dry sense of humor."

"Henri, that is a friend." I smiled at him, hoping to take the sting out of my comment. "We do have a great friendship." He was perhaps one of my best friends even. After his help at the hospital, it felt like he had seen me at my worst.

I didn't have anywhere lower to go, so I had just been myself. It was liberating to know whatever he felt, it was about the real me, not some best-projected version of myself. Not many people were okay with the real me right now.

Henri continued, "See! We even argue with each other well. Seriously, I think about you all the time. I can picture us in the future."

I laughed. "You are with me all the time! You haven't said anything about me you couldn't say about a sister." I mean, I felt the same way about him, and it certainly wasn't sexual.

"Well," he grumbled, "I never said I was lusting after you, just that I loved you." A hint of exasperation was creeping into his tone. He finally got up from bended knee, brushing off the dusting of snow that clung to his jeans.

"Don't you think that would be important in a marriage?" There was no snarkiness in the question. I genuinely wanted to know if he could be happy in a relationship that lacked physical attraction. Would we avoid sexual contact altogether, or would it become a chore, something we did because we were supposed to? Could he enjoy sex with me anyway, since I'm lacking a Y chromosome?

We continued to be stuck in his house. We both knew that would change if I just said yes. Not that we had discussed the fact — probably because we both knew that "yes" would be a mistake. We were doing what we could to avoid cabin fever. Henri struggled more than I did. He spent hours going on increasingly long walks.

I was honestly happy to have an excuse to hole up for the most part. My only regret so far was that I missed both *The Tempest* and *Pirates of Penzance*. It hurt to not get to support Kella after all she had done for me.

But now that we were entering December, missing holiday festivities was making everything harder. Henri's family tradition was to go to the tree lighting ceremony in the town square each year. He mentioned it so wistfully that Paulo and I decorated an entire swath of the forest. We had our own lighting ceremony. The Magic, or the weather, depending on how you wanted to think about it, helped us out with an early snowfall. The twinkling lights and the snow certainly felt like something out of a fairy tale. Now Henri was proposing to me under the centerpiece of it . . .

Henri was quiet for so long, I thought he had given up for the day. "Maybe we should give it a try."

Huh? Give what a try? A relationship? Sex? Henri leaned forward and pushed my red, fur-lined hood a bit further back on my head. Then he cupped my face gently in his hands.

Oh, this.

Around us, the muffled quiet of the snowy forest stilled further.

I knew it would take almost nothing — the slightest shift in weight or a single word — to break the gentle hold of his hands, but his gaze was another matter. He stared at me intently. The question of whether I was comfortable with his touch was as present as the gold flecks in his green irises. I gave him a tentative smile and a small nod, one he would feel more than see.

I appreciated his patience. All our casual contact was making it easier for me to be touched, but I still wasn't sure when something might set off panic rather than pleasure. But this was good; I felt cherished even.

He whispered a kiss against my lips, giving me a chance to pull away. I stepped toward him, rising onto my toes to follow his retreat, letting him know we could continue. It would be so much easier if this worked . . .

His warmth curled around me, chasing the tingle of wintry air from my skin. The cinnamon scent of our hot apple cider swirled around us as our breath mingled. A soft graze, our lips brushing in tiny sips. I let myself commit to the experience, tangling my fingers into the chunky knit of his sweater.

He angled his head, his nose nuzzling mine, and laced his finger in my hair. My eyes drifted close. The kiss deepened, and his lips were now a firm pressure. His tongue flickered along the seam of my mouth before finally sliding slowly inside.

Our tongues swept along each other's before he retreated to softly nibble on my lower lip, his hands drifting to settle on my waist. His lips lingered against mine for a moment more before he ended the kiss and leaned his forehead against mine.

We finally leaned back, breaking apart.

Both of us took deep breaths.

Henri gave me an intense look.

"Damn, that didn't work at all did it?" he asked, crestfallen.

I shook my head.

Henri had expert technique. We didn't bump teeth or awkwardly miss lips. It wasn't too wet. It should have been a perfection of fireworks, but there was nothing there. I once dated a guy whose kissing reminded me of a car wash and had more heat with him.

"Maybe we should try again?" he sounded hesitant.

I gave a little shrug. "I don't mind trying again, but it probably won't change anything. There just isn't any . . ." I struggled for the right word — a kind word, ". . . tension there." He was absolutely perfect in every other way.

Henri drooped a bit but nodded.

We had played this game of hope for over a month now. We kept telling ourselves this story — that surely something would grow between us with enough time and proximity — like we were sticks being rubbed together to create a spark. Except it just never happened.

"Henri, I think you are a wonderful man. But we aren't right together. Sexually, I mean."

"Is this where you promise to stay my friend?" His lips twisted into a wry smile to show there were no hard feelings.

I laughed, surprised, the peals chasing the silence away through the snowy tree branches. "I'd like that."

"So, what do we do now?"

I'd been considering the question for weeks. "We could call Connor and discuss alternatives. Maybe he has contingency plans?"

"Is there time for an alternative? I thought we only had until Christmas Eve, or at the latest Valentine's Day, when the whole stepmother thing becomes official."

"I know. But I am currently out of ideas." It was frustrating.

"And there is still Liam to consider."

"I am aware of that." Still jumping at every creak in the house, remember?

"And then there's the fur issue."

Right. My presence was supposed to be fixing that, too. But it didn't matter. We would be awful romantic partners.

Henri considered, "You know, I actually think we should still get engaged." I started to protest. "Wait, hear me out. I'm not saying we should get married — just engaged. We don't have to set a date. We can wait until the Magic has moved on to someone else and break it off. They don't show the wedding in most of the Disney movies, do they?"

I considered the idea.

Henri was getting excited about his plan. "It should be enough to get rid of the hair. Liam will move on if he thinks the Magic is settled. This might work."

"Wait, would we tell everybody it was a fake engagement?"

It was Henri's turn to shake his head as he interrupted. "It won't be fake. It will be a real engagement, it just won't be followed by a wedding." That was splitting hairs a bit . . .

"What about telling a few people?" My brain fired off a list of people. Grandmother and Henri's mother before they planned the whole wedding; Connor, so he could work out his quantum formulas; Kella, so she wouldn't be hurt that I had lied; Paulo, so he wouldn't give up all hope . . .

The excitement in Henri's eyes faded. "I don't think it will work if we do."

Ouch. The plan wasn't without merits, but . . . Would the Magic know we were faking things or was the official announcement of an engagement enough? Even then, all the lies . . . Hurting people I cared about wasn't high on my to-do list.

I tried to make it work.

"We could say we are planning a long engagement so we can get to know each other better." What a weird reason in any other situation! "We could emphasize we have no plans to set a date for the wedding any time soon."

Would it be enough for the right people to read between the lines?

Henri scrunched his nose and one eyebrow shot up. "That *might* work."

"Want to run it by Connor and see if he thinks an engagement will be enough?" I'd hate to do this if it wasn't going to work, but there wasn't a tactful way to say that.

Henri must be having similar concerns. He jumped on the idea. "Yes! That sounds like a good plan. Why don't we go call him now? Maybe I can take you to see *The Nutcracker* after all — I felt terrible you were going to miss it."

"That would be fun." But I was still stuck on the flaw in the plan. "Do you think the Magic will know if we aren't really in love — that we aren't planning to get married?"

I wondered idly what would happen if I did say "yes." Would I get a light show where Henri would get lifted into the air and spun around as his hair melted away? I almost giggled to myself as I thought about the confused look in his eyes as he spun around, he wouldn't be unconscious like the Beast . . . Oh, shit.

"Wait. This is all wrong. I can't just agree to marry you. I have to leave first. And you have to almost perish, so I come back and throw myself over your prostrate body, and declare my undying love."

"Oh!" He cleared his throat. "I mean, I may be bored to tears if you leave, but 'prostrate with grief' might be a bit much."

I couldn't help but laugh at him. "I don't know about all that either." I sobered quickly. "Although, the alternative is fighting Liam and almost dying after you kill him."

"Now *that* I would consider."

Oh, wow.

Henri continued. "How could we forget you need to go back to your family for a few days?"

"I'm not going back to my father's house." I wasn't willing to budge on that.

"I bet your grandmother's house would work. We need to plan carefully though. We need to keep you safe from Liam. We should probably involve

Connor to help plan, too. I'll set up a meeting as soon as possible." He was staring into the distance. I could see his mental gears clicking as he made plans.

I took a larger step back from him and planted myself. "Henri."

He snapped out of his cogitations.

"I get to be involved in planning this, too."

". . . Right." That didn't sound as solid as I would like.

"I hope you aren't considering setting up something to catch Liam and telling me not to worry my pretty little head about it." I gave him Grandmother's best hairy eyeball look — not that she would have called it that.

"Of course not." He hemmed and hawed. I stared at him. He straightened before continuing. "I promise to involve you. It is your story too, and your life. You should obviously get a say in how it turns out."

"That's more like it. Now, let's go make some phone calls."

CHAPTER 32

"Henri, I am going to be fine. Really!" He was taking the overprotective thing a bit far. He asked me to check in once I got to Grandmother's, but he called my cell phone before I even arrived.

"I wish I could have dropped you off. It sounds like your grandmother is cranky because of her physical therapy. It might be hard living with her again . . ."

"Mm-hmm. What are you actually worried about?"

Henri heaved a sigh. "Liam."

"Henri, you planned the guard rotation yourself. And Chief Duncan has a police car out in front of the house. It is only for a week, and I don't plan to go anywhere. Remember? I am going to be painting. You helped pack all my art supplies into the car."

"I know." Wow! He sounded miserable! Maybe he would manage to do the whole pining away thing – or at least worry himself to death.

"I've been with you for over a month. Honestly, you should be glad to get rid of me!"

"I've gotten used to having you around." He sounded surprised; I wasn't sure if it was by his emotions or because I thought he wouldn't miss me. "And it is going to be lonely without you here."

"You need to cheer up, or I will have to share some of the jokes Connor sent me. You don't want me to do that."

"Connor sent you jokes?" His tone noticeably brightened.

I sighed, "Alright: why did Cinderella get kicked off the soccer team?" I paused for a moment before answering my own question. "She kept running away from the ball."

"Ouch, that was bad!"

"I've got worse. How did Jack know how many beans his cow was worth? He used a cowculator!"

Henri laughed. "So bad. Classic Connor. What about this one: 'Why should you never trust an atom? Because they make up everything!'"

I chuckled. "You think you are going to be okay, or should I get him to come over and cheer you up? I'll only be gone for a week. Grandmother is already having a hissy fit about us living together before we are married." Stanley gave a cough from the front seat that sounded suspiciously like a laugh. Talking with Henri about Grandmother in front of her employee, however much more he was than the gardener, felt weird and inappropriate. And wow, I was channeling Grandmother. She was infecting me!

Henri was laughing, "Yeah, my mother isn't loving that either. Don't worry, they'll manage to deal with it. I mean, Mom is still excited about finally having a daughter. To be honest, I'm feeling a bit guilty." Ouch. I did too.

"Oh, man! That is going to be hard to explain later, Henri. Are we sure we want to do this?"

Silence. "I can't think of any alternatives. And maybe it will work out."

I sighed. "Right. Hey, I need to run, we just arrived. Which means I am here safely and have let you know. So you can stop worrying now."

"Thanks for indulging me. If you call me later, I will know you got inside safely . . . ?"

"I need to be away for a week, Henri!" I laughed at him. "It won't count if I am on the phone with you the whole time!"

"Don't worry, I have a plan for how to fill my time. I'm going to adapt all the great classics to give a proper voice to my despair." He heaved a melodramatic sigh. "*O Loren, Loren. Wherefore art thou, Loren? Deny thy family and refuse thy species; Or, if thou wilt not, be but sworn my love, and I'll no longer be a Beast.*"

I was laughing so hard that I had trouble responding. "You are ridiculous. And you need new material. We've debated this already. Romeo and Juliet were just horny teenagers, it's not romantic."

"Hmm, how about this? 'It is a truth universally acknowledged that a single woman in possession of a great deal of beauty must be in want of a beast.'"

"I repeat: you are ridiculous. Bye, Henri!"

"I sure am! Love ya! Bye, Loren!"

I ended the call before he said anything else absurd, shaking my head.

I got out of the car and hadn't even finished greeting Millie before being engulfed in a hug. "Oh, it's so good to have you back here where you belong."

I was surprised to hear Millie felt that way. I caught myself scuffing my shoe in the gavel. "It's only for a week, Ms. Millie."

"Well, I guess we will have to take what we can get." She sighed heavily. Wow! The melodrama setting was apparently on high today.

Stanley opened the trunk and started unloading my things. I went over to rescue my canvases. It wasn't that he wouldn't be careful with them, but he couldn't possibly be as careful as I would be.

"Why don't we get your things inside? Your grandmother cleared the morning room for you to use as a studio while you are here. Although she called it an atelier."

"That was kind of her!" That room definitely had better light than the bedroom I was in the last time.

I was girding my best princess posture and Emily Post manners when Millie casually mentioned Grandmother was with her physical therapist, and that she would need a nap afterward. I wouldn't be seeing her until lunch.

Ms. Millie gently poked my back as I let the steel drain out of my spine. "Best to practice, so you don't get caught unawares."

"Yes, Ms. Millie. I just can't believe Grandmother isn't here to greet me!"

"Don't you dare tease her about it," Ms. Millie's tone was almost sharp. "It took way too much work on my part to keep her from canceling therapy. She needs every bit of it she can get. Besides, you aren't a guest."

"I don't think the rules work that way." I held my hands up before she could lecture me. "But I agree they're silly. I promise not to say anything!"

"See that you don't, young lady!"

"In the meantime, would you mind terribly if I got straight to painting? Connor said I might be able to manage it this week since it is Belle going back to her old ways . . . I don't want to waste a moment!"

"Hmm. I think that would be smart. Want me to bring cookies along in a bit?"

I grinned. "Would a smart person turn down your cookies, Ms. Millie?"

"Harrumph. Shoo, off you go to get your work done."

She didn't have to tell me twice. I couldn't wait to paint.

I scurried along and set up my drawing board. Then laid out all my freshly sharpened pencils, and found my eraser. Watercolor tray next, and a cup of water . . . I was all set. It was a beautiful feeling. Everything would go well this week; no trepidation about my skills like when I tried at Henri's house. I ran my fingertips around the tip of a brush, bringing it firmly to a point. I breathed in the smell of my paints. I had missed this.

Which plant should I draw first? I reviewed my list: pumpkin, apple, two roses, rampion, pea, and wheat. Hmm, there were two rose images to complete. Perhaps one of those would be a good segue from my own tale back to school work.

I examined my notes and the photo from last time. I sketched lightly with a pencil, but as I worked, I couldn't seem to bring myself to focus on the topic. Images of wolves painted with ink kept interrupting my mental concept of the project. The petal I was outlining turned into a haunch and bent back leg. And was that a leaf with a serrated edge, or a tail? I frowned as I erased it.

Let's try that again.

After a few moments, I stared at the page in dismay. I'd seen art depicting green men before, but never the canine equivalent. Yet there was one on my page — petals arched to create shadowy eyes, a leaf as a cocked ear, stamens forming the nostrils. This was supposed to be my week. What was happening?

Was this the Magic at work, or was this just what was occupying my thoughts? I'd not practiced any mental discipline recently. Maybe I needed to work on my focus? Should I try again on the rose, or let the wolves loose? If I finished the wolf, would it let me get back to my thesis work?

I clutched the brush so tightly it bit into my hand, snagging my skin. I stared at the blood welling up in a bubble around the splinter in my finger. I know some artists said they bled for their work, but this was ridiculous.

Where would I find a Band-Aid around here? I just needed to make sure not to smear blood on my paper. Maybe the little break would help me pull myself together.

I sighed as I sat back down to my work.

Right, let's try really focusing. Roses. The arch of the petals. Sharp points of the thorns. Sinuous curve of the vine. The shading from ochre shadows to pale lemon on the petals. The wolf's form needed more depth. Hmm . . . I could do a fabric collage or papier-mâché to help actualize it properly.

ARGH! Wolf?!

Focus, Loren. Roses! What if we focus on the details . . . buds, sepals, stipules, petals, petioles, paws . . .?

That was it. Fighting it obviously wasn't going to work. It didn't matter why, the project needed to happen.

And honestly, I kind of wanted to do the wolf project. I shrugged to myself. Wouldn't be the first time I chose to work on a project I wanted to, over the project I should be doing. The biggest problem was that I didn't want to interrupt things to go to the store. Where could I find some fabric? Maybe Millie?

Oh! Oh . . . I could feel my cheeks stretch as a Cheshire grin spread across my face. How poetic. What a lovely way to fire back at the Magic. Belle and her damn blue clothes . . .

Now, where were my scissors?

CHAPTER 33

"Hey, Loren! Can I come in?"

"Hmm?" It was hard to pull myself out of my project.

"Loren?"

"Oh, Connor! Um, hi." He laughed at me as I looked up and sat blinking at him, trying to change gears and focus. "What are you doing here?"

"Your grandmother wanted to discuss her ideas for the ball with me. She is trying to respect your plans. I thought I would check in with you." He nudged a cup of coffee in front of me.

"Respect my plans?" That was new. Was it wrong of me not to trust that entirely? I peered into the coffee cup. Heavy on the cream, just how I liked it. I took a sip.

"Yes. She even has Kella working on a yellow ball gown and gloves for you."

"Oh, this coffee is good. Thank you. I think I can even deal with talking about more Belle things now."

"You're welcome. You don't sound thrilled."

"Well, I'm still not sure if I'm making the right decision." I had, in fact, been considering calling it all off. Though, it seemed like I should talk to Henri in person first.

"Oh. I thought things between you and Henri were going well?"

"It's just, umm . . ." How did I explain without sharing secrets? "Let's just say we are counting on the Magic for a happily ever after and true love more than I am comfortable with."

"Hmm." Connor's intense contemplation had me concerned. Goodness knows where that mind of his was going, or what he would come up with.

I stood casually. "I mean, I like Henri. He's a great guy!" Sheesh. That was convincing, Loren! "Umm. It's hard to explain without disclosing some details — well, they are kind of bigger than details — pretty big things that aren't mine to share."

"Huh. Did I tell you about how I learned about werewolves actually existing?"

"No . . ." What did that have to do with anything?

"When we were kids, I found Henri chasing a wolf puppy one day. I couldn't believe he didn't tell me about getting a pet. Of course, the puppy was Liam, but I didn't know. Next time we went over, the puppy wasn't there, and both of my cousins were cagey. Henri was my best friend, and I was hurt he was keeping secrets. So, I pestered them for weeks.

"Liam eventually caved — he said I wasn't being fair to Henri, and he was sick of it. He told me all about werewolves. I later learned he was taking on responsibility for any damage that came to the Pack through my knowledge of their secret. I should have been grateful. Instead, in the irrational indignation only a child can manage, I was angry I hadn't been told before. I was mad they left me out of the Pack. I didn't care about the facts: that being a werewolf was genetic, or that you had to be an adult before you could go through an invocation ceremony. I did what I always did, and researched to learn everything I could on the topic. It led me to instances of cynocephali throughout history, like some hieroglyphs of Anubis, Duamutef, and Wepwawet in Egypt, not to mention those in the Greek and Chinese –"

Whoa. I was quickly getting lost. I interrupted gently, "Umm, Connor, I don't understand where this is going . . ."

"Sorry, I got a little off track there. What I meant to get around to is that sometimes learning a secret can change your entire life. Things were never the same for me after learning about werewolves. It is almost like a rebirth or a whole separate phase of your life. Everything is divided into before and after . . . I bet finding out about the tales is like that for you — and perhaps whatever it is you can't share with me now."

I considered that. "You may be right about the fairy tales . . . But not so much the other thing." It should be a problem, but honestly, it was a relief to have a reason for the relationship not working.

The truth was I didn't want to be having this discussion. There was so little time left this week, and so much to fit in. I wasn't sure what I would be able to do once I went back to Henri's. I usually enjoyed Connor's company, but right now I wanted him to leave so I could work. Although to be fair, I wasn't working on my thesis illustrations. I was purging my emotions on canvas. It was still important to me, but I couldn't explain it in a way that justified asking Connor to leave so I could work. I looked back at my painting, hoping for some sort of inspiration to make Connor understand. A wolf peered back at me from underneath a fern. He merged with the plants in the background.

Connor didn't say anything. He was waiting for me to make sense of it all. I tried again, "Henri and I — it doesn't quite feel right." It wasn't just that Henri was gay. Maybe . . . "Will what happened with Liam affect my story? Nothing like that happened in the original French story, and things went way beyond what happened between Belle and Gaston in the Disney version. And my Dad was supposed to be happy, but when I told him, he was irritated because Emilia went ballistic and said I was trying to steal attention from their engagement. Maybe we were wrong to try to switch tales. Maybe I am Sleeping Beauty or Snow White. The whole taking liberties with an unconscious person lines up better with those tales, doesn't it?"

Connor sighed. "I wish I knew. You can only get so much information from a journal or an interview. I understand that what happens during these tales is highly private, so people don't want to talk about it. Yours is the only tale I have witnessed firsthand."

"Oh, right." And he didn't have all the data about my tale, either. Sheesh.

"I still think we can assume we are on track for 'Beauty and the Beast.' We have checked off a lot of the plot points, like Henri's hair, and we should cement it even further when you two are reunited. Also, if it was either 'Sleeping Beauty' or 'Snow White,' you would be getting engaged to Liam, not Henri."

That alone was enough reason not to break things off with Henri until I was sure about what was happening. His comment made me feel like the numb Ice Queen instead of Belle.

"Connor, can you tell me more about the last Sleeping Beauty? My mother . . . I want to know what happened with her."

Connor cleared his throat. "Well, I don't know all the details. Your father wasn't interested in talking to me." I just bet he wasn't. I snorted. "That left your grandmother to tell me what happened. Apparently, she asked your father to try kissing your mother. He took things significantly farther than she intended." He glanced around the room, not meeting my eyes. "Your grandmother has recently indicated she pushed for it to happen, and that she deeply regrets her actions. I believe she told me what little she did, to convince me that trying to control the tales is a mistake."

I took a deep breath, trying to calm myself. I was so angry with both my grandmother and my father.

Connor knew trying to control the tales might be a mistake. I understood he thought he knew enough to make it work, and I hoped he was right. I wasn't sure I would be able to forgive him if he was wrong.

But Grandmother . . . I tried to remind myself she was from a different time with significantly different values. A time that valued the mythical intact hymen over a woman's happiness for the entire rest of her life. But seriously, it was ridiculous! We don't even need dragons or towers to keep people locked up. No, who needs those, when we have social mores? Don't see any knights tilting at those!

Connor was watching me carefully. "Umm, did you get cleared to start cerebral activities again? You could review my notes?"

"That shouldn't tax my system too much." I smiled, trying to keep it from having a sharp edge. "No need to turn into worrywart Cogsworth on me."

Connor opened his notebook and passed it over. "Right, I probably shouldn't even be here because of my role as Cogsworth. But, well . . . would it be —" Connor hesitated. "Can I look at your paintings before I go? I am curious to see what you have come up with."

"I don't mind, go ahead." I gestured at the wall my canvases were leaning against. Connor only had half my attention though, because I was scanning his notes about my mother.

I flipped through the pages with growing frustration; there was no new information here. I had already pieced the worst of it together. The one or two extra facts I gleaned from the notes lacked the impact of the photos I had found in the library. Was that the last of it? Hmm, blank page — maybe he skipped it accidentally? I idly flipped to the next page to make sure there was nothing else.

Huh, this must be one of Connor's poems. I read with growing interest. It was clearly based on the Sleeping Beauty tale. Had he written it about my mother?

It seemed to be an early draft, with lines crossed out, and arrows wildly bisecting the page. One stanza stood alone in the middle of the page, free of edits:

> Do you wonder if the curse lay in the sleep
> or the enchanted kiss?
> Although you lack time to find the answer,
> the prince is demanding gratitude for rescuing you
> neglecting to mention he stole the chance
> to be yourself before a piece of an "us."

Well, that was interesting. I wanted to turn the book sideways to read the next verse, but I felt like I was spying. I hadn't asked to look at his personal work. I looked up guiltily, to make sure Connor hadn't noticed my snooping. He was still looking at my paintings. I could ask him about it, but it felt private.

I scrubbed my face and checked my partially finished painting. This week hadn't gone the way I'd expected, but it had been cathartic. Freeing. It was frustrating Connor brought me back to real-world issues. Why was I letting anything sidetrack me? Why was I giving anyone else control? I wouldn't let him, or the tale, sidetrack me. Well, I mean besides the subject I was painting. I mentally shook my head at myself as I went back to painting.

Ignoring Connor while he poked around was easy. I managed to forget about him as I continued working.

"Loren." I jumped when he said my name. How long had I been working? "These are astounding."

I snorted. "Don't sound so surprised. I'm going to think you didn't expect me to have any talent at all."

"It's just . . ." He floundered. "I mean, I've seen some of your previous work, and it was good. But it was different — highly technical, analytical. These are so much *more*."

"Huh?"

"I mean, I have seen a LOT of fairy tale art, but it's generally focused on the surface plot of the tales, or on how beautifully the princess can be presented. These go so much deeper. They capture the duality and darker nature that isn't often explored. Like this one, it's almost like the sleeping princess is being held captive by the roses surrounding her . . ." He picked up the canvas. "It's not all rainbows and kittens peacefully waiting for true love. She is struggling to be free even in her dreams. And this one — I can't tell if this is an embrace between the prince and princess, or if he captured her and she is pushing him away. Every time I am certain, I am suddenly convinced it is the other way around. It makes me curious about how often the princess wants to be in the relationship in her tale. I knew this all intellectually, before. I even knew this was your struggle. But now I *feel* it, too."

"Oh. Wow. Thanks." I hadn't aspired to go beyond being informative with my art before. The realization hit me like a physical blow: I hadn't trusted I could elicit an emotional response with my art. I'd been scared to try and fail.

Technical illustrations just needed to convey information. They were safe. Did I actually want to be a technical artist, or was it the best I thought I could do?

"And this one, where Little Red Riding Hood and the wolf kind of smear into each other." He made some elaborate swiping hand gestures to show the section he meant. "It makes me think about their duality, about how they exist as both separate individuals, and as a merged unit. You should open a gallery or something!"

Never mind, I hadn't been playing it safe. I laughed. "That is supposed to be Belle and the Beast. I guess I let Disney get to me with the red cape Belle wears while she is at the Beast's castle."

"Oh. The idea could apply to both tales. You couldn't have either story without both of them, and how they interact."

"Nice try. I'm not sure you saved yourself there. Besides, why do you need both? Why can't the story have just been 'and she grew up and lived happily ever after?'"

Connor shook his head at me with a gentle smile. "There's no conflict. It's not interesting. Nobody would read it."

"Oh, but you are wrong. I would! I want to read a story where the woman creates her own agency and lives happily ever after. One where there isn't some sort of an inciting incident to force her into fighting for it."

Connor's smile was sad. How did he do that? "It doesn't work that way, Loren."

"Why?! Why doesn't it work that way? Why can't women just be happy, why do we have to pay for our happiness with trauma or loss? Hell, even if it's only marriage, women historically give up everything — including their names! Why?"

My mind mulled the possibilities. Is it because it's not possible to be in a relationship where both people blossom, where one isn't subsumed? How would a truly equal relationship play out? Do women only get the shit end of the deal because of biology and babies? Or were we taught to let our needs be subsumed? Why didn't I feel I was allowed to prioritize the things that made me happy?

I was questioning my foundations again.

If you know you want a change, but you don't know what that change needs to be, what do you do?

Most stories for women are about situations where they have no control. Is it that most people aren't proactive about creating their happiness? Do people seriously not ask themselves what being happy would look like and then go after it?

How ridiculous! I wasn't going to be that way any longer. Oh, um, except what *did* I want?

I didn't have a clear picture anymore. I used to think finishing my degree and starting my business would make me happy. Now I didn't know. I was immediately swamped with guilt. Ambushed by all the expectations I wouldn't meet and the things I should be doing, instead of hunting down the tentative desires lurking in the darkest, most tucked away corners of my mind. It felt selfish.

I banished the guilt. It wasn't like I was asking for it to be all about my happiness. That would lead to becoming a sociopath, like Liam. I can't believe you just went there, brain. Seriously, there has to be a middle ground. I mean, Liam had obviously gone to one end of the spectrum in only caring about himself, but had I gone as far in the other direction? Wow. That was a lot to untangle.

Connor touched my arm.

"What?!" When did he cross over here to me?

"You spaced out there, everything all right?" Connor asked.

"Yes," I mean, not really. No, things weren't okay. "I don't know. I may be having a quarter-life crisis – do such things exist? Sorry, I have a lot to think about."

"Being an adult isn't quite what I thought it would be, either."

"I still don't feel like an adult. When does that happen?"

Connor shrugged, "I'll let you know when I get there?"

"But you have a real job, and a house, and everything!"

"I haven't completed my coming-of-age quest. Even if I had, I still don't think I would feel like a grownup. I thought they had answers and knew stuff. Maybe they are only faking it?"

I considered the people I considered grownups. "I don't know, somehow I don't think Grandmother or Ms. Millie are faking it. Maybe we just need another thirty years to get there?"

"That's an awful thought. I'm hoping to feel grown before my body starts giving out."

"I guess I need to think about what being an adult even means. I've got lots to figure out."

"Right. Well, I am guessing it would be best if I left you to it then?"

I nodded. "I'm sorry, but yes."

"I'm the one that should be sorry. I thought I would be able to help more, but so far I'm not doing a great job of making things easier."

"Connor –"

"No, it's okay. I wasn't saying that so you could make me feel better. I wanted to –"

"Connor." I laughed at him, "Seriously, shut up for a minute. Listen, didn't you just tell me that if it was easy, if there was no conflict, no one would be interested?"

"Oh. I did, didn't I? It seems I have some considering to do, myself." He was looking intently at the ground, brain already going a million miles an hour. He could probably tell me the exact speed of a synaptic connection and its quantum implications. I couldn't help but smile. He was so earnest, it was impossible to stay mad at him.

"Connor, your thoughts are really loud. Any chance I could get you to at least have them over there?"

"Oh! . . . No." No? I raised an eyebrow. Connor explained, "I mean, I need to head out anyway. If I can help in any way, please let me know?"

"You've got it. Absolutely."

But first, I needed to help myself.

CHAPTER
34

I tapped my fingernails against the kitchen counter, waiting impatiently for Henri to answer his phone. Was that paint under my nail? Ugh. Belle didn't have fingernails to get paint under so maybe it wouldn't count against me?

I couldn't wait to show Henri my paintings, especially the one inspired by Connor. It would make him laugh. It was of a knight fighting a dragon, but all the figures were made up of inked numbers with a color wash over them. Even the chain mail was made up of interlocking numbers. The body was proportioned according to the Fibonacci sequence. I'd left the lines and math measuring the golden ratios as part of the painting. The dragon the knight was fighting was coiled into a golden spiral. Equations were evident in the swirls of motion his sword made.

Five rings now, was the Magic irritated? Since I was delayed, I hoped the Magic hadn't jumped ahead in the story to where the Beast is lying senseless somewhere. Wasn't that part of the story though, me being late? No reason for the Magic to be snarky about it. Unless it knew I was strongly reconsidering the plan, that part of me wanted to tell Henri I was calling the whole thing off . . .

I pulled my cell phone away from my ear to double-check which number I had dialed. Yup, that was his cell phone number. Was it lost on his desk in a stack of papers again? Should I have called the house line?

"Hello?" Finally! Henri sounded distracted.

"Hi, Henri! It's Loren."

"Hey, Loren! Sorry, I was on the other line with Mom. She was trying to convince me we needed an engagement dinner in addition to the formal announcement at the ball." He sounded amused.

"I hope you told her that wouldn't be necessary."

"Maybe she will believe you." Yikes. This was blowing up quickly.

"I can try to talk her out of it. But I was actually calling because I am running late. I'm so sorry, but I got caught up in my work and didn't notice what time it was. Give me twenty minutes to pack, and I will head right over!" I remembered the state I had left my temporary studio in. "Uh, maybe I should make that forty minutes?"

"No worries. Why don't you take your time, and give a holler before you head over?"

"Okay. Do you want me to wait a bit longer for the rain to stop? Maybe let you do the whole prostrate with grief in the garden scene, without drowning or getting struck by lightning?"

"Oh, I don't know. The rain will make it easy for me to act miserable." I could hear the laughter in his voice. "Don't worry about any of it, the delay or the rain."

"If you say so . . ."

"I do. On a more serious note, I am looking forward to seeing you. I've missed having you around."

What did he mean by that? Was he trying to confuse me? This wasn't real, did he remember that?

"Henri . . . I, um, I don't know how to respond to that."

"I didn't mean it that way! It was intended to be friendly." It would be impolite to heave a sigh of relief, wouldn't it? "Please don't worry. I don't want things to get weird between us. We can talk when you get here; you know how much I hate being on the phone."

"I sup– "

"Liam! What the hell are you doing here? I can't believe you—" There was a muffled thump and then a sharp crackle of static.

"Where is she? She is supposed to be HERE." There was a sharp stabbing pain in my chest as I heard Liam's voice over the phone line. I put a hand out to steady myself. I noticed myself gibbering mentally, floating away on a litany of no, no, no, no!

Come on! Get it together. There isn't time to fall apart, Loren. Help Henri. Get him help. Where was Paulo? Right. Not there, so he didn't have to see our romantic reunion.

Who did that leave?

Did I risk the Pack's secret and call the police? Did I know anyone else in the Pack? But I didn't know anyone's number off the top of my head. I couldn't hang up on Henri — I needed to know what was going on.

Thank goodness Grandmother still had a landline. I careened over to the phone. My heart was pounding, and it was making me lightheaded.

I put the cell phone down and stabbed the speaker button. Then I picked up the handset for the landline and dialed with shaking hands.

"Why would she choose you over me? Why does everyone *always* choose you over me?" Liam was being irrational.

"What are you talking about?" Seriously, Henri? You are too smart to sound so baffled. Don't you know how insecure your brother is?

"9-1-1 What's your emergency?" Heavens, I wish I knew the dispatcher. What did I say to get the right people there?

There was a crashing noise.

"You need to tell Chief Duncan or Officer Ramos that Liam Randolph is at his brother Henri's house. Please tell them to hurry. It is sounding violent."

"Ma'am. Where are you? Are you safe?"

"Yes, yes!" I was practically yelling. "I'm not there."

Millie hurried into the kitchen with her eyebrow raised. I think she was about to fuss about my volume. I didn't have time for a lecture. "Listen, I was on the phone with Henri when Liam barged in. You have to get Henri help."

Millie's other eyebrow flew up and the color drained from her face. She scurried from the room.

"Stanley, Stanley!" I heard her calling. Apparently yelling was allowed in emergencies.

"You aren't better than me. I was willing to make a real commitment. And you'd prefer to be fucking Paulo! She *chose* to date me, but it took Magic to make her stay with you!" More tinny crashes and static pops came from the cell phone speaker. "Once you are gone, the Magic will stop forcing her to be with you!"

"Liam, you need to put the gun down. We can talk about this. You know I'm not interested in Loren."

"Ma'am, ma'am!!" The 9-1-1 lady was yelling in my ear; I hadn't noticed.

"He has a gun! Tell the chief! They are at Dr. Henri Randolph's house." I put the handset down distractedly, ignoring the muffled squawks coming from it.

I picked up the cell phone. The loud scuffling noises and meaty thumps sounded like the guys were brawling. What happened to the gun?

"Liam, don't hurt him!" Well, that wasn't helpful, Loren. How will you wanting Henri safe make Liam feel better about all this? "If you hurt him, you will go to jail, and then we can't be together." Right, that was pathetically obvious. I rolled my eyes at myself. Loren, think! You have got to be more convincing.

Stanley and Millie came running back into the room.

"You have to go to him!" Millie was practically shoving me out the back door. "If you aren't there when the fight ends . . . Well, you are the one who *has* to be there. I don't know what the Magic will do otherwise."

Oh! The castle rooftop fight scene! How had I missed it? The weather was perfect for it. I was an idiot. Disney was winning out despite Henri's efforts to go with the Lang or Villeneuve version. I guess not having the requisite sisters was a problem for that version anyway.

There was an ear-splitting crash and silence from my cell phone. I stopped letting Millie herd me into the car to glance frantically at the screen. Millie looked at it, too. Call lost. "Shit!"

"Loren!" The rules about cursing hadn't been let go of along with the ones about yelling.

"Ms. Millie, make sure the police come. Please!"

"I will! Go!" Millie almost closed the car door on me.

Stanley came close to peeling out of the gravel driveway. I'd never seen him drive so fast, but it would still take too long to get there. This was going to be the longest twenty minutes of my life.

CHAPTER
35

Where were they — all of them? Was Liam still here? What about the police? Was I going to get myself shot running around? Today was not showcasing my best decision making skills.

I threw the car door open as soon as we pulled into the courtyard, and hopped out before Stanley put the car in park. I opened my mouth to yell Henri's name, wait — was that another bad idea?

Stanley got out of the car stiffly. "Go," he said, waving his arm, "find him."

"What about Liam? What if he is still here?"

"He won't be able to hurt you. It's not a part of the story. Go find Henri."

His conviction was so absolute, I ran toward the house. "Henri?!"

My thoughts raced faster than my legs were able to. Where would he be? My mind flashed to an image of 'Beauty and the Beast' illustrated by Mercer Mayer I'd seen at some point in my childhood. The Beast was lying amongst the brown roots and the canes of roses . . . The garden? Or the roof? I eyed the roof of the house warily. How would they get up there? I listened and didn't hear anything. Instincts Loren, follow them. Roses? Check the garden.

I hurried around the side of the house, slowing so I didn't slide off the stepping stones but ignored the grasping limbs of brush reaching out to slow me, tangling in my hair and skirts.

I burst into the clearing at the back of the house. It was hard to see anything with the rain and mist. "Loren!" I whipped my head around. Was that Paulo?

Paulo was gesturing from the balcony that made up the roof of the sunroom. Of course! The roses grew all along the trellis and twined over the railing. I pushed through the back door into the kitchen and hurried up the backstairs, leaving a trail of muddy footsteps behind me. I flew to the open door of the balcony, grabbed the doorframe to keep myself from skidding, and braced myself for what I'd find.

It was worse than I expected. I could feel myself deflating, my hand fluttering up to cover my mouth. Henri was a crumpled heap on the ground, and the puddle around him was tinged pink with blood. Paulo was draped over him, slumped shoulders heaving.

As soon as I reached his side he let go of Henri and grabbed me by the shoulder. He pulled me around, his intense gaze unnerving. The light was oddly diffuse, catching on all droplets sliding down his face and in his lashes.

"You have to save him!" He didn't shake me, but his firm grasp pulled me off balance. Me? But I nodded, unsure what else to do. Of course I would help.

He pushed to his feet and stumbled off.

"Wait! Where are you going?"

He shook his head. "I can't do anything here, I am going to go make sure they catch Liam."

He took off at a sprint before I could ask who "they" were.

I turned back to Henri. His nose was mushed out of its normal configuration. It looked more like bread dough than anything else, the swelling puffing out into his cheek and around his eye. I gently laid a hand on his chest. I felt it rise and sobbed with relief.

"Henri?" No response. "Oh, what did he do to you? I'm so sorry I got you involved in this."

Where was the blood coming from? I needed to figure it out. The hot tears slid down my face along with the cool rain, as I ran my hands through his hair and along his neck. Nothing there.

"Loren?" It was barely a whisper. "You came back?"

Unbelievable! He was still following his lines?! A strangled chuckle escaped before I could rein the hysteria back in.

"Of course I came back! If only I had gotten here sooner!"

"It was better this way, he couldn't hurt you."

What a noble idiot. I shook my head at him, "No! We are together now. Everything is supposed to be fine. I'm tired of others getting hurt in my story." He stopped me by raising his hand to my cheek.

"I am tired of hurting people in my life, too. At least this way no one else will be hurt."

His hand fell away as he groaned. He curled around his side slightly before stiffening. What little color was left in his face drained, then his eyes rolled up in his head. He lost consciousness.

"No, no, no." I felt an upwelling of panic, not love. It couldn't end this way. How was I going to save him if I didn't love him romantically? Was this punishment for trying to interfere with the Magic? Or for reconsidering the plan? "No, please! Henri, you can't die!"

A gust of wind blew rain and leaves into my face. The wind swirled around us. Oh no, what was that mixed in with the leaves? Shit, shit, shit – those weren't leaves at all. Rose petals. Hundreds of them settled around us in a near perfect circle. The wind calmed and the air surrounding us crystalized expectantly; time itself waiting for my next line.

Even if it meant I ended up married to Henri, I couldn't just let him die. I had better give it a try.

I flung myself across Henri and let the tears and panic loose.

"No, please don't leave me, Henri! I love you!"

I was a horrible actress. Was it enough?

The calm fractured in a ferocious rush — a windy vortex filled with flying rose petals. I pulled Henri to me to protect him, but I couldn't see anything. My hair was whipping into my face, making it impossible to see anything. I closed my eyes and hung on tightly until it subsided.

Henri groaned again. I pulled back and lowered him to see what was wrong.

Oh. Goodness. It had worked. No way! I stared in amazement.

Henri slowly opened his eyes and smiled beatifically. He haltingly lifted his hand to his forehead. "That feels so much better." Then he noticed his hand. He pushed up onto one arm with a small, unbelieving laugh.

"It's gone! We did it!"

Henri pulled me into a hug. "Was there a light show?" he asked as he let me go.

Even his face looked significantly less puffy. His nose was back to its proper shape and there was no bruising. I studied the sharp line of his cheekbone as a raindrop slid over it. It was a shame I wasn't attracted to him.

"Is everything okay?" Oh right, he had asked me about something . . .

"Yes, of course!" I stuttered. "I'm just relieved you're okay."

It was only a partial truth. I mostly felt numb.

CHAPTER 36

The numbness didn't let up either. The protective trance lasted all day, through the arrival of the police and the paramedics, through being questioned, through the emergency room doctors reporting the litany of Henri's injuries: broken fifth metacarpal, mild concussion, broken and bruised ribs, a broken nose, ruptured kidney, contusions, and lacerations. But in the evening, when the wind started rustling branches and leaves outside, the numbness receded, and panic took its place. The prospect of Liam lurking outside broke through my stupor.

Each time the wind rattled a window or blew a branch against the house, tiny jolts of horror ran through my brain. I paused the show we were watching. I couldn't ignore the issue any longer.

"Henri, what happened to Liam?" I asked.

Did he die like Gaston? Would Henri be in trouble if he had? And why was no one telling me what was going on?

The look on Henri's face went from polite inquiry to smugness. "He went over the edge of the balcony when I punched him. I wish I could take full credit, but the guards distracted him when they got there."

"What?! Wait, I didn't know you still had guards at your house while I was gone!"

Henri shrugged and then winced. "We couldn't be sure he would know you left, and you were supposed to be back already."

"Oh, right." How did I phrase this delicately, "So what happened after he fell?" That was good! I managed to not accuse him of killing his brother.

"I'm not sure, I passed out. Paulo said he would come by tomorrow and fill us in. I do know the Council has Liam though."

"Oh!" The panic drained away in a rush, much faster than the way it crept in. It left me dizzy.

"You didn't know?"

I shook my head. "I –"

Henri's cell phone rang, interrupting. He glanced at it dismissively as he set it aside, then turned back to it.

"I'm sorry, it's Connor. I should probably answer." I nodded, and Henri answered the phone. As he raised it to his ear, his splinted pinky finger stuck out like he was keeping it raised to drink a cup of tea. I ducked my head to hide the grin the thought brought to my face. Was there a proper way to hold a phone? Oh man, I can't believe I was seriously considering the issue. I rolled my eyes at myself.

"Hi, Connor."

Henri listened for a few moments before standing and starting to pace.

"Couldn't it wait until tomorrow? I don't have anything set up." He sounded doubtful. What sort of problem was Connor raising now? Hadn't we done everything we were supposed to, followed all the rules?

"Right," Henri scrubbed his free hand over his face. "Okay, send her over. I'll see what I can manage."

I wished I could hear the other side of the conversation.

"No, that isn't fair to him." He sighed, "It should be coming from me, anyway."

Henri barely let Connor speak before he interrupted.

"Connor, it's just . . ." a frustrated sigh from Henri, "He must be tired, too. I've got it. Really."

. . .

"Wait, how long?"

Henri glanced at his watch.

"Right." This time the word was resigned. "Next time, a little more warning would be nice. I've got to go. I have things to do here. We can talk tomorrow if you feel the need."

I could hear a murmur with its pitch rising as Henri pulled the phone from his ear and glared at it in disbelief.

He raised it back up to his ear and spoke over whatever Connor was trying to get out. "Tomorrow. Goodnight, Connor."

He hung up and turned to me. "My mother is going to be here any minute."

"What?!" I looked at the boxy t-shirt dress I had pulled on when I finally got home and was able to shower. I hadn't done anything with my hair but run a comb through it. "But I'm not dressed for company!" I was so tired, my damp and bedraggled clothes still needed to be dealt with — and he wanted me to deal with meeting his mother?

Henri threw his head back and laughed. He reached out and pulled me to him so he could kiss my forehead. "Sweetheart, you look lovely. This is fine." He cracked a lopsided grin, letting me know whatever came next was what he had found so amusing. "Your grandmother is getting to you."

He smoothed a finger down my nose as it wrinkled in disgust and lightly bopped the tip of it.

"That said, if you want to change, there is time for it."

I didn't want to change, but I didn't want to meet his mom for the first time dressed like this. I sighed, "I do want to change."

"Right, well, we have about ten minutes. I'll put on a pot of coffee, or would you prefer some tea?"

"Either is fine," I answered distractedly. I was already mentally trying to figure out what an appropriate meet-the-parent outfit was.

Henri was laughing at me again. "I'll make both. And maybe see if I can find some cookies." That got my attention and I smiled at him gratefully. He winked at me as he walked off.

Right, pep talk time! Let's get going Loren, what can we do with ten minutes?

My mind was way ahead of my body, reviewing outfits as I was still walking along the hall. It was evening, which dictated a more formal outfit, but I didn't want his mom to think I was stuffy and sat around the house dressed to the nines every night. Ugh. And wow, why was I overthinking this? I wasn't going to marry Henri. It would be all right if his mother didn't like me. I took a deep breath. But wait, I didn't want his mother to think less of Henri because of me. Any which way, she would think Henri had decided he liked me enough to be engaged to me. Shoot. It did matter.

I walked into my room and stopped short. Laid out on the bed was the perfect dress for tonight's occasion. It was green, so an appropriate Belle color for her time with the Beast. It was soft, and the sack dress styling made it seem casual, but a gorgeous beaded mesh overlay dressed it up. The best part was it was one of my own dresses. It wasn't one Grandmother or Kella picked out.

Who had laid it out? I looked around the room as if I expected to have missed someone sitting there, but I was alone. Perhaps it had been the hob? There wasn't any time to figure it out.

I threw the dress on, along with my ballet flats. What else? The dress didn't need jewelry. Right. My hair. A glance in the bathroom mirror proved that Henri was dead wrong. It wasn't a "fine" situation.

I threw my hair up in a low bun Kella had shown me. Right, I need to pull a few small wisps out around my face to appease the Belle's-hair-is-always-falling-in-her-face requirement.

I poked my head out of the bathroom to peek at the clock on the nightstand. Any time left for makeup? Nope. I grinned, aw shucks . . . what an awful thing. The thought spurred guilt, so I grabbed some pink lip gloss and ran it over my lips. One final check in the mirror before heading back downstairs. Huh, not bad for ten minutes' effort.

I walked back into the den, but Henri wasn't there. "Henri? Is your mother here, yet?"

I heard a throaty chuckle from the direction of the living room. "Yes, she is," a feminine voice answered.

I wandered into the living to find a woman sitting on the couch alone. I would have known this was Henri's mother without anyone telling me. He resembled her — from the cheekbones to the gold-flecked green eyes. If I were going to be marrying Henri — why was that hard to remember? — I could have been pleased he would age well.

She stood, coming toward me with a hand extended to shake. "You must be Loren. I'm Margarete, Henri's mother." She was smiling, but it didn't seem genuine. Maybe her feelings for me were as complicated as mine were for her, our ties being through both Henri and Liam.

"I've heard so much about you! It's a pleasure to meet you." I said dutifully, optimistically hoping it wasn't a polite lie. I wish this could have happened when I wasn't already exhausted.

She motioned over her shoulder with one hand, the gesture a graceful movement that wouldn't be out of place in a ballet studio. "Henri went to finish getting the coffee ready. He should be back in a minute."

I sat, mindful of modestly tucking my skirt underneath me and crossing my ankles. Margarete resumed her seat and continued. "Actually, I'm glad I've got a minute to talk to you alone." My stomach plummeted. There was little chance something good would follow that statement. "I talked to Liam tonight. He claims he knew something about the murder of Charles Gifford, and that Henri tried to kill him to protect you . . . to keep him from telling the police about it."

"What?!" I spluttered. That rat bastard! I was so angry a wash of red clouded the thoughts zinging around my brain. I couldn't pull words out of the emotional maelstrom to defend myself. A not-so-small part of me wished Liam had died. I mean, Gaston wasn't supposed to come back to haunt Belle and cause problems for her! Why couldn't I catch a break here? Maybe I should have watched the sequels of the Disney movie, but they didn't seem canon, so I hadn't bothered. Did Gaston come back in one of them?

"Mother." I jumped a little, but Margarete only flinched. I suspect more from the tone of his voice than from being surprised.

"Yes, dear?" She turned her head toward Henri with a calm smile but didn't take her eyes off me. She didn't look at all ruffled. "I was just getting to know Loren. I have to say, from what I've seen, she doesn't seem your type."

What was that supposed to mean? What she had seen? Did she mean my outfit or the fact that I was a woman? Did she know about Paulo?

"Liam attacked me. He tried to kill me." His words were emphatic. "Protecting Loren had nothing to do with it."

"Hmm." That small moue of hers spoke volumes. She didn't believe Henri . . . at least not completely.

To be fair, I didn't believe it the way he had phrased it either. He was being protective, but it was more of a white knight protecting a damsel in distress protection — not a keeping a dirty secret kind of thing. There was no secret there! When would people believe that?

Henri set the tray down with a sharp rattle of teacups on saucers before sitting next to me.

"Mrs. Randolph, I had nothing to do with Charles Gifford being killed." There was a slight wobble in my voice.

"Loren, you don't need to defend yourself." Henri reached out and pulled me to him as he spoke. His movements were gentle, but his voice was like a steel cable. "I can't believe Liam is still finding ways to hurt you. Or that my family is involved!" Ooh, glad his glare wasn't directed at me!

"Why would Liam want to marry me if he thought I was a murderer?" I asked. Big freaking hole in his story there!

"I assumed he found out after you rejected him." Mrs. Randolph calmly replied.

"Rejected him? I haven't even spoken to him since Halloween!"

Henri spoke at the same time, "What was she supposed to do after he raped her?"

"Hmm, perhaps that was a poor choice of words. I should have said after marriage was no longer an option." Damn. The woman was unflappable. As horrified as I was, I was a bit jealous. I could use a little bit of that skill myself.

"Unbelievable!" Henri pushed his hands through his hair in frustration. "Mother, you seriously can't still believe him?! I mean, I know he got away with this shit when he was a kid — always some excuse or reason that made it okay when he did something wrong. But there is nothing he can say to make what he did to Loren all right. If you don't want to take my word for it, I suggest you talk to Chief Duncan or Connor. I don't know what ridiculous way he has twisted things, but I'm not letting Loren be hurt by his manipulation. I would like for you to leave until you get your facts straight."

Oooh! That got through the calm. You're a bit shocked now, aren't you? I mean, I would have been gaping like a bug-eyed fish, and she was only mildly surprised. It still felt like a moral victory. And wow, this was not a good start to my relationship with Henri's parents. Although, so far it wasn't as bad as the ogre mother-in-law in the original "Sleeping Beauty," who tried to kill her grandchildren and daughter-in-law, and then serve them to her son for dinner. So perhaps I should take it as a win? Maybe she would come around?

Mrs. Randolph stood stiffly and was still looking a little shocked. Shit, what was the etiquette for this? Did I say something? What would Miss Manners say to do when the host throws a guest out of their home? Did she even cover such a topic?

She walked toward the door without saying a word. Ugh! I hated that Henri was unhappy with his mother. My brain knew it wasn't my fault, but there was still a little part of me that felt some ownership in the situation, and therefore, guilt.

"Henri," I whispered to him behind his mother's back. "I can leave if you want to talk to your mother. I don't want you two fighting because of me — you need each other." He closed his eyes and sighed. I could almost see him weighing his options.

He stepped into me and kissed my forehead. "I'll be right back." Then more loudly, "Mom, let me see you out."

Henri came back about fifteen minutes later. "She asked me to apologize to you. She would have done it in person, but I told her it would be best for me to relay it for now." I gave a tight nod. "I feel like I am making excuses when I say this, but I think she is confused. She doesn't like that, and you were a convenient scapegoat. I'm not saying that makes it right, but I wanted to make sure you understand it wasn't about you."

I didn't know what to do with that information, and Henri was waiting expectantly for a response. Guess the truth it was. "It's just . . . I have a lot going on already, and I keep having to deal with other people's emotional issues. I don't have the energy for it, but I don't have a choice." I mean, forget bone-tired. I was exhausted on a cellular level.

"I'm sorry." Henri engulfed me in a giant hug and gently rocked back and forth. "I don't know if it will make anything better, but Mom believes you since you didn't smell guilty."

What? I pulled back from Henri's embrace to make sure my hearing wasn't blocked this time. "Smell guilty? What?"

"I told you about that." At my confused look he went on, "We talked about a heightened sense of smell, didn't we?"

"I thought that was when you were a wolf!"

"Well, it is significantly greater as a wolf. But, in human form werewolves are still more aware of what our sense of smell can tell us."

Oh, man. "Really?" That felt like an invasion of privacy. Even if I put a calm facade on, my raging emotional swings would have been obvious to most of those around me recently. Oh god, that would mean everyone knew about the times I was hot and bothered about Liam.

Henri must have seen something in my face. "Loren, I'm not sure what's wrong. It just means I have extra information about your feelings. They are part of the Loren package, and I think you are an amazing person. In fact, there is something I want to show you."

Why was he taking me to the dining room? There was nothing in there; we had emptied it to make space for our dance lessons. Oh! It wasn't clear anymore. Wow. Hundreds of fat pillar candles flickered around the edges of the room and flower petals were scattered across the floor.

Henri ducked his head, bashful. "It's not much, but I only had a few minutes. Mom helped me get all the candles lit. She also brought me this." He pulled a ring out of his pocket. "It was my grandmother's. I have something I want to ask you." He pulled me into the room, my stiff resistance from surprise, not reluctance. I thought we agreed to stop these displays.

Henri dropped to one knee. "Loren Roselle Hughes, will you do me the honor of becoming engaged to me?"

"But I've already agreed to that! You didn't have to do all of this!"

"But I wanted to! I know you would have preferred a different plan to deal with the Magic. I know you settled on this one because you took what was best for both of us into account, not just what is best for you. You deserve special treatment, and a lovely engagement story."

I had been feeling pretty good until that last line. How much of this was about me, and how much was about the story? What would I tell other people about his proposal? It made me sad Henri was living his life as much for the people around him as he was for himself. But he just said the same thing about me. Pot and kettle much, Loren? Well, that was something to consider later.

"So," Henri grinned up at me, "what do you say? Shall we get engaged officially? Oh, but also quasi-*un*officially, so your grandmother doesn't skin me alive for not doing it as a big reveal at her ball?"

The image made me laugh. "Of course. You didn't doubt that, did you?"

"Nope!" Henri replied as he popped up to give me a hug. "Let's see if this ring fits. Wow, it's like it was made for you."

"Or like magic?" I asked, rolling my eyes.

"Yes. One could put it that way. Quite the magical day all around."

That was accurate. And we were both exhausted. Going back to watching television felt anticlimactic. We agreed to turn in for the night and to work on plans the next day.

Getting engaged should have been effervescent, with happy sparkly feelings. But the evening hadn't gone that way. Dread lurked around the edges all night. I had been trying so hard not to center the thought, to make it not matter. Now with the prospect of lying on my own in a dark bedroom looming, I couldn't pretend anymore.

There was no way I would sleep with the question haunting me. So I padded down the hall in my nightgown, to knock on Henri's door.

"Come in."

I peeked around the edge and saw Henri reading in bed. He gestured me over, so I went and sat on the edge of the bed.

"What's up?"

"Henri, what are they going to do with Liam?"

"I don't know, Loren. And I really wish I did."

"Oh." The tears I had managed to suppress all day finally overcame my defenses and slid in hot tracks over my cheeks. Henri pulled me into a hug, and let me sniffle into his pajama shirt until even the hiccupping sobs were finished.

His touch was void of lust and stayed well within the realm of comforting. Despite that, it was the first time since getting engaged I hadn't felt like I was living a lie. It was such a relief, I fell asleep. I don't know if the decision was intentional on his part, but Henri didn't wake me. We slept together all night and well into the next day. It would have been lovely, except Paulo found us there together in the morning when he came to check on Henri.

Couldn't anything go right?

CHAPTER 37

Chief Duncan's earlier phone call was damaging my ability to stay calm. I couldn't help but speculate about what information he had to share, and why he wanted to give it to me in person. When I talked about needing to schedule with Grandmother's attorney though, he said it wouldn't be necessary; they weren't planning to ask me any questions. Had they found out what went wrong with the hunter?

I spent the morning trying to read in the library to distract myself. The fact I could see the drive from the library's windows had nothing to do with it, really. When the police cruiser pulled up, it managed to both spike my anxiety level and be a relief at the same time. The mixed feelings were doing weird things to my stomach. It felt like it was being tumble-dried. I tried not to vomit.

Henri showed the chief and Officer Ramos into the library, then came over and gingerly lowered himself to sit next to me on the loveseat. His ribs must still be sore. He wanted to be there for moral support. It seemed like it would be the thing to do if we were engaged, so I had agreed. Maybe I shouldn't have though. He should be resting. Hmm, wonder if he remembered to take his anti-inflammatory this morning?

I saw Chief Duncan's lips purse as he noticed the ring on my hand. I could see questions flickering behind his eyes, but they didn't make it past his lips. His face had locked down.

Officer Ramos caught the look. She grinned at Henri, "Looks like congratulations are in order?"

Henri nodded. "Thank you. I'm the luckiest of men. We haven't officially announced it yet, but I'm excited for everyone to find out at the ball." He reached out and took my hand before raising it to his mouth to kiss. Laying it on a little thick there, aren't you? I pasted a smile on my face for the chief's sake. Happy couple here, see?

"What a beautiful ring, Loren!" Officer Ramos bubbled. "I'm so happy for you two."

"Thank you."

"I know you and Henri are engaged now, but some of the information we have to share is of a personal nature. You might prefer we do this in private." The chief's words were gruff, but they also felt protective. That was interesting.

"Um? Oh . . . no. Henri can stay." It will keep you guys from ganging up on me. And while we are at it . . . "Won't you both take a seat?" Victory! I got to say it this time. My house, my invite! My internal maniacal evil laugh was getting better. I shouldn't have to practice if it was in my head, should I? Oh, wait. Henri's house. He should do the inviting. Whoa, was it weird I just did that? Was that the Magic kicking in? Focus, Loren. I mean I was still a hostess, right? Right?

"Would anyone like some water?" Yup, that was me playing at being hostess again. Paulo had left a tray that came straight out of *Better Homes and Garden* – right down to the beaded condensation on the pitcher and the lemon and mint sprigs. After pleasantries and the water were finished being passed, Officer Ramos got the ball rolling.

Good cop first, apparently.

"Right, let's get down to business." She waved a manila folder.

I swallowed, trying to create some moisture in my suddenly dry mouth, and settled for nodding. Please don't let there be any gruesome pictures. Nothing dead – human or animal.

"We got the results of your sexual assault evidence collection kit back this morning."

That was the last thing I had expected.

"But . . . You said it could take more than a year if I was lucky?" If they had told me that before doing the kit, I'm not sure I would have gone through with it.

"We decided to send it to a private lab . . . with a rush order." Officer Ramos said it dryly, and wait, was she giving the chief side-eye? What the hell was going on here?

Why the special treatment for my kit? It was bewildering. I turned to the chief in confusion.

"There were reasons not to have the results in the public database," he responded. What? My mind raced. He leaned forward in his seat and clasped his hands, not meeting my eyes. "I may have, um, leveraged that fact, to procure funding not available in our budget."

"That, and the other 89 tests still waiting for the state lab to get around to them." It seemed like Officer Ramos was gently mocking the chief. My bewilderment grew.

"Well, it couldn't look like we were giving one kit special treatment. It would have been suspicious. Besides, they prefer to run those things in batches anyway. Seems to be what holds them up." He sniffed like his delicate sensibilities had been offended.

Henri caught on faster than I did. "Wait. You blackmailed the Council?" I couldn't tell if he was aghast or in awe of the chief.

Chief Duncan turned red. Was he blushing? "I'm tired of this happening in my town." Oh. Nope, that was anger. "I wasn't willing to let this slide. The Council agreed to pay for a private lab. I keep the data private until it is necessary for prosecution. Everyone wins."

The Council . . . oh! Werewolves. Was their DNA different? I felt like I was lacking information understood by everyone else in the room.

"Not as if they can't afford it," Henri harrumphed. "I'm glad you got things moving."

Officer Ramos flashed the chief a look. He deflated a bit as he settled back into his chair. Then she turned to me and flashed me one of her trademarked dairymaid smiles. "How about we focus on you right now, Loren? We can talk about the rest later."

Focus on me? Chief Duncan submitted all the rape kits, including mine. It made me feel like there was at least one person in the system that cared about how badly society was failing at handling rape. That *did* affect me. It was important information. It gave me hope. How could she not see that?

The circumstances surrounding my rape were lucky. Ugh! What an awful, loathsome thought — but it was true. First off, there were witnesses — it's unreal that was lucky. I'm an introvert, not an exhibitionist. Secondly, most of the people in my life believed me when I said it happened. I also had police assigned to the case that cared, which felt like it should be standard, but it wasn't. I could afford therapy. I also got test results back in less than ten years. It made me livid that those things weren't the norm. I took a deep breath.

Was now the time to argue about this? Did I have the energy to fight this battle and hear the test results? Chief Duncan met my eye and gave me a nod, acknowledging my rage. He saw me. He shared my anger. It was enough. I released the deep breath I had marshaled to power a verbal tirade. I was going to let this go for now.

"Are you ready?" Chief Duncan asked, his voice quiet.

I wasn't, not really. I so badly wanted to say, "No, not yet. Perhaps not ever . . ." But I had to know.

I took another deep breath. "Yes."

Henri's hand found mine and squeezed. I was grateful for the show of support, but I needed the anger. Without it, I might turn into a blubbering wreck. It might happen in any case; I hate that I cry when I get mad.

I realized I was sitting with my back as rigid as a poker. I'm not sure if I was braced for the news, or if Grandmother's training was finally sticking.

Officer Ramos opened the folder on the coffee table, but she didn't even glance at the papers in it. "First of all, there was ketamine in your system. It is an anesthetic sometimes used as a date rape drug."

"We've actually known that for a while." The chief cleared his throat. "I've been working on tracking down where he got it."

Officer Ramos shot him a quelling look as she continued. "Ketamine can cause hallucinations. Since you previously expressed concern about your mental state, I thought knowing drugs were involved would help."

My body relaxed a fraction. Yet another thing it was ridiculous to feel lucky about. I wasn't going off the deep end. I had just been drugged against my will. Great. Officer Ramos was focused on me, obviously expecting a response. I didn't have one, but she was going to wait. I nodded. It must have been enough because she continued.

"DNA traces from the suspect were found in several locations on your body, including the vagina." The information knocked all the air from my body. I cringed and noticed the chief did, too. I didn't turn in time to catch Henri's reaction. Officer Ramos's face was carefully blank. "Only skin cells were found, there was no sign of sperm. Additionally, your DNA was found in samples from the hand, mouth, and penile swabs." She finally looked up from the report to meet my eyes. "There is enough evidence that the prosecutor is willing to take it to trial for sexual assault."

I could feel tears burning like acid, but I refused to let them fall. I just wouldn't blink — ever again, if need be. Liam didn't deserve any more of my tears. He better hope I never saw him again, though. I had plenty of rage that needed venting.

Officer Ramos continued, "There is still some discussion over whether to push for first degree rape, which is a class B1 felony and carries a penalty of 144 months to life in prison, or a second degree rape, which is a class C felony and carries a penalty of 44 to 182 months in prison."

As the word "rape" was said, it suddenly felt official. No wondering how far things had gotten or what exactly happened. The reality was as horrible as I had dreaded. The void this caused was collapsing all my internal organs, starting with my heart. I closed my eyes. Just breathe. I tentatively sucked in a lungful of air and let it out. I could do this.

"You have to catch him first though, right?" Henri spoke up, his voice hard.

"Yes," Chief Duncan responded. "We are still working to apprehend him. If it doesn't happen soon, we will have to upload his DNA to local, state, and federal databases." The chief held Henri's gaze as he said it. Henri nodded his understanding. I was missing something. I was going to have to force Henri to explain what was going unsaid as soon as everyone left.

Officer Ramos was determined to force me into the center of things. "Loren, do you have any questions?"

I shook my head, working on speaking. I finally managed to croak a single word, "No . . ." Everyone seemed to expect more though; they were all staring at me. "Actually, could I get a copy of the report?" I could tear it into shreds or burn it if I decided I didn't want it around. Maybe the task would give everyone something else to focus on, something to do so they could feel better about it all, and leave me alone. I needed to process things without everyone watching.

"I will make sure you get a copy today," Officer Ramos replied.

Henri glanced at me then turned to address the officers, "Was that everything you needed?"

"Oh, yes!" Officer Ramos said, glancing at me. "I suspect you might like some time to process all of this, Loren. We will go ahead and take off. Please don't hesitate to reach out if you have any questions later."

Chief Duncan nodded in agreement. They both stood and moved toward the door.

Henri got up off the couch much more easily than I had three days after breaking my ribs. Harrumph. Must be those special werewolf healing powers. I made a mental note to ask about that later. Who could I talk into giving me Werewolf 101? Although dumped in the deep end like this, maybe I should cram and ask for a higher-level option. Were there any 500-level classes?

We all moved into the hall — Henri and I planning to see our guests out. Paulo popped into the room as we left. He was probably planning to grab the tray of water glasses he had left for us earlier.

Chief Duncan paused right before leaving. "I want you to know I will do everything in my power to see that William Randolph is caught." He cleared his throat, seeming slightly embarrassed by the strong sentiment.

"Thank you."

"I also intend to find out where he got the ketamine. I am going to get to the bottom of all of this. The missing pieces are finally falling into place."

I barely managed to avoid giving Henri a knowing glance. How interconnected was it all? What else would the chief unravel?

"I'll be glad when this is all over," Henri said, saving me from having to think of an appropriate response.

Chief Duncan nodded and walked out to the cruiser. I wasn't surprised to see he was driving, and Officer Ramos was relegated to the passenger seat.

Henri closed the door and we exchanged the glance we hadn't been able to earlier. Henri spoke first, "Well, this is going to get interesting quickly."

"Which definition of interesting you are using there? I suspect it's not the fun kind."

Henri started to reply when Paulo found us and interrupted, "I need to talk to you both." He appeared miserable.

"What's up, Paulo?" I asked outwardly calm. Inside I was cringing. Was I seriously going to have to do something else emotional? I wanted to go hide in my room for a bit.

"I think Liam stole the ketamine he used from the Council's medical supplies."

Henri groaned and turned white. "Oh no!"

"What? Why would the Council have ketamine?" I asked.

"We keep it on hand in case someone is injured badly in wolf form. Sometimes it is hard to remember to shift so you can heal if you are in enough pain. It can also be used in a dart to take out anyone who loses control without killing them. Several of us in medical fields divert it whenever possible."

"That means we could be the reason . . ." Henri was looking at me helplessly.

"Don't even go there, Henri." There was a sharp, impatient edge to my voice. "No one is responsible for what Liam did but Liam." I glanced at Paulo to make sure he was getting the message, too. "No one."

Henri wanted to argue with me, "But—"

I was spared repeating myself by his cell phone ringing. He pulled it out of his pocket and glanced at its screen. "It's Dad. I'm sorry, I need to let him know about this, or I wouldn't take it."

"Right. Go ahead." I barely kept myself from sighing.

Henri mashed a button. "Dad, hi. I'm glad you called. I need –"

I watched the color drain from his face as he listened to his father.

"What?! How did that happen?"

He was listening again. Paulo looked concerned, while I waited impatiently to hear what was going on.

"No, it definitely took someone else's help. Maybe he blackmailed –"

He wasn't having much luck with finishing sentences in this conversation.

"Yes, I know Dad! Maybe we can use it to our advantage? If he is getting information from someone, maybe we should make sure he is getting the information we want him to — set a trap."

A trap? But the only person we might need a trap for . . . No. It seriously couldn't have happened.

"I'm happy to help come up with a plan –"

If this call went on for much longer, I might throttle Henri.

"Right." Henri's shoulders slumped. "I'll set up a guard rotation. Please have someone report any changes to me as soon as possible."

Hang up already!

"Yes."

I mouthed, "What is going on?" to Henri and he held up a finger to ask me to wait.

"Right. Bye, Dad."

I pounced the minute he took the phone away from his ear. "What is going on, Henri?"

"Liam escaped. Again."

Paulo nodded while I simultaneously shrieked, "What!?"

Henri sighed. "Dad thinks someone helped him escape. He wants to feed false information to the Pack and have only a few people he trusts waiting to capture Liam."

I was angry, seeing red even. But . . . The thought calmed me a bit, that was progress. I was angry. Not scared. There was no panic attack in sight. I marveled over the fact while the guys continued the discussion.

"Well, there are a few problems with that," Paulo said. "What if he is blackmailing someone your dad trusts?"

"I know. He isn't ready to hear it yet, though. So, for now, I am going to do the only thing I can: plan more guard rotations." He looked at Paulo, smiling tentatively. "Would you consider staying here? I would feel better knowing I had your help and that you were safe . . ."

Paulo sighed. "Yes, I'll stay. But Liam needs to be caught soon, for all our sakes."

Henri and I couldn't do anything other than agree.

CHAPTER 38

I ripped another strip off the report Chief Duncan had brought and wadded it into a ball. I was surrounded by small glass jelly jars filled with watered-down glue, all tinted in various green hues. I thought I was done yesterday, but I changed my mind after everything dried. Good thing I saved my decoupage mixtures.

Hmm, I examined the thorny beast climbing out of the canvas. It only needed one or two more strips. That was a shame; I had plenty of the report left that needed destroying. I didn't set out to do this painting, but the image had been haunting me. It was probably a good thing I hadn't lost my artistic abilities when I got back to Henri's. I needed to get this out of my system. I poked the sodden paper strip into place and then shoved the painting away. It reminded me a bit of Arcimboldo's fruit and vegetable people — not a direction I would have ever expected my art to take.

For that matter . . . I glanced around the room at the paintings I managed to finish over the last three weeks or so. I was still shocked by them. Most were like nothing I had created before, different in both style and in that I had poured buckets of emotion into them. Some of them were perhaps melodramatic, slipping into clichéd, but I didn't care. I needed to make them and that was reason enough for them to exist. That said, I wasn't sure I was going to let Henri and Paulo view the art they had inspired.

What had emerged, almost unbidden as I sketched, was Paulo adrift in lake water. I had spilled color onto the canvas — inky swaths of teal and cerulean water, dotted with bright pinpricks of bubbles in a spiraling swirl to give the water chaotic motion. Curling strands of hair wrapped around his reaching arms. Paulo's chin was lifted, his whole being focused on reaching the surface. His determination was obvious. However, I wasn't sure I wanted him to see the piece because of the not-so-subtle metaphor about him being lost.

I was certain I didn't want Henri to see the artwork he had inspired. I didn't want anyone to see it, actually. Stylistically, it was the offspring of Da Vinci's notebooks and something by M. C. Escher — a line drawing done in sepias and browns. The piece reminded me a bit of Russian nesting dolls. A tree filled most of the page. A portion of its trunk peeled back, but instead of the usual tree rings, a wolf was revealed. The wolf's fur was split along the middle and Henri was underneath. But Henri's figure opened to nothingness. There was a hollow void inside — or perhaps he contained the entire universe. I wasn't sure. I don't think Henri would know which was true either.

I was staring at his painting when Henri knocked on the door and popped his head into my studio. "Mind if I come in?" It was weird to have him ask. It was his house, but he had given me the space to use as a studio and treated it as sacred.

"Sure." I casually turned the painting toward the wall.

He gazed intently around the room as he came in. I had been lying to myself earlier. Other people's opinions did in fact matter. I desperately wanted Henri to like my work.

"Wow!" He gave me a distracted hug and kissed my temple as he said it. "These are phenomenal. You are an amazing artist!"

A fuzzy glow spread through me, and I could feel my cheeks flushing. I needed to work on being better at taking a compliment. Just say thank you, Loren. No really. Say it. "Thanks, Henri. I appreciate the compliment."

"I love having you here — even just all the little things you notice and share with me are special."

I laughed. "You are kind for humoring me. I'm glad to know it's not too much trouble when I make you drop everything to look at random things."

Henri was shaking his head. "No, seriously. Loren, I don't know how to explain it so you will understand. You have this unique way of seeing the world. You find this . . . transcendence in the smallest, most ordinary things — the way a leaf moves in the wind, dew drops in a spider web, the color of the light . . . I didn't know light could have a color before I met you! I had no idea what I was missing. I see the world differently now. It is so much more achingly beautiful than I ever knew. You should be called Beauty if only because of how much beauty you have brought into my life."

"That's sweet. But it was there all along, Henri. Maybe you just finally took time to stop and notice what was around you?" I heard what I just said. Well shit, so much for managing to take compliments well.

"I wouldn't have noticed without you here to point it out. And you do it again with your paintings. You peel back the surface; there is a deep truth in each of them. Even when it is an ugly truth, you somehow help me accept that it is still part of the beauty of the world."

Yikes. Would he still say that if he saw the painting of him?

He continued, "You are awe-inspiring, and I am truly honored to be getting engaged to you tonight."

Oh shit! Engaged, as in at Grandmother's ball! "Oh no! What time is it?"

He laughed at me. "Don't worry. That's why I came up — to remind you it was time to start getting ready." I heaved a sigh of relief. "In case you had lost track of time . . ." He raised an eyebrow at me.

I raised my hand. "Guilty as charged there. Thank you!"

"If it's possible, we should leave a bit early. The forecast is for snow and I'd prefer not to rush if road conditions are poor."

"Sure thing. Let me clean up here and then I will pull myself together." I glanced out the window. "It feels weird to put on formal clothes and go out in the snow."

"Tell you what, why don't I grab your boots and an extra jacket, and stick them in the car? That red cape won't be warm enough in an emergency."

"I might wait and change into my gown when I get there. It will keep my dress from getting crushed. But that still sounds perfect. Belle's normal clothes aren't warm, either. Thank you."

"I'll leave you to your tidying then."

I smiled as he left, but let it fall off my face the minute he was out the door. I turned Henri's picture around again and looked at it.

I sighed, if only Henri could get past his fear and do what would make him happy . . . Oh wow. It hit me like a ton of bricks — or perhaps a ton of fairy tale books — I wasn't any better. I was doing the exact things Henri was doing. I was letting all the 'what ifs' I was afraid of control me.

What if my technical drawing skills never came back? What if the Magic tried to make me marry Liam? What if I didn't love Henri? What if the Magic made something horrible happen? But it went further back, before the Magic, even. What if people didn't like my art? What if I turned into the proverbial starving artist? What if my father was right and I should have done something to contribute to the world, like run a non-profit for starving orphans or saving the rainforest? Not that he meant those things when he said it . . .

And what happened? I had done everything I was supposed to: dotted all my metaphorical i's and crossed my t's, said please and thank you to the universe *and* the Magic. And everything was a mess anyway. All the polite pretenses and rule following and pretending everything was okay . . . I was wearing a mask, too. And nothing was okay with this situation. There was a gaping void inside me, and Henri wasn't the right way to fill it. Just pretending would make the void bigger.

Any way you examined it, it was wrong. Doing something you know is wrong in a fairy tale is not smart. Ugh — that is a cop-out. Loren, just own it. You aren't saying it's wrong because the Magic will punish you. It's wrong because you can't do it and be true to yourself.

Of course, that left me in a bit of a pickle. Maybe Connor could do some equations to help figure out the ramifications of it all. He could tell me what the consequences might be or verify that I was on the right track.

Why did that thought seem wrong?

What was it Connor had said? Something about how we don't ever interact with the objective world, only with our subjective beliefs about the world. How did that work? No two people inhabited the same world because we all had different expectations and beliefs. Even if several people went through the same thing, their experiences would be different. It hurt my head to consider the first time I heard it, but it did have serious implications. Maybe it was time to work through it all.

It would mean we were only interacting with things in our mind, our own imagination. We were creating our experiences, our stories . . .

I was the only person seeing my entire story, the only one fully aware of the lens I was seeing it through. I was the person who built this world, and no one else could be an authority on it. Not Connor, not Marie D'Aulnoy, and not the Jungian collective unconsciousness.

I closed my eyes in disbelief at how wrong I had been. All the rules I followed, the cultural conditioning. All the times I listened when people said to stay on the right path or terrible things would happen. Ruled by fear . . . that was no way to live.

Why had I been waiting to be saved by a prince? I was writing this story. I was in control. Why was I going along with the flow of things, hoping for the best?

I prayed this didn't end as dramatically as most choose-your-own-adventure tales did! Not that it mattered. I was done being dictated to.

There had been several defining moments in my life, moments like Connor mentioned, touchpoints that break everything into 'before' and 'after.' There was my mother's death, before and after the big reveal about the Magic and the tales, pre- and post-rape. I knew this was going to be another seismic shift: the day I realized I wasn't the Princess, but the storyteller.

The Magic was going to force a tale on me, but could I take the story elements we had lined up, and rearrange them to tell a different story? Perhaps the desires of my heart could create a new path to follow, or not follow as the case might be.

CHAPTER
39

Whoever designed Grandmother's staircase certainly had grand entrances in mind. I didn't disappoint with my arrival. The only thing missing was a teapot singing "Tale as Old as Time." It's funny how much easier it was to sweep in once you decided it didn't matter if you did it properly or not. Of course, it also helped that Kella had worked her own special magic, and I knew I looked amazing. I floated effortlessly down the stairs. From my hairpins to the light glinting off the gold applique adorning my gown, I was every bit the glittering princess.

Henri waited at the bottom of the staircase, snazzy in his tuxedo. The appreciative awe on his face felt genuine. He reached out his hand to guide me down the last few stairs, then pulled me into a hug.

"You are absolutely stunning!"

I laughed. "Thank you. You were supposed to let me curtsey." I teased gently.

He leaned in for a kiss. It was awkward, chaste — empty. Well, that kiss would have convinced me to change courses if I hadn't already. It was such a tempting thing, this beautiful lie. But it would be disappointing in the long run, like finding out your chocolate Easter bunny was hollow. I wanted to fill the void the Magic left in my life with joy — with people and activities that reminded me of the substantial beauty to be found in life. Henri might even be one of those people, but not in the role of fiancé or husband.

Henri put a hand on my shoulder and turned us to face Grandmother. I hadn't noticed her off to the side of the foyer. She was beaming. I hurried over to hug her, careful of her cane. I leaned awkwardly to avoid crushing my skirt. I half expected her to fuss about my posture, but she didn't.

"Loren, you are lovely."

"Thank you. You look pretty wonderful yourself!"

She waved my compliment off. "You are too kind. I am going to go check the ballroom to make sure the musicians are situated correctly. I want everything to be perfect after the debacle with the cellist in 2002." She thumped her cane. Her arsenal for displaying her disapproval just kept growing. "I will be back here in twenty minutes to receive guests. I assume you still plan to join me?" It was phrased as a question, but I knew she didn't mean it that way.

"Yes, Grandmother." She nodded before calling Millie to join her in the final preparations. I gave Millie a little wave as they left.

I turned back to Henri and gave him an impish grin. "All right, now that we have done our duty, I have a surprise for you. Come with me."

His eyebrows shot up. "A surprise?"

"Yes." I took his hand and led him along the hallway.

"Where are we going?"

"You'll see."

"You really aren't going to tell me?"

"Nope! Just be patient. It won't be long!" I laughingly refused to say anything else until I got to the kitchen. I nodded at the caterers but continued straight to the back door. Great! Ms. Millie had stashed our outerwear as requested.

"Here." I handed Henri his wool overcoat and then let him help me with my cape. I took a deep breath, steeling myself against heading out to the patio. I could do this. I wasn't going to let what Liam did spoil the patio or my agenda. I didn't need the extra layer of panic; I was already nervous about my plans for Henri.

"Everything all right?" The gentle concern in Henri's voice almost undid my fragile composure.

"I'm sorry. Give me a second." I squared my shoulders. Liam didn't get to steal this from me. I was the one telling the story, not him. Right. "Okay, I'm ready."

"Are you sure?"

"Yes. I am. Come on." My smile was more genuine as I pulled him outside. I paused on the patio. "I've spent a lot of time thinking about fear and its repercussions. You know how they say fear is a deadly sin? It's because if we aren't careful, fear keeps us from doing what we know to be right and true. It makes us doubt ourselves. It keeps us from pursuing the beauty we might otherwise find in life."

I gestured at a sleigh standing thirty feet away. It was beautifully decorated with greenery, it came straight out of a holiday card. "Grandmother arranged sleigh rides through the forest for the guests. She has the forest lit with lanterns and little twinkly lights. The effect is magical and very romantic. Rides don't officially start for a few hours, but I arranged for an early ride as a surprise."

Henri's brows drew together, and he stared at me, mouth hanging open. "But . . ."

I couldn't help but laugh. I knew all the ways he wanted to finish that sentence but couldn't for fear of hurting my feelings, ruining the tale, or perchance offending the Magic.

"But you have no desire to go on that ride with me, huh? Here's the deal," Oh boy, deep breath, "The plan isn't for me to go with you." Confusion washed over Henri's face. "Henri, this thing between us — it isn't going to work. We both know it. I realized this afternoon I could do what was expected of me, or I could do what would make me happy. But I couldn't do both at the same time — I think the same is true for you. I've decided I can't live my life for everyone else. I'm not going to let anyone else direct my life. I deserve to be happy, and so do you."

Henri stared at his feet and his shoulders drooped. Oh god, he looked so defeated.

"I would change any way I could to make this work!" It was an anguished admission.

"But that's just it, Henri!" I hoped that felt like gentle exasperation and not criticism. "You shouldn't *have* to change. The Beast changing is bullshit! We should both be with someone who loves us for who we are. Not what we could be, not the polite social front we put on for society, but who we actually *are*. That's a special kind of love."

I paused, unsure how to continue. I couldn't steal someone else's happily ever after. I slipped his grandmother's ring off my finger and held it out to him. "You know, you didn't have to get engaged to me for your spell to end. You had the perfect story before you met me. This is a pale imitation."

Henri's face crumbled. "Shit! It was perfect, and I let him go! That has got to be the worst decision I've ever made! I am such an ass!"

I couldn't help but chuckle. "That seems a bit harsh. I'm also pretty sure it isn't too late."

"Really? I don't care about anything else if you think that is possible."

"Yup, in fact . . ." I raised my voice and called out, "Hey, Paulo?"

Paulo stepped out from behind the pergola where I had asked him to wait. He stared directly at Henri and opened his arms. Damn, he wore a tuxedo well. How could Henri say 'no' to that? He was too intelligent not to go for this.

Luckily, Henri made the right choice. He ran and launched himself into Paulo's arms.

I stepped back to give them some privacy. I didn't need to hear all the confessions of love and the apologies Henri was making, but I did want to remind them there was a sleigh ride awaiting. Although the driver didn't seem to mind. He was grinning so widely that it looked like his face would split. I was glad to see there was at least one Pack member that wasn't upset by Henri and Paulo's relationship. The driver caught my eye and winked before ducking around behind the sleigh. I wished I could disappear to give the guys some privacy, too.

Paulo pulled back a bit, placing his hands on Henri's shoulders. "I love you . . . but I can't hide it anymore."

"I know. I should have never asked you to keep our relationship a secret. It doesn't matter who knows."

"What about the Pack?"

"Screw the Pack!" The stunned look on Paulo's face was priceless. "If they can't accept me as I am, then why should I sacrifice everything for them?"

Paulo gave a giddy laugh, and the men embraced.

Henri smoothed Paulo's hair out of his face. "I just want you — always. And I want everyone to know that. Everything else will work out if you are by my side." They melted into a tender kiss.

Was that . . .? Holy shit! They were glowing. Now we got the light effects. Henri and Paulo slowly rose off the ground as the light show increased. The Magic spun them around three times before settling them back on the ground.

At first, the guys were too absorbed in their kiss to notice what was happening, but they caught on at the end. We were all still for a moment, incredulous.

"Well, I have to say I think the Magic approves." I threw my arms around them both in a giant hug. When I pulled back, I gave the guys a gentle push. "Now, go enjoy your sleigh ride."

Paulo turned to me, "Thank you, Loren."

"It was nothing," I waved his thanks away. "You two were meant to be."

Henri stepped up to me, looking grim. He whispered, "I hate to do this, but I have another favor to ask of you. Would you see if your grandmother would let me propose to Paulo tonight? As a replacement for our engagement announcement? I'd like to do that for him."

My face felt like it would split, I was smiling so hard. "I'll find a way to make it happen!" I promised.

"You are seriously the best. Thank you." Henri had turned away, but he whipped back around. "Wait, what about you and your story?"

"It's not your problem anymore, Henri," I said gently but firmly. "I'll figure it out. I already have a plan. Now go. Go enjoy your happily ever after.

Henri gave me a big hug, "This means the world to me. Thank you." I could see Paulo beaming at us from over Henri's shoulder. I smiled back at him.

Wait.

What was in the forest behind Paulo? It was so dark . . .

Was that Liam!? No! No, no, no! I pushed Henri away in horror as panic washed over me.

"Paulo, behind you!" I cried out.

CHAPTER 40

Paulo didn't have time to react. Liam grabbed him around the neck and held a knife against his throat. Shit. Shit!

Where were the guards? Why weren't they here? Oh, no, no, no. I changed our plans. We weren't expected outside yet. How could I make such a careless mistake? But still, guards were surrounding the house, including a handful hidden in the forest. How had Liam slipped past them?

The blood was rushing so loudly in my ears that I couldn't even hear what Liam was saying. It made my vision fade slightly around the edges. My mind scrambled to make sense of the light and dark shapes — pale faces shining in the night's darkness, the men's dark clothing a sharp contrast against the snow. My brain locked onto its target, the danger — Liam. Liam with his face twisted and snarled by hate. Paulo pale, his abject terror noticeable from ten feet away. Henri begging, arm stretched out . . .

No. Fuck that.

It wasn't supposed to happen this way. I was supposed to be in charge of this tale.

Perhaps if I was Snow White, I would be so disgustingly sweet that birds and small mammals would follow me around. Then I could send them in a wave of attacking claws and beaks and teeth. But I didn't have animal minions.

I searched for anything to help: guards, extra guests, a convenient weapon . . . There was nothing but snow. Snow and a stick. A big stick. Not ideal, but it was something. Liam wasn't looking at me. I snatched it, hiding it behind the folds of my skirt.

"Don't take another step!" Liam was yelling at Henri. He jerked Paulo back, the blade pressing against his throat. Paulo's hands scrabbled at Liam's arm.

A primal scream caught in the back of my throat. It reminded me of Led Zeppelin's "Immigrant Song," which seemed like an appropriate soundtrack for the moment. No, that didn't seem formal enough. Three of us were in black tie attire after all. Maybe something from Wagner – "Ride of the Valkyries"? Seriously Loren?! Where is your brain?

"Loren, come here sweetheart. Don't worry. I won't let them hurt you. They can't keep you from me anymore. I'll keep you safe."

Wow! He was delusional! What a self-centered prick! How could he rationalize things that way? He was the person I needed protection from! I edged closer to Liam.

I had never been so grateful for Grandmother and all those lessons that now permitted me to keep a smile pasted on my face. It was better than the dread I was feeling. If I could get close enough . . .

Liam gazed adoringly as I approached. I noticed Henri trying to edge closer in my peripheral vision. He wouldn't be able to get close enough to help without causing problems. Hopefully, I could.

I called out, "Henri, please don't try anything!"

Liam whipped his head around. "Don't try anything! I will kill him. You kept me from my love, I won't hesitate to take yours away." I crossed the rest of the distance between us as Liam yelled at Henri. Please don't look this way . . . I just needed one more step.

I raised the branch. The motion caught Liam's attention, but it was too late. I brought the branch down in an overhead swing like I was chopping wood. His eyes widened with horror as the connection was made with a meaty thunk.

Liam crumpled on top of Paulo. Oh god, what had I done? Did he hurt Paulo? I fumbled frantically to roll Liam off Paulo. But Paulo was already digging himself out. Henri made it across the clearing and scooped him into a panicked embrace. Oh, thank goodness! I crumpled in the snow, relief making my knees weak. Paulo wasn't hurt, or at least not seriously.

A movement caught my attention. Liam was struggling to sit up. Shit! I hadn't hit him hard enough.

A gunshot rang out. I stared in surprise at the warm spray of droplets that spattered me, a stark contrast against my pale skin. I waited for the pain, but it never came. I gathered my courage to check myself for holes. There weren't any. Oh . . . Oh. Liam was the one who was shot. Who were all the men with guns?

"Where were you?!" Henri was demanding angrily.

"You shot him!" Paulo sounded shocked.

Someone mumbled an indistinct reply.

"No, you could have hit Loren!"

One of the men walked over and held out a hand. I looked at it numbly, taking way longer than I should have to realize what he wanted. I let him pull me up from the ground.

Everyone was talking at once. I caught bits and pieces as discussions, plans, and arguments swirled around me.

Someone leaned over Liam and checked his pulse. "He's still alive."

Someone else scoffed, "Not for long at the rate he's losing blood."

"Shit!" Henri exclaimed. "We can't let him bleed out here. The house is full of people! We have to move him. Cover up the bloody snow. Or scoop it up. Get rid of it!"

Paulo faced Henri squarely, "You won't be able to face your parents if you let him die."

Henri closed his eyes. "Damn it."

A guy in camouflage was making hand signals at two of the men to pick Liam up. He interrupted, "You all have to get back to the party. We'll take care of him."

The men lifted Liam with quiet grunts. The Pack faded back into the forest. Paulo turned and started to head out with them.

"Where are you going?" Henri asked.

Paulo turned around stiffly. "I have to go, I'm the Pack doctor." His voice was flat, his face blank. It was frankly scary how shut down he was.

"No," Henri's reply was firm. "No, you don't have to go. You don't have to take care of him after everything he did to you. That is ridiculous."

"But..."

"No! Toby is perfectly capable of dealing with a gunshot wound. And if not, I honestly don't care at this point. I'm not letting our evening fall apart — especially not for him."

I wasn't sure it was the right thing to do, but I piped up. "I have to agree with Henri. Besides, it will be suspicious if you disappear. Don't you need to worry about keeping the Pack's secret?" I wasn't sure that was sound logic, but it seemed like an argument that might convince Paulo. I didn't add that Liam could rot for all I cared.

Paulo turned to look at me. "But... *Dios!* Loren, you are covered in blood!"

I touched my dress numbly. The teeny tiny droplets smeared as I ran my fingers across them. I must have stared at my hands for a bit, as the next thing I knew, Henri was there with his handkerchief wiping my fingers off.

"Don't worry Loren, we'll help you." Henri was speaking softly like I needed handling. I didn't need handling. I didn't. Pull it together, Loren. "Right, Paulo?"

Paulo sighed and nodded, capitulating to their previous argument by extension. "I bet we can find something for you to wear. Or we could call Kella?"

I guess it was a good thing I wasn't planning to have that iconic waltz around the ballroom with Henri. I would be scrambling to find another dress as it was. Needing to find one in Belle's iconic yellow... Well, that would only be accomplished with magic, which is exactly what I was trying to avoid. Besides, I didn't have time before — "Oh no! No! I was supposed to join Grandmother in the receiving line. I am not going to hear the end of it!"

"Why don't we focus on getting you changed first? If anyone sees this blood, we will have a whole different set of problems." Henri turned in a circle, "Where's your cape?"

I scanned the area and pointed. "It's over there. It must have come off earlier; I didn't even notice."

"You were too busy going all Valkyrie to notice such trifling details, huh?" Henri laughed. "I wish you could have seen yourself. It was epic." He laughed, but the sound was raw.

Paulo headed over to get my cape. Henri squeezed my hand and whispered, "You saved him. I don't know how I will ever repay you."

I rolled my eyes at him. "I guess you'll have to name your first-born child after me or something."

"Kids?" Henri's face went blank.

"Breathe, Henri! Sheesh. I was joking."

"It's not that, I just realized I want to have children with Paulo. Not right away or anything, but I want children with him."

"I am sure you two will figure something out. Now, you should back away before you get this . . ." I gestured, "all over your tux."

"Got it," Paulo walked up with my cape folded over his arm. "Let's get you inside."

Henri eyed me critically. "We can't fix this."

"Hmm," Paulo said. He pulled the dress handkerchief out of his lapel pocket and eyed it dubiously.

"Don't even think about spitting on it first," I said.

Both guys laughed. "How about some melted snow?"

I shivered at the idea but nodded.

"I only need to make it up the back stairs, anyway."

"Yeah, but you won't make it past the first caterer you meet in the kitchen right now," Henri responded.

"That bad, huh?"

"Yes," Henri and Paulo replied in unison.

"Here," Henri said reaching for the handkerchief. "I can do that. You have a better chance of saving Loren's hair than I do."

A few minutes later the guys pronounced I was as good as I was going to get. I took a breath. Liam got everything off track. That wasn't allowed. I was the storyteller here. It was time to act like it.

"Right," I said. "Paulo, can you escort me to my room? Henri, can you tell my grandmother that there was an emergency and ask her to come to my room?

Then maybe you can take over greeting people for her? With any luck, she won't miss many people."

Paulo nodded. Henri shrugged, "Sure, I can do that."

"Then I want you two to come out here and take the sleigh ride. Damn it! This is supposed to be your night!"

"Yes, ma'am," Henri said with a chuckle.

Paulo attempted a smile, before saying, "Well, if you insist."

"I do! Now, let's get this done so you have time to enjoy your evening!"

CHAPTER 41

Getting to my room was easier than I anticipated. We managed to breeze past the caterers with the men blocking me from view. No one else had been on the back staircase or in the hallway. Everyone must be in the ballroom.

Paulo saw me to the door of my room. He turned to walk away, but I wasn't done with him yet. We needed to talk. I let go of the doorknob and reached out to stop him. "Paulo, you need to tell Henri everything."

He looked blank.

"Everything to do with Liam."

"Oh. But . . ." His shoulders slumped. "You're right. I know you are. I've been avoiding it. I don't want to hurt Henri. Knowing what Liam did is going to break him. Do you think he will hate me for not telling him before?"

"No! Absolutely not. None of this will change what Henri feels for you. He loves you – all of you. You know that, right? But, if you don't tell him now, I think he will worry you don't trust him. That would hurt him deeply." Paulo's eyes widened a bit as I said it. Good. That hit home.

"I suspect there is something else you need to tell him about Charles Gifford, too?"

He deflated further. "How did you know about Connor?"

"Connor?" What did he have to do with anything?

"You know, the scar on his foot. From jumping out of a tree onto a garden rake when he was a kid . . .?"

Huh? Scar? Oh . . . Chief Duncan's phone call about the paw print? "Wait! Connor is a werewolf?"

"He's not. It's different. You will have to get him to explain it to you. It has to do with metaphysical stuff no one else has been able to figure out."

"Um, okay." Huh. Well, that was interesting. It made things easier . . .

Paulo interrupted my musings. "Wait, what were you talking about if it wasn't Connor?"

"The squid. I thought you might know who had eaten squid and then bitten Charles Gifford. It's the only thing I can't explain yet . . ."

"Oh, hell. You are right." He sighed. A door opened along the hall. Paulo frantically pushed me into my room. "I promise to tell him, now go. Get cleaned up! Before we get caught out here."

He turned to walk away for the second time when the realization hit me. Had Liam used my name when he was talking to Margarete? Perhaps he only said Henri was protecting someone he loved? "Wait!"

Paulo paused in closing the door between us, cocking a questioning eyebrow.

It didn't matter which way Liam phrased it, Margarete would probably take issue either way. "Whatever you do, don't let Henri's mother find out about the stuff with Gifford."

"Why not?" He was glancing over his shoulder as he said it.

"Please, trust me on this one. I can explain later when we have time."

"Okay. Now go change!" He was trying to shoo me back into my room. "I don't want to have to explain what happened on the patio to anyone!"

"Yes, sir!" I grinned as he walked away, shaking his head at me.

Right, time to deal with my own mess. I dropped the cape on the floor and assessed the state of my gown. Oh my god. I was covered in hundreds of drops and spatters. It looked like it had been airbrushed. The crimson smears over the gold organdy were a gorgeous color combination. I was both disgusted and intrigued by how I might replicate the effect with paint. What a ridiculous thing to get distracted by. Of course, realizing it was my brain creating a distraction meant the exact visual I was trying to avoid popped up front and center in my mind. I swayed, light-headed for a moment before I could cram the thoughts back into their box. Fix things now. Panic later.

But where did I start? I didn't ever want to see the gown again, so I didn't need to worry about getting the blood cleaned out at least. I could throw it in the nearest trash can, or I could burn it. Was that extreme since the blood might wash out — would anyone else want it after this? Wait.

Shit! Did I need to worry about evidence? I had assaulted Liam, and then he was shot. There was a good chance he would die. Was I an accessory to murder? I was.

Why was I just realizing that? Was it still self-defense if you were protecting someone else?

Breathe Loren, breathe. A wave of dizziness washed over me. No, slower. Deep breaths. There you go.

Right. I would change and then go talk to Henri. Or was his dad here — should I talk to him as Council leader? Was there an official Pack stance I would need to corroborate? Was I willing to do that? The situation just kept getting more complicated. I didn't want anything to ruin the announcement tonight . . . Maybe tomorrow would be a better time to deal with it?

I walked into the bathroom. The image in the mirror made me realize how lucky we were to avoid running into anyone on the way to my room. There were faint red smears on my face in addition to the Jackson Pollock creation on my dress. Nausea hit me hard. I needed to get it off. Shower first. Anything else could wait. It was frustrating that it would have to be a quick shower; I would have liked to scald and scrub myself until Grandmother's considerable hot water tank ran empty.

I was drying off when there was a knock at my door. "One moment!" I called out. I threw on my bathrobe and hurried over. I opened the door a crack and checked to see who it was. Grandmother. Right, here we go. I opened the door and gestured for her to come inside.

Grandmother took in everything from my wet tangled hair down to my bare feet in one glance and shook her head before hobbling into the room. I shut the door as soon as I could without catching Grandmother's skirts, hiding us away.

"What is all this about, Loren? Henri said there was an emergency of some sort?"

When I opened my mouth to explain, I was shocked to find myself abruptly crying instead. Oh, Grandmother was going to love that.

"Goodness. It seems you have had some sort of upset."

I started laughing and sobbing at the same time. Understatement of the year.

Grandmother raised her eyebrows. She reached out a hand, awkwardly patting my back. "There, there. Have a good cry, and when you are finished, we can straighten it all out."

I gulped back a hiccup and blurted, "Liam attacked us, and they shot him."

"Those are some distressingly vague pronouns, dear."

I sniffled. "Liam attacked Paulo, Henri, and me. One of the guards who was supposed to be protecting us shot him." I realized I left something out. "Umm, after I hit him. Liam, I mean. With a stick."

"Oh. Well. I assume Liam is dead?"

"No. At least he wasn't yet. They carried him off."

Grandmother sighed. "I suppose that would have been entirely too convenient."

"Grandmother!"

She allowed herself a disdainful sniff. "Don't be sentimental. It would have been easier all around if he had been decent enough to die and not left his mess for others to deal with."

"You don't mean that!" I underestimated how ruthlessly practical she was.

"I do. The Council can't turn him over to the police. Keeping him locked away hasn't turned out to be the most viable option. I'm not entirely sure how they will handle him. It would have been easier for his family to not have to make those sorts of decisions. Perhaps I should have been more explicit when explaining the situation to the Pack members guarding the house. The sleigh driver ought to have been close enough to be of assistance at least."

"Oh. I think he was the one who shot Liam. Maybe if he had been closer . . .?" I shrugged.

"It sounds as if he needs to work on his marksmanship." Grandmother sniffed delicately. "So, there was almost a murder on the back patio that will need to be dealt with. You still haven't explained why you are *en deshabille*."

"Blood sprayed all over me when Liam was shot."

"That is problematic. I don't believe your gown can be cleaned in time for the announcement. Were there any suitable alternatives when Kella was going over the options with you? Perhaps we should call her."

"I could put the dress I wore to the theatre on again, I left it in the closet here . . ."

Grandmother sighed. "No, you can't wear the same dress twice in a row. Besides, doesn't your gown need to be yellow or at least gold?" Was Grandmother seriously more upset about the suggestion I re-wear a dress, than by murder?

"Umm, I need to talk to you about that."

"Oh?" There was that eyebrow again!

I needed to perfect the move. I wanted it in my arsenal. Right. Focus. I discreetly let out a calming breath. "Henri and I aren't going to announce our engagement tonight. In fact, we aren't engaged anymore." I rushed on. "Please don't tell me I should marry him or that this is a bad idea. I would pay for it with my happiness."

Grandmother pursed her lips and gave a small, tight nod. She reached out and cupped my cheek in her hand. "I believe that is a wise decision."

I threw my arms around her and buried my head in her neck. "Thank you."

She hugged me back and spoke into my hair. "I am relieved that you have stopped trying to steer the direction your *contes des fées* is taking." Umm, about that . . . "Trying to control the Magic had disastrous results when I tried years ago."

I locked my jaw to keep my mouth from falling open. Is that why she resisted our plan?

"You mean with mom?"

"Yes." Grandmother inhaled sharply. "I couldn't bear losing my daughter to an enchanted sleep. I thought she was safe after she got engaged. I was wrong — the Magic took her anyway. I tried having her fiancé kiss her, but she didn't wake. Your father was one of her doctors. I was desperate; he was the seventh person I asked to try. I still don't know if it was the timing, or if it was because it was the seventh — all these significant numbers in *les contes des fées* make it hard to tell. I don't understand how things went as far as they did. She was pregnant and still unconscious, the way the old story went, waking upon giving birth. We stubbornly insisted on marriage. It was too late though, we couldn't set things right. Your father's medical license was revoked. Your mother pulled further and further away, and, well, I understood why it was almost impossible for her to forgive me. Then she made the same decision to try to interfere . . . And then again, with Connor and his math. Who was I to say it couldn't work, simply because I failed? But that didn't mean I wasn't concerned. I still am."

Whoa. That was a lot of new information to take in. And there was no time to process before I made decisions.

"I still don't want the Magic to control my life, Grandmother. But I can't figure out how to work around the Magic without failing somewhere else . . . I don't know what to do."

"Sometimes the best you can do in life is to choose which problems you will have to deal with. There isn't always a perfect solution. You should choose whichever path will bring you the most happiness."

"Really? Even if it will mean everyone will think poorly of me?"

"Yes. I am beginning to believe that is another way to be brave."

I hugged Grandmother again, sniffling back tears. Of course, Grandmother had a handkerchief handy. At the rate I was going tonight, there was going to be a whole load of those in the laundry.

"Speaking of problems, the timing of your decision is a bit unfortunate. I have been hinting about the big announcement we would be making all week. We are going to have to think of something to share with everyone."

I laughed shakily through sniffles. "I'll try to figure things out sooner next time. But, I have a substitution for you."

"You do?"

Grandmother's values tended to be old-fashioned, for obvious reasons. I wasn't sure how she would feel about my request. Homosexuality wasn't something we ever talked about. "I believe Henri would like to announce his engagement to Paulo tonight . . . If you are willing?" I tried for nonchalant, but neither of us bought it.

Grandmother threw her head back and laughed. I had never heard such unrestrained joy from her. When she finished, she dabbed her eyes and sniffed delicately. "I've always wanted an excuse to ruffle everyone's feathers." Were her eyes glinting mischievously? I had seriously underestimated Grandmother. "What a lovely scandal. No one will dare decline an invitation to one of my parties after this."

I laughed. It was a shaky laugh, but it was a start. Although considering what happened so far . . . "Please don't misunderstand Grandmother, but so far, I have found your parties to be a little too exciting. I may strongly consider turning down your next invitation."

"I was hoping tonight would make up for the last event." She sighed. "Still, I hope you will be around for the announcement. I have a rather special surprise planned."

There was a knock on the door. I looked at Grandmother to see if she was expecting anyone, only to find her gazing questioningly at me. I shrugged and walked over to the door.

"Yes?"

"Loren, it's Kella. Can I come in?"

I opened the door to find Kella standing there with a garment bag. "Henri called and said you had a wardrobe crisis?"

"Oh, bless him!" He'd thought ahead and taken care of the issue. He would have been an amazing partner in so many ways. Paulo was a lucky man.

Kella spotted Grandmother. "Good evening, Mrs. Dalton. Thank you for inviting me tonight. I can't wait to see the ballroom. I hear your decorating is simply magical!"

Grandmother cleared her throat delicately, "I may have borrowed the skills of your set designer."

"Isn't he incredible?" Kella asked conspiratorially.

Grandmother nodded. "I didn't want Phyllis Baulstraude to get her claws on him, so I secured him with a contract of exclusivity – for social events, of course. I would never try to keep him from working in the theatre."

There was a stunned silence in the room for just a moment before Kella laughed. "That is high praise indeed."

Grandmother stood and gently thumped her cane on the ground. "Well, it seems the situation is under control." It was a statement, but she expected confirmation.

"Yes, ma'am," I answered.

"In that case, I shall return to my guests." I heaved a sigh of relief. We hadn't gotten into the messier implications of canceling my engagement. I was fairly certain Grandmother would not approve of my plan. Begging forgiveness later would be easier than convincing her about it now.

Almost as if she read my mind, Grandmother stopped and turned, "Loren, we can discuss the ramifications of your decision later if you would like, but you seem to be clear in your vision. I have faith everything will work itself out."

Tears misted my eyes. I hopped up and gave her a gentle squeeze, careful not to jostle her. She stood stiffly, not entirely comfortable with my exuberant display of emotion, but not entirely displeased either.

"Thank you, Grandmother. Knowing I have your support means a lot."

"Well, I am glad to hear it was useful since I made the effort of climbing all those stairs." She nodded and finished leaving the room.

Kella chuckled. "That woman has some serious moxie. Phew!"

"That she does." I agreed. "I'm hoping it rubs off." I gestured at the bag in her hand. "Are those dresses for me?"

"Dress actually, just one. Henri said it didn't need to be gold?" She was asking about more than the dress color. She unzipped the garment bag.

"No, it doesn't. You will understand later tonight after the announcement is made." I couldn't wait to see her reaction. I gave her a mischievous grin.

"But everything is all right?" She wasn't buying it.

"I don't know about all right, but at least as it *should* be."

Kella stared at me, willing me to spill everything. I wasn't going to cave though. "It's not my secret to share."

She narrowed her eyes. "But you promise to explain it all tomorrow?"

"Um . . ." I considered her request. That should be enough time. "Sure."

Kella took a deep breath. "On to the dress then. Henri said fast was more important than perfect, that any ball gown would do. I hope he meant it. I happened to have this on hand because I told the costume designer I would fix some torn lace. I kind of miss doing the costumes . . ."

"Uh-huh." Why was Kella practically babbling?

"Anyway, it's not important . . . I just want you to be aware it's not what I would have picked out for you. In fact, it's completely wrong, except I'm pretty sure it will fit."

Kella pulled the garment bag away from the dress. She gave it a shake and held it up. Heaps of white tulle and lace fell into place. It took me a moment to piece out the froth of white before me. The bodice was covered in beaded and embroidered lace applique. The high empire waistline fell in mounds of tulle that skimmed the floor with a scalloped, lace edge. It had the smallest of trains in the back. The skirt must have made up ninety percent of the dress.

The dress screamed precious and innocent. I would look all of about fifteen wearing it. It was the perfect image to project, given what I had just done. And, come to think of it, what I was about to do.

The thought made me burst out laughing — I was going to be dressed as a bride on the night I was giving my fiancé away. The anxious look on Kella's face turned to confusion. "Is it that bad?" she asked.

I waved a hand at her to stop. I managed to gasp out, "No. It's great. You have no idea how perfect this is."

"You aren't getting married tonight, are you?" Kella demanded.

"No. I'm not."

Kella muttered. "I can't think of anything this is perfect for besides a wedding."

"A first communion?" I offered.

"Not helping."

I shrugged.

"Let's get you into this and see what we can do with your wet hair." Kella gave me a gentle push toward the bathroom.

"Yes, ma'am."

"Don't ma'am me!"

"Yes, ma– Umm. Whatever you say, Kella." I wasn't facing her, and I could still tell Kella was rolling her eyes at me. I grinned. "Have I told you recently what an amazing friend you are?" I asked.

"Uh-huh," she said skeptically.

"I mean it."

"You are freaking me out a little. You *promise* you will tell me everything tomorrow?"

I turned and nodded, still grinning like a maniac. Between Grandmother and Kella, my spirit was recuperating. The bone-deep certainty I had felt earlier in the day was returning. It was bubbling up in my being, and crackling across my skin.

Kella examined me. "Why do I feel like you are getting ready to color outside the lines?"

"Because I am?"

"Hmm. I think I like it."

"Thanks. I like it, too."

I hoped I would still feel the same way tomorrow.

CHAPTER 42

When I walked into the ballroom, I understood why Grandmother was going to extremes to secure the services of the event designer. The room had been transformed into a forest.

Hundreds of branches, both bare and evergreen, were set against the walls to create the feeling of being amongst ancient trees. Hanging from the branches were thousands of hand-blown glass icicles. There were also artistically arranged snowflakes made from Austrian glass beads, Swarovski crystals, and pearls. Tiny lanterns glowed and glinted off the decorations, creating sparkle and warmth.

The whole thing was elegant and magical. I felt the tiniest of pangs at giving the moment over to Henri and Paulo, no matter how much they deserved it. I allowed myself one small sigh. It wouldn't do to mope; my surroundings were too beautiful. There was also too much to do — like playing hostess. Besides, there was an easy solution — Grandmother would just have to find a way to top this if I ever decided to get engaged.

"Mr. and Mrs. Bainbridge! How delightful to see you tonight. Oh, your dress! That color is gorgeous!"

I continued across the room, exchanging pleasantries as I went. I had passed right over fashionably late — the party was in full swing. At least I was in time for the announcement.

As I finished chatting with the Darringtons, I stepped back and jostled the chair at the table behind me. I turned around to apologize. Oh, dear.

"Mrs. Randolph! I'm so sorry I bumped you!" I pasted on the smile I directed at Henri's mother. "And this must be Mr. Randolph?" They both nodded. "Sir, it is so lovely to finally meet you."

Mr. Randolph stood and pulled out the empty chair next to him "Won't you sit with us for a moment?"

I sat and got my first glimpse of the centerpieces on the table in front of me. Candles appeared to float above the snowy table linen in clear glass vases. Each fat pillar had snowflakes carved in the wax. There were easily a dozen candles on the table and no two looked alike.

Mr. Randolph deftly pushed my chair in. "Dear, under the circumstances, perhaps you would consider calling me Nickolaus."

Oh no. No one told them yet. "Oh!"

"Or perhaps . . . Dad?" Yikes!

I gave him my best social smile and tried for bubbly. "Why don't we discuss that after the announcement is made? We've got a surprise planned. Even for you two!"

"Oh?" Mrs. Randolph asked.

"Yes," I said firmly. "And I actually have something related to that I need to take care of. I hate to run but . . ."

"Of course, dear. We can talk later. I look forward to getting to know you better." He seemed sincere. Interesting. Did no one tell him what Liam had said?

"That would be lovely, Mr. Randolph. I sincerely hope you enjoy the announcement." Did that come across as too fervent? I stood and slipped away before they could ask any more questions.

I found Millie in the kitchen.

"Ms. Millie." She turned toward me. "Is there a bedroom with a fireplace?"

I could see her face change from wondering what I was doing in the kitchen to why I had changed dresses. "A fireplace?"

"Yes." I wasn't going to bother trying to make the request seem logical.

"There are several rooms with fireplaces. The one at the end of the west wing on the second floor is free."

Of course it would be in the west wing, how very forbidden of it. I refrained from sighing or rolling my eyes. "Can I use it tonight?"

"Certainly, Loren. But –"

"Is there someone who could light the fire for me?" The speculation was clear in Ms. Millie's eyes. "I promise to explain everything later."

"Do you need it done soon?" She was the picture of patience with my odd demands.

"Yes, please."

"It's a good thing we have extra help tonight." Her smile was only a bit frazzled.

"Thank you, Ms. Millie."

Millie smiled at me. "You should go enjoy the party." She glanced at her watch. "Your big announcement is soon." Interesting, Grandmother hadn't told her yet, either.

"What time is it?"

"Nine forty-five."

"Fifteen minutes. I do need to head back in soon." There were just a couple of things to grab first. Better use the back staircase. It was a more circuitous route, but I wouldn't need to stop for chitchat every few seconds as I would if I walked through the ballroom. There wasn't time for small talk.

As it was, I only made it back into the ballroom with a minute or two to spare. I spotted Grandmother on the staircase landing, getting the microphone ready with one hand while clenching Henri's arm with the other. Henri was looking grim and panicky. What was going on? Where was Paulo?

I made my way toward them, but Grandmother figured out the microphone before I could reach the bottom of the stairs.

"Good evening." The lights dimmed and a spotlight came up on Grandmother. How had she managed that? "I wouldn't normally interrupt the dancing, but I have a bit of a surprise planned, for which I would appreciate everyone's attention. This ball is one of my favorite evenings of the year, and it means so much to me that you took time out of your busy holiday season to be here tonight. Some of you have been attending this event for years, and it is my absolute pleasure to have each and every one of you join me.

"Over the last few months, I have enjoyed the company of my granddaughter as she explored Lointaine and met its residents. Her youthful energy, and the new generation she has brought into my life, have been delightful. I hope you too have enjoyed having them here tonight."

There was a round of polite applause. Grandmother waited for it to peter out before continuing.

"I have with me tonight an especially close friend of Loren's. For those of you that don't know, this is Henri Randolph. Now, it is my understanding he has developed a tendre for someone and there is an important question he would like to ask. When I heard, I felt tonight would be the perfect opportunity." She smiled like the Cheshire Cat.

The crowd near me turned with expectant grins. Boy, Grandmother was setting them up. I gave everyone a tentative smile back.

Was that why Henri had looked upset earlier? A bit of revenge, or theatrics on her part? He didn't know I talked to her, did he?

"Loren, would you be a dear and come here? Is Dr. Martín about? Perhaps you could escort her?"

Oh, she was devious.

I met Paulo at the bottom of the stairs. His face was blank. No way to tell what he thought was happening. He offered his arm and genteelly led me up the stairs. I trailed my fingers along the banister, careful not to disturb the greenery or the crystals decorating it. Paulo didn't use the banister at all. He walked with the steady poise of Baryshnikov.

When we reached the top, Grandmother held out a hand to me. She pulled me toward her. Paulo started to turn to rejoin the audience. Ouch. Grandmother held the microphone down at her side. "One moment, young man. I am going to need an escort." He dutifully came and stood next to us.

Grandmother lifted the microphone again. "I'm going to turn things over to Henri now. I hope you enjoy both the surprise I planned, and the one he has planned for you. Good night."

During the light round of applause, Grandmother handed the microphone over to Henri, then tucked her hand into my elbow.

Confusion and surprise showed on faces across the crowd as we came down the first few stairs from the landing. I turned to watch over my shoulder. The amazed shock on Paulo's face made my night.

Grandmother paused, too. She turned to look at Henri. "Young man, you are supposed to get down on one knee to do this properly." That was hardly a stage whisper. I had to laugh.

"You are absolutely correct, Mrs. Dalton." Henri promptly dropped to one knee and reached for Paulo's hand.

I allowed myself to beam as Grandmother and I glided down the stairs. It was time to leave the stage to the guys.

Henri waited a moment before beginning.

"Paulo, I've made some mistakes in the past. I let fear keep me from sharing large parts of my life with my friends and family. But I'm not willing to hide any longer, because the truth is beautiful. I treasure our love. I would regret it for the rest of our lives if I did anything to make you doubt that. Paulo, I know in my heart that you are the only one for me. I promise no one will work harder to make you happy or cherish you more than I will. Your face is the first thing I want to see in the morning, and the last thing I want to kiss at night. When you love someone that much, the only sensible thing to do is to marry him."

I reached the bottom of the staircase in time to turn and watch the grand finale.

"So, Paulo Lukas Martín, will you please marry me?"

Wow, all those practice proposals were paying off. Paulo owed me.

Paulo laughed and pulled Henri up and into his arms. "Yes, yes!" he said through tears.

I heard a whir that sounded like a hair dryer from above. What was that? I watched in awe as snowflakes drifted down into the ballroom. One landed on my cheek and melted. It was real snow. Wow. A gentle flurry was turning the ballroom into a snow globe, with Henri and Paulo at its center. Grandmother must be Henri's fairy godmother. Tears ran down my face. My makeup wasn't going to survive this.

I turned to Grandmother. She was glowing in triumph. "You are amazing." I enveloped her in a giant hug. I wasn't in the mood to worry about dress creases. I even snuffled into her ear.

Grandmother hugged me back briefly before setting me back from her. "Thank you, dear. But the evening isn't over yet. I need to go make sure this tale spins out the proper way."

I stared after her as she processed away. Where were Henri and Paulo? They both needed giant hugs, too. I turned and almost plowed Connor over.

"Loren," Connor was looking intense, as usual. Oops. Another person we should have told about the changing plans. "I thought you were announcing your engagement?"

"Umm, well, our plans changed a bit."

"Yes, I noticed that."

"Right. More than a bit, actually." The whispers were already rustling through the crowd, and speculative glances were being shot my way. "Can we maybe talk somewhere private?"

I caught sight of Paulo out of the corner of my eye — time to do my part to nip gossip in the bud. Everyone expected Henri to propose to me; I didn't want there to be any negativity toward him because people thought I was hurt or jilted. "I just need one second first . . ."

I let myself beam as I practically skipped over to Henri and Paulo, making my glee obvious to our audience.

Paulo's smile slipped off his face when he saw me. No, we couldn't have any of that. I threw my arms around both of them in a giant hug. "I am so happy for you two! Oh shoot, I just know I am going to mess this part up. Let's see, it's crass to tell the bride she made a good catch so . . ." I turned to Paulo, "All the best wishes!" To Henri, "Congratulations! You are a lucky duck to land such a great guy! Was that right, or did I get it backward?"

Connor must have followed me over; he spoke up now. "No, you followed the rules. Assuming Paulo is the bride."

"Hmm, we might have to change those terms. What about the proposer and the proposee?" I offered.

Paulo shook his head at me. "You can congratulate us both. It's about time some of those old etiquette rules got updated, anyway. Fairy tales too, for that matter!"

Connor lowered his voice, "Apparently! You two have seriously wrecked my model. I'm going to have to make some big changes." Henri laughed in disbelief. "I don't mind though, because you look so happy, Henri. Thank you for that, Paulo." Though his words were simple, they were clearly heartfelt. My smile became a little wobbly. Ugh, I couldn't tear up again — people would take it the wrong way.

Speaking of people . . . "Umm, it looks like everyone else wants to talk to you guys, too. I feel like we are monopolizing your attention."

Henri looked up and paled. His parents were bearing down on us.

"I think we are going to slip off so you can talk to your parents, Henri . . ." I said. Paulo looked panicked. I gave him a quick hug and whispered, "You've got this! Chin up."

I took the advice myself. It was time to push through all the metaphorical barriers in my way. It was my turn.

CHAPTER 43

I pasted a smile on my face and took Connor's arm, leading him through the crowd to the kitchen door; it was the fastest way out of the room. Connor was thinking hard, so it didn't feel rude to check to see how Henri and Paulo were doing, instead of making small talk as we left. I desperately wanted things to go well for them.

Hmm, Henri was talking, and things looked awkward, or even tense — Paulo was nervous, Mr. Randolph seemed perplexed, and Mrs. Randolph's face was blank. It was definitely a flaw in the plan that this discussion had to happen in public. Wait — Mr. Randolph was smiling! That was good! My attention was diverted as Connor stopped to exchange small talk with an older couple and introduce me. By the time I glanced around again, the Randolphs were nowhere in sight. How much could I look for them without spurring gossip? Well, I was about to leave the party, and that was sure to cause gossip. I needed to let it go. Time to focus on my own story.

Connor didn't make it far down the hall before the questions started. "Exactly how much of a change in plans are we talking about here? We don't have a lot of time left before the whole stepmother situation becomes a factor. I don't know if we can find another Beast that quickly."

"We could knock Emilia off to buy some time," I offered dryly. "Why should the evil stepmothers get to have all the fun?" Connor's eyes grew wide. I couldn't help but laugh. "I'm joking, Connor! I know time is short. I have a plan, but I'd like to wait to discuss it." I didn't trust him not to stall as his brain worked overtime. An audience would make that difficult, especially if he forgot to worry about his volume when debating the merits of this new course of action.

Connor sighed impatiently. "Wouldn't any of these rooms do? What abo–" I bet he had an entire list of concerns he wanted to share.

"I have a specific one in mind. It's on the second floor." Connor was quiet as I guided him along the hallway. "Here we are." I gestured toward the appropriate door as we neared it.

He opened the door and held it for me, the gesture was so ingrained he probably wasn't aware he was doing it. After Connor stepped into the room, he started to close the door but paused, asking, "Should I close this?"

I nodded. I watched him consider whether to turn on the overhead light. He left it off. The fire and lamp lit the room in a cozy way, but it was still an interesting choice. We sat in the armchairs flanking the fireplace.

"All right," I could see him reining his thoughts back in. "Why don't you update me on the change in plans."

Wow, I hadn't been expecting him to let me go first. I thought he'd need to explore solutions to inconceivable problems before I got a chance to talk. I really was in control of the story.

"Well . . . Henri needed to propose to Paulo instead of me," I began.

"I caught that part." His tone was dry.

"You didn't know Henri was gay, did you?" I asked.

"No, I didn't." He rubbed the back of his neck. "I wouldn't have planned Henri as the Beast for you if I had known."

"Well, I'm glad to hear that." I managed not to roll my eyes, but barely.

He frowned and shrugged. "Why didn't he tell everyone earlier?" He sounded a bit hurt.

"He was afraid of how it would affect the Pack, and the other people he loved."

"He should have known it wouldn't have mattered to me." There was no real anger to his words, just exasperation.

"I suspect that is true for the rest of Henri's family, too. Henri and Paulo have their happily ever after waiting for them, but I don't." I took a deep breath. "As much as I want to say to hell with the Magic, it doesn't seem like a good idea. I believe I have come up with a compromise between what *it* wants and maintaining some agency."

"We don't have a lot of time. At the very least, we need to find someone for you to get engaged to. Oh . . ." He gulped. "Did you mean, um, m–"

I didn't let him finish that sentence, so he wouldn't dig himself a hole. "I don't want to marry someone or get engaged just for the sake of the Magic."

"Oh." I could practically see his attention drawing inward as the possibilities unfurled in his brain. It was fascinating how much time he spent up there. It had taken me a while to accept that I lived in my own world where only I knew my story. With Connor, that was obvious to anyone who knew him.

"So," I gave Connor time to come back to the discussion before I continued. "I started thinking about fairy tales with female protagonists but no nuptials."

I had been all geared up for this, but I was suddenly hesitant. What if I couldn't handle this? What if he wasn't willing? The nerves showed as I babbled, delaying getting to the point.

"There aren't many well-known options, which seems to be a requirement. So, nothing like 'The Seven Ravens,' even though it would be cool to get a whole slew of brothers. 'Hansel and Gretel' isn't a good idea. I couldn't figure out how to get trained bears for Goldilocks. I considered a dirty play on words and trying to twist 'Puss in Boots.' But it's the wrong time of year for bathing naked in a river, which is how that story begins. The tale might morph into 'The Little Matchbox Girl' with this weather." Connor started to speak but I cut him off. "Which isn't an option, either."

I took a deep breath, and Connor took the opportunity to ask, "So, did you come up with something?"

"I did. But there might be some problems."

"Which I am here to help you figure out?"

"Yes."

"What is the tale?"

I blew my breath out in a puff that wouldn't be Grandmother-approved, but it would have done the Big Bad wolf proud. I finally got to my point, "'Little Red Riding Hood.' I realized I have spent my whole life sticking to the proper path for fear of what might happen if I left it. The Magic has given me all the pieces. I'm just choosing to see them as jumbled and rearranging them to channel the path of the Magic. Not so much fighting my fate, as choosing it."

All the *what-ifs* that herded me through life . . . It was infuriating. You can't get a fine arts degree because it means you will be asking about wanting fries with your meal; can't wear that because it's not in style; can't say that for fear of hurting someone else's feelings, so repress your own pain. It was maddening to remember all the times I let other people's opinions keep me from pursuing my own happiness.

"Oh." Connor cogitated for a moment. He cleared his throat. "I assume you don't want to literally be eaten and are going for the more metaphorical interpretation?"

I nodded, "Yes, as is suggested by the moral verse at the end of the Perrault version. The whole bit about gentle wolves being the most dangerous of all for well-bred young ladies . . ." Most modern children probably had no clue the tale was initially propaganda for purity culture.

But Connor wasn't listening. He was wrapped up in his own ideas. "Or were you thinking of going with the Grimm version and counting Liam as the first wolf? In which case we are going to need to figure out how to boil someone as the second wolf, without hurting them . . ."

"Huh, I hadn't considered that option." I pondered the matter. Could we just dump Liam down the chimney and not worry about hurting him? Damn. As much as I liked the idea, it wasn't the end of the internal journey I was on. "It doesn't feel right. It's not what I have been building toward."

"Right, in that case . . . Wow . . ." It was his turn to be at a loss for the right words, he pushed his glasses up, and scratched the back of his head.

"So, I have some concerns. I don't want Grandmother eaten. Also, I'm not a virgin. That seems like it could be problematic for a morality tale about losing your virginity."

"Huh . . ." Connor was taking his time to consider, and the anticipation was killing me. "I think you are safe on the grandmother issue. She already got wolves when she was expecting her granddaughter tonight. It's close enough. I'm also not worried about your virginity. It's more about breaking with societal expectations and the repercussions as you suggested. All of the princesses were theoretically virginal, too. Best I can tell, it only seems to matter for the duration of the tale."

Well, that was a relief. "At least I am dressed for the part?" I gestured to the sweet, white dress.

He nodded. "I wondered about your outfit." Then he cocked his head to the side. "You aren't worried about the wolf dying?"

"Not really. Men never seem to be punished for sex in a fairy tale, not even for rape. I figure maybe someone would burst into the room to 'rescue' me. Worst case scenario, everyone is a bit embarrassed."

"That does seem about right. You know there is a version where Little Red Riding Hood escapes on her own, right?"

I laughed. "Yes, but she still gets into bed with the wolf. Running home naked through the woods seems like a good way to freeze to death. It's not escaping at all, just delaying her downfall. I think it is time to reject Perrault as a Puritanical, prune-faced, misogynist. Maybe Red wanted to step off the path. Maybe she did so happily — with great joy even. I plan to pick the damn flowers."

Connor was surprised by my vehemence. "Wow, I feel like you aren't Little Red — maybe you are the Wolf?!"

"I'm not."

"But –"

"Look, I'm willing to consider that stepping off the prescribed path might make me a wolf as far as society is concerned. If that is the case, I'll deal with the repercussions. But I'm not following rules, just because other people say they are the rules, anymore."

It was time to excavate what I wanted from the heap of societal expectations burying me alive. I just needed some help to get around the Magic that was insistent on manifesting those expectations.

I continued, "But I'm pretty sure you are wrong. I'm not the one who changes into a wolf." I paused briefly to give him a look for not sharing the information with me earlier. I raised one finger, and then more as I made my points. "I'm not the one who has put on Grandmother's nightgown. I'm not the one who has been trying to figure out where the girl is headed, to manipulate where she ends up." I was getting loud. Shit. I scrubbed my face.

I hadn't meant to say anything to compel Connor to help. It wasn't fair to put him in the same position I was trying to claw my way out of. Also, I didn't want to ever have regrets because of feeling like I forced him in any way. It would make me no different than Liam, and that would destroy me.

"Loren —"

"No, wait. I'm sorry. I didn't mean to pressure you in any way. I can figure out someone else to be the wolf." Although, Connor was the only person I could imagine in the role. He knew my history, so I wouldn't have to explain. I could trust him to respect any boundaries I set. He was safe. I liked him as a person — a lot even. But that wasn't enough to make this easy. This might be impossible without him. There was no way I could tell him that, though.

"Um, maybe we could skip the whole bedroom scene." I was babbling again. "Make it extremely metaphorical. Perhaps I could decide to throw getting a degree out the window . . . Maybe go live in an artist colony somewhere?"

Connor blinked several times. ". . . I can run some equations if you want, but my gut instinct is that you already know where the tale is going and what it needs to be."

He was right. I did know. "It wouldn't be enough." I sighed. "I'm pretty sure this is an all-or-nothing situation." I was ready to reclaim the power to control my life, not just from societal expectations, but also from the harm done by Liam.

"So, are you willing to help me?" I gestured toward the bed. The nightgown, which Liam had tricked Connor into putting on before, was there. I pushed the thought of Liam away, crammed it into a box, and shut the lid firmly. I couldn't think about him or this whole thing might fall apart. My red Belle cape lay next to the nightgown.

Connor closed his eyes. "Are you sure this is what you want? Are you up for this?"

"Yes. I'm not willing to be damaged any longer. I need to move forward." I blew out a shaky breath, "I will need somebody who can be patient, though."

"I can be patient." He paused. "I just want to make sure I'm clear here. You are asking me to help rescue you, by having sex with you?" I couldn't tell if he felt that was a good thing or a bad thing.

"You could put it that way . . ." Although really, I was rescuing myself. I was the one being brave.

Laughter burst out of him. He gasped, "I'm sorry, it's just this feels like it came straight out of pornography of some sort — a badly written one even."

His comment broke the tension that had been growing in the room. I laughed along with him. But he was wrong again. "Bad writing would be more like this . . ." I sauntered over with as much hip sway as I could manage. I took his hand in mine and trailed my fingers up to his bicep. Then in my best breathy voice, I said, "My, what big . . . arms you have."

Connor stared at his arm. He gave a strangled laugh. "That would qualify, too."

"Can you guess what the following lines would be?" I gave him a mischievous grin and raised my eyebrow.

"I can, indeed."

"So, are you okay with this, or should I start considering alternatives?"

He shrugged helplessly. "It's my quest — rescuing princesses from their stories. If this is what you want, if it will help . . . of course I will."

"That's not . . . Umm, I don't want you to do this if you feel like you have to. I can't do this unless you want to – unless you will enjoy it."

Connor gaped at me. "Loren, of course I will enjoy it. I mean . . ." He gestured to me helplessly. He wasn't going to be a dick and make this about looks, was he? I raised an eyebrow, and he gulped. "I promise, I am happy to do this. I am fairly certain I am going to enjoy this immensely. Umm," he glanced up at the ceiling, perhaps desperate for a change in topic, "I do have some concerns that the Magic might try to pair *us* off instead — the tale is so similar to 'Beauty and the Beast,' but I'm willing to risk it if you are."

I shook my head at him. "No, that's not how the story goes. Once there was a young girl. Through hardship and toil, she found her way to her grandmother's house beyond the dark and dangerous forest. She was expecting to find her grandmother in need of care. Instead, she found you. Lying in bed, waiting . . ."

Startled awe washed over Connor's face. "Your hair just turned red."

"It did?" I pulled a strand of hair forward so I could see it better. It was a deep garnet red. "Umm, wow. I guess the Magic approves. See? No worries, 'Little Red Riding Hood' for sure."

Connor got up and locked the door. "If we are doing this, I would prefer not to be interrupted." He turned toward me and shrugged out of his tailcoat. He folded it and draped it over the back of his chair. Now luminous in his white waistcoat and dress shirt, he unbuttoned his waistcoat and asked, "Would you pass me the nightgown?"

"Umm, sure." I turned and went to retrieve our costumes, exquisitely aware of Connor even as my back was turned. I heard him sit in the chair. I waited to hand him the nightgown as he took off his shoes. The shiny patent leather caught and threw the reflection of the firelight as he tucked them under the chair. He tugged his socks off and pushed them under the chair with his foot.

For some reason, the sight of Connor's bare feet suddenly made the theoretical situation evaporate, and left the real one in its place. Holy moly, this was happening. I tucked my shaking hands under the cape. I was going to do this, no thoughts to the contrary allowed.

His task finished, Connor took the nightgown and cape from me and laid them across the chair's arm. Connor reached out and lightly held my fingertips in his hands. "I don't want to do anything to make you uncomfortable. Maybe it would be better if you were in control?"

"But Little Red Riding Hood wasn't in charge. Don't we need to stick to the story?"

Connor was already shaking his head. "I think the important thing is that you are . . ." Even in the dim firelight, I saw the blush wash across his face. ". . . devoured." He made air quotes as he said it. He ducked his head as he continued. "I thought it might be easier if you set the pace."

Oh. Taking control would be difficult, ever so much harder than just letting things happen. Although Connor probably was correct. I was probably less likely to freak out if I knew exactly what was happening . . . And control was what I said I wanted. Did I actually mean it?

I did.

It was time to be brave.

I nodded, not trusting my voice to work. I tugged my fingers out of his hand and then reached up to undo his bow tie. My fingers were shaking. I let my arms fall, hands clenched in fists to hide my panic.

Goddamn it. This was Connor. He wasn't a threat. And I *was* going to do this.

Forget what happened. Don't think about where this is leading. Focus on right now, this moment.

You are just taking a bow tie off. You can do that.

Let's try that again.

The weave of the tie was almost rough under my fingers as I pulled the bow free. Hah! I had managed the first step.

Hmm. What else is holding Connor's outfit together? I was working on getting us to the point where we could both fall apart. The thought was almost enough to make me smile. It got me through undoing both his cufflinks and the studs in his dress shirt. My fingers were clumsy, but I managed not to drop any of the formal accessories.

Right, I couldn't do much more with Connor sitting. I slid my hands into his and pulled him to his feet. I found myself staring at his chest, at the exposed vee of skin where his collar was open. The shadowy dip between his collarbones. Oh god. I drew in a calming breath. Umm . . . Right. Suspenders next.

There was nothing for it — the shirt was next. I almost expected to have to push through tension building between us as I reached out to tug his shirt free of his pants. Except it didn't pull free . . . Oh right, shirt tabs. A few months ago, I wouldn't have known about those. I bet Grandmother didn't expect her lessons on proper white tie attire to come into play in quite this way.

I was going to have to slide my fingers under the edge of his pants to unbutton those.

Intently focusing on the details of each step was the only thing keeping panic at bay. It also made me realize that Connor's formal attire had the minimal amount of ornamentation required to be acceptable. There were no ribs, texture, or pattern on his silk socks. No pleats in his trousers, and only one satin stripe down the side rather than two. A single-breasted waistcoat, a bib front shirt instead of a pleated one, no boutonniere, and lace-up oxford shoes — of course, the idea of Connor in pumps with grosgrain bows was just amusing.

I was able to give Connor a small smile as I slid the sleeves off his broad shoulders. I let the shirt drop to puddle on the floor.

Oh . . . Um, I didn't expect to be affected this way. Firelight flickered across Connor's body, creating interesting pools of light and shadow. The suspenders hanging from his shoulders were extremely suggestive. I was torn as to whether I most wanted to touch him or sketch him.

The strong attraction was a bit frightening. The last time I felt this way . . . No. We aren't going there. Stay in this moment.

This moment is good.

Connor turned and collected the nightgown. "Well, this ought to make me look sexy."

"We can stick to the metaphorical side if you prefer . . ." I offered.

Connor shook his head, "I don't mind, and I'd prefer to play it safe. The closer we can stick to the tale the better. I just want you to know I am much sexier when I am not wearing shapeless women's garments."

I laughed, which was probably his intention. "Right. Duly noted." He didn't need to worry, his mischievous grin would more than make up for the outfit.

Connor dropped the fabric over his head. As the hem bunched and caught on his waistband, he unzipped his pants and pulled them down, allowing the nightgown's length to simultaneously fall to the floor. He stepped out of the pants and picked them up.

Connor was decidedly wrong about the nightgown. The body I had been admiring earlier was backlit by the fire creating a silhouette against the thin linen. It was dead sexy.

I swallowed. So much for Connor being safe.

"Right," he picked up the cape and held it up in invitation. "Your turn."

I stepped forward and Connor swirled the cape behind me and around my shoulders, closing the clasp under my chin with delicate movements I could barely feel. He stepped back and waited. Right, I'm in charge here. I put my hands on his shoulders and rose onto my tiptoes to kiss him.

The mechanics of the kiss weren't sophisticated; it was just a gentle press of lips. Despite that, it was everything: a secret, a prayer, a promise, a storm. In the seconds our lips touched, we wrote volumes containing both tragedies and joyful endings.

This wasn't supposed to be an emotional connection. I went into this with the hope we would at least enjoy each other's company, but that kiss . . . I never prepared for that.

Connor and I stared at each other, stunned.

"That wasn't part of the plan," I told Connor.

Connor smiled, creating laugh lines around his eyes. I loved them, and that his sense of humor had marked him in such a wonderful way. Somehow those creases in his skin let me know everything would work out.

"What if . . ." Connor took my hands in a loose hold, "What if we stop planning and calculating, and just see what happens?"

Umm, wow. Connor was asking us to be in the moment. If he could manage to turn his brain off, surely I could too. I took a deep breath. "I'm willing to try."

Connor tugged lightly on my hands to pull me toward him. "I am going to go get into bed over there to play my part." He laid a soft kiss on my forehead. "And in a moment, you should join me. But first, you need to take off your clothes and burn them."

Right. It was another piece of the 'Little Red Riding Hood' puzzle. Putting it into place would help set the Magic, but Kella wasn't going to be happy with me. I was going to have some groveling to do. And a dress to buy. I hoped she would understand.

Connor was waiting for a reaction, so I nodded and squeezed his hands. Connor moved the fireplace screen aside before heading toward the bed in the shadowy corner of the room. I stepped out of my shoes before reaching behind me to start undoing the zipper of my dress. He threw the covers back as I let the mounds of tulle slip over my body to the floor. This was going to be a fire hazard. I compacted the dress into a tight ball and carefully placed it on the burning logs. Maybe another log on top? Sure. And then the grate in front. And now that the sartorial symbol of my innocence was on its way to being destroyed, there was nothing to distract me from the more literal act.

I turned toward Connor and the bed. The earlier tension had dissipated a bit; I was nervous again. The cape mostly covered my body, but we both knew I was nearly naked underneath it. As I crossed the room, I allowed myself to be distracted by texture: the cool satin lining of the cape brushing my bare midriff and the lightest prickle of the oriental carpet felt through my silk stockings.

Soon enough, I reached the edge of the bed. Connor was tucked in but sitting against the headboard. Since I could only see him from the waist up, the nightgown looked more like a period shirt for an old pirate movie than anything else.

I paused, what was I supposed to do again? I went blank. Right, my line was: "Grandmother, what big eyes you have!"

Connor gave the appropriate response, "The better to see you with, my dear." He paused, "I feel like I should leer at you. That was weird. It's getting a little weird at this point, isn't it?"

I raised an eyebrow and nodded.

"Why don't we get the corny lines out of the way then?" Connor suggested.

"Yes, let's do that please." Connor gestured for me to go ahead. I sat on the bed next to him, "Oh my . . . Grandmother, what big arms you have."

Connor waggled his eyebrows at me. "The better to hug you with." He put an arm around my shoulders and gently pulled me into him.

"Oh my, what big teeth you have, Grandmother!"

"The better to eat you with!" Connor leaned in to nuzzle the skin along my neck. He gave a slight nip and then trailed a line of ice and fire as he brushed kisses along my jawline. The tension was back and rising. Thank heavens.

Connor stopped and sat back, visibly reigning himself in. "I hope I can talk you out of that cape soon . . ." His voice was rough with passion, almost a growl.

The chances of that were high, it was as certain as fate.

CHAPTER 44

Connor was tracing a lazy circle on my shoulder blade. I was so sensitized, it was enough to send tickly frissons racing across my back. Connor chuckled — pleased with himself, pleased with how he affected me.

We were lying in a twisted jumble of sheets. Our skin was still glowing from the exertion of our previous activities. Neither of us wanted to get up. Perhaps it was the firelight playing across the room . . .

I rolled over. "You know turnabout is fair play, right?" I asked. He was propped on one elbow, leaving prime tickling spots unguarded. I trailed my fingers along his side, ending with a playful poke in his ribs. Hmm, I might deserve an award for not allowing myself to be distracted by his chest.

"Ooomph." He laughed. "Oh, don't do that. I think I pulled something earlier." He collapsed over onto his back and rubbed his side ruefully.

"Did I hurt the Big Bad Wolf?"

"Maybe." He said it with a grin, but seriously. "I'm not sure."

"Oh no. Want me to rub it or something?"

"I think I just need to lay still for a moment."

"Okay . . . Couldn't you heal by shifting? How does all that work, anyway? I still don't understand."

"Oh no, what I do isn't shifting physical matter like the wolves, it's shifting energy levels. Like an electron switching orbits or ice melting into liquid water."

"Huh, so no magical healing?"

He shook his head. Then his eyes widened dramatically. "Oh, wow. Your hair is blonde again. It must have faded slowly. I can't believe I just noticed."

"Well, you were a little occupied." I grinned at him, sitting up to examine my hair. It was back to its original color. Huh. I shrugged. "I didn't notice either. It's not blonde really, more of a strawberry blonde. Still somewhat red?"

"Guess you were distracted, too?" He chuckled and then groaned as it pulled his injured muscle.

"Does this mean the tale is over?" I asked. "Wait — if I was Red Riding Hood, shouldn't my hair stay red? My hair doesn't match any of the Disney princesses now . . ."

". . . Loren, did you have a tattoo before?" Connor asked. "I don't think I would have missed that."

"What? No!"

Connor reached out and ran a finger gently across my breast, over my heart.

It could have been a birthmark or henna from the rosy taupe color, but the shape was a detailed rose. A five-petaled rose. What in the world . . . ?

"It was literal. In the journals — they meant 'marked by the tales' literally!" Connor sounded as astonished as I felt.

"What, are you saying the Magic did this?" I asked.

"I can't think of anything else," Connor replied. "Can you?"

"But why a rose? That makes no sense for 'Little Red Riding Hood.' Is the Magic saying I'm Belle?"

I mulled it over; I suppose Connor was thinking it through, too. He looked a bit green and had his hand over his eyes. Was he freaking out because we might be hooked to each other now? That sucked. I hadn't meant to trick him into anything. My heart sank. I wasn't sure I was happy either. Maybe it wasn't what he, I mean what *we* thought . . .

I brainstormed aloud. "Of course, there are other tales with roses. They are in 'Sleeping Beauty' — which we know isn't the right tale, 'The Wild Swan,'

'Snow White,' and 'Rose Red,' there is even a weird little one by the Grimm brothers called 'The Rose.' Oh, wait! Little Red Riding Hood strayed from the path to pick flowers. That must be it — I metaphorically stepped off the path and pursued the flowers!"

"But," Connor pursed his lips, "The Big Bad Wolf didn't tell you to stop and pick flowers."

I rolled my eyes. "I know we talked about females lacking agency in fairy tales, but give us some credit. Little Red Riding Hood could have chosen to stay on the path and she didn't. She might have ignored the dictates of society even without the wolf. I may not have complete control over what happens to me, but I plan to choose joy in every way within my power, even if it means diverging from expectations. I love a rose as an emblem of that, especially with its historical and cultural symbolism and how it ties me to my female ancestors."

"But, a rose for Sleeping Beauty ties you to your ancestors, too . . . And it would mean you got a happily ever after."

I started to laugh. "But I don't need a happily ever after gifted by the Magic. I have the power to do that myself." I paused to see if Connor wanted to weigh in. He was focused on the tattoo though, lightly tracing the edges of the petals. "Besides, what other symbol would you have the Magic choose, a wolf? That seems a bit sadistic. Besides, a rose is also perfect because of its thorns. I don't expect my journey to be without its issues; there are often briars when you leave the trail."

Connor gasped. I looked down just in time to see thorny vines and leaves unfurling from the rose tattoo, appearing out of nowhere and flowing across my skin. Connor jerked his hand back as if the tattoo was scorching hot, or perhaps like he had been pricked by a thorn.

"Oh no." His skin was actually almost gray now.

"Connor — I may have a panic attack if you don't tell me what is going on." Why did he look guilty?

"Shit. How did I miss that? Umm, Loren, I know there were certain things you were trying to avoid, but, well . . . to make a long story short, I think the Magic may consider us paired off."

"But how?" That didn't make any sense. Unless we managed to accidentally do 'Beauty and the Beast.' And, well . . . I finished the thought out loud, "We clearly and carefully just finished 'Little Red Riding Hood.' My hair turned red. Red doesn't end up with the wolf. Unless . . . well, if you are a reformed wolf, that could be a variation on 'Beauty and the Beast.'"

Connor cleared his throat. "Can we talk about the why later? I'd rather discuss the repercussions . . . How do you feel about being stuck with me?"

"*Stuck* with you? How am I stuck with you? You make it sound like you are some sort of consolation prize. People shouldn't be used as awards ever. That's gross."

"Well, I mean, you only asked for one night, and I don't know how you feel about me, or being with me, let alone for an entire happily ever after . . ."

Several different ideas raced through my head, but the one concerning how I might have hurt him took precedence. "Connor," I smoothed some of the exasperation out of my voice and reached over to touch the side of his face gently, waiting until he turned toward me. I met his gaze squarely with my own. "I like you. I wouldn't have chosen you to help me if I didn't."

What had Connor thought this was? A booty call?

"As for us being stuck together," I laughed. "Neither of us needs to worry about that. No one is throwing me out because I am ruined, forcing me to marry you, or forcing you to marry me. No shotgun weddings at all. Only you and I have any say about whether or not we stay together. Now, if you want to discuss extending this . . ." I circled my hand as I struggled for an appropriate word, "connection?" Connor nodded his agreement with my word choice. "Then I am happy to. I enjoyed this. I enjoy you."

I was watching Connor's reaction carefully. His eyes were shining, and all those delightful lines were crinkling their corners. His broad grin told me he wasn't averse either. But I wasn't done yet.

"However, I refuse to run out and get married or announce our engagement, just because of a tattoo."

Connor's laugh turned into a groan. "Oh man, something isn't right." He rolled over and vomited over the edge of the bed.

Huh, that certainly wasn't the reaction I was hoping for.

EPILOGUE

That obnoxious beeping noise . . . Why hadn't I turned my alarm off? I reached out a hand to hit the snooze button, but my bedside table wasn't there. What was pulling on my hand?

"Hey, hey. Shhh. It's okay." What? I had a woman stay over? That was unexpected.

Opening my eyes was an impossible task. Each lid had weights attached — megagram weights from the feel of it, and it seemed there was some sort of adhesive involved also. For that matter, everything was heavy. Perhaps this is what gravity on Jupiter would be like.

The shushing noises continued, but I blocked them out to focus on my abdomen. With every breath, I felt tugging along a linear stretch of skin; it wasn't painful necessarily, but it was peculiar. The pain was deeper, spreading through my abdomen like tentacles. The pain was the catalyst that let my thoughts fall into place.

I was damaged enough that I was in the hospital. The rhythmic beeps, stiff and crackling sheets, and the antiseptic smell – all confirmed my suspicions. And the woman sitting helplessly by my bedside was Loren. Interesting. The last time we were here together, the roles had been reversed.

Laughing was a horrid idea, given the pain it would cause, but the Magic sure had a sadistic sense of humor. Apparently, the Big Bad Wolf got punished after all. That should make Loren happy, except it wouldn't. She would probably feel guilty. I bet the surgeon that took my appendix out was even a member of Modern Woodmen of America or maybe moonlighting as a lumberjack champion specializing in speed carving. I would have to do some research to confirm, but later. Right now, everything was too hazy. My thoughts were fading in and out, and it was hard to concentrate. Some sort of painkiller, surely.

Perhaps I could kick-start my synapses with some simple math. Two squared is four. Four squared is sixteen. Sixteen squared is . . . I know this. Maybe prime numbers. One, two, three, five, seven, eleven, thirteen, seventeen . . .

The tactic appeared to be working. Right, we had finished Loren's tales. Tales, plural. That seemed wrong.

Nineteen, twenty-three, twenty-nine . . .

The tattoo. The rose. It negated the other tales we tried to force. And yet, I still ended up here in the hospital for my part as the wolf. Was it 'Little Red Riding Hood' because it was Loren's story to tell?

Oh. Loren wasn't going to like my theory. She was Sleeping Beauty all along. How had I overlooked all those themes? Had it been all about how we couldn't escape our fate?

Thirty-one, thirty-seven, forty-one . . .

I was never going to hear the end of it. I could practically hear what she would have to say. Her romantic fairy tale involved getting crushed by a "creepy hunter" and "a dog lick" for her enchanted kiss! At least she already knew I could turn into a wolf.

Loren did have a wonderfully dry sense of humor. Maybe she would find it amusing?

What did this mean for us? Were we joined as a couple now — would we get married? It wasn't necessarily part of the original tale.

Forty-three . . .

Wait? Marrying Loren?

I was okay with that. Beyond okay. Being married to Loren would be incredible. And it wasn't because of last night. Or not only about last night — it wasn't the mechanics of sex. It was the intimacy — how she had dropped all her masks and let me see her courage and playful wittiness. Of course, I also couldn't stop thinking about the indent of her navel, or the soft shell of her ear. It would be incredible to wake up to her, to share a hundred small moments with her, every day. I expected the shift from bachelor to husband mentality to be harder. Why was that? I mean I could shift from man to wolf, but getting married would be hard?

Too bad shifting didn't heal me like it did Pack members. I need to figure that out. And what the next orbital level was, too. I was willing to bet it was a wolf head on a human body . . .

Forty-seven, fifty-three . . .

Maybe the Magic was making the mental shift easier? But the Magic didn't need to force the issue. It was also more than likely finished, both with us and with the tale, that's what the tattoo meant. Probably. I awakened Sleeping Beauty with an approximation of a kiss and slept with her. That should fulfill the major requirements. Especially since Loren hadn't given birth to twins in order to wake up, I wasn't already married, and my mother wasn't an ogre. That would allow us to avoid the gorier fates in the original tale — hopefully, we were done with Loren's story. Do we need to take care of the Disney version too, just to be safe? How would we manage a color-changing dress? Fiber optic lights?

Or perhaps the next energy level was a human body with a hawk head. Did the animal head have to do with cultural geography?

Fifty-nine, sixty-one, sixty-seven . . .

A reason to dance with Loren. This time she would actually be my date. The thought made me happier than I had been in a long time. Loren was pretty magical, all on her own.

Seventy-one, seventy-three, seventy-nine . . .

We had done everything backward. I hoped she would be able to overlook the Magic's interference to see there was a genuine attraction. Even if she kept insisting her tale was "Little Red Riding Hood," it seemed like there was a chance she'd consider me if she was interested. I could cover myself in rose tattoos and be some of the flowers she picked.

Eighty-three, eight-nine, ninety-seven . . .

There was an astounding bravery in what Loren had done by rejecting societal narratives, in finding her own path to follow. I couldn't wait to see where it led her. Once upon a time, there was a girl who decided to live happily ever after. If I was lucky, she might let me be a part of that.

Acknowledgments

Like many epic tales, my journey to becoming an author had a rocky start. I began things by going in the completely wrong direction and getting a Master of Science. This turned out to be one of those traps – you know, the kind set by an evil fairy, where you are sucked in because everything is golden and easy, and yet when you stop to consider for a moment, you realize it is utterly unfulfilling at the same time. I wrote my way out of the spell, starting with reports and procedures, brochures, and booklets about environmental regulations. My story probably would have concluded there, if it weren't for my husband and Julya Mirro of little independent artists (LIA).

My husband helped me create space in my life for writing, saw hope in my earliest drafts, made my computer behave, found precious files that were lost on my hard drive, and was happy to help me talk through world-building problems.

Julya Mirro helped me find faith in myself, breaking the last vestiges of the evil spell that had me convinced I wasn't really a writer. Spell Borne would have never made it to publication without her. I'm so grateful for her championing of my work.

I'd also like to thank my mother-in-law for helping with my children during writing retreats, my children for (usually) understanding that I needed time to write, and all the people that encouraged my writing along the way, including my parents and my teachers.

I'd be remiss if I didn't thank my Beta and Delta Reader teams for pointing out when things were just in my head, and not on the page. Gratitude to readers Michaela Adams, Victoria Barnes, Brian Clark, Christine Jones, Jan Joyner, Ariel Palmer, those who read unofficially, and extra special thanks to those who stuck around for multiple drafts.

And lastly, thank you – the reader – for taking a chance on a new author, and being a part of my happily ever after.

About the Author

Photo by Julya Mirro

Auden Llyr is the author of Spell Borne. She grew up in the Blue Ridge Mountains, steeped in the magic of nature and a steady stream of fairy tales. After obtaining her master's degree, Auden spent several years as a technical writer before realizing her true vocation lay in writing fiction. She now lives in North Carolina, raising two boys (or perhaps small dragons, as they seem to have similar destructive capabilities) along with her husband.

Made in the USA
Columbia, SC
20 April 2023

8ef9b94f-252d-4e76-9519-963754b02920R01